English for International Business
—— Negotiation & Communication

国际商务英语
谈判与沟通

主编 蒋磊

副主编 王 莉 马玉梅 马兰萍 李青山

编 者 刘彩霞 王 绚 高晓红 李青山

马兰萍 马玉梅 王 莉 蒋 磊

高等教育出版社
Higher Education Press

图书在版编目(CIP)数据

国际商务英语判断与沟通/蒋磊主编 .—北京:高等教育出版社,2007.8
ISBN 978 – 7 – 04 – 022204 – 3

Ⅰ.国 ... Ⅱ.蒋... Ⅲ.国际贸易 – 贸易谈判 – 英语 Ⅳ.H31

中国版本图书馆 CIP 数据核字(2007)第 121278 号

策划编辑 周俊华 责任编辑 张春超 封面设计 王 峥 责任印制 毛斯璐

出版发行	高等教育出版社	购书热线	010 – 58581118
社 址	北京市西城区德外大街 4 号	免费咨询	800 – 810 – 0598
邮政编码	100011	网 址	http://www.hep.edu.cn
总 机	010 – 58581000		http://www.hep.com.cn
		网上订购	http://www.landraco.com
经 销	蓝色畅想图书发行有限公司		http://www.landraco.com.cn
印 刷	北京未来科学技术研究所有限责任公司印刷厂	畅想教育	http://www.widedu.com
开 本	787×1092 1/16	版 次	2007 年 8 月第 1 版
印 张	17.5	印 次	2007 年 8 月第 1 次印刷
字 数	430 000	定 价	24.00 元

本书如有缺页、倒页、脱页等质量问题,请到所购图书销售部门联系调换。

物料号 22204 – 00

前　言

随着全球经济一体化和中国经济的快速发展,中国对外商务合作的前景日益广阔,大商务格局的经贸活动日益频繁。目前,国际谈判与沟通已成为经济活动中非常关键的一个环节,谈判与沟通也成为很多大中型企业日常工作的一部分,对谈判策略与技巧的灵活应用已成为提高企业和商品竞争力的重要因素。为了适应新的形式,满足各大专院校复合型外语人才培养以及社会各层次商务工作者的实际需要,我们编写了《国际商务英语谈判与沟通》一书。

《国际商务英语谈判与沟通》是一门主要研究国际商务谈判具体过程及实务的课程,是一门实践性很强的综合性应用课程,是国际商务学科体系中的一门基础课程,也是商务英语专业的骨干支撑课程。该课程针对国际商务谈判的特点和要求,从实践的角度,分析研究国际商务谈判相关的国际惯例和国际商品交换过程的各种实际运作,以从事国际商务谈判的主要业务环节为主线,系统介绍各环节的操作规程和国际惯例。本书科学地把商务知识、谈判知识、现代沟通的内容及形式与英语语言综合技能融为一体,目的在于帮助更多的学习者通过系统的商务英语谈判的学习,掌握商务谈判的基本理论知识,借助于灵活多变的谈判技巧,熟悉各种谈判活动,了解不同商务活动的人文背景、规范以及具体操作程序,从而提高商务谈判中分析问题和处理问题的能力。基于这种理念,本教材在编写时特别注意把握好商务谈判活动主题的涵盖面、商务知识的系统性与完整性,以及语言技能与商务知识的平衡,力求体现语言技能的训练与商务知识的学习融为一体,使得学习者在英语应用能力的同时掌握商务专业知识,从而实现培养复合型人才的目标。

全书采用英文编写,旨在使学生在国际商务英语的语言环境中直接、系统地学习国际商务谈判的专业基本理论和知识,了解不同人文背景下商务活动的规范以及具体操作实务,并通过对国际商务知识的学习,强化商务英语这一专门用途英语的技能,掌握商务领域的英语术语、文体和语言特点,从而提高学习者用英语分析和处理谈判业务的能力。

教材结构安排:全书共十四章,涵盖商品销售、商品合同、项目投资以及技术转让等有关的谈判与沟通的内容与过程,主要包括:商务英语谈判与沟通的基本理论;商务谈判与沟通的原则;商务谈判与沟通的形式与过程;商务谈判与沟通的策略与技巧;商务谈判中的口头沟通;商务谈判中的书面沟通;电子通信沟通;销售谈判;投资谈判;技术贸易谈判;国际商务合同谈判;商务活动中的跨文化意识;不同商业文化的谈判与沟通等。

章节体例安排:(每个章节的基本结构大致如下)

● 学习要点(Learning Goals):每章的学习目标,简明扼要地概括本章节的知识点,使学习者在开始学习之前对本章节有一个全面的概括性了解。明确重点、难点,有的放矢地学习。

● 生词(Lead-in Words):课文中出现的主要生词,以帮助学习者排除课文学习的困难,掌握词语的意义和用法。

● 课文:以谈判与沟通业务环节为主线分别介绍各环节的操作规程和国际惯例,使学生在学习完课文后能较准确地掌握有关专业术语、英语相关表达方式和专业知识。此内容均选自较为权威的书籍和刊物。

● 实践活动(Practical Activities)：包括案例分析、角色扮演、微型谈判。结合各章节的知识点，精心挑选了经典的实际案例，有助于学生将理论知识与实践相结合，能客观和理性地处理业务中的问题，从而学到"活"知识。

● 谈判秘诀(Negotiation Tips)：结合各章节要点介绍2至3个谈判小技巧。

● 拓展练习(Extended Activities)：帮助学生把所学的知识灵活地运用到实际中。每章后面都附有针对性的练习，帮助学生巩固最基本的词汇、专业术语和相关的专业知识，强化学生专业知识点的理解和运用。

本教材由蒋磊教授任主编，各位作者编写分工如下：

蒋　磊：第1章	李青山：第2、12章	刘彩霞：第3、10章
马兰萍：第4、13章	马玉梅：第5、8章	王　莉：第6、9章
高晓红：第7、11章	王　绚：第14章	

本书的出版得到了高等教育出版社的鼎力支持和热情帮助，在此我们表示衷心的谢忱。

在本书编写过程中，我们参考并借鉴了国内外出版的有关书籍和资料与相关的网站资料，在此一并感谢。

由于编者水平有限，书中不足之处在所难免，敬请国内外专家、学者和广大读者批评指正。

编　者

2007 年 7 月

Table of Contents

Part 3　Practical Business Negotiation

Key to the Exercises

Part 1

ABC to Business Negotiation & Communication

Chapter 1

Fundamental Theories of Business Negotiation & Communication

Learning Goals

Upon completion of this chapter, you will be able to:
- ☞ recognize the important role of communication in bussiness;
- ☞ identify the components and nature of communication;
- ☞ define concepts and motivation of business negotiation;
- ☞ recognize the key elements of international business negotiation;
- ☞ distinguish the major characteristics of business negotiation;
- ☞ present the different types of business negotiation.

Lead-in Words

infinite *adj.* 无限的

vital *adj.* 至关重要的,致命的,根本的

territory *n.* 领土,领域

concise *adj.* 准确的,简明的

divergent *adj.* 不同的,有差异的,有分歧的

confrontation *n.* 对抗,敌对

trigger *v.* 激起,引起,引发

tackle *v.* 应对,处理,应付

option *n.* 选择

plead *v.* 请求,恳求,央求

bargain *v. n.* 讲价,讨价还价

agenda *n.* 议事日程,章程

embodiment *n.* 体现,显现,化身

Section I   Introduction to Business Communication

As an element of human behavior, negotiation depends on communication. Communicating effectively in speaking and writing extends across all areas of business, including management, technical, clerical, and social positions. And now in the 21st century, business has become truly global and the electronic age has made possible instantaneous communication. The phenomenal growth of international business also creates the need for us to understand international communication.

1. Business Communication & Its Nature

In general, communication is the transferring of message and understanding of meaning among people. But communication is more than just the spoken or written words. At its best it is multifaceted through which we exchange information with the world around us. We use communication skills in every aspect of our lives: at work, family and friends, even with ourselves.

As for business communication, it differs to a certain degree from other forms of communication even though they do share something in common. Sun Yao-yuan（孙耀远）explained that *international business communications mean the exchange of trading messages that relate to buying or selling, understanding or being understood, with the use of traditional or advanced technology*. Xu Xian-guang（徐宪光）in his *Business Communication* defined it as: a dynamic, multi-channeled process, which covers internal as well as external communciation in a given organization. This definition has included those essential elements like dynamic, multi-channeled process in nature.

First, business communication is dynamic because it is always changing with the changing business. Every day business people from CEO to employees should take part in all kinds of business activities inside or outside the organization in an oral or written way. They communicate with different people for different reasons or purposes trying to solve all kinds of problems — some between individuals, some between the individual and the management, some between the organization and the public, and still some between organizations. Besides, from time to time, they will hold meetings or give presentations to people inside and outside the organization. Moreover, every day business people either receive or send many business letters, memos, faxes, e-mails, etc. However, we could hardly believe that business communication would involve so many aspects in its applications. All these and more have constituted nothing else but the dynamic nature of business communication.

Second, being multi-channeled is another important feature of business communication. It is highly advantageous for business people to get in touch with each other in a multi-channeled way in their daily management of business communications. Sometimes they choose the form of telephone or video conferences to discuss important issues. Still sometimes they have their activities recorded or produced on a tape or disk, so as to make it portable and convenient for promotions (like a product presentation or a TV promotion) or for distribution. When a GM (general manager) has something in his mind and he wants to discuss it with someone, he has a number of choices. He may choose a face-to-face way so as to make the talk more impressive or emphatic. He may simply pick up the phone if he wants to save time, or he may write a memo, even send either e-mails or faxes to the relevant person(s) instead.

In a word, being multi-channeled leaves much room for business people to choose the most effective way for their intended communication, which is highly necessary for business people today. It won't be hard for us to find out — and to understand as well — what an active role business communication may play in our versatile business activities.

2. The Role of Business Communication

First, communication is the "lifeblood" that makes every organization go around. And without effective communication organizations cannot function. An organization is a group of people associated for business, political, professional, religious, athletic, social, or other purposes. Its activities require people to interact and react, that is, to communicate effectively.

Second, most managers and office staff spend more than 70% percent of their working time on communications for their daily business, including writing and reading letters, faxes, e-mails, and proposals, making and receiving phone calls, and having meetings etc. Their job, promotion, and professional reputation often depend on doing well in both written and oral communication. Therefore communication is often regarded as a primary responsibility in many careers such as customer relations, labor relations, marketing, personnel, public relations, sales and teaching. Even in the accounting profession mainly with figures, the ability to communicate to those who read his / her financial reports is essential. And this is also the reason why strong communication skills are found in the job descriptions, as a valuable job requirement, listed by numerous companies advertising positions.

3. Components of Communication

Communication is dynamic. Simply stated, it is a two-way process of exchanging ideas or information. In this process, a number of components have been involved, each of them plays an important role in the promotion of communication. These factors interact in the communication processes, affected by various contextual conditions and decisions. This chapter only covers several main elements such as context, sender-encoder, message, medium, receiver-decoder, and feedback, each has different implications and functions.

(1) Message

A message carries ideas from one person to another and it can be delivered either in a verbal way or in a non-verbal way. Verbal message can be further divided into oral form like a face-to-face talk, a phone call, voice mail, TV conference, speech making, and written form, etc. In fact, for a better and more effective communication, the two forms should go hand-in-hand according to the actual situation.

(2) Sender & Receiver

Sender refers to the person who sends the message, and receiver is the one who is supposed to receive the message. As far as the sender is concerned, there are two factors to be taken into consideration: what message should be composed and how to send it out. A message comes from an idea, yet it is not equivalent to an idea. A sender should be wise enough to compose a message in an appropriate way. And then he should choose the right channel to send it out.

In order to make the message well understood and to minimize the probability of misunderstanding, the sender should put himself in the receiver's shoes when designing the message. Suppose a manager wants to send a message to his employees about the rescheduling of the work. Before he actually sends it out, he should think about the likely responses positive or negative — he might get from them, and then decide in which way he should create the message. This will help him to minimize the possible complaints from the employees.

On the receiver's part, although he is entitled to give his feedback in whatever possible ways he likes, he should not give the feedback in a casual way if he really cares about getting the right message from the sender. When he is not clear or not certain about the message, he should not hesitate to ask for clarification. In this way, it will be possible for the receiver to minimize any misunderstanding resulting from vague messages.

In addition, as a good understanding of the interchangeable nature will help us think from both sides — the sender's and the receiver's, the study on the interchangeable nature of both sender and receiver is significant. As a receiver, we all expect the message to be clear and well composed (better not too long); and as a sender, we should do a good job in composing the message before we actually send it out, and none of us would expect any misunderstanding from our receivers. The explanation or reexplanation is not only time-consuming, sometimes, it may result in loss of some opportunities or failures in our planned action.

(3) Channel

The term channel is used technically to refer to the means by which the encoded message is transmitted, that is, the ways of sending and receiving messages. Today, you might feel more comfortable using the word "media". The medium or channel, then, may be print, electronic, or the light and sound waves of face-to-face communication. Different messages naturally ask for different channels for transmission, for example, when the message to be sent is urgent and asks for an immediate reply, the oral channel will be the best choice. As the oral channel is characterized by its intimacy, directness, promptness and impressiveness, many people prefer oral channel.

When the message is formal or worth keeping, another channel is preferable, i. e. the written channel. Written channel helps people to memorize the message. It also serves as a data source. In addition, it can supply legal evidence when required. That is why no one could say "no" to written channel in spite of its time-consuming efforts and cost, although people are getting busier and busier with each passing day.

In fact the oral channel and the written one should not be taken as conflicting ways of message transmission. Actually, they often compensate each other when required. For example, when time is tight, a manager may not be able to give a detailed explanation about some decisions. Then it is high time for him to use the written channel — sending each of his employees an e-mail with his new idea. Sometimes the receiver may not have enough time to go over written message, especially when the message is too long, he may use the oral channel — asking the sender to give him the general idea of the report. Still sometimes both channels are required. That is, when something is really important, the employment of both channels would ensure the desired effect. That is the reason why a copy of the agenda is provided to everyone for a meeting, a brochure distributed for an exhibition and a handout given to each participant before / after a presentation.

Channels within an organization can be further divided into formal and informal ones. Formal channels comprise three kinds of communication — downward, upward, and horizontal, which will be discussed in the following chapter.

(4) Feedback

Feedback refers to the reaction from the message receiver to the message sender. Feedback can be presented in various forms — verbal or non-verbal, formal or informal, positive or negative, etc. It can also be an action, such as receiving in the mail an item you ordered. Senders need feedback in order to determine the success or failure of communication. The actual choice depends both on the message received and on the preference of the receiver. Feedback is important as it gives the original message sender the responding message. Feedback makes communication a two-way or interactive process, but only when the reader responds to a survey or writes a letter to the author does feedback occur.

In another way feedback can be further divided into two pairs: positive feedback vs. negative feedback; internal feedback vs. external feedback. Positive feedback refers to the response that has an encouraging impact on the sender, while negative feedback refers to the corrective reaction from the receiver to the sender. Internal feedback refers to the feedback initiated by the sender. External feedback is often called feedback, as many people have little knowledge of internal feedback. The coupling of internal feedback with external feedback is an ideal model for communication, as it can maximize the effectiveness of the feedback as a whole.

(5) Context

The final component of communication is context. Context is a broad field that includes country, culture, organization and external and internal stimuli. Generally, context can be defined as the environment in which the communication process takes place and which helps to define the communication. If you know the physical context, you can predict with a high degree of accuracy much of the communication. For example, you have certain knowledge and expectations of the communication that occurs within churches, temples, and synagogues. At times, you intentionally want to place your romantic communication in a quiet, dimly light restaurant or on a secluded beach. Again, knowing that a person is being stopped by a police officer for speeding is enough to predict much of the communication.

Every country, culture and company or organization has its own convention for processing and communicating information. As context, every culture has its own worldview, its own way of thinking of activity, time, and human nature, its own way of perceiving self, and its own system of social organization. Knowing each of these helps you assign meaning to the symbols. In this point, the choice of the environment or the context helps assign the desired meaning to the communicated words; certain things are likely to be said and done; other things are very unlikely. It also helps you recognize that the extent to which the source and receiver have similar meanings for the communicated symbols and similar understandings of the culture in which the communication takes place is critical to the success of the communication.

Section II Basic Concepts of Business Negotiation

According to Robert Maddox, author of *Successful Negotiation*, negotiation is the process we use to satisfy our needs when someone else controls what we want. For example, suppose you were a small child and you stood in the aisle of a store and pleaded with a parent for the purchase of a toy, a candy or a game, you were negotiating. You may have been promising you'd be good; you may have been articulating that the item was needed. Your persistence may have been the biggest bargaining chip you held in these dealings with grown-ups. In a word, negotiation is a basic human activity as well as a process people undertake every day to manage their relationships such as the relationship between husband and wife, children and parents, and buyer and seller. Negotiation is a fact of life. People negotiate something at work, at home, or as a consumer every day even when they don't think of themselves as doing so.

1. Motivations of Business Negotiation

Although human beings live in a finite world, their appetites are oriented to the infinite. As a result, man's unlimited demand has constantly given rise to conflicts between such demand and limited, scarce natural resources. To find a way out, the science of economics has been developed to study alternative ways to use scarce and limited but productive resources to produce goods and services to satisfy man's unlimited demand. Man's endless need and demand not only produce confrontation against nature but trigger conflicts among themselves. As we know the long lasting negotiations between Israel and Syria on returning of Israeli occupied territory — Golenhigh site an example to the point. On the 11% of the territory Israel agreed to return, there is a lake providing fresh water to Israeli people. Because of scrious shortage of fresh water in that area, the lake becomes vital to the people of the both countries. Israeli government's target in the negotiation was to make sure that after the returning of the territory, Israel could continuously fetch water from the lake. So the water issue became the focus of the negotiation and increased complexity of the talks.

Water conflict in the Middle East is simply one typical issue among countless disputes of similar nature among countries and nations. There are also other serious confrontations and conflicts induced by social, religious, cultural and political events, however the majority of the conflicts have direct and indirect economic background.

How to resolve and tackle these problems has always been the chief concern of all countries and states. Generally speaking, two approaches have been applied to conflict settlement: military means and peaceful means. Countless battles and wars, both worldwide wars and regional wars have been fought resulting in loss of millions of lives and ruin of property. As an alternative to military forces, weapons and guns, negotiations have also been employed to manage conflicts and settle disputes, thus negotiations are also referred to as peaceful means or political approaches. The two approaches have always backed each other and functioned in an alternative way. However, after the World War II, the devastating consequence of the war has made people all over the world realize a solid fact that coordination through negotiations is no doubt a better option for various conflicts and disputes.

It is misleading to conceive that negotiations are only applied to significant issues. As a matter of fact, negotiations are applied to all situations of conflicts, arguments and bargaining arising in the normal course of business, personal relations and daily life.

More and more occasions require negotiations; conflict is a growing industry. Everyone wants to participate in decisions that affect him; fewer and fewer people will accept decisions dictated by someone else. People differ, and they use negotiations to handle their differences. Whether in business, government, or the family, people reach most decisions through negotiations. Even when they go to court, they almost always negotiate a settlement before trial. Negotiation is such a common phenomenon, it is of great importance to define the meaning of negotiation and generalize activities that can be negotiations in a more concise way called definition.

2. Implications of Business Negotiation

With the further development of economic globalization and integration, negotiations have been widely practised in social life of all kinds, particularly in business activities. Then what is business negotiation?

Generally speaking, business negotiation is one of the important steps taken towards completing import and export trade agreements. It is a bargaining situation in which two or more players have a common interest to cooperate, but at the same time have conflicting interests over exactly how to share. In other words, the players can mutually benefit from reaching an agreement on an outcome from a set of possible outcomes, but have conflicting interests over the set of outcomes. In import and export trade operations, the buyer and the seller confer together to reach a mutually satisfying agreement on a matter of common interest. This is because each of the parties has his own objective in trade operations; e. g. the seller intends to sell the goods / services at a higher price, while the buyer intends to buy the same goods / services at a lower price. Each party presses for the attainment of its own goal. But some elements of cooperation must be presented, otherwise there will be no agreement at all and the opportunity to take part in the activity will be lost. Therefore, business negotiation is a dynamic process of adjustment between governments, trade organizations, multinational enterprises, private business firms and buyers and sellers in relation to investment and import and export of products, machinery and equipments and technology.

Take the following as example. Jane owns a car that she values at $100, 000 (which is the minimum price at which she intends to sell), while Mark values this car at $80, 000 (which is the maximum price at which he intends to buy). If trade occurs at a price that lies between $100, 000 and $80, 000 —— that is, if Jane sells the car to Mark — the seller and the buyer would each become better off. In this situation, there lies a common interest for the two individuals to trade. But, at the same time, they have conflicting interests over the price at which to trade: the seller would like to trade at a higher price, while the buyer would like to trade at a lower price. Any exchange situation, such as the one just described, in which a pair of individuals (or organizations) can engage in mutually beneficial trade but have conflicting interests over the terms of trade, is a bargaining situation.

The main problem that confronts the players in a bargaining situation is the need to reach an agreement over exactly how to cooperate — before their actual cooperation. On one hand, each player would like to reach some agreement rather than no agreement. But, on the other hand, each player would like to reach an agreement that is as favorable to him as possible. It is thus conceivable that the players will strike an agreement only after some costly delay, or indeed even fail to reach any agreement.

3. Elements of Business Negotiation

Negotiation is a social phenomenon and a special embodiment of human relations. It is a process of information exchange between two sides. They are counterparts of matched qualification and rather independent in material force, personality and social status. etc. Due to mutual contact, conflict and differences in viewpoints, needs, basic interests and action mode, both parties try to persuade the other party to understand or accept their viewpoints and to satisfy their own needs. It concerns the following elements: It is an element of human behavior and depends on communication, that is, it occurs between individuals; it takes place only over negotiable issues; it takes place only between people who have the same interest; it takes place only when negotiators are interested not only in taking but also in giving; and it takes place only when negotiating parties trust each other to some extent.

In negotiations, both parties should know the following:

(1) why they negotiate;

(2) whom they negotiate with;

(3) what they negotiate about;

(4) where they negotiate;

(5) when they negotiate;

(6) how they negotiate.

4. Characteristics of Business Negotiation

And no matter what the negotiation is about, there are some of the characteristics of business negotiation:

(1) Negotiation is at the heart of every transaction and, for the most part, it comes down to the interaction between two parties with a common goal (profits) but divergent methods.

(2) These methods (the details of the contract) must be negotiated to the satisfaction of both parties. It can be a very trying process with confrontation and concession.

(3) Both parties share open information. In this case, both parties sincerely disclose them and listen to the other's objectives in order to find something in common.

(4) Both parties try to understand each other's point of view.

(5) Both parties know that they have common and conflicting objectives, so they try to find a way to achieve common and complementary objectives acceptable to them both.

(6) There's no such thing as "take it or leave it" in international business. Everything is negotiable. It all depends on the expertise of the negotiators.

(7) Intenational business negotiation is known as the zero-sum game. One side's gains are directly the other side's losses. Your counterpart attempts to achieve the maximum concessions while leaving you just enough to keep you interested in the deal. Behind all of the smiles, handshakes, and banquets lurks the reality that both parties are trying to "beat" each other. It's an accepted, yet unspoken, fact.

5. Types of Business Negotiation

So far as the types of business negotiation are concerned, we focus on four areas to prepare you for the fundamentals: sale of goods / services, investment, technology transfers as well as bussiness contract.

(1) Sales of Goods / Services

Sales negotiation is an increasingly important part of the sales process. Negotiation starts when a buyer and a seller are conditionally committed to the sale. Negotiation generally results in a compromise between seller and buyer on price, i.e., the seller reduces and the buyer increases the price from their starting positions.

Due to the status differences of the two parties, generally the negotiator shall discuss the export business on the basis of analyzing the relation between supply and demand in international market, making proper strategic objective to achieve the desired results. No matter in what situation, the goal of the negotiators is to provide / get the right product in the right place at the right time at the right price. For the exporter, he must make sure that he gets paid for the product, and for the importer, he must be assured that what he'll get is exactly what he orders.

To achieve desirable results in a sales negotiation, one must consider a variety of factors: product, quality, quantity, packing, price, shipping, quotation, offer and counter offer, insurance, payment, claim and arbitration, etc.

(2) Investment Negotiation

The creation of joint venture is probably the most widespread and complex investment negotiations that exist nowadays. Here, we just quote the negotiation of joint ventures as a example of investment negotiation.

Literally, setting up a joint venture is a long and complicated process that involves four stages: preliminary investigation, pre-negotiation, negotiation and implementation. The preliminary investigation covers the initial approach to the market. This exploratory stage is mainly a phase for collecting infomation before acting. The pre-negotiation phase includes making the first contacts with the company that could be a partner, assessing the compatibility of the two parties' objectives, ascertaining if they have common views on market strategy, conducting the feasibility study, and signing a letter of intent. When the feasibility study has approved by the authorities, the full negotiation can take place. At this stage the parties concerned discuss everything necessary to set up and operate the future joint venture, such as the rights and obligations of each party, as well as the respective contribution of capital, technology, expertise and other resources. The negotiation also addresses issues concerning the management of the joint venture, its decisionmaking structure, its policy for personnel management and the conditions for its termination. At this stage, parties also explore such issues as domestic and export pricing of the future products for sale. This phrase is rather difficult with more than 50 issues, involving a large number of negotiators, lasting a long time and be subject to multiple unexpected events.

The last stage of the whole process concerns the implementation of the agreement. It would be logical to think the negotiation is over, but this is usually not the case. At this stage, surprises crop up on a daily basis because, for instance, the working conditions or supplies of raw materials may undergo dramatic, unforeseenable external changes, as a matter of fact, numerous renegotiation may take place.

(3) Technology Transfer

For different environmental and developmental reasons, technological advances in different countries have always been unequal. The disparate nature of technological progress throughout the world provides the very basis for technology transfer. In the past few decades, international technology transfer has multiplied in leaps and bounds.

Technology transfer is a means of transferring research findings from within the institution to and for the benefit of the public. There are three principal legal methods that can be used to import technology. The first one is through assignment, which is the most expensive among the three as it entails the purchase from the owner all his exclusive rights to a patented technology, trademark or know-how. The second method through a licensing agreement or contracts more flexible and less expensive, hence more suitable to our national conditions. The third method is signing a know-how contract. But more often than not, the purchase of know-how alone is not enough. It takes place together with the purchase of equipment or technology and therefore can be included in the license contract.

A number of unique features in technology transfer as following: First, commercial technology transfer is highly monopolistic. Second, a single technology can be traded multiple times, as the transfer does not involve ownership but only the right to use. Finally, technology transfer does not simply follow the basic market rule of exchange.

(4) Business Contract Negotiation

A contract, in the broadest sense, is simply an agreement that defines a relationship between one or more parties. A business contract, in simplest terms, is just an agreement made by two or more parties for the purpose of transacting business. The contract which is generally adopted in import and export business is the formal written contract. Written terms may be recorded in a simple memorandum, certificate, or receipt. Because a contractual relationship is made between two or more parties who have potentially adverse interests, the contract terms are usually supplemented and restricted by laws that serve to protect the parties and to define specific relationships between them in the event that provisions are indefinite, ambiguous, or even missing.

Section III　Practical Activities

1. Case Study

● Case Study 1

Background

A fair and equitable deal can be reached quickly, with a minimum of effort on even the most complex issues. It depends on who the major players are, how motivated they feel and whether lawyers play an active role. If you think there is a little unfair to attorneys, you might be right. However, most of the lawyers I've worked with agree with me, off the record, of course.

There are businessmen and businesswomen out there who still do things in the old-fashioned way. Their negotiating style is much the same as it was when they were kids. They know the rules, that to give value. All they want is a reasonable profit. When you run across a company like this, you should go out of your way to keep them happy.

In the following dialogue, Jeffrey is an honest old-fashioned businessman content to make an honest living. He wants to buy some big screen TV sets distributed in the U.S. Marilyn has often contacted Jeffrey and tried to sell him electronics, but this is the first time she is meeting Jeffrey in person and she is hopeful Jeffrey will actually buy from her.

Jeffrey: Hello, come in. I've been waiting for you.

Marilyn: Thank you. I'm not late, am I?

Jeffrey: No, no, no, not at all. It is just that I've been looking forward to meeting you.

Marilyn: Well, thank you, but it is not all that hard to do, you know. I've been calling your office and sending you proposals for about two years, and you've never responded before.

Jeffrey: Ha, ha, ha! Yes, I guess I deserved that. Let me explain, OK?

Marilyn: Please, I wish you would.

Jeffrey: Well, as you probably know I buy from a selected group of suppliers and don't, as a rule, deal with new people.

Marilyn: Yes, I know that. It is why I've been trying to become one of those suppliers. I hear you are a good man to do business with.

Jeffrey: I've very old-fashioned. I believe in loyalty. Once I start a sales relationship with someone, I stay with him or her, and we do most of our business on the phone. I expect their absolute best price possible and don't haggle. But if I find out they screwed me over, then I find another supplier.

Marilyn: That's pretty much what I heard.

Jeffrey: Well, those are my terms. As long as you honor them, we do business. If you break faith and try to take advantage, I'll find someone else to work with. Can you live with that?

Marilyn: No problem at all, Jeffrey, just give me the chance.

● Case Study 2

Ikea, a well-known Swedish home improvement store opened a Home Furnishings store in Shanghai last year, and has attracted many visitors every day.

Ikea's Rule

Xu Mei and her husband have just moved into a new apartment and the couple wanted to add some more pieces of furniture in the apartment. As Xu Mei's husband once lived and studied in Sweden for some time, the couple decided to go to Ikea for the selection. They found what they wanted: a set of leather sofa. However, they were told that they should pay the total sum of money right there before the furniture was sent to their home.

In Shanghai, the popular way for the purchase of furniture is to pay 10 percent of the total sum as a deposit, and the remaining is paid upon the arrival of the furniture. After some negotiation, Ikea employees gave up their original request but insisted on a 25 percent deposit for the sofa.

In the course of this process, the saleswoman's arrogant attitude and her repeated expression "It's Ikea's rule ... " almost spoiled the transaction. Nevertheless, the couple filled in the order form for the sofa. They asked the saleswoman to tell the deliverers not to forget to bring the receipt with the sofa.

Three days later, the ordered sofa was delivered to the couple's apartment, which was on the fifth floor. When the husband asked for the receipt while paying the deliverers the outstanding balance, they told him that they were from a home-removal company and Ikea would send the receipt to him the next day. In this case, the couple asked to keep the ¥1,000 until the next day. When the deliverer phoned Ikea up for the answer, they were told to bring the sofa back if the outstanding balance was not fully paid, as it was the rule from Ikea's financial department. The deliverers brought the sofa down from the fifth floor.

No message came from Ikea the next day.

(Adapted and translated from People's Daily, Overseas Edition, Jan. 7, 1999)

Questions:

① You are a friend of Xu Mei. After hearing Xi Mei's story, what would you do to help her? Why?

② You are the newly-arrived manager of Ikea. As soon as you arrive, you hear the whole matter, what do you think of this? And what action would you take to handle it (as the media is concerned about it)? Why?

③ As a potential consumer of Ikea furniture, how do you feel about this after reading the case above? Do you think that Ikea has its reasons for reacting in that way?

2. Role Play

For your Information

Having a reputation for honesty is important in doing business and following the advice above will go a long way, but that is not everything.

The following is an example of just how easy it can be. It could be face to face or over the phone. Jack is selling speakers made in Taiwan, and Mary works for an American distributor.

Jack: Mary! How are you? It's good to hear your voice.

Mary: Thank you, Jack, it is always a pleasure doing business with you.

Jack: So how are things in the land of the free and the home of the brave?

Mary: Great! And, how are things in your neck of the woods (你的地盘)?

Jack: Things are so great here. I almost smiled myself to death last week. One of my coworkers had to give me CPR (心脏复苏术).

Mary: Oh, Jack, I have missed your sense of humor. Ha, ha, ha! Nobody else sees things quite like you do. It's your gift.

Jack: Or a curse.

Mary: Nope, it is a gift. Anyway, we need some more of those mid-range speakers you tricked me into buying last time.

Jack: That, my dear, was classic sales technique delivered by professionals.

Mary: Are you still gouging (欺诈,勒索) your customers the same price per unit?

Jack: Heck no, we doubled the price, but because it's you, I'll let you have them at 50% off. Heh, heh, heh! How does that sound?

Mary: You silver tongued devil. Can't you ever just answer a question with a simple yes or no?

Jack: I could but there's the fun in that!

3. Mini Negotiation

Background

You are the chairman of the Machinery Import and Export department of the company "Bright Path". There are 200 people working in that company. After lengthy internal coordination and discussion, "Bright Path" is going to invested in a set of new special machinery to expand their productivity.

In the end, you opted for the offer of "Information Highway", a Japanese supplier. Even though the price of "Information Highway" is high, you hope to save time and money in the long run since the geographic proximity of "Information Highway" will make the maintenance of the machinery easier.

The new machines were delivered over the last two weeks. On the last five days an installation team of three engineers from "Information Highway" came to "Bright Path". They installed the machines, conducted tests and finally a take-over-protocol was signed.

The representative of the installation-team, Mr. Tanaka, came to your office for the last half hour of the final installation; you drank some tea together and had a lively *conversation. The technical director of "Bright Path" could have asked more detailed questions. But at the moment he is out of the city on a business-trip.*

Generally speaking, your long hours working on the weekend were worthwhile: The new machines are installed and the Monday morning-shift will start the production. This is very important since orders for the new product have already come in: the first delivery to one of your longstanding key customer must be completed in one week.

On Monday morning, not long before the morning break, you receive a phone call from the assembly shop. The excited shift leader tells you that there was an accident with the new machines. An electric shock injured two engineers of your company. An emergency doctor and an ambulance have already been called for. The machines' provider, "Information Highway", had also already been informed. They promised their support as quickly as possible. The new machines don't work! The engineers of "Bright Path" are helpless. You leave your office in order to go to the assembly shop. The two engineers affected seem to be "OK": Some minor burns on their skin, they escaped with no more than a fright. It could have been a great deal worse! About two hours later, you receive a phone call from the factory security service: A visitor from "Information Highway" is waiting at your company's security gate in order to see you. You hurry there. Approaching the gate, you recognize the competent Mr. Tanaka. He smiles.

Directions: *Supposing the given situation takes place in China. Please discuss the questions below in small groups and afterwards select a person (playing the part of Information Highway) from one group who will then role-play the conversation with a person from another group (playing the part of "Bright Path"). You'll have about 20 minutes for discussion and preparation.*

Questions:

① How will you act towards the head of the installation team, Mr. H.?

② Should the situation arise, what will be your steps against the head of the installation team, Mr. H., and what are the steps against "Technology Corp."?

③ Please explain your approach.

Negotiation Tips

● Be Prepared 充分准备

Preparation is the single most important element in successful negotiations. In negotiation, information is power. The more relevant information you have, the better your position is. Preparation for your negotiations can not be overdone. Allow yourself adequate time to prepare prior entering any negotiation.

● Negotiation Involve on Going Relationships 谈判着眼长远关系

With the exception of large purchase, most negotiations involve parties involved in a long term relationship. Whether the relationship is family, friends of business associates, it will be necessary to continue to deal with your "adversary" outside the context of the negotiation. Always be sensitive to the potential impact of your negotiations on these relationship.

● Understand the Needs of Your Adversary 了解对手的需求

Your adversary in this context is the other party in the negotiation. Your relationship with this party may not normally be described as adversarial（敌对的，对抗的）, but for the purposes of this discussion we will view the negotiation as an adversarial relationship. Put yourself in your adversary's shoes. What would they like to gain from the negotiation? Write down as many possible goals as you can think of. Prioritize（区分优先顺序） your list in the order that you believe your adversary would. Identify the items you are willing to negotiate and those items which are non-negotiable.

Extended Activities

I. Situational Group Talks.

A director of garment factory and the dean of the director's office receive a businessman and his foreign trade customer who come to visit the factory to see how garments are made from selecting material, cutting to sewing and the whole process of making garments.

II. Decide whether the following statements are true(T) or false(F).

1. Negotiation is a way of dealing with human relationship and resolving conflicts.
2. If conflicts give rise to negotiations, then the conflict itself is caused due to clash of stakes or interests held by each party.
3. A negotiation is a process of communication between parties to manage interests in order for them to come to an agreement, solve a problem or make arrangements.
4. Negotiation on price is normally the key part of a business talks.
5. The most important part of pre-negotiation planning is determining your objectives that need to be achieved.
6. In negotiations, you should pay attention to your verbal and non-verbal communication skills as well as get feedback properly.
7. Technology transfer simply follows the basic market rule of exchange.
8. Feedback can be further divided into two pairs: positive feedback vs. negative feedback; internal feedback vs. external feedback.
9. Managing position means knowing how to make concessions.
10. A conclusion or an agreement should be reached to finally close the negotiation.

III. Translate the following sentences into Chinese.

1. Never forget, everyone who sits down at the negotiation table is there for one simple reason:

they want something the other side has.

2. If you are armed with knowledge you can face your negotiators with confidence.

3. Success in negotiation is seen not to be measured in points scored off one's opponent, but in the contribution that the negotiation makes to the successful operation of the activity as a whole.

4. The entire process of negotiation is founded on the premise that both are interdependent, that is, one party cannot get what he / she wants without taking the other into consideration.

5. Negotiation is a function subservient to the general commercial interests of the parties involved and it is directed towards the achievement of their overall objectives.

IV. Translate the following sentences into English.

1. 谈判并非独立于整个交易之外,而是整个交易活动的一部分。

2. 谈判者需要通过就共同的利益来交换意见从而调整各自的想法。

3. 共同以及互补的目标对谈判产生直接和积极的影响,而相互冲突的目标则对谈判进程产生消极的影响。

4. 谈判高手认为创造一个建设性的氛围和建立彼此尊重的人际关系是至关重要的。

5. 谈判的关键是结果,其他的一切均为装饰。

V. Read the following passage and fill in the blanks with the given words.

bargain	cooperation	agreement	lost	interests
objective	mutual	lower	risk	negotiator

Negotiation is a dynamic process of adjustment. In import and export trade operations, the buyer and the seller confer together to reach a mutually satisfying ___1.___ on a matter of common interest. This is because each of the parties has his own ___2.___ in trade operations, e. g. the seller intends to sell the goods / services at a higher price, while the buyer intends to buy the same goods / services at a ___3.___ price. Each party presses for the attainment of its own goal. But some elements of ___4.___ must be presented, otherwise there will be no agreement at all and the opportunity to take part in the activity will be ___5.___ .

The dual elements of conflict and cooperation are described here: it is in the ___6.___ interest of participants to come to some agreement and this provides a cooperative aspect; however, the ___7.___ of participants are opposed, and this is the basis for rivalry. The ___8.___ is pulled in two directions at the same time: towards holding out for more with the ___9.___ of losing all; towards agreeing to his opponent's demands and securing the ___10.___ with sacrificing the chance of a possible higher reward.

Chapter 2

Principles of Business Negotiation & Communication

Learning Goals

Upon completion of this chapter, you will be able to:

☞ identify the 6Cs principles of business communication;

☞ grasp the connotation for the 6Cs principles;

☞ understand the 5 principles of negotiation;

☞ learn how to build trust in negotiation.

Lead-in Words

ambiguous *adj.* 不明确的	indentation *n.* 缩排
inevitable *adj.* 必然的,不可避免的	accurate *adj.* 精确的,正确的
goodwill *n.* 好意,信誉	distract *v.* 转移
demolish *v.* 破坏,推翻	hasty *adj.* 匆忙的,草率的
clear-headed *adj.* 头脑清楚的	redundant *adj.* 多余的
abbreviation *n.* 缩写;缩写词	multiplicity *n.* 多样性
jargon *n.* 行话	evaluate *v.* 评价,估计
acquainted *adj.* 知晓的;有知识的	explicitly *adv.* 明白地,明确地
terminology *n.* 术语	resourceful *adj.* 足智多谋的
visual aids 视觉教具	masculine *adj.* 男性的,阳性的
tabulations *n.* 表格	collaborative *adj.* 合作的
italics *n.* 斜体字	empathy *n.* 移情作用,[心]神入
obstacle *n.* 障碍,困难	formidable *adj.* 令人敬畏的,可怕的

Section I   Principles of Business Communication

To be a successful negotiator, we need to understand the basic principles of business communication and negotiation. Basically, there are six principles of business communication: clarity, correctness, conciseness, completeness, courtesy and consideration (6Cs principles).

In order to convey effective and readable information, 6 principles must be followed in business communication, which provide guidelines for choice of content and style of presentation, adapted to the purpose and receiver of your message.

1. Clarity

Clarity means to make the information clear so that the reader can understand what you are trying to convey. The meaning the reader gets is the meaning you intended. If the information is ambiguous, the reader has to guess the right one; it is quite probable that misunderstanding or even mistake will be aroused at last. Therefore, further exchange of messages for explanation will be inevitable, your effort and the reader's time will be wasted and your organization's goodwill will be demolished.

To maintain clarity in your message, you should first be clear-headed about what you are trying to say. Don't rely on inspiration; take notes to list all the details before writing a letter, making a presentation or even a phone call.

Second, choose precise, concrete and familiar words. When you have a choice between a redundant and a simple word, use the short, familiar one that the reader will quickly understand. But that does not mean to use a lot of abbreviations like a fax does. In a formal message, abbreviations are not widely welcomed. Use synonyms instead of unfamiliar Latin terms. Also, avoid using technical terms and business jargon in some professional situations, when you communicate with a person who is not acquainted with the terminology. If you must use such terms, define them briefly and clearly.

Third, organize effective sentences and paragraphs. The suggested average sentence length should be about 17 or 20 words. And one sentence has only one main idea. Writers must choose correct sentence structure to emphasize the main idea properly. In a complex sentence the main idea should be placed in the main clause; the least important points are in subordinate clauses or phrases. In addition, some visual aids can be applied, including: headings, tabulations, itemizations, graphs, pie charts, underlining, italics, indentations, colored capitals or italics.

2. Correctness

Correctness means the writer should not be distracted by mistakes in grammar, punctuation or spelling. All of the information in the message is accurate.

In order not to make mistakes, you should use the right level of language. Formal writing is often applied in scholarly writing, legal documents, top-level government agreements and so on. The style is impersonal and contains complicated sentences. Informal writing is more typical of business communication. The words are usually short, well-known and conversational.

Errors of fact should be paid attention too. For example, errors with name of article, specifications, quantity, trading terms, price quotation, sales discount, currency option, payment modes, etc. are often made. These errors are usually caused out of one's inattention and carelessness such as careless typing, insufficient proofreading or too hasty correction or erasures of mistakes on the computer. Errors can also be made because reference books are not consulted when necessary.

So your message must be checked carefully before it is sent out.

3. Conciseness

Conciseness refers to say things in the fewest possible word. That is to say, you say things briefly but completely without losing any other information. Then a busy reader will not waste any unnecessary time. Try to keep your sentences short, avoid unnecessary repetition and eliminate excessive details.

To keep your sentences short, you can change a long one mentioned before into a shorter name, an abbreviation, initials or even a proper pronoun. All the useless repetition of phrases and sentences should be avoided.

In addition, you should make sure to include the relevant information only, so that the redundant details will be cut out. Stick to the purpose of the message, delete irrelevant words and loose sentences, omit information the receiver already knows, avoid long introductions, unnecessary explanations, excessive adjectives and prepositions, these are all good methods to be concise.

A concise message is not necessarily a short one. Sometimes your message deals with a multiplicity of matters. In this case it cannot avoid being long.

4. Completeness

Completeness means your message contains all details you plan to convey to your reader. In a complete message, all of the reader's questions are answered. The reader has enough information to evaluate the message and act on it.

One way to help make your message complete is to provide all the necessary information the reader needs. Whenever you reply to any inquiry, answer all questions, including explicitly stated and also implied questions. Sometimes you must do more than answer the reader's specific questions. They may not know that they need or their questions may be inadequate. So you should provide some extra when desirable.

5. Courtesy

Courtesy means using social skills to show your respect for the reader. The courteous message should be sincere, friendly, thoughtful, cultivated and resourceful. It helps to build a good image of your company and deepen the business relationship.

You can use tactful, respectful and appreciative words or expressions to build goodwill. The value of goodwill or public esteem for the firm may be worth a great amount of money.

Non-discriminatory language reflects equal treatment of people regardless of gender, race, ethnic origin, and physical features. In business communication, you should try to avoid any masculine words.

Courtesy is not mere politeness. It's not neutral or negative. Courtesy is of positive value. If the occasion demands firmness, deal it that way, but not show your anger. Prompt and punctual handling of your business communication is also a way of courtesy.

6. Consideration

Consideration means that you prepare every message with the reader in mind and try to put yourself in reader's place. This will also show you look at things from the reader's point of view, emphasize what the reader wants to know, respect the reader's intelligence, and protect the reader's ego.

When communicating, you had better try to use "you" or "your" instead of "we", "our", "us" and "I", etc. This thoughtful consideration is called "you-attitude" approach. The reader will feel being cared about by you.

Section II   Principles of Business Negotiation

As a significant social activity, negotiation is a means of dealing with human relationships and resolving conflicts and has never been non-exist. As a product of social competition, negotiation has got its different meaning and content with the development of the times. There are normally five principles of negotiation: principles of collaborative negotiation, principles of interest distribution, principle of trust in negotiation, principle of distributive & complex negotiation and win-win principle. We will deal with them separately.

1. Principle of Collaborative Negotiation

Collaborative negotiation is also commonly known as Harvard Principled Negotiation, which is developed by Roger Fisher and William Ury in the book *Getting to Yes*. The core of the principle is to reach a solution beneficial to both parties by way of stressing interests and value not by way of bargaining. Negotiation is to negotiate with the other party in order to solve problems. It involves people with diverse interests working together to achieve mutually satisfying outcomes. Negotiation in itself is a kind of sincere collaboration. Through it both parties are seeking an alternative arrangement of a business situation so that at the end of the negotiation they feel this result is much better than that when they first started. Therefore the goal of collaborative negotiation is to minimize the dispute so that the outcome is more constructive than destructive. In achieving this, both parties are making concessions. They foster communication, problem-solving, and improved relationships. They are clear that it is through their sincere cooperation that the best result can be achieved.

Collaborative negotiation consists of four basic components:

People — separate the people from the problem

Interests — focus on interests not positions

Gaining — invent options for mutual gain

Criteria — introduce objective criteria

The four components are interrelated with each other and should be applied to throughout the whole course of the negotiations. The four components are explained in the following:

(1) Separate the People from the Problem

It is generally understood that in negotiations, problems will be discussed and resolved if talks are going on in a friendly and sincere atmosphere. Unfortunately more often than not high tension is built up due to negotiators' prejudice against the other party or poor impression on each other or misled interpretation of the other party's intention. It is conceivable that negotiations would be directed to personal disputes and both sides say something hurting each other when such prejudice or misunderstanding exists. As a result negotiators' personal feeling is mingled with interests and events to be discussed. For example, you may feel very uncomfortable when your counterpart appears arrogant and superior, so you probably throw out something to knock off his arrogance, which may further irritate him and make him take irritation action. The focus of negotiation is shifted from interests and issues of both parties to personal dignity and self-respect, thus the attacks and quarrels end up with nothing. In other cases your counterpart may misunderstand your intention and openly show his emotion when you make comments on his opinion and events he has described. For situation as such, collaborative negotiation develops three steps for both parties to follow, which are:

✦ Develop empathy:

We put ourselves in their shoes;

We avoid blaming them for our problems;

We help them participate in the process.

✦ Manage emotions:

We allow them to let off steam;

We do not overreact to emotional outbursts.

✦ Communicate:

We listen and summarize what we hear;

We avoid trying to score points and debating them as opponents;

We do not berate them about what they are doing wrong.

The best time for handling people problems is before they become people problems. To do so, negotiators need establish a working relationship with the other party. Be "partners", not "adversaries". One specific technique that works is to change the shape of the table rather than sitting opposite your "opponents", and arrange the seating so that all the parties are sitting together facing a flip chart or blackboard where the problem is presented. That makes it clear that all the participants are facing the problem together. Instead of "us" against "them", it has become a case of "all of us" against "it".

(2) Focus on Interests Not Positions

Conflicts of interests bring people to negotiation table. Negotiating parties holding on to their own positions is for the purpose of having their interests realized or protecting their interests or gaining more interests. Successful negotiations are the result of mutual giving and taking of interests rather than keeping firm on one's own positions. The method of focusing on the common interests of negotiating parties works well because firstly, there's always more than one way of fulfilling each other's interests, and secondly, both sides can always find out certain common interests, otherwise they will not sit together discussing and talking. Negotiating parties can try the following methods in order to concentrate on interests not positions.

✦ Identify the self-interests:

Explore and recognize the interests of the other party that stand in your way;

Examine the different interests of different people on the other side;

Respect your counterparts as human beings and recognize the needs and interests that underlie their positions.

✦ Discuss the interests with the other party:

Give your interests a vivid description and be specific;

Demonstrate your understanding of the other party's interests and acknowledge them as part of the overall problem that you are trying to solve;

Discuss the problems before proposing a solution;

Direct the discussion to the present and the future. Stay away from the difficulties of the past;

Be concrete but flexible;

Be hard on the problem but soft on the people.

(3) Invent Options for Mutual Gain

The first two components look at the relation between people and problems, and interests and positions, which are conductive for negotiators to establish an objective view on those important factors in negotiations. The third component of inventing options for mutual gain provides an approach to fulfillment of two parties' demands.

Why are negotiators easily trapped by their own positions? The explanation is that many negotiations simply focus on a single event and the solution to the event is either win or lose, for example, price of a car, size of commission, or time limit of a loan. The distributive nature of interest gaining limits people's scope of thinking and causes people to insist on their own stance. In such case, there is one way out, which is to jointly make the cake of interests as large as possible before cutting it apart so that both sides may get what they desire. To this end negotiators should be able to provide creative options and alternatives to unaccepted solutions. There are in fact always alternative solutions to problems to be solved, which is, unfortunately, often not fully understood.

There are four major obstacles that prevent negotiators from creative thinking: premature judgment; searching for the single answer; the assumption of a fixed pie; thinking that "solving their problem is their problem".

(4) Introduce Objective Criteria

The first three components advocate the benefits of considering both parties' interests and designing a distributive pattern that would satisfy both sides' demands. However, conflicts and disputes of the two parties over interest gaining will not disappear no matter how considerable the two sides try to be and how creative in providing options. When the two sides can not decide which option is reasonable and rational, looking for an objective criterion will be a way out. The guidelines for objective criteria are:

✦ Independent of wills of all parties;

✦ Legitimate and practical;

✦ Acceptable for all parties.

The next important step is to choose a fair procedural standard, the way of implementing the criterion, when an agreement is reached upon such a criterion. A good example for "fair procedure" is the way to divide a piece of cake between two children: the one who cuts the cake must let the other choose first. The fair procedures may also include "doing it in turns", "drawing lots" and "looking for an arbitrator".

Every negotiation is different, but the basic elements do not change. Collaborative negotiation can be used whether there is one issue or several; two parties or many; whether there is a prescribed ritual, as in collaborative bargaining, or an important free-for-all, as in talking with hijackers. The method applies whether the other side is more experienced or less, a hard bargainer or a friendly one. Collaborative negotiation is an all-purpose strategy. Unlike almost all other strategies, if the other side learns this one, it does not become more difficult to use; it becomes easier. The success of collaborative negotiation does not rely on playing tricks or negotiators' resourcefulness but on fairness, objectiveness and mutual understanding.

2. Principle of Interest Distribution

The purpose of negotiation is to reach agreements between parties with different interests. Negotiation can take a variety of forms. While the traditional competitive approach to negotiation tries to maximize one party's gain over the other party's loss, the collaborative approach focuses on parties with diverse interests working together to achieve mutually satisfying outcomes. However, no matter what form a negotiation may take, its goal will never change: interest realization.

Any negotiations occurred at home involve two levels of interests: personal and organizational; at the international level, there are three: personal, organizational and national. To what extend these interests can be coordinated, integrated and balanced determines largely the progress and outcome of negotiations.

(1) Personal Interests VS Organizational Interests

Personal interests may include such major aspects as realization of personal value, promotion to higher positions, increasing personal income and pursuing comfortable life. Comparatively speaking, personal interests can be easily brought into line with that of organizations since realization of one's personal value, social status and his reputation in others' expectation are linked closely with his performance and achievements done for the organizations. Therefore there is an interior connection between personal and organizational interests, so realization of organizational interests means fulfillment of personal interests and vice versa. By virtue of this linkage, negotiators will make his utmost efforts to achieve interests of organization he represents in the negotiation.

However, personal interests are not always in convergence with interests of organizations particularly when individuals place their own interests before interests of the organizations or when their own interests are in conflict with interests of the organizations, which are often of momentary nature.

(2) Personal Interests VS Organizational & National Interests

Personal interests are found easier to be brought in line with interests of organizations by reason of close linkage between the two, but may be frequently in conflict with interests of the state. For individuals, national interests appear to be quite remote and directly connected with individuals' and thus they are often looked upon as a general guideline. However, when an individual represents his country in binational negotiations, he will definitely defend the interests of the country and make every effort to gain state interests, since on such occasion state interests are so overwhelmingly important that any suffering of state interests will bring heavy losses not only to the state but to organizations and individuals as well.

Organizational interests and national interests should be in convergence well coordinated, too, since national interests represent organizational interests fundamentally. When dealing with issues involving bilateral relations of two countries, organizations have to get the support from the government because bilateral or multilateral relations of countries are so complicated that they are beyond organization's abilities and authorities to manage. By requesting assistance from the government, organizations can still have strong influence on government's decision-making.

The government will give its full support for the realization of the interests at both the organizational and national level.

Organizations, on the other hand, paying undue attention to their own interests at the negotiating table will undermine or jeopardize national interests. Such cases are not uncommon in resent years. For instance, some companies imported scrapped cars causing air pollution; some enterprises manufactured products such as disposable chopsticks for export at the expense of valuable national resources.

National interests should always be of top priority. When there is a conflict between organizational interests and national interests, organizational interests must be subordinate to the national interests. In almost no exception government will give its full support to the realization of the common interests of both the nation and the organization.

3. Principle of Trust in Negotiation

Trust is of great importance in negotiation. Trust between group leader and group members as well as trust between two negotiating parties is a decisive element of shaping relationship of all sides. Low trust leads to poor relationship and thus low degree of cooperation, on the other hand, high trust leads to good relationship and high degree of cooperation. When people trust one another, relationship and cooperation are enhanced and when they mistrust each other, relationship and cooperation suffer. We can not underestimate the corrosive effects of mistrust.

There are basicaly three types of trust in professional relationships:

① Deterrence-based trust: People trust or expect that they will be punished if they do or do not do something based on consistency with past behavior.

② Knowledge-based trust: people trust or expect that the other person will act in a certain way based on what they have learned about that person. Predictability is based on their understanding of the other person's action, thoughts and intents, not just his past behavior.

③ Identification-based trust: People trust or expect that they can act on behalf of the other person because they share the interests, values and concerns of the other person very well. It involves substantial internalization of the other person's desires, intentions, values, and so on.

4. Principle of Distributive & Complex Negotiation

Negotiations according to issues discussed and parties anticipated may fall into two categories: distributive negotiations characterized by single issues and only two parties, and complex negotiations involving more than two issues and multi-parties.

(1) Distributive negotiation

Distributive negotiation, also called positional bargaining, claiming value bargaining, zero-sum bargaining, or win-lose bargaining, is a competitive approach that is used when there is a fixed "pie" — a finite limit to a resource and negotiators have to decide who gets how much of it. The negotiators assume that there is not enough to go around, and they cannot "expand the pie", so the more one side gets, the less the other side gets.

Distributive bargaining is important because there are some disputes that cannot be solved in any other way.

Information is the key to gaining a strategic advantage in a distributive negotiation. A negotiator should do his best to guard his information carefully and also try to get information out of his opponent. To a large extent, the negotiator's bargaining power depends on how clear he is about his goals, alternatives and walk-away values and how much he knows about those of his opponent. Once he knows these values, he will be in a much stronger position to figure out when to concede and when to hold firm in order to best influence the response of the other side.

(2) Complex Negotiation

① The Underlying Reasons for Complex Negotiation

A complex negotiation is so called because it involves:

✦ A number of parties: in addition to two parties anticipated first, third parties will join or a coalition of multi-parties will be established;

✦ A number of issues: instead of single issue in distributive negotiation, a number of issues related with one another together become the focus of negotiation, which require clarification of linkage among several issues and trade-off between issues;

✦ A number of interests: this demands a careful choice of priority among several interests;

✦ Different interests: personal negotiators' interest differs from the party interests.

② Five Principles for Complex Negotiation

It is more difficult to reach rational agreement in a multiparty negotiation than in two-party bargaining. Negotiators need to consider the varying interests of more people and deal with the possibility of forming coalitions. They are:

✦ To think carefully about the distribution rule to be used in allocating resources among the parties;

✦ To avoid majority rule in group negotiations whenever possible;

✦ To avoid strict issue-by-issue agendas whenever possible;

✦ To focus on the differing interests and preferences of group members to facilitate creative integrative agreements;

✦ To recognize that coalitions are inherently unstable, often leading to agreements that are not in the best interest of the organization.

Group negotiations are becoming increasingly common in and among organizations. To effectively manage these negotiations, one needs to look more carefully for integrative opportunities, be aware of barriers to integrative agreements, and be sensitive to the impact of decision-making rules on the quality of group outcomes. Negotiating as a group allows one to take advantage of the knowledge, information, and perspective of each member to reach a creative and integrative solution.

5. Win-win Principle

In this approach, parties collaborate to look for a solution that maximizes joint gain and allows everyone to walk away feeling like they have won something. The basic idea is that both sides can achieve their objectives. It focuses on developing mutually beneficial agreements based on the interests of the negotiators. Interests include the needs, desires, concerns, and fears important to each side. They are the underlying reasons why people become involved in a conflict. Win-win approach is important because it usually produces more satisfactory outcomes for the parties involved than positional bargaining does.

Win-win approach is a collaborative process and the parties usually end up helping each other. It facilitates constructive, positive relationships between previous adversaries. To apply win-win approach to negotiation, the first step is to identify each sides interests and find out why the other side wants that. The bottom line is that you need to figure out why people feel the way they do, and why they are demanding what they are demanding. Be sure to make it clear that you are asking these questions so you can understand their interests better, not because you are challenging them or trying to figure out how to beat them.

When you are clear about the other side's interests, you might ask yourself they perceive your demands. What stands in the way of their agreeing with you? Do they know their underlying interests? Do you know your own underlying interests? If you can figure out their interests as well as your own, you will be much more likely to find a solution that benefits both sides.

Win-win approach has proved to be successful and effective in many tough negotiations because it takes into full consideration of both sides' interests, which contributes greatly to the mutual understanding of negotiating parties, therefore, it can bring about positive results that both parties expect. However effective win-win model can be, not all people in all situations will be guided by this concept by by virtue of one deep-rooted dimensional concept of win-lose, therefore there is still a long way to go since it is a formidable task for people to establish a new concept.

Section III　Practical Activities

1. Case Study

● Case Study 1

Background

　Good performance will lead to promotion. But sometimes, it was not necessarily the case, why? Let's study from Mr. W's story.

Failure in Promotion

Mr. W works for HTD Company in China. Two years ago, he was assigned to be in charge of a farm construction project at WGF Farm, which is located in a city along the Yangtze River. As an experienced and skillful engineer, he did a good job for this project. Therefore, he won praises from the management.

Mr. Rishman, the CEO of HTD Company, wanted to know how everything was going on at WGF Farm. When he got there, he found that there was a channel around the farm, whose opening led directly into the Yangtze River. He was worried about the possible spillover of the Yangtze River flood, as he has seen from TV news. Therefore, he asked Mr. W to start taking measures and record the water level of the channel every day at 7:00 A.M. However, he did not explain the reason for this.

Mr. W did not understand why he should make such a record. He thought that the record would probably be used by the Company as normal statistic data in the future. He had done a good job in recording the water level exactly as he was asked to for almost half a year.

However, one day he overheard that there was a big valve controlling the flow of channel water in / out of Yangtze River. It was obvious that the record on the channel water level was different from that of Yangtze River. Feeling puzzled, Mr. W called his line-manager an explanation. Unfortunately, his line-manager was too busy to pay attention to his question. Mr. W did not follow it up. He just went on with his recording of the channel water level.

Three months later, Mr. W was assigned to work on another farm project. However, when his successor came, he learned about that valve was from the local people. Immediately he sent a written report to his line-manager, who passed the message on to Mr. Rishman. The 9-month recording on the channel water level was stopped by the new comer's line-manager, who had received the directive from Mr. Rishman.

At the end of the year, Mr. W received no bonus, not to speak of promotion, though he had done a good job on the quality control of the farm project. Again, Mr. W felt puzzled. He asked himself: why?

Questions:

1. What would have been the appropriate action for Mr. W to take when he first received the directive from Mr. Rishman and later on failed to receive any explanation from his line-manager?

2. What would you appraise in Mr. W's performance if you were Mr. Rishman? Why?

3. If you were Mr. W's line-manager, and someone tells you that Mr. W is not to blame for the valve and for keeping the recording on the channel water level, what would you say?

● Case Study 2

Background

People routinely engage in positional bargaining in a negotiation. Each side takes a position, argues for it, and makes concessions to reach a compromise. The following is the classical example of the kind taking place in a secondhand store:

Don't Bargain over Positions

Customer: How much do you want for this brass dish?

Shopkeeper: That is a beautiful antique, isn't it? I guess I could let it go for $75.

Customer: Oh, come on, it's dented. I'll give you $15.

Shopkeeper: Really! I might consider a serious offer, but $15 certainly isn't serious.

Customer: Well I could go to $20, but I would never pay anything like $75. Quote me a realistic price.

Shopkeeper: You drive a hard bargain, young lady. $60 cash, right now.

Customer: $25.

Shopkeeper: It cost me a great deal more than that. Make me a serious offer.

Customer: $37.50. That's the highest I will go.

Shopkeeper: Have you noticed the engraving on that dish? Next year pieces like that will be worth twice what you pay today.

And so it goes on and on. Perhaps they will reach agreement; perhaps not.

Any method of negotiation may be fairly judged by three criteria: It should produce a wise agreement if agreement is possible. It should be efficient. And it should improve or at least not damage the relationship between the parties. Taking positions, as the customer and the shopkeeper do, serves some useful purposes in a negotiation. But those purposes can be served in other ways. Positional bargaining fails to meet the basic criteria of producing a wise agreement efficiently. In contrast to positional bargaining, the principled negotiation method of focusing on basic interests, mutually satisfying options and fair standards typically results in a wise agreement.

2. Role Play

For Your Information

The 6C principles in business communication are also applied in making a telephone call. In order to get the right information, the receptionist should "double-check" the information, esp. the spelling of the name and numbers.

The following is a phone call between a receptionist and a caller.

A: Hello. Ultimate Computers. May I help you?

B: Yes, this is Jack Kordell from Hunter's Office Supplies. May I speak to Elaine Strong, please?

A: I'm sorry, but she is not in today.

B: Can I ask when she is back?

A: Uh, yes, she would be here until late afternoon, perhaps 4 o'clock. Can I take a message?

B: Yes. Ms. Strong sent me a brochure detailing your newest line of laptop computers with a description of other software products, but there wasn't any information about after-sales service.

A: Oh, I'm sorry to hear that. I will inform Ms. Elaine Strong as soon as she comes back. Would you like her to fax the information about after-sales service to you?

B: Yes. But our fax machine is being repaired at the moment, and it won't be working until around 2:30. Could she try sending that information around 3:30? That should give me time to look over the material before I call her again, say, around 5:00.

A: Sure. Could I have your name, the telephone and fax number?

B: Yes. Jack Kordell, the phone number is 560 - 1287, and the fax number is 560 - 1288.

A: OK. Jack Kordell. Is your name spelled "C-o-r-d-e-l"?

B: No. It's Kordell with a "K" and two "l"s.

A: All right. Mr. Kordell. And your phone number is 560 - 1287, and the fax number is 560 - 1288.

B: Yes, it is.

A: All right. I'll inform Ms. Elaine just when she gets back.

B: Thanks, bye.

3. Mini Negotiation

Suppose you were Mr. Zhao from the China National Complete Plant Import and Export Corporation. Now you're discussing the price of an import project with Mr. DuPont, marketing manager of a French company.

A: Good morning, Mr. Zhao.

B: Good morning, Mr. DuPont. Did you sleep well last night?

A: Yes, very well. I'm now fully recovered from the jet lag and ready to discuss business with you.

B: Good. Let's get down to business at once.

A: I believe you have studied our proposal about the project. What do you think of it?

B: After a careful study of your project proposal, we find that there are some points that need further discussion.

A: Good, further discussion will certainly be useful. The purpose of my coming here is to discuss the proposal with you further.

B: First of all, we find your quotation much higher than we expected.

A: If you take everything into consideration, you will find that our price is very competitive.

B: To be frank, we are also discussing the project with some other companies. The quotations they have offered are much lower than yours. So the success of the negotiation depends largely on your price.

A: But you have to admit that our equipment is of superior quality. If you take quality into consideration, you will find that the price is fair and reasonable.

B: If you insist on the original offer, I'm afraid the chances for us to conclude the deal are remote as your price far exceeds our budget.

A: How much is your budget?

B: I'm sorry I can't tell you that. It's confidential.

A: Then could you give me some idea of the price you regard as acceptable?

B: To get the business done, you should at least reduce your price by 25%.

A: 25%? You are not kidding? It's impossible for us to reduce the price to such a great extent. But to pull through the business, we are willing to cut the price by 10%.

B: But your price is still a bit higher than we expected. If you can make a further reduction of another 10%, we can probably come to an agreement.

A: Do you mean a 20% cut? To be frank, it is impossible. We would rather not join in the project than make such a big cut.

B: How about meeting each other halfway, say a further reduction of 5%, so that business can be concluded?

A: OK, to show our sincerity in doing business with you, we accept your counter-bid. I hope this transaction will pave the way for more future business.

B: I'm glad we have reached an agreement on price.

Negotiation Tips

● Never Lie 讲究诚实

Very few negotiations are a single contact event. With the possible exception of making large purchases, most parties involved in a negotiation have continued contact after the negotiations are completed. When you are caught in a lie, and it is inevitable that you will be, your future credibility will be lost.

● Be Flexible 随机应变

Understanding that negotiation frequently involves compromise. Look for creative solutions to the problems presented in the negotiation. Make tradeoffs in order to gain those elements you most desire.

● Winning Isn't Everything 赢不是唯一目的

It is easy to get caught in the competitive spirit of a negotiation. Remember that the point of negotiation is to reach a common agreement on how to move forward. While it may be possible to bludgeon your adversary into agreeing to your terms, this does not create the "mutual agreement" that makes for a truly successful negotiation.

Extended Activities

Ⅰ. Situational Group Talks

Student A: You are Mr. Richen. Call Mrs. Jones to make an appointment for next week. If she is not available, leave a message.

Student B: You are Mrs. Jones' secretary. Take messages and make appointments if necessary. Don't forget the caller's name and phone number.

Ⅱ. Multiple Choices

Directions: There are ten incomplete sentences in this part. For each sentence there are four choices marked A, B, C, and D. Choose the one that best completes the sentence.

1. Success or failure here would be _____ to his prospects.

   A. critical   B. crucial   C. critic   D. criticized

2. The Town Hall was built in a(n) _____ position on a hill where everyone could see it.

   A. domestic   B. overwhelming   C. dominant   D. metropolitan

3. We have not _____ information to state the exact damage.

   A. equal   B. efficient   C. satisfied   D. sufficient

4. The example set by their brave commander _____ the troops to take the hill despite heavy enemy fire.

   A. encouraged   B. inquired   C. inspired   D. acquired

5. TV, if properly used, can _____ a child's imagination.

   A. stimulate   B. cause   C. incite   D. arise

6. After a long lunch hour, business _____ as usual.

   A. responds   B. resumes   C. delays   D. resurfaces

7. The State Secretary _____ to newsmen that an immediate agreement in the Middle East was nowhere in sight.

   A. confessed   B. concurred   C. admitted   D. conceded

8. Some school authorities _____ a teacher's achievement or his ability by the number of his students who pass their public examinations.

   A. assess   B. access   C. estimate   D. compute

9. Although this is very poor just now, its _____ wealth is great.

    A. prevalent   B. potential   C. previous   D. profound

10. The federal _____ must be approved by congress; without formal approval its financial plan would be invalid.

    A. budget   B. economy   C. construction   D. development

Ⅲ. Read the following statements and fill in the blanks.

1. Win-win approach is a collaborative process and the parties usually end up _____ each other.

2. _____ allocation rules divide the resources equally among the group members.

3. Trust is hard to build, but easy to _____ .

4. The purpose of negotiation is to reach _____ between parties with different interests.

5. Negotiation in itself is a kind of sincere _____ .

Ⅳ. Decide whether the following statements are true(T) or false(F).

1. When you are caught in a lie, and it is inevitable that you will be, your future credibility will be lost.

2. When you are not clear about the other side's interests, you might ask yourself they perceive your demands.

3. Make tradeoffs in order to gain those elements you most desire.

4. Think carefully about the negotiation rules to be used in allocating resources among the parties.

5. Remember that the point of negotiation is to reach a common agreement on how to move forward.

Ⅴ. Translate the following sentences into Chinese.

1. Negotiation is a function subservient to the general commercial interests of the parties involved.

2. I suggest we meet each other half way so that the business can be concluded.

3. We're glad that the deal has come off nicely and hope there will be more to come.

4. Negotiations is not treated as an isolated event but as an integral part of the total business activity.

5. Good negotiators consider it very important to promote a constructive climate and respectful personal relationships.

Chapter 3

Process of Business Negotiation & Communication

Learning Goals

Upon completion of this chapter, you will be able to:

☞ learn about verbal and non-verbal behavior in business communication;

☞ employ both oral and written methods to communicate in business;

☞ be sensitive to the differences between internal and external communication;

☞ grasp the five planning steps for writing a business letter;

☞ be clear about the procedure of negotiations;

☞ know about the steps of business negotiating summary.

Lead-in Words

inter-complementary *adj*. 相互补充的	subtle *adj*. 微妙的,敏感的
show one's colors 表明某人的观点	spontaneous *adj*. 自发的
inter-dependent *adj*. 相互依赖	posture *n*. 身体的姿势,体态
disseminate *v*. 散布	multidimensional *adj*. 多面的,多维的
shareholder *n*. 股东	horizontal *adj*. 水平的
colleague *n*. 同事	dual-functional *adj*. 双重作用的
business contacts 业务往来的人	inadequate *adj*. 不充分的,不适当的
deploy *v*. 拆开,撤开	venue *n*. 地点
rapprochement *n*. 恢复友好关系	neutrality *n*. 中立
integrative *adj*. 完整的	subsequent *adj*. 随后的
deduce *v*. 演绎,推论	resort *n*. 手段
reiterate *v*. 重申	fluctuation *n*. 波动
minute *n*. 会议纪要	majeure *n*. 不可抗力

Section I   Forms & Approaches of Business Communication

Generally speaking, different cultural background demands different forms of business communication. But it is almost the same process of how to put business communication into practice. On both sides, you need to distinguish a form of business communication and apply it according to the planning steps.

1. Forms of Business Communication

Our values, priorities, and practices are shaped by the culture in which we grow up. Different cultural background nourishes a different form of communication. Successful multicultural business encounters depend to a large extent on a properly chosen form of communication.

(1) Verbal & Non-Verbal Business Communication

Verbal communication is an essential part of human communication. Of course, language is the most important channel of communication in human interaction, but it is not the only one. Many non-verbal symbols are necessary in communication. In fact, business communication is effected both verbally and non-verbally. Ignorance of non-verbal messages will result in incomplete communication. Verbal and non-verbal communication together forms the whole process of communication. They are inter-complementary and inter-dependent.

① Verbal Business Communication

Verbal business communication refers to the communication that is carried out either in oral or written form with the use of words (Xu, Xianguang, 1997).

To live in society, people have to communicate. As a businessman, you spend an average of 30 percent of your working hours in speaking. On each working day, you have to communicate orally with colleagues, clients and business contacts. And you have to write a letter of enquiry, send an e-mail to make an offer, or fax to your long-standing suppler to confirm a date for next month's product discussion. Periodically, you have to write a monthly, quarterly or yearly report to show your company's overalls to the shareholders. Still other times you may make a presentation to group of visitors in your organization, or negotiate with other groups of people outside of organization. Those are varieties of verbal business communication, to name but a few here.

As a result, verbal communication works as a fast and efficient way for business people. It's quite sure that they express ideas, show their colors, disseminate and keep information, all through language. If possible, learning another language will assist you in business communication. First, learning another language will give you at least a glimpse into the culture. Culture is one of the most enduring, powerful, and invisible shapers of human being's behaviors. Communication is the basis of all human interaction. It will develop into an advantageous relationship between you and your business partner without language problem. Second, learning some of the language will help you manage the daily necessities of finding food and getting where you need to go while you're there. Finally, in business negotiations, knowing a little of the language gives you more time to think. You'll catch part of the meaning when you hear your counterpart speak; you can begin thinking even before the translation begins.

② Non-Verbal Business Communication

As to what is non-verbal communication, different people have different definitions. Generally speaking, non-verbal communication refers to the information that is transmitted from senders to receivers when the dominant meaning is not conveyed by the use of words.

Non-verbal communication includes several major categories: spatial distance, facial expressions, postures or gestures. All of these elements constitute the basic components of non-verbal communication. Non-verbal communication is a subtle, multidimensional, and usually spontaneous process. Sometimes we are not aware of most of our own non-verbal behaviors, which is enacted mindlessly, spontaneously, and unconsciously. We all take these non-verbal behaviors for granted, but they do exert an immense impact on communication.

As important as verbal language is to a communication event, non-verbal communication is just as, if not more, important. For instance, research shows that when we meet someone for the first time, only 7% of our initial impact on others is determined by the content of what we say, the other 93% of our message is made up to body language (55%) and the tone of voice (38%).

Non-verbal communication encompasses more than one function. First, non-verbal communication behaviors are used to reinforce verbal messages. While coming to an agreement, you may smile and shake hands with your clients. You are telling them that you are satisfied with the business. Second, verbal signals may be used to emphasize a portion of verbal messages. Or sometimes they are used to take the place of verbal messages. Third, non-verbal signals are often used to verify whether the listener understand the verbal message. An example of this might be our asking someone to "come here", and then mentioning with our hand or arm. This is usually done out of habit, and has little to do with the listeners' intelligence. Fourth, we often regulate and manage communication by using some forms of non-verbal behaviors: we nod to indicate to the speaker to continue talking; or remain silent for a while and let the silence to send the message that we are ready to begin the speech. In short, non-verbal behaviors help people to control the situation.

(2) Oral & Written Business Communication

If fact, oral and written business communication are two branches of verbal communication. Because both of them are seized of the same of characteristic: using words to implement the process of verbal communication. While in practice, they go hand in hand with each other.

① Oral Business Communication

Oral communication refers to communicate with spoken words. So it involves variety in your own voice, including pitch, rate, volume, stress and tone of voice. Common forms of oral business communication are such as: presentation, telephone, interview and conference. Several strategies will lead you to a successful oral communication (Refer to Chapter 5).

② Written Business Communication

On the contrary, written communication means using the written words to fulfill verbal information transmittion. It contains business letter, e-mail, fax, memo, minute, message, note and so forth (Refer to Chapter 6 and 7).

(3) Internal & External Business Communication

We have learnt that being multi-channeled is a prominent feature for business communication. Two fully opposite directions of communication will make a forceful explanation about this feature. They are internal and external business communication.

① Internal Business Communication

Internal communication refers to the kind of communication that takes place within a given organization. It can be subdivided into three categories: downward communication, upward communication and horizontal communication.

Downward communication is the communication which goes from the superior to the inferior, from the management to the subordinates. It plays a leading role of the three internal communications as it often carries decision, instruction, suggestions and announcements. Whether to choose an oral way or a written way for downward communication depends on the consideration over the efficiency of the communication, organization's customers and also actual requirement.

In adverse, upward communication refers to the communication is from a lower lever to a higher lever. Upward communication prevails when there is a democratic atmosphere in an organization. As in most cases, it may come from the employees' own initiatives, suggestions or reports. Upward communication makes it possible for the management to hear the voice of their subordinates, which is beneficial for the managerial level to check the correctness of their decisions. But is the freedom of the subordinates' own will. So quite often the management feels frustrated as they could not get the desired messages from their employees. The difficulty lies in the subordinates' doubt or distrust in the management.

Horizontal communication refers to the communication at the same level. It is characterized by its informality, closeness and speed. The latest news and comments will be exchanged through this casual way. Horizontal communication is dual-functional in nature: it could have a positive role if appropriately guided; but also may have negative impact upon the morale of employees at a particular level. Therefore, horizontal communication is worth special attention from the management.

② External Business Communication

External communication is defined as the kind of communication outside the organization. An organization cannot survive without communicating with the outside. In order to make it better, many organizations may set up a department called public relations which helps to heighten the popularity and to perfect their organizations through exchange with the public.

2. The Five Planning Steps of Business Communication

In order to have an effective business communication, you need to follow the five steps:

(1) Identify Your Purpose

The identified purpose is the very target you want to reach. Suppose you want to write a letter, you should first of all be clear about the purpose: Is it to persuade people to take some action, to inform them of something they don't know, or simply to entertain them?

(2) Analyze Your Audience

The purpose of analyzing your audience is to prepare your message from your reader's point of view: try to understand their needs, views, interests, attitudes, culture, social values and so on. This will help you to find a proper way to communicate.

(3) Choose Your Ideas

The ideas you include depend on the type of message you are sending, the actual business situation and the cultural context. Functionally speaking, major ideas serve as the nucleus of the message, as it best represents your purpose. Therefore, it is highly necessary to have a clear mind as to what you are writing or saying.

(4) Collect Your Data

Be sure to collect enough data to support your ideas. For this purpose, you must determine what kinds of specific fact, figures, quotations, or other forms of evidence you need. Make sure you know every detail of your company. Remember to check your data on individual names, addresses, dates, and statistics.

(5) Organize Your Message

To organize your message, you should firstly outline your ideas, and then decide which approach you will use and at last do it according to the 6Cs principles.

Section II Procedure of the Negotiation

The procedure of business negotiation is complicated and arduous. It consists of three different stages. A stage is defined as a specific part of the procedure and covers all actions and communication by either side relevant to the negotiation. The three different stages are: pre-negotiation stage, integrative bargaining stage and decision-making & action stage.

1. Pre-negotiation Stage

Far too many business negotiations fail because of inadequate preparation on one side or the other. So it is important for the participants to make a good job of preparation before the negotiation begins. Preparation is necessary to achieve the highest level of success in business negotiation. In a word, there is no substitution for advance preparation in negotiation arena.

(1) Establishing Issues & Targets for Negotiation

Establishing issues and targets for negotiation is very important. It means that negotiators should know well their desired results according to their own practical conditions, and should not be willfully manipulated by their counterparts.

The first step that you take in your preparation is a simple and straightforward one — it is that of deciding what it is that you want to achieve. It seems obvious, does it? But you'd be surprised how many people don't do it.

The desired results, which should be decided in business negotiations, have three different targets: the best target; the intermediate target; and the acceptable target.

The best target is to achieve all desired results planned at the beginning of the negotiation, which will benefit you best. If the world market is beneficial to you and you can firmly maintain the desired objectives to the end, then you will probably obtain the best target.

Usually it is not easy for the negotiators to get the best target, so, when such a target can not be achieved, you had better make a good preparation to achieve your second target — the intermediate target, which is fair for both sides, although it is slightly lower than the best target.

When you find that you do not have the advantage in the world market, you have met a skillful negotiator in the business activities or you have to export or import some products, you have to face the reality — to accept the acceptable target gradually. However, you should always remember that this should not be known to your counterpart until the last minute.

(2) Forming Negotiation Team

Negotiation is a team sport. It requires the specialized skills, communication ability, team spirit and gamesmanship found in any professional sporting event. If a negotiating team is structured properly and is deployed in an effective and timely manner, it can play a critical role in achieving victory at the bargaining table.

If you expect your negotiating team to be effective, it must be organized at an early date, preferably as the first step in preparing for a transaction. The members can foresee the areas covered by the negotiations, and have the technical expertise to deal with the problems effectively. They should also be compatible in temperament.

(3) The Selection and Size of the Negotiating Team

The negotiating team should include members in each of the following areas:

① commercial: responsible for the negotiation on price, delivery terms, and commercial policy of risk taking

② technical: responsible for the area concerning specification, program and methods of work

③ financial: responsible for terms of payment, credit insurance, bonds and financial guarantees

④ legal: responsible for contract documents, terms and conditions of contract, insurance, legal interpretation

If it is an important negotiation, the negotiating team will be comprised of negotiators responsible for the above mentioned areas. Other members for the negotiation include some functional specialists. The negotiator's function is to negotiate, while the functional specialists provide specialist advice or information.

For negotiation of lesser significance, one negotiator would cover two areas after having been fully briefed on the subject with which he was less familiar. For instance, the legal negotiator might cover the financial area. Team of four could be reduced to two; it should not be reduced to one, no matter how well qualified the negotiator is.

However, the negotiating team should not be too large. At any time it should not exceed five. It becomes extremely difficult for the team to be kept under control, if the team numbers is beyond five. And it is difficult for its activities to be directed towards a single outcome. Arguments are likely to develop between the members of the team themselves during the negotiation session.

It is preferable that a negotiator has the support of an assistant to make notes, do calculations and remind him of any points that he has missed. And this does not leave him to handle the whole bargaining process by himself.

(4) Team Leader

The team leader is always the full-fledged member of one group as well as the main speaker during the negotiation. It is his full delegation to lead and organize the negotiation which will have a great effect on the final result. So it is very discreet to choose the team leader. In general, the team leader should meet the following requirements:

① He should be capable of organizing and managing as well as cooperative spirit;

② He should be of good psychology and decision qualities as well as strong meeting contingency abilities and public relations, more ideas and more decisions;

③ He should be of wide scope of knowledge and capable of dealing with the other negotiators from abroad around the negotiating table;

④ He should have a high rank in his company.

The duties of the team leader are to select the remainder team members, prepare the negotiating plan, conduct the negotiations and make decisions on concessions, selection of trade-off items, and etc. He is also to make the bargain with the other side, to ensure that the bargain is properly recorded, and to issue the negotiating report.

Additionally, a leader has more general functions to perform. He is the person who generates enthusiasm in his team, maintaining the morale under all conditions and obtains the maximum contribution from each member by his own example.

(5) Creating the Information Base

Once the negotiating team has been organized, the first and most basic step in preparing for a specific transaction is creating an information base.

Negotiations are conducted under a system of law and within a particular economic, cultural and political framework. The framework of international negotiations is derived from two or more sources that will be in conflict with one another to a degree. Knowledge of this and the ability to apply the knowledge are essential to the achievement of a successful outcome to the contract. Note that it is the performance of the contract that is significant, not just the negotiation itself.

Factors related to the foreign country, its economic and physical resources, infrastructure, climate and geography will affect the way in which the work can be performed and the program of implementation. And they will also affect the cost and the importance of specific contractual terms. It is only possible for these to be assessed if the negotiator is fully informed as to their applicability.

① Negotiators should identify all issues that may be relevant

+ The political system: the extent of state control of business enterprises and its organization; social stability; they extent of political interest in the contract, and etc.
+ Religion: the predominant religion of the country and its social influence.
+ Legal system: the legal and judicial system; their influences on business, the relevant laws on establishment of a local company and on employment, and etc.
+ The business system: business conduction; significance given to contract, roles of professional advisers; negotiation proceeding; and the counterpart of the negotiation, and etc.
+ The social system: social behavior concerning business.
+ The financial and fiscal system: the country's foreign exchange reserves; the commodities exported for foreign earnings; the currency freely exchangeable within the territory and its restrictions; procedures for obtaining payments in foreign currencies; the country's record on honoring payment obligations including likely delays; the type of Letter of Credit used in the country; the applicable tax laws, restrictions on remittance of the final payment; regulations on the payment of customs duties; other fees concerning the contract and etc.
+ Infrastructure and logistical system: the availability in the territory concerning labor,

materials for construction; the availability of finding a competent and financially sound sub-contractors; restrictions on importation of labor, materials and plant; local logistical problems relating to transport; problems relating to weather.

② The negotiators should select those issues relevant to the particular negotiation

This is a matter of obtaining an understanding of some of the points referred to in the above mentioned section so that the negotiators can recognize both the degree of their importance and the extent to which they are interrelated.

The negotiators can obtain data from the following sources in order to understand whether a problem exists or not:

+ From the organizations in the country and its provincial committees, foreign trade corporations, banks with particular interest in the territory and newspaper articles;

+ From overseas, for example, Chinese Embassy and Chinese local companies, local banks, the agents, other businessmen operating in the territory, local newspaper articles and etc.

③ The negotiators should get detailed knowledge of relevant

The only way to obtain such knowledge is visits to the territory concerned made by suitable qualified personnel. It is necessary to get generalized data on the territory as much as possible beforehand and try to see something of the country first-hand during the visits without relying on second-hand data. The visitors should retain an objective in mind and do not allow particular events to affect their judgments. And the visitors should also record the facts impartially and refrain from making judgments in an unbalanced manner.

+ Choosing the location of negotiation

Generally speaking, negotiation sites can be divided into three categories: host venue, guest venue and third party's venue.

+ Host venue

Host venues can be one party's own country, own city or own office building or any other places where the party hosts the negotiation. As the host party, it can enjoy several advantages that it may not otherwise, for instance waiting at its ease for exhausted counterpart, familiar surroundings with no novel and foreign attractions distracting its members' attention from their tasks, assistance ready at hand and feeling of security, comfort and relaxation. The host side may also create pressure or obstacles to its counterpart if there is the necessity by making use of the decorations of the meeting room, accommodation and other devices.

+ Guest venue

When negotiations take place at counterpart's country, city or office buildings, they are conducted at guest venues. For the gust party, almost all advantages enjoyed as the host are reversed to be the barriers and difficulties. In such cases they guest party has to be more patient, steadfast and perseverant. However, as the saying goes every coin has two sides, the inconvenience to sufficient information for sound judgment and absence of authority for a decision can always be explored as acceptable excuses for asking for a halt or even withdrawal from the on-going negotiation.

✦ Third party's venue

The negotiation is held neither in the host party's places nor in the guest party's locality, but rather in the third party's place which is directly or indirectly related with the two parties. The third party's site is preferred frequently out of the following concerns:

- The two negotiating parties are hostile and antagonistic to each other, or even engaged in a fighting against each other. Since there is no direct channel for dialogue between the two parties in such a situation, and it is impossible to invite one party to come to the other party's territory, hence a third place is chosen as a result.

- When a negotiation goes into an impasse and there is no sign of rapprochement, it is apparent that it would be impossible to carry on such negotiation in neither party's places. A third place has to be considered if the two sides wish to resolve their conflicts through peaceful means.

- None of the two situations is in existence, nevertheless a third place has to be chosen due to the dispute that both parties demand strongly to host the negotiation, therefore, a place of neutrality is the only choice for settling the disputes.

Choosing a right place for negotiation is part of the negotiation strategy, the importance of which can not be neglected. Once the site has been selected, reasons for the selection and local conditions should be stated, and impacts on the environment should be studied.

(6) Designing Agenda for Negotiation

Agendas are fantastic control devices. Creating the agenda is an advantage to you even if you are not in charge of the meeting. Some useful guidelines to writing an agenda may be found below:

① Make a list of all the important issues to be covered. Write down all elements you wish to talk about and everything you wish to find out about that you don't already know.

② Check off all elements you want on the agenda. Ensure all information you wish to extract from your counterpart goes into your private notes and not on the written agenda for everyone involved in the negotiation.

③ As soon as you know what you wish to discuss, determine the order. It is suggested that you start the negotiation off with something on the agenda that is less emotional and easy-going.

④ Ensure you have enough copies of the agenda for everyone attending. Make extra copies for unexpected people that wish to attend the negotiation of whom you were not made aware.

⑤ It is important you realize that an agenda only suggests the order in which issues will be discussed. This is not cast in stone and therefore does not dictate the order.

(7) Making a Feasible Negotiation Plan

A feasible negotiation plan can be very critical to a team's success. It will serve as the negotiating team's guide.

The format of the plan will be common to each of the negotiating situations although the details are different.

The negotiating objective will usually be expressed in terms of the expected return on sales, taking into account the risks involved in performing the contract. If any of the risks are changed, the degree to which the margin may be changed should also be expressed.

In defining the initial strategy and stating the possible measures or tactics, set down some basics and allow flexibility in different situations. The first offer and counter-offer is very important. In the beginning, make high offer and negotiate for the best target. Generally speaking, those who firmly maintain the desired objectives to the end can obtain the best deal. Don't begin negotiating at too low a price. Your quotation is to be a little lower each time. Do it step by step. The acceptable result is the minimum level both sides can bear and generally it has already been stated in the brief. The minimum should not be exposed to your counterpart at the beginning of the negotiation. The team should keep it in mind.

The negotiating team should be given as much time as possible to complete the negotiations in order to avoid time pressure. The trade-off in the reduction in margin because of time costs and time spent on negotiation should be made clear.

The plan should state the names and job titles of the team members. It should also indicate any duties performed outside of their own function.

2. Integrative Bargaining Stage

When the preparation and planning for the negotiation have been carried out, the actual conduct of the negotiation will be considered. The period covered by the negotiation will be divided into three stages: opening & its review; bidding & bargaining; settling & ratifying.

(1) Opening & its Review

In the opening stage, negotiators are getting to know each other and identifying the issues involved. After that, the review is followed. The negotiators then modify their negotiating plan as necessary to take account of any factors disclosed in the opening of which they had not previously been aware.

① The Opening

It is time for the initial presentation in accordance with the terms of the negotiation plan. One party may be in the situation to take the initiative and submit a proposal required by the other party or to respond to one already provided by the other. Thus the negotiation begins by submitting a written proposal / answer supplemented by face-to-face discussions or sometimes without verbal discussion, and alternatively by presenting verbal proposals at a meeting.

The opening phase is influential because energy and concentration are naturally at a high point at the start of any activity. The choice of opening topic and the form in which it is discussed sets a precedent for the way the subsequent topics will be approached and tackled. It creates the conditions for a later battle between the parties.

The parties' attitudes are being formed at this time. Each party is reading signals from what the other says and does, making continued judgments about the other's character, and framing its own behavior in response. The skilled negotiator would take the advantage of this important period to attain his goal.

The objective at the opening stage of the negotiations may be described as exploration without commitment. The negotiators want to ensure that the whole of the area to be covered by the negotiation is exposed, together with the opponent's views on each point. But at the same time they do not want to be drawn into making too firm a commitment of his position on any individual issue, and try to avoid any agreement or concessions. And most probably the parties would agree on the agenda and the pacing of the negotiation.

② The Review of the Opening

If the parties are presenting the initial proposal at the end of the opening phase, the negotiators should know which parts of his offer that the opponent is likely / unlikely to accept. They can deduce the strength of the opponent's opposition on any issue and predict the general form of the optimum bargain on each issue the opponent is likely to accept.

Before proceeding further with the negotiations, the party should review the results achieved from the opening phase. And then decide whether the negotiations can be placed on a bargain acceptable to both sides which can be identified immediately, or a bargain acceptable to both sides is foreseeable which will need further negotiations to achieve, or no bargain is foreseen acceptable to both sides.

If the bargain can be identified immediately, the negotiators should resist by making an immediate proposal of concession from his initial offer. They should not appear overeager, which lead the opponent to believe they have personal reason for early agreement. Otherwise, the other party may believe they can achieve further concessions by prolonging the negotiations. The negotiators are proposed to decide on some intermediate step, e. g. provide the chance for the opponent to make a responsive concession and judge his next move according to it.

If the bargain is foreseeable, it is possible to identify the total negotiating area. The party should seek to establish the resistance points for each major issue based on his original planning and what he has learned from the opening. This enables him to make an estimate of the loss he would suffer either now or in the future, or of the probability of incurring the loss if he were to concede. And he should also estimate the loss he would suffer by maintaining the resistance or the probability of giving away the negotiation without making the concession. What else he should consider is the value of the bargain without making the concession.

At the conclusion of the review stage, the party should have achieved to define the negotiation area, establish his points of resistance and make an estimate of those he believes likely to be adopted by the other party. The party should also arrive at a close approximation of the time period for the negotiation, and update his previous forecast of the probable form of the final bargain.

If no bargain is foreseeable, the negotiation can break off the negotiations and withdraw. This is the last resort that the negotiators should come slowly and with reluctance, because they know that there are competitors waiting in the wings only to eagert take their place.

And the second possibility of negotiators is to continue the negotiations on minor issues and seek revised authority from the senior management, which they believe will be sufficient to secure eventual agreement. The third is to influence the other party and then to seek revised authority from senior management. The influence given to the other party is to persuade them at least to modify their demands to some degree. The important point is that the negotiators should not allow the other party to be aware of their seeking revised authority.

(2) Bidding & Bargaining

This stage covers a broad period of bargaining in which concessions are made and advantage are gained, so that the gap between the two sides is narrowed to a point. Bid is a kind of offer. It has two forms: firm bid and non-firm bid.

In the course of transaction negotiating, when the seller's goods sell well or when the seller is unaware of the market situation and is not sure whether the buyer is willing to buy, he usually asks the buyer to offer first, and this offer made by the buyer is called bid.

In this stage of bidding and bargaining, each side starts significantly to adjust its demand and attitudes to the observed behavior of the other. The process of adjustments by the two sides within the framework of the variables leads to considering the preference of one demand to another.

As a result of the initial contacts between the tow sides, it is probable that each side will modify its original objective, reassess the potential outcomes and the time taken to achieve each of these. These will enable each side to determine the conditional value for each outcome and to estimate the probability of success. And then negotiating strategy will be selected to maximize the expected value.

In making the next move each party's concern is with the degree of commitment he attaches to any issue. On very minor points, there may be almost immediate agreement. On more significant points, both sides will reiterate and expand on their previous proposals with varying degrees of commitment, but without closing the door totally on the possibility of finding some way in which their respective viewpoints may be reconciled. The gap is gradually narrowed, and the outlines of the compromise maybe clear. They are ready to move to the phase of identifying the bargain.

(3) Settling & Ratifying

The final stage of business negotiations involves reaching an agreement and contract signing.

The final concession should be made at the right time, neither too early nor too late. For the purpose of timing, it can be divided into two parts. The major part of concession should be made just before the other party is to review and consider the deadline. One minor concession should be held as a final benefit and offered at the very last moment if it is absolutely necessary. The final concessions put emphasis on their finality.

Unless the concession is a total acceptance of the other party's current demand, the team must signal to the other party, either before or in the course of making their final concession, that they expect the other party to respond. One way is to agree to such a bargain provided that the other party will reciprocate. Another way is to indicate their willingness to make a concession against a concession from the other party.

Different terminology, the use of words and differences in language contribute to misunderstandings. The two sides should make sure to have identical understanding of the terms to which they are agreeing when the bargain is being made. Here are some points the negotiators should pay attention to:

① Price: Does it cover taxes, duties and other statutory charges? If so, who pays? Is the currency fixed against exchange-rate fluctuations? Is it clear what contract price does not include?

② Completion: Is it clearly defined? Does it include customer testing of the system? When can completion certificate be issued? On what conditions?

③ Claims settlement: What is the scope of the settlement? Is it a final bar to any future legal proceedings?

Last but not the least, the record of negotiation should be made in written form and initialed by the two sides before they depart.

3. Decision-making & Action Stage

As the negotiation moves to the final stage, the negotiator will expect to receive / send signals from / to the other party so as to decide whether a deal could be concluded or not.

Who makes the decision?

The difference between a successful and an unsuccessful negotiator is the ability to close a deal when it has reached its maximum level of distributing "enough" among all participants. The deal is best closed when the agenda has been exhausted.

The final concession should be made at the right time, not too early or too late. For the purpose of timing it can be divided into two parts. The major part should be made at a time allowing the other party to review and consider before the deadline. One minor concession should be held as a final "benefit" and offered at the very last moment if it is absolutely necessary. The final concessions put emphasis on their finality.

(1) Wrapping up

It is quite necessary to have a thorough and systematic summary of the finished negotiating work, whether the negotiation is a success or a failure. The summary should start from the preparation and go through to the end of the negotiation. The whole negotiating process should be reviewed, analyzed and evaluated in order to improve the negotiating level.

① Content of negotiation summary

Among the far-ranging content of business negotiation summary, the following are important:

+ Aspects that have direct relation with negotiating process: preparation work; illustration of gains and losses; negotiating efficiency and results; advantages and disadvantages of the procedure, time and place; main experiences of the success.

+ Aspects concerning the opponent: Evaluate the opponent including the impression, the working style, efficiency and the things that are liked or disliked. To those who are important or have long-term cooperative relations, establish files to put the negotiation experiences, style, tactics, skills as well as the disadvantages into written form to learn the merits and avoid the shortcomings for future negotiations.

② Steps of business negotiating summary

Business negotiating summary is generally composed of the following steps:

+ Review the negotiating process and go over the minute.

+ Analyze and evaluate the negotiating, find out what is well done.

+ Give suggestions of improvement.

+ Write the summary report.

(2) Drawing up a Written Contract

One who drafts the contract plays a leading role in the negotiation especially when both parties speak in different languages. Here are some of the reasons: First, when drafting the contract, the negotiator could make the terms in compliance with domestic laws and regulation. Second, when the disputes arise, it's much easier for the negotiator to settle the problems with domestic laws and regulations. Third, it could make the negotiation go smoothly and avoid too many revisions. Fourth, without giving the chance to the other party to prepare the draft, the negotiator could avoid being cheated. Sometimes when the other party prepares the draft, he might overshadow something we can not foresee. And it seems that the other party makes a concession when we intend to modify some of the terms. So the negotiator should make every effort to take initiative. In order to draft a perfect contract, don't forget that working in team is also very important. The reason is that all-round talents proficient in the knowledge of trade, investment, insurance, law and so on are not very easy to be found.

Normally speaking, the contract for international business includes three parts: opening, body and ending.

+ Opening includes the name of contract, contract number, signing date and address, names and addresses of the parties, and so on.
+ Body includes basic clause (quality, packing, price, shipment, etc) and general clause (insurance, inspection, claim, force majeure, etc).
+ Ending states the legal effect of contract, the enclosures and signatures of both parties.

(3) Contract Signing

Before signing the contract, the negotiator shall check if the contents of the contract are the same; if it is in agreement with the negotiation terms; if the documents are complete; if the contents of the contract are in conformity with the ones in the documents. Provided faulty documents are found, one should notify the other, try to communicate with each other and avoid misunderstanding.

Once it is signed, the contract is binding upon both parties. Neither of the party could modify the contracted terms nor be in breach of the contract. So signing the contract is a crucial part of business negotiation.

Section III　Practical Activities

1. Case Study

● Case Study 1

Background

Nobody wants to cause offence but, as business becomes ever more international, it is increasingly easy to get it wrong. Consider the following example.

Business between Chinese and Arabs

Company H is a large company and its products are among the best of the same line in China. They have already extended their businesses into several regions overseas, however, the Middle East remains blank, as they have no experience in doing business with Arabs.

One day, a delegation from Dubai visited Company H. Mr. L, the chief representative of the company, received them. As the delegation was interested in the Company's products, both sides sat down for a negotiation on the products.

As the negotiation went on, Mr. L felt confused and bored because the Arabs asked for a break every hour. Then they went to the toilet to wash their hands and faces. When they came back, they knelt down to pray. As there was no towel in the toilet, the Arabs prayed with wet hands and faces. Mr. L found himself in a dilemma, because he did not know whether he should withdraw from the scene or not.

When it was time for lunch, the Arabs were treated to a rich dinner. When everyone was seated, the waitress started introducing the different dishes in English to the Arab visitors. They all looked surprised and pleased at the variety. But this did not last long. When the waitress mentioned some specially cooked pork, the smiles disappeared from all those visitors' faces and all of them looked blue — no one said a word. Quickly they stood up and left the dinner table without bidding farewell to anyone, though there were some important Chinese local guests present. The same day, this Dubai delegation left the city without notifying Company H.

A few days later, the bad news reached Mr. L — this Dubai delegation had signed a contract with their competitor — Company C, and the contract was the very one which was being negotiated between Company H and that Dubai delegation. Mr. L got a strong blame from his boss for losing the opportunity to their rival's hand.

Three days later, Mr. L took the following actions:

1. Start a training program for all waitresses and persons involved in communicating with Middle East business people, and invite some professors to give lectures on the Islamic culture and customs.

2. Invite some Arabic teachers to teach the waitress simple Arabic to communicate with Arabs.

3. Set up a separate dinning room with special set of dinner dishes for Arabs.

4. Set up a special room close to the meeting room. This room would be used only for praying by those Middle Eastern business persons. In addition, he also put some compass and small carpets in the room.

5. Prepare some small towels in the toilet for the Arabs to dry their hands before praying.

Half a year later, Company H had five customers in Middle East. All of them had visited Company H and were impressed by their understanding and respect for the Islamic culture and habits. Company H has been expanding their market share in the Middle East ever since.

Questions:

1. List all the conflicts in the case.

2. What do you think of Mr. L's actions after his first failure? Which one impressed you most? Why?

3. What is required for a modern business person with reference to a globalized economy and business? Why do think that way?

● Case study 2

A salesman arrives at the doorstep of a woman's house. He talks away glibly, trying to persuade the lady to buy his product.

Striking a Bargain

A: Good morning, Madam. If I could just take up a moment of your time, I've got a proposition that I'm sure will interest you.

B: Well, I'm rather busy.

A: Yes, Madam, but the whole basis of what I'm proposing to you is to make you less busy. Perhaps not immediately, but in the long run. Just a moment of your time now, and it will save you days of work.

B: What is it then?

A: Madam, have you ever thought about your pipes?

B: My pipes? What do you mean?

A: Well, pipes go everywhere, don't they? Through walls, under the floor, over ceilings. Everywhere in a house there are pipes.

B: Well, yes I suppose there are.

A: And have you ever thought about how, little by little, those pipes get clogged up? Thousand of cubic centimeters of water run through them every day. And each of those cubic centimeters leaves a little deposit, a little smear ... Until finally the day comes when no water flows at all.

B: I suppose so.

A: Now, all over the world, other housewives forget about their pipes. And what has been the result? Impure water?

B: I suppose it is a little worrying.

A: But now a new era has dawned! Thanks to Franco's Flush Fast Water Mixture. Our new invention has made clogged pipes a thing of the past. You no longer need to put on a tap with the hidden worry:"Will the water flow or will it not?" By administering Franco's to your water tank at regular intervals you can be assured of a clean system.

B: Yes, perhaps ...

A: And all it costs is two pounds for a whole set of Franco's Flush Fast Water Mixture. A dozen sky blue containers set in a cream plastic case with two pages of clear instructions on how Franco's Flush Fast Water Mixture should be used.

B: It sounds like a good idea.

A: It is a very good idea, Madam, and it only costs two pounds! A real bargain if I might say so.

B: Yes, two pounds. Here you are!

A: Thanks, Madam. And here are your specially designed cream plastic cases. I'm sure you'll never forget it. Good luck, Madam. You deserve it. I envy you the thrill of feeling that your pipes are clean at last!

B: Now, I want a moment of your time, sir, and I've got a proposition that I'm sure you'd be interested in.

A: What do you mean, Madam?

B: Well, you see, I'm a business person. I run a shop selling all kinds of household goods. I might buy your Franco's Flush Fast Water Mixture in quantity if the quality is good and the price is right. Are you in a position to make decisions?

A: Yes, I'm the sales representative of the firm. There's no doubt about the quality, Madam. You can try it before placing your order. I think you should have the box of Franco's Flush Fast Water Mixture free. Let me give you back your two pounds. As for the quantity discount, Madam, it depends on the size of order.

B: Of course I know the price varies according to the number I order. Suppose I want over a thousand. What will the price be?

A: Then you can have it at one pound and fifty, I think. That's a bargain price.

B: Come on, one pound and fifty! That's not cheap at all! Let's say fifty pence each.

A: Fifty pence! You must be joking! Why, that's less than the manufacturing price! No, it really is. I honestly don't see why we should go below one pound twenty-five pence.

B: Really? Well, if you say so. Well, you know I may not be able to place an order at that price. Besides, I haven't tried the product yet.

A: Hmm. That would be a pity. Well, perhaps we'd better think it over. Shall we meet again sometime next week? By then you'll be able to tell if the quality is good. And both of us may be able to come to a decision of some kind.

B: Good idea. And I hope it will come to something. It really will be a pity if it doesn't!

2. Role play

For Your Information

How to make a reservation is a priority for business people to other countries.

A: Hello, this is Sheraton Hotel, may I help you?

B: Yes, I'm calling from Westwood Corporation. I'd like to make a reservation for Mr. and Mrs. Brent, please.

A: Fine, Madam. When will Mr. and Mrs. Brent be arriving, and how many nights will they be staying?

B: From January 23rd to 30th for a week under the name of John Brent and Helen Brent.

A: Well, no problem.

B: By the way, how much is it?

A: $290 a night, we're near the center of town. And we have a shuttle service to attractions.

B: What is the room like?

A: It is furnished with indirect lighting. It faces to a garden, which is treed and flowered. And a hairdryer and an iron are available. It is very convenient.

B: Sounds wonderful. How should they handle their account?

A: Credit card is required.

B: OK. I see. Thanks for your help. Bye.

A: Bye-bye.

3. Mini Negotiation

A: Hello, Mr. Thompson. We are very glad that you have come here in person to discuss the project with us.

B: We believe that a face-to-face talk will make it easier for us to get to know each other better and also facilitate the settlement of problems. Besides, it can be more efficient.

A: Absolutely right!

B: I think you must have studied our proposal. May I know your opinions about it?

A: Thank you for sending us the proposal. After reading it, we find we need to exchange views on some points in order to find some common ground.

B: Our proposal is merely a basis for further discussion. We certainly welcome you to put forward your proposal.

A: First of all, we find your price much too high. It is almost 20% higher than those offered by other suppliers.

B: But you have to admit that our products are of top quality. And if you take everything into consideration, you will find our quotation reasonable.

A: But the products offered by other suppliers are also of good enough quality, and can well meet our production requirements. So the business depends very much on the price.

B: Then could you give me some ideas of the price you regard as acceptable?

A: To get the business done, we think you should at least reduce the price by 15%.

B: To be frank, a 15% reduction is more than we can accept. However, to show our sincerity in doing business with you, we are ready to make some concessions and reduce the price by 8%.

A: We think the price is still too high.

B: This is really our rock-bottom price. We can't make any further reduction.

A: If that's the case, I'm afraid we'll have to go somewhere else to buy what we need.

B: Well, to get the business done, I will make it an exception and reduce the price by another 2%. If you are still not satisfied, I'm afraid I could do nothing more about it.

A: All right, we accept.

Negotiation Tips

- ● Quit While You Are Ahead 见好就收

Too many people have to see just how far they can push a negotiation. They have to try to get just one more concession. This attitude can be a deal breaker. The best negotiations are brief and to the point. Get agreement on your major points and stop. Additional items can be addressed in subsequent negotiations.

- ● Don't Tip Your Hand 不要摊牌

Uncertainty is your key advantage in most negotiations. If your adversary knows what you desire most, your negotiating position is not as strong. Play it close to the vest.

- ● Learn to Be Surprised 学会诧异

The objective of this tactic is to make the other person feel uncomfortable about the offer he or she just presented. For example, a supplier quotes a price for a specific service. Being surprised means you respond by exclaiming, "You wan how much?" You must appear shocked and surprised that the supplier could be bold enough to request such a high figure. Unless the supplier is a well-seasoned negotiator, he will respond in one of the two ways: He will become very uncomfortable and try to rationalize his price, or he will offer an immediate concession.

Extended Activities

Ⅰ. Situational Group Talks.

Student A: You are in the staff of the manager of a car hire firm at Dublin Airport. A small car costs £14.5 per day, or £35 for a weekend, a family car costs £19 per day, or £39.99 for a weekend, and no luxury cars are available this weekend. Your firm is open 24 hours a day. You need a name, contact number and credit card number for all reservation.

Student B: You are Mrs. Jones' secretary. Call the car hire firm at Dublin Airport and reserve a car for Mrs. Jones from Friday evening to Sunday evening. Ask about the fee.

Ⅱ. Multiple Choice.

Directions: There are ten incomplete sentences in this part. For each sentence there are four choices marked A, B, C, and D. Choose the one that best completes the sentence.

1. Our quotation _____ 50 metric tons of groundnuts is valid for 6 days.

    A. to   B. for   C. with   D. in

2. Please quote us your lowest price _____ CIF London basis for 100 pairs Sport Shoes.

    A. on   B. from   C. at   D. for

3. His offer is subject to your reply _____ us before May 6.

    A. is reaching   B. reaching   C. reached   D. reach

4. Our offer is firm _____ May 6, 2005.

A. on   B. in   C. before   D. till

5. No discount will be allowed _____ you could place an order for more than 500 dozen.

A. until   B. unless   C. besides   D. except

6. We will place another _____ you in the near future.

A. in   B. with   C. for   D. on

7. We are making you our best offer for Leather Shoes _____.

A. as follow   B. as following   C. as follows   D. follow

8. We are not in a position to offer firm, as the goods you are interested in are _____.

A. out of stock   B. in stock   C. without stock   D. no stock

9. In _____ of quality, our make is superior.

A. term   B. terms   C. view   D. relation

10. The letter we received yesterday is an enquiry _____ Walnuts.

A. for   B. at   C. in   D. to

Ⅲ. Fill in the blanks with the words given in the box.

automatic	dial	dialing tone	directory	engaged	exchange
operator	receiver	trunk code	Yellow Pages	subscriber's number	

You need to make a telephone call? Then make sure you have your correspondent's number close at hand. Telephone numbers consist of a ___1.___ and a ___2.___ . If you don't know your contact's number, look it up in the telephone ___3.___ or the ___4.___ . The latter contains the telephone number of businesses and traders in your area.

The next thing you do is to lift the ___5.___ and ___6.___ or press the number. You will then hear a ___7.___ . If the number is ___8.___ , you will hear an engaged tone. Bad luck, you will have to ring back later.

In a company, the first person who answers the phone will often be the ___9.___ . He, but usually she, will put you through to the person you require. The operator operates the telephone ___10.___ . In an increasing number of businesses, however, manual exchanges are replaced by direct lines or ___11.___ exchanges.

Ⅳ. Decide whether the following statements are true(T) or false(F).

1. Establishing issues and targets for negotiation is very important.

2. Negotiation is a team sport. It requires the specialized skills, communication ability, team spirit and gamesmanship found in any professional sporting event.

3. Knowledge of negotiation and the ability to apply the knowledge are essential to the achievement of a successful outcome to the contract.

4. The major part of concession should be made after the other party is to review and consider the deadline.

5. Without giving the chance to the other party to prepare the draft, the negotiator would be cheated.

Ⅴ. Translate the following sentences into Chinese.

1. Please quote us your lowest price for 100 metric tons of Rice CIF Guangzhou, stating the earliest date of shipment.

2. To enable you to have a better understanding of our products, we are sending you by air 5 copies of our catalogue and 2 sample books.

3. As a rule, we usually get 5% commissions from the European suppliers.

4. Should your price be found competitive, we intend to place with you an order for 300,000 yards of cotton cloth.

5. If your quality is good and the price is in line with the market at our end, we would place a large order with you.

Chapter 4

Strategies & Background of Business Negotiation & Communication

Learning Goals

Upon completion of this chapter, you will be able to:
☞ identify the roles of cultural systems and social customs play in business communication;
☞ choose suitable styles and modes;
☞ establish strategies of negotiations;
☞ make concessions;
☞ make a final offer.

Lead-in Words

instability n. 不稳定性	superstition n. 迷信
taboo n. (宗教)禁忌,避讳	ambivalent adj. 有矛盾看法的
default v. 违约,缺席	consensus n. (意见)一致
platoon n. 组,小队	hierarchical adj. 等级的,阶层的
facilitate v. 助长	compel v. 迫使
genuine adj. 真正的	persuasive adj. 有说服力的
pros and cons 利弊	

Section I Background of Business Communication

Before we make business communication or go to a business negotiation, we need to be clear about the culture background of the organization: its economic system, political system, legal system and social customs system.

The international business communication exists in a certain background. To pay more attention to the background around the organization will make any forms of business communication possible.

1. Economic Systems

Economic systems refer to the way in which the products that meet the material needs of the people are produced, distributed, and consumed. To understand the differences between capitalism and socialism will help you do better in different economic systems.

2. Political Systems

The political system is mainly based on dictatorship, constitutional monarchy, inherited rights, elected procedures, or consensus. It is the special system of a given government. Political stability is the key factor in determining the stability of a county. Companies should pay more attention to political changes and instability, which will influence the willingness to do business in a country with a certain political environment.

3. Legal Systems

International or government laws and regulations affect people and business. Legal systems are another background of business communication. You should be clear about which laws are followed, the home country or host country.

4. Linguistic Systems

Obviously, unless both sender and receiver understand a common language, the opportunities for successful business communication are significantly limited. Try to learn another language. You get a much warmer response when you travel and command one respect in business when you speak another language.

5. Social Customs Systems

There is not one aspect of human life that is not touched and altered by culture. Culture and communication, although two different concepts are directly linked, because culture is learned, acted out, transmitted, and preserved through communication. If fact, culture is communication, communication is culture. Social customs are linked with greetings, verbal and non-verbal communication, use of humor, superstitions and taboos, dress and appearance and so on. While it is impossible to identify all customs of a particular culture, certain customs should be paid attention in your daily life. (Refer to Chapter 13)

Section II Strategies and Tactics of Negotiations

Strategies and tactics are crucial to business negotiations. They are acting guidelines and policies of the whole negotiating process and are subject to modification with the progress the negotiation. Since different organizations work in different ways, and each has a characteristic style of negotiation, negotiators need training and experience before they can successfully handle the different styles of other parties. No single style of negotiation "wins". It is the more skilled negotiator who will prevail.

1. Choosing Suitable Style and Modes

As tactics are closely related to negotiation styles, each negotiating team and each negotiator should choose a style that will best serve their goal. The same style will not work in every situation, nor will every situation permit every style. Negotiators and teams must be flexible, able to change styles as easily as they change locations.

(1) Personal Styles

There are several kinds of negotiating styles and rarely does a person use one style to the exclusion of all others. There is a great deal of crossover. Negotiators strive to be believed, and they must believe in their own words if they are to be successful. Potential negotiators must research their own talents and virtues to determine which style or combination of styles best fits their personality and the team goals. The followings are the styles often used in negotiations:

① Aggressive: Negotiators of this style run roughshod over opponents with little regard for their counterparts' positions. They focus on their own goals, and don't want to make concessions. Skilled negotiators will assume an aggressive posture only when supposedly non-negotiable points are being discussed.

② Compliant: Negotiators of this style demand that many points are readily conceded early in an effort to draw the aggressor farther into the process. Major points are purposely kept off the agenda until late in the negotiations when the aggressor believes that they will continue to receive concessions.

③ Passive: Passive negotiators are not always what they seem. They convince the opposition to put all of their cards on the table in the belief that everything is mutually acceptable. Once all has been revealed, the previously passive negotiators start their attack.

④ Impressive: Impressive negotiators are purposely unreadable. This style has been successfully used by skilled negotiators around the world for centuries. By creating an image of being indifferent to either winning or losing on any particular point, impassive negotiators cause their counterparts to believe that some secret is being withheld.

⑤ Technical: Technical negotiation centers on the data of the product or service under discussion, and it counts on the opposition being worn down by the onslaught of technical details. Many negotiation teams purposely include a member who is highly knowledgeable about technical processes.

⑥ Secretive: Many negotiations are conducted wholly or partly in secret. This style can be used to keep counterparts from seeking outside assistance or information once negotiations begin.

⑦ Exploitative: All opponents have weaknesses that can be exploited. Negotiators must determine for themselves which weaknesses to exploit and when. If best practiced, the exploitative style involves a careful study of counterparts before and during discussions. As exploitative styles generally involve using deceptive tactics, therefore they rarely survive long-term scrutiny.

⑧ Ambivalent: Ambivalence is something that negotiators never consciously choose as a style, but it is often there as a character default. Most ambivalence stems from a lack of research concerning the particulars of the deal at hand.

⑨ Social: Negotiation is certainly a form of social contact, but some participants choose to emphasize its social aspects in an attempt to sway counterparts. Lavish receptions with important guests, private dinners at popular venues, choice seats at sporting events, etc. are designed to make opposition believe that their best interests are being looked after. The message is "let's be friends first and business partners later".

(2) Team Styles

Besides the above personal styles in negotiations there are also team styles. Teams must make a conscious effort to maintain a unified front. This can be accomplished through a variety of styles, with specific choices based on member talent, cultural background, and personality type.

① Consensus: It allows the team to share authority and responsibility. The group sets policies and makes decisions. The group is consulted on issues both large and small. It is a very time-consuming style, but it has the virtue of being difficult to penetrate. Every decision made by the team requires a form of voting. Counterparts will find it difficult to pry apart positions that appear seamless, but they may also be worn down by the slowness of the decision-making process and grant concessions simply to keep things moving.

② Platoon: This style runs with small sub-teams. The team leader must be able to organize and supervise a team of its own. This style is very useful when large numbers of technical specialists must be brought along for negotiations. Team leaders are in charge of the specialists and handle applicable negotiating sessions or side trips.

③ Hierarchical: This style is used by the teams which choose to pass all decisions through the chain-of-command for approval. Although it is safe, it is not necessarily effective. Since all the decisions come from a single source, which can ensure consistency within the team, it defeats the purpose of doing fieldwork for negotiators. One of the advantages of this style is that it acts as a training ground for novices while the disadvantage is that it is slow.

④ Divide and conquer: The easiest way to keep the negotiation under control is to control the counterparts' position. Of course, the counterparts will try their best to prevent that from happening. Team negotiation can effectively adopt this style either as the overall strategy or as simple tactic for specific agenda points. All negotiators must be on the lookout for signs that it is being used against them. The style depends on either gathering information from a counterpart who has been strategically separated from the group or consistently exploiting the small mistakes in a counterpart's position.

Every style has its pros and cons. Negotiators should do some research work before negotiations on their counterparts and choose the suitable styles and modes in order to achieve their goals.

2. Strategies of Pre-Strategies of Presentation

In the bidding presentation of the negotiation process, there are three guidelines to the way in which a bid should be presented firmly, clearly and without comment.

The opening bid needs to be put firmly, seriously and without reservations or hesitations. At the time when both parties are sensing and judging from each other's words and facial expressions to inferring the other party's intention, every hesitation or reservation presented in either party's bid will raise the attacking confidence of the other party.

It needs to be understood clearly so that the other party recognizes precisely what is being asked. In the process of the negotiation, it's better to have the quotation typed on paper and to ensure the clarity and nicety of the bid, to show the other party a sense of seriousness and legitimating. Even though it's a kind of oral bid, after a precise oral expression, the party should also see to it that the quotation be written on paper to show to the other party for a visual impression. In doing so it can avoid possible confusion by merely memory later on.

There is some controversy as to who should be the first to make a bid. Most people take the first bid to be a good idea. The first statement in the bidding carries a durable influence. To some extent first bid is more influential than responsive bid.

Some other people believe the first bid might have its disadvantages. A disadvantage is that when a party hears another party's opening bid, they can then make some final adjustment in their own thinking. A new element of information is provided about regarding a party's starting point, providing modification to their own bidding to gain fresh advantage.

Another disadvantage is that others may try to concentrate on attacking our bid, trying to drive us down and down without giving us any information about their own position. This is something we must resist — we must make them bid and not allow the negotiation to become a fight on our first offer.

As a matter of fact, it's not necessarily that to bid first will either on the upper hand or in the passive position. It is always possible for those who bid first or after to gain or lose. What really counts is the role that played by either side's economic force, negotiation capacity, knowledge scale, negotiation tactics and some comprehensive factors.

3. Strategies of Responsiveness

At this stage first party should fully aware that he has put a bid, and he has a perfect right to know what the other party is prepared to offer in return.

In general, the other side will not respond by accepting but to react in this or that way. Thus both parties are entering a bargaining period. The case is more intense. Both sides at this time are trying to move the negotiation to a more favorable direction to their own side. So, it's quite necessary to do some research work of studying the other side before responding to the bid. In responding to bids by the other party there is a need to distinguish between clarification and justification.

The competent negotiator first ensures that he or she knows what the other party is bidding. On this basis, he or she must have an idea how to satisfy the other party in gaining their interests and at the same time have to figure out what are the interests that really belongs to them and what are the things they expect to get.

4. Offensive and Defensive Strategies

Offensive strategies are designed to take the initiative while defensive strategies are the counter to offensive ones, and they are the springboards from which a counter-offensive can be launched.

Negotiators can not rely on defensive strategies only, because no defensive is ever perfect, a weak point will be found upon which the opponent can concentrate his attack.

(1) Offensive Strategies

① Asking questions

There four kinds of questions involved: probing, specific, attacking, and "yes" / "no" questions.

The probing questions are difficult to answer because they are phrased in general terms. They are intended to gain information for one party to make sure the weak point in the opponent's propositions before a major attack. For example, "We have had a look at your quotation, but perhaps you could explain rather more fully the way in which you have arrived at the increase in price."

The specific questions are designed to force an admission based on the information gained from the probing question and data already known. For instance, "What is your program for manufacture and testing?" These questions are simple and short without disclosing all facts.

The "yes" / "no" questions should never be asked unless the questioner has prepared the ground in advance, and is satisfied that the answer he will obtain is the one he wants to hear. They are designed to set up a direct attack. The attacking questions are designed to force a concession based on the answers to the specific questions and other data, such as "How can that be valid?"

② Making the other side appear unreasonable

It is a method of challenging the validity of a proposition. A case is found in which application of the propositions would be absurd, so the person who posed it is challenged to redefine it in more limited terms.

③ Pulling the pig's tail

It is a colloquial term referring to the result of the activity that the animal pulls as hard as it can in the opposite direction. One party will over emphasize the apparent importance to his securing a particular point when his real objective is the direct opposite. Some negotiators are suspicious of any proposal made by their opposite partner.

④ Use of commitments

The use of commitments is needed to persuade the opponent of the truth of the statements the party is making. It is a major offensive negotiating tactic that both sides will use. When the commitments are of different rank, the higher will normally prevail.

⑤ Discovering interests

As negotiating about interests is a better way to conduct technology trade negotiations, discovering the other side's interests becomes a paramount necessity. This simply means asking questions:"Could you tell us . . . ?" "Why do you need . . . ?", "So your real interest is . . . ?"

To facilitate the search for options, both sides should not only try to find out the real interests of their counterparts but also state explicitly those of their own, giving reasons wherever necessary.

⑥ Presenting arguments

In negotiations, a party often feels the need to show to the other side that they know exactly where the other's real interests lie and will not compromise theirs. The valid reasons must be put into some kind of an order. Each point should be stronger than the one before until the argument reaches its climax.

⑦ "The right answer" strategy

When the two parties have conflicts of interests, which are pretty difficult to resolve, they may try "The right answer" strategy, which works in this way:

Agree that a state of deadlock exists;

Step out of the role of negotiators;

Study the problem objectively;

Seek the right answer;

Agree on the right answer;

Return to the role of negotiators and see if the right answer offers acceptable solutions.

This strategy is particularly useful to business people. Whenever the other side suggests something doubtful, ask about it until it is absolutely justifiable.

⑧ **"The best alternative" strategy**

This is often used in tender business. After a receiver receives a number of offers, he decides which company has made the most attractive offer and then negotiates with the other companies with a view to improving his "best alternative". Once he can improve it no further, he begins negotiation with his first choice, now negotiating from a much-strengthened position.

　(2) Defensive Strategies

① **Minimum response and pretended misunderstanding**

The most effective of defensive strategy in negotiation is to say just enough to compel the other side to go on talking. The more they talk, the more they will reveal, the more they will feel compelled to reveal in order to be persuasive, and the nearer they will come to exposing their genuine motives and the real level of their minimum negotiating objective.

② **Side-stepping**

If one party does not want to answer the opponent's question directly, he may seek to side-step the issue. So, in answering to a question "Can you guarantee completion by a specified date?", the party might reply "Here, have a look at the program, then I can show you how we have arrived at the end date and you can see for yourself the problems."

③ **The "Yes-but" technique**

If the negotiator faces a question that he wishes to answer in the negative, but he does not want to give offence, he may use the technique of "yes-but". The affirmative part of the answer should appear to align the negotiator alongside his opponent, and so establish the negotiator as someone who is cooperative and appreciative of the viewpoint of the other side. The negative part is intended to identify some of the reasons that prevent the negotiator from doing what the other side would like him to do.

④ **The counter questions**

If the opponent uses questions as offensive tactics, the party's correct response is the counter questions. The questions are designed to compel the opponent to limit the scope of his inquiry and to reveal more of his own position.

⑤ **Straw issues**

A straw issue is one that is of no value to one party in itself, but it is raised with the intention to be lost, thus provides the opportunity for the party to secure a genuine concession from the opponent in return. Securing a particular concession from the opponent must allow the opponent something in exchange. By including one or more straw issues in his initial demands, the party ensures that he has something in the bank to allow the opponent as compensation for the opponent abandoning or modifying his own initial demands. The party must view the problem through the opponent's eyes in deciding on what to select as a straw issue.

⑥ **Exposing dirty tricks**

It is quite common in negotiations that the negotiators find their counterparts playing dirty tricks. First, they must recognize that what is happening is in fact signs of dirty tricks. Next they must show their counterparts that they understand the game by exposing it.

5. Strategies of Making Concessions

Making concessions is one of the most popular strategies used in the bargaining process to keep the negotiation on going. Making concessions however has a lot to do with many other factors. Every concession is very closely connected to a party's own interests. Although it depends mainly on the negotiator's flexible usage of the tactics of making concessions, it also is constrained by some basic principals. The following principals are often used:

(1) A concession by one party must be matched by a concession of the other party;

(2) It's better for the pace of concession to be as little as possible and the frequency of concession to be slow. What's more, the pace of concession must be similar as between the two parties;

(3) A party should trade their concession to their own advantage, doing their best to give the other party plenty of satisfaction even if concessions are small;

(4) A party must help the other party to see each of their concessions as being significant;

(5) Move at a measured pace towards the projected settlement point;

(6) Reserve concessions until they are needed.

6. Towards Settlement

When the parties become aware that a settlement is approaching, they should make the final offer. Characteristics of this final offer are:

(1) It should not be made too soon. Otherwise it will be taken as just another concession — one of many still to be hoped for;

(2) It must be big enough to symbolize closure. Rounding off a bid sufficient yet not too generous would certainly have the required impact;

(3) Negotiating to our advantage demands the last halfpenny. If you do not squeeze the final 1 / 4 per cent off his discount or the final two days off his delivery — he will not have the satisfaction of believing that he has taken you absolutely to the limit;

(4) Give him that satisfaction.

Finally, at the end of the negotiation:

(1) Summarize;

(2) Produce a written record;

(3) Identify action needs and responsibilities.

Section III　Practical Activities

1. Case Study

● Case Study 1

Background

Some Chinese students studying at a business school in the UK were asked by their professor to study a case written by an American and then make a presentation. What happened then?

Overseas Chinese Students

The case was about a JV project in a coastal city in China. The American described dinners given by the Chinese and some of the indirect ways Chinese people have at the negotiation table. The Chinese students realized that the American businessman's report was prejudiced. It was clear that he did not understand the Chinese culture. Furthermore, the Chinese students saw that his description caused some of their Western classmates to believe that the Chinese only liked rich food and were not sincere when doing business. They got this feedback, subsequently, from casual talks in the classroom. The Chinese students decided they needed to correct their classmates' misunderstandings. They decided their case analysis should include a more accurate description of Chines culture and worked very hard on theire preparation.

In their presentation to the class the following week, the Chinese students began with a brief introduction to Chinese hospitality. They explained the Chinese guest-treating culture with a quotation from Confucius, the ancient Chinese educator: "What a pleasant thing it is to have friends coming from afar." They described how the Chinese people care more about hospitality than about the money spent on the guests. The Chinese students then talked about the Chinese way of negotiating with Westerners. As they talked, they noticed some of the Western students nodding their heads in understanding and even heard occasional "wows" in a low voice. Their presentation caused great excitement and won a big round of applause. More importantly, it cleared the misperceptions the Western students had had about the Chinese.

Questions:

1. List your way of entertaining guests.
2. What do you learn from this case?

● Case study 2

Sometimes both sides have to make concessions so that the deal can be closed. Study the following case and see if we can learn something from it. Mrs. Smith(S), a textile dealer from London, is met by Ms. Yang(Y) in the showroom. Looking at the samples, Mrs. Smith negotiates business with Ms. Yang:

Can We Meet Each Other Half Way?

S: What do you have there, Ms. Yang?

Y: Some of our new products. Would you like to have a look at the patterns?

S: Yes, please.

Y: Here they are, Mrs. Smith.

S: I like this printed poplin. How much is it a yard?

Y: 45 pence per yard, CIF London.

S: Your price is higher than I can accept. Could you come down a little bit?

Y: What would you suggest?

S: Could you make it 40 pence per yard, CIF London?

Y: I'm afraid we can't. This is the best price we can quote.

S: Let's leave that for the time being.

Y: Are you interested in our pongee?

S: Yes. Please show me the latest product.

Y: Here it is.

S: The quality is very good. But nowadays nylon is pushing this material out.

Y: I don't think so. We've sold a lot this month.

S: Well, anyway, I'll book a trial order. The price?

Y: Same as we offered last time.

S: What about the quantity?

Y: 200 pieces for September shipment.

S: All right. I'll take the lot.

Y: How about the printed poplin, then?

S: There's still a gap of 5 pence. Will you give me a trade discount?

Y: Sorry. Can we meet each other half way?

S: What do you mean?

Y: Let's close the deal at 43 pence per yard, CIF London.

S: You dive a hard bargain, but I'll accept this time.

Y: We will provide good service and quality.

S: That will be deeply appreciated.

Y: Shall I make out the contract for you to sign tomorrow?

S: Fine.

2. Role Play

For your Information

In the conversation, the caller (B) is complaining about the problem of a digital video. How will the seller (A) deal with this complaint?

A: Hello.

B: I bought a digital video here three days ago in your company, but it doesn't work. I come to see what you can do about it.

A: What's the matter with it?

B: The photoflash lamp does not work. Can I get my money back, because ...?

A: Do you have the warranty?

B: Sorry, I lost it.

A: We must have the warranty.

B: Can you fix it?

A: No, we don't have repairs here.

B: It is ridiculous. I want my money back.

A: We never give refunds.

B: It seems you can do nothing about it. It is ridiculous!

A: We may send it to the factory for repair. It will take two or three weeks. And you have to pay for the repair because you have no warranty.

B: Two or three weeks! I will be on holiday next week, and I want to take it with me.

A: Sorry, you have to wait.

3. Mini Negotiation

Discuss the mini negotiation and answer the question after it.

A: We have studied your case and with our policy you are entitled to $3,300.

B: I see. How did you reach that figure?

A: That was how much we decided the car was worth.

B: I see. What standard did you use to determine the amount? Do you know where I can buy a comparable car for that?

A: How much are you asking?

B: Whatever I am entitled to under the policy. I found a second hand car like mine for $3,850. Adding sales and excise tax it would come to about $4,000.

A: $4,000! That's too much!

B: I'm not asking for $4,000, or 3 or 5; just fair compensation. Do you think it's fair and I get enough to replace the car?

A: OK, I'll offer you $3,500. That's the highest I can go.

B: How does the company figure that?

A: Look, $3,500 is all you get. Take it or leave it.

B: $3,500 may be fair. I don't know. I certainly understand your position if you're bound to company policy, but unless you can state objectively why that amount is what I'm entitled to, I think I'll do better in court. Why don't we study the matter and talk again.

A: OK, I've got an ad here for a 1985 Fiesta for $3,400.

B: I see. What does it say about the mileage?

A: It says 49,000, why?

B: Because mine had only 25,000 miles. How much does that increase the value in your book?

A: Let me see, $150.

B: Assuming the 3,400 as possible base, that brings the figure to $3,550. Does that ad say anything about a radio?

A: No.

B: How much extra in your book?

A: That's $125.

B: What about air conditioning? ...

(30 minutes later, B took home a check for $4,100.)

Question:

What strategies does B take in the negotiation?

Negotiation Tips

● Ask Your Customer More Questions 多询问客户

You need to learn as much about the other person's situation as you know about your own. This is particularly important for salespeople. Ask your customers more questions about their purchasing behavior. Learn what is important to them, their needs and wants. Develop the habit of asking questions such as, "What made you consider a purchase of this nature?", "What time frames are you working with?", "What is most important to you about this?".

● Negotiate at Every Opportunity 不失时机谈

Most people hesitate to negotiate because they lack the confidence. Develop this confidence by negotiating more frequently. Ask for discounts from your suppliers. As a consumer, develop the habit of asking for a price break when you buy from a retail store. Be pleasant and persistent, but not demanding. Conditioning yourself to negotiate at every opportunity will help you become more comfortable, confident, and successful when the time comes to negotiate for your business.

- ● Maintain "Walk-away" Power 保留退出谈判的权利

It is better to walk away from a sale than to make too large a concession or give too deep a discount. This particular strategy gives salespeople the most leverage when dealing with customers. It might be challenging to do when you are in the midst of a slow sales period, but remember — there will always be someone to sell to.

Extended Activities

Ⅰ. Situational Group Talks.

Discuss with your partner and decide which words and expressions should be used when telephoning.

Making a call	
Taking messages	
Handling complaints	

Ⅱ. Multiple Choice.

Directions: There are ten incomplete sentences in this part. For each sentence there are four choices marked A, B, C, and D. Choose the one that best completes the sentence.

1. As we are one of the importers in this line, we are _____ to handle large quantities.

    A. at a position   B. of a position   C. on a position   D. in a position

2. We offer you the following items _____ your reply reaching here by May 21 our time.

    A. subjecting to   B. to subject to   C. subjects to   D. subject to

3. _____ your prices be in line, you will find a ready market for the products.

    A. Should   B. To provide   C. Provided   D. Provide

4. We confirm our e-mail of yesterday, _____ as follows.

    A. reads   B. read   C. which reads   D. which reading

5. We _____ your letter of Nov. 4 asking us to make a quotation.

    A. go over   B. have read   C. check up   D. refer to

6. Our offer _____ firm till May 8.

    A. could be   B. is   C. for   D. /

7. FOB should be followed by _____.

    A. port of shipment   B. port of destination

    C. port of transshipment   D. port of calls

8. In CIF, the _____ has to procure insurance against the buyer's risk of loss of or damage to the goods during the carriage.

    A. seller   B. buyer

    C. freight forwarder   D. receiver

9. The _____ term can only be used for sea and inland waterway transport.

    A. CPT   B. CFR   C. FCA   D. CIP

10. The Youth Pens are _____.

    A. on scare supply   B. in short supply

    C. not preparing   D. with abundant supply

Ⅲ. Choose from the phrases and sentences listed below to complete the conversation and then practice the dialogue with your partner.

---

a. I see. How many would you like?

b. Yes, do that and then perhaps you'll call me back.

c. Yes, but we had 7.5% last time and Mr. Kell said it would be 5% higher for a repeat order.

d. What discount would you offer on an order for 1,007?

e. Speaking.

f. That's good. We give a better discount on a repeat order.

g. We're thinking in terms of 12.5%.

h. Well, it depends on your terms. Is your May price list still valid?

A: Hello, Mr. Wood.

B: 1. _____

A: I'm ringing from Computer Sales Ltd. We'd like to order some A12 Printers.

B: 2. _____

A: 3. _____

B: Oh yes, until the end of the year.

A: 4. _____

B: You've done business with us before, haven't you?

A: Yes, and this is our second order for this type.

B: 5. _____

A: 6. _____

B: Oh, we don't normally go over 10%.

A: 7. _____

B: I see. Well, I'd better confirm that with him.

A: 8. _____

B: Yes, we'll contact you afterwards.

Ⅳ. Decide whether the following statements are true(T) or false(F).

1. Potential negotiators must research their own talents and virtues to determine which style or combination of styles best fits their personality and the team goals.

2. As a matter of fact, it's not necessarily that to bid first will either on the upper hand or in the passive position.

3. Offensive strategies are designed to take the initiative while defensive strategies are the counter to offensive ones, and they are the springboards from which a counter-offensive can be launched.

4. Making concessions is one of the most popular strategies used in the bargaining process to keep the negotiation on going.

5. It is worse to walk away from a sale than to make too large a concession or give too deep a discount.

Ⅴ. Translate the following sentences into Chinese.

1. We are studying the offer and hope that it will keep open till the end of the month.

2. Because there is a brisk demand for the goods, the offer will be open only for 5 days.

3. You are cordially invited to take advantage of this attractive offer. We are anticipating a large order from the United States, and that will cause a sharp rise in price.

4. All quotations are subject to our final confirmation. Unless otherwise stated or agreed upon, all prices are net without commission.

5. In reply to your inquiry of July 21, we have the pleasure of offering you Children's Bicycles as follows.

2

Practical Business Communication

Chapter 5

Oral Communication in Business

Learning Goals

Upon completion of this chapter, you will be able to:
☞ grasp the general oral delivery skills;
☞ understand the forms of oral communication;
☞ follow up the strategies for successful oral communication;
☞ comprehend the dual-direction of oral communication.

Lead-in Words

feedback   *n.* 反馈,反映
minute   *n.* 会议记录
elaborate   *v.* 精心制作,详细描述

stage fright 怯场
gender   *n.* 性别
statistically   *adv.* 统计上地,统计地

Section I   Forms of Oral Communication

Statistically speaking, a businessperson spends an average of 30 percent of the working hours in speaking. An effective speech will win honor both you and your organization. But a poor one will dishonor both.

1. Oral Presentation

In general, humans had mostly expressed their thoughts and feelings in the form of oral speech before writing was adopted. Oral communication includes such media as face-to-face conversations, speeches, meetings or conferences, presentations, telephone conversations, teleconferences and others.

An excellent presentation starts with excellent content. For your presentation to be a success, identify why you are speaking about your topic and to whom you are delivering the message. That is, the first thing you will should do is to know the precise purpose of the presentation. Will you inform, persuade or entertain? Make a detailed analysis of your audience: their interest, education, gender, approximate ages and so on. The next thing to do is to gather support for your topic, organize your points and write a draft of the presentation. Plan how you will present, prepare speaking notes and create audiovisual aids.

(1) Analyze the Audience

Analyze your audience and think about who they are.

✦ How interested might they be in the topic and how could you attract their interest and make the information relevant to them?

✦ What do they know or not know about the topic you will present?

✦ What questions might they ask that you might need to address in the presentation?

(2) Create an Outline and Write a Draft

It is important for your presentation to be well-organized. Jot down your ideas and organize them into an outline. Then, write a draft of your presentation. Writing a draft helps you clarify your thoughts on the topic, become familiar with the topic and decide on appropriate transitions between the different points. You can use this draft to help you write a formal report if you are required to submit one. When you write the draft, pay particular attention to the introduction. In the introduction you gain the audience's interest, state the purpose of the presentation, and give an agenda or outline of your major points. In the body of your draft, make sure you use clear transitions that will indicate to your audience you are moving from one point to another. The draft should include a conclusion or summary.

(3) Devise a Presentation Plan

Once you are clear on what you want to say in your presentation, you can plan how you will present it. A presentation plan helps you organize your time, know when to incorporate activities for the audience to do, and decide on the types of audiovisual aids to use. Note that each section of the presentation should have an estimate of the amount of time it will take to complete, a note of the type of audiovisual aid you will use, and what type of activity you will do, if applicable.

(4) Prepare Speaking Notes

If you know your material well, you could use the presentation plan to prompt you during the presentation to ensure what you want to say. However, you might feel more comfortable by using speaking notes to jog your memory. Speaking notes summarize the key points in your draft and are more detailed than a presentation plan. During your presentation, you will glance at the speaking notes and then elaborate on each point from memory. Your audience will find it easier to pay attention to you if you talk to them rather than if you read to them from a draft of your presentation.

But actually, public speaking may scare you, as we call it as "stage fright". To get over nervousness, the best requirement for you is to be self-confident. Besides, do a good preparation for the speech, so after having finished the draft, you can rehearse your talk for several times. Be sure to arrive earlier than the scheduled time, deep breath before the speech are all good suggestions for you to fight stage fright.

2. Dyadic Communication

Dyadic communication is also defined as interpersonal communication. To be exact, it is the kind of communication between two or more persons.

(1) Interviewing

A self-assessment is the first step for an interview: your likes and dislikes, merits and demerits, attitudes towards work, habits of life, willingness to the place of work and so on. Creating a good CV will help you win the first impression from the interviewers. Many interviewers may use a traditional approach in which they ask you to elaborate on your resume content and evaluate your own capabilities. They may use open-ended questions like "Tell me about yourself." or closed questions like "Are you willing to travel?". These questions often exam your perceptions of yourself and your goals, the motivation behind goals and decisions, and connections between your background or qualifications and the employer's need will have the most effective impact.

One of the most important ways of preparing for an interview is to anticipate questions you may be asked and practice them before the interview. Traditional interview questions are as follows:

① What is important to you in a job?

② Why do you want to work for this organization?

③ We have a lot of applicants for this job, why should we appoint you?

④ How long do you think you'd stay with us if you were appointed?

⑤ What do you think your strength and weaknesses are?

⑥ Which is more important to you: status or money?

⑦ How do you spend your leisure time?

⑧ Where do you want to be five years from now?

⑨ What are your salary expectations?

⑩ What would you do if . . . ?

⑪ What type of position are you interested in?

⑫ Could you tell me something about yourself?

⑬ Do you have any questions about the organization or the job?

⑭ What has been your most valuable experience?

⑮ How would you describe your personality?

⑯ Why do you want to leave your present job?

⑰ What makes you think you'd enjoy working with us?

⑱ What are the most proud of having done in your present job?

⑲ What was the worst problem you have had in your present job and how did you solve it?

⑳ What are your long-range goals?

㉑ Describe your present job — what do you find the most rewarding about it?

㉒ What do you think is your ideal boss like?

(2) Telephoning

Telephone communications have now become an indispensable part of any business offices. Many profitable business deals are completed with good telephone skills. The way to handle them does far more to enhance or impair the image of a firm than is often realized.

If you don't have much experience of making phone calls in English, making a business call can be a worrying experience. Prepare for an important phone call in a foreign language, you should make notes in advance. They will help you to remember what will be said when you are talking.

In general, four steps should be followed when opening a call: greeting; asking for a connection; identifying yourself; and stating your purpose. Remember the following when making phone calls:

① Sound efficient so that the other person will get a good impression of your firm.

② Pausing is vital to establishing effective communication on the phone.

③ Unless you know the person you are talking to, don't try to be funny.

④ Be sure to use proper phone etiquette (friendly, polite etc.) through the whole call.

⑤ Don't interrupt the other person. Let them finish what they want to say.

⑥ You should always end a call on a positive tone by thanking the other person for his or her time.

⑦ When answering a business phone, try to pick up the phone within two or three rings and be sure to identify yourself.

⑧ Remember to call back if you say you will.

(3) Business Meeting

A group for the business meeting may demand more people, at least three and perhaps far more than that.

Formal business meetings are run under strict rules or procedures. Motions must be made formal before a topic can be debated. Each point is settled by a vote. Minutes record each motion and the vote on it. Informal meetings, which are much more common in the workplace, are run more loosely. Votes may not be taken if most people seem to agree. Minutes may not be kept. Informal meetings are better for team-building and problem solving.

Planning an agenda is the foundation of a good meeting. A good agenda indates: whether each item is presented for information, for discussion, or for a decision; who is sponsoring or introducing each item; how much time is allotted for each item.

According to the agenda, you then decide on whom, what, when and where to distribute the announcement for the meeting.

Pay attention to people and process in the meeting. At informal meetings, a good leader observes non-verbal feedback and invites everyone to participate. At the end of the meeting, a good leader must summarize all the decisions and remind the group who is responsible for implementing or following up on each item. Short breaks are planned in a long meeting.

3. Effective Ways of a Conversation

On social occasions, if we are planning to establish business relations with a potential partner, it's quite often that we would approach them and greet them so that we can have conversations with them.

(1) Starting a Conversation

On social gathering or other occasions, we may start conversations with strangers (our potential bussiness partners) by commenting on the following topics, then introduce yourself and other people with you to each other.

✦ the weather (the rain, the snow, the sunshine, etc.)

✦ the food and drink (the Italian food, the Chinese food, the Indian food, etc.)

✦ the journey (the train, the bus, the air, etc.)

✦ the city (when travelling, the destination)

✦ the event (the party, the trade fair, the exposition, etc.)

e.g.

(It is) a nice party, isn't it?

What a nice day, isn't it?

Excuse me, would you mind ...?

Say, don't you think we've met somewhere?

Excuse me, is anybody sitting here?

(2) Maintaining a Conversation

If we want to establish business relations with our potential business partners, we need to know each other. One of the best ways of maintaining a conversation is for us to ask each other questions, when we meet face-to-face, is by exchanging information, which is also a good way for us to know each well.

✦ Yes / No questions — The replay can be *Yes* or *No*

　Is your company a state-owned?

✦ Alternative questions

　Is your company a newly established one or an old one?

✦ Wh-questions — Information questions

How long have you been in this line?

(3) Ending a Conversation

At the same time, we also need to end our conversations politely before we say good-bye to each other.

e.g. OK, good talking to you.

I hope to see you again.

I've enjoyed talking to you.

It was very nice talking to you.

4. Major Advantages of Oral Communication

It is generally believed that oral communication has the following major advantages:

(1) Directness

Spoken form tends to be direct. You face the partner in a visit, or speak to an audience on the phone, which furnish your message directly. It is easy for both parties to read the body language of each other in the case of a dialogue or meeting, and to hear the tone of mutual responses in the case of a telephone conversation.

(2) Exchangeability

In most spoken ways you can get your audience involved with your topic, speaking first and then listening, exchanging your ideas with listeners before speaking again.

(3) Confidentiality

Since voice tends to be temporary and perishable, and your audience is usually a selected group, it can be more confidential than written channel.

(4) Immediacy

Both non-verbal cues and verbal communication supply immediate feedback. You can reach a collective decision since you have immediate feedback from each other. The immediateness is obviously a physical outcome of both directness and exchangeability.

Section II   Strategies of Oral Communication

In business negotiation, many times when negotiators restricted by particular time, place, and atmosphere, can not say directly then and there, tactical expressions will succeed. The common tactical expressions in oral communication include euphemistic presentations, fuzzy wording, merit demonstrations and polemic statement, which can relieve the tension of negotiating climate and break the deadlock when a negotiator expresses his different opinions, or gets the negotiation to be stuck.

1. Euphemistic Presentations

Euphemistic presentation is an effective negotiating means for both sides. Find a need of your opponent's and meet it. Don't have to give him the hard shell. All that's necessary is to shade your case positively in a way that makes clear to your opponent how much he will benefit. There are many devices for euphemistic presentations, which includes the following:

(1) Adopt Softened Wordage

People can use softened wordage to express indirectly and inoffensively. A negotiator can, by the strategy of hedging, make sure that he is not completely committed and also soften the tone in case of hurting the opponent. The expressions such as "I'm afraid", "we would say", "it seems to me", "we would suggest", etc. turn the strong into the moderate tone, thereby gaining the mild, euphemistic effects.

(2) Adopt Empathic Technique

The main empathic technique is to look from the opponents' point of view. In business negotiations, by imagining how opponents feel, it improves the bargaining climate. If used skillfully, it fools opponents into thinking you care about their problems in order that they will reciprocate. It is powerful in that one thing from different person's point of view, showing that speaker's empathic consideration for others. The empathic technique somehow helps negotiators to better understand each other. This understanding often leads to better proposals and more satisfactory agreements.

(3) Give Partners an Out

It is very common for negotiators to refuse other's offer, even criticize other's inappropriate needs. In this case, euphemistic speech plays a somewhat lubricating role in business negotiation. For the sake of saving an opponent's face, negotiators can give the opponent an out by way of euphemistic speech in business negotiation.

(4) Adopt Passive Voice

A passive voice often express vaguely due to the omission of the agent, which gives much more possibility to guess who is responsible for the deeds. It is possible to be the speaker, or the superior or someone else in charge. Even though the speaker refers to the opponent, in his mind, the passive voice seems more polite especially when the speaker thinks the opponent gets wrong in some regards.

2. Fuzzy Wording

Fuzzy wording is multifunctional and can often be used as a kind of politeness strategy, which usually plays some unexpected positive part in business negotiation. Usually it is difficult for negotiators to force others to reach an agreement. Therefore, they must leave some leeway to each other so as to change their position or standpoint without loss of their face. Fuzzy wording can leave room to negotiators' maneuver, avoiding the "win-loss syndrome" deadlock. By using fuzzy wording, speakers satisfy the opponent's negative face without interference in other's freedom of action. Fuzzy wording can, undoubtedly, not only improve the negotiating climate, thereby helping the negotiation go on smoothly, but also sound the opponent out about the question, in an effort to know the other's real intention. On the basis of this "dodge" strategy, the negotiators seek and enlarge the common points, hoping for the ultimate agreement.

Fuzzy wording can also help negotiators to win the opponent psychologically, for example:

I'm sure you'll find out our price most favorable. Elsewhere prices for hardware have gone up tremendously in recent years. Our prices haven't changed much.

In the above sentence, "most favorable", "tremendously", and "much" are all fuzzy words. Here the negotiator emphasizes the fact of price rise in hardware, indicating their price most preferential.

(1) Direct Utterance Avoided

In international business negotiations, fuzzy wording can sometimes be used to avoid any direct utterance to either the speaker or the opponent. By avoiding direct utterance, the speaker can increase flexibility of his speech and avoid coming into deadlock. When one asks the opponent's management policy and enterprise credit with respect to some secret considerations, the negotiator doesn't answer directly, but also cannot neglect the other. Then he says:

① *Well, our business policy is very clear, and our enterprise credit is also known to all.*

Here the "all" is very flexible, which can refer to anyone, what is known to all is also explained in various ways. Therefore, the above example does not let out any concrete information.

② *In this case, if a sort of testing agent is just available to put into it, the result would be much better and satisfactory.*

In sentence ②, "a sort of", "better", and "satisfactory" are all fuzzy words, they do not provide the opponent with any concrete information at all.

(2) Hedging Words Used

By definition, hedging words make things fuzzier in some sense, which can be classified into two kinds: hedges used to reduce the degree of truth value or alter the related scope of an utterance, such as "sort of", "kind of", "somewhat", "really", "almost", "quite", "entirely", "a little bit", "some", "to some extent", "more or less" and etc., and the other kind of hedges used by the speaker to judge subjectively what is said or to access indirectly what is said, according to some objective evidence, such as "I think", "no wonder", "I believe", "I assume", "I suppose", "I am afraid", "probably", "as far as I can tell", "seem", "hard to say" and etc. In business negotiation, negotiators deliberately put their statement in terms that are tentative or vague. For example:

① *Anyhow, I am afraid the implications of these two terms are somewhat different.*

② *Well, the design is generally based on the calculation of Professor Thomson. He once said that even the most efficient steam engine was only about 20% efficient.*

③ *And I think we can probably just make shipment before May ... As far as I can tell you right now, we stall at once.*

④ *I caught the eleven something plane.*

In the sentences above, the speaker makes use of "something", "somewhat", "on the calculation of", "I think", and "as far as I can tell" to better hide the speaker's inefficiency and inadequacy in some regards. These hedging words can leave some leeway for the speaker and save his face.

(3) Authorization Limited

Limited Authorization can be a big advantage in negotiation to be murky. By invoking the tactic of authority limits, the negotiator gives himself some more time to consider the deal. At least, he takes this as an excuse to refuse the opponent without hurting mutual face. Therefore it is very useful to provide a good way of maintaining good relations with your opponent when you have to say no or intend to keep opponents off balance, or want to retreat from previous concessions, etc. The usual technique he is to pass the opponent to successively higher-ranking people, for example:

① *To be honest, the problem you put forward may be solved if I have the final. But I am sorry, I have no such a right to decide.*

② *You know, this is not my personal affairs. To tell you the truth, the conditions you put forward just now are something new to my company, in fact, it's the first time for us to handle. I think, if you can lower your requirements, I shall try what I can to report to the Head Office and persuade my boss to agree to your terms.*

③ *As for the problem of specification modification. I'm afraid it's difficult for me to give you my opinion right now. Because this is not a problem of my own institute only, but relates to other factories in connection with the product. However, if you can add another 5% of the total products to be sold in your own country, I shall try my best to meet your requirements by reporting to the department concerned and consulting with other relevant factories.*

3. Merit Demonstrations

Driven by the mixture of strength policy and profit, negotiators readily demonstrate their merits, their advantages and past accomplishments, etc. This overstatement often seems forward and aggressive in the opponent's presence. Therefore, attention should be paid to the question of how to say one's merit appropriately negotiators. In business negotiation, negotiators should present merits skillfully and appropriately in order to achieve much more effective results. Usually understatement is preferable, which obeys the modesty maxim and indirect politeness strategy. The speaker endeavors to praise others and dispraise himself despite of his merits. It can emphasize a fact by deliberately understating it, impressing the listener or the reader more by what is merely implied or left unsaid than by bare statement.

There are some useful devices of understatement listed below.

(1) Limiting Direct Comparison

Remember that a negotiator should not contrast his strengths with his opponent's weaknesses directly. The head-on comments are not commendable, for the deliberate depreciation of others is not only impolite acts, but also reflects the speaker's moral inefficiency in listener's eyes, for example:

① *As a big factory, we have rooms to move about. And with a number of newly-developed products, we need to open overseas markets, and have had a group of foreign cooperative partners. While that EFG Company is a small one, they have insufficient ability of technical development, and their products are mainly for domestic market. So they now cannot begin to talk about the cooperation with foreign firms.*

② *This kind of instrument of ours is small in dimension, high in sensibility and easy to operate; while your product is bigger in volume and lacking of one percent in sensibility and without the automatic control function.*

Example ① emphasizes the size, production ability, and marketing conditions in direct comparison. From the listener's angle, the speaker pushes himself too forward to be approved, whereas, example ② gives prominence to the speaker's strengths in terms of the technological qualifications.

(2) Minimizing Exclamation

Minimizing exclamation is powerful in condition of demonstrating merits in the opponent's presence. Showing merits and worth, negotiators should attach great importance to the mood and tone, for the arrogant airs probably evoke the opponent's negative assessment such as disagreement, dislike, and hostility. As a result, exclamation and imperative sentences should be avoided as much as possible, for example:

① *Through repeated experiments, we have at last obtained these data which we have been longing for. It's certainly no easy job!*

② *We failed several times, but finally we succeeded in getting these experiment data.*

In the first example, the speaker somehow shows off his achievements and advantages. In general, such self-praise sounds impolite, and even sharp to listeners, whereas, the second example is mild, plain and objective. Thus it is more acceptable.

(3) Attenuating Subjective Coloring

When mentioning our own merits, we readily stress "we", "ours", "none but ours", etc. However, these expressions sound as if others were exclusive, they seem to flaunt to the speaker's power. Therefore, it violates the cooperative spirit of business negotiation. Compare the examples below：

① *Our enterprise has been developing rapidly, and well known in China and overseas. Our products are extremely welcomed by the customers.*

② *Our factory's economic beneficial results have in fact been tripled in the last three years. There's a special report about our factory carried in Beijing Review last month. You know, Beijing Review is weekly published in more than 20 languages and distributed to over 180 countries and regions. At present, a number of buyers especially name our factory as their only supplier, and we're just worrying how to meet the needs of the customers at home and abroad.*

The first example is effusive in the subjective color. The words "we", "our", "we think" give the listener a parading impression; while the second one seem concrete, objective and creditable, the negotiators manage to express "merit" modestly by showing objective situation. In fact, they intend not to dispraise themselves, but to describe their merits skillfully. By eliciting objective responses from opponents, the negotiators save their own positive face and improve the negotiating climate.

(4) Lessening Flowery Language

In business negotiation, flowery language sounds false and incredible, even repugnant. Those exaggerating and inflated modifiers such as "good", "optimal", "big" "first-rate", "super", "unique", "second to none", "incomparable" etc. should be used as less as possible. Typical fact and precise data can exactly reflect the nature of merit, and play a more persuasive and convincing role in negotiating, for example：

① *This kind of lighter has good performance and can be used for a long time.*

② *This kind of lighter can operate continually more than 40,000 times a piece.*

In comparison with the above-mentioned sentences, the second example is stated in a matter-of-fact way. The modifiers "big", "good", etc. can not work better than the plain fact-based or number-based statement.

4. Polemic Statements

Polemic statements play a powerful role in business negotiation. The key of polemics lies in "speak" and "state". Polemic statements should be definite; the grounds of arguments should be sufficient and logical. There are many devices for polemic statements. We mention several ways as follows.

(1) Furnish Appropriate Examples

When giving a polemic statement, the speaker should attach great importance to appropriateness, that is to say, he should furnish appropriate examples to support his points, for example：

"... *if I'm not mistaken. I understand what you asked in your question is about the problem of my Frequency Standard's Configuration. To answer your question, I'm afraid something must be stated here clearly:*

"Firstly, we have acknowledged the original proposal of making a Frequency Standard by ... This is clearly indicated in my paper. Please see the Reference No. 3. And in my talk just now, I once again mentioned the reference.

"Secondly, I supposed you must have noticed the differences between the proposal by ... and our actual experimental methods and the obtained results, especially the dimensions of the cavity in the Configuration. So far as the theoretical considerations are concerned, I'm afraid, ours is entirely different from what was proposed by ... Here are some curves of our measurements and the general diagram.

"Thirdly, the proposal made by ... was published in 1981. It's already more than twenty years since then. I think it's natural to have any ideas and techniques developed and advanced progressively.

"So, I don't quite understand what you're driving at by 'refurbished version'. And I ... "

In the example above, the speaker gives an appropriate and reasonable polemic statement toward the problem of "Refurbished version", it sounds mild and persuasive.

(2) Unleash Psychological Attacks

Looking from the opponent's angle, a negotiator shows that he understands and cares about the opponent's problems, and establishes a mood of trust and rapport with him, thus a kind of psychological communication between them can be formed, for example:

We appreciate your products very much, and we really need them, too. But it's too bad that we now have some difficulties to afford such a big sum. We were wondering whether you could take a more flexible policy toward that.

The example above shows the negotiator's interest in the opponent's products. Naturally, there is much more cooperation than conflict.

(3) Retreat in Order to Advance

To retreat means making some concessions to meeting some of the opponent's requirement. In the course of business negotiation, sometimes, a negotiator should retreat in order to advance; while to advance, put forward some requirements. It is quite common that the opponent reciprocates your good concessions for your meeting some of their requirements, for example:

We have met many of your requirements in the scientific survey to the forest regarding the visiting area and the time of stay there. To all this, you may be clear. So, if we can more appropriately solve the problem of the investment proportion, I'm afraid then, there should not be too much trouble for solving the transportation problem in the forest according to your requirement.

From the above example, the speaker, first of all, states that he has met many of the opponent's requirements, and then he takes advantage of "retreat" — solving the transportation problem, in an attempt to make the opponent cooperate with him in terms of the investment proportion.

(4) Take Advantage of Contradictions

In polemic statement, negotiators take advantage of contradictions or competitions between different rivals and counterparts, lead them to compete with each other in an effort to control them. For example:

① *Frankly speaking, the businessmen from America, Japan as well as from France are trying to contact us. But to us, we are going to compare commodities from different producers, treat them equally without discrimination, and choose among the best.*

② *At present, the products from Philip are attractive to us; but we are also very much interested in those from Matsushita. We hope that you can offer your competitive price.*

(5) Give Tit for Tat

Negotiators can adopt a tough and decisive tone of voice — "tit for tat" in making a polemic statement. It is an effective negotiating means in business negotiation, sometimes you have to give your opponent the hard shell in order to make him give up. In most cases, this technique can serve the progression of business negotiation, if the negotiator deals with it appropriately. It can usually fool the opponent into making concessions and closing the deal. However, it is aggressive and risky. For example:

① *Personally, this is our rock-bottom price, Mr. Green. I'm afraid, it seems that we can't make any further concession.*

② *It seems that the gap between us is too great whether the dispatched personnel could enter and work in the "center", although I can not say that we will call off this battle. However, if there is no flexibility on that from your side, I'm afraid I can not see any necessity of talking of sending personnel any more.*

③ *As the matter stands now, I'm afraid what we can do is only up to here.*

Section III   Practical Activities

1. Case Study

Background

In many international companies, groups exist because people working together can accomplish more, and they can make better decisions than the same number of people who work individually. It is known to that "the total is greater than the sum of parts".

Business Meetings in an International Company

But, in an international organization, what is the effective way to improve the coordination of all members in one group? Although there are many ways to select, I think an effective way to go is to have staff meetings. In our company, nearly all working groups have weekly staff meetings. It was designed by our top management to help all staff to learn some aspects about business, and then to make the management and their subordinates better understood each other. A well-managed weekly staff meeting is the key to effective performance management.

In our company, a weekly staff meeting is a meeting between a supervisor and his subordinates, which is the principal way to maintain their relationship. Its main purpose is mutual teaching and exchange of information. By talking about specific problems and situations, the supervisor teaches his subordinates his skills and know-how, and suggests other ways to deal with the same problem. Meanwhile, the subordinates tell their supervisor what is going on and what they are concerned mostly about in a detailed way.

Take my group as an example. We always hold a staff meeting once a week. After some regular meetings, I have found that good communication in small groups leads to better group decisions, which are superior to individual members' initiatives, encourage them to think and assist attitude development and change. What is emphasized at the group meeting comes out of a good consideration of several factors by all members, not out of someone's personal ideas.

A key point about a staff meeting is that it should be taken as all members' meeting, with its agenda and tone set forth by them, and there is a good reason for it. As the project leader, I need to prepare for each meeting, which is very important because I am forced to think in advance about all the issues and points I plan to bring up at the meeting. In this way, I feel better for the meeting. Moreover, with an outline, I know at the very beginning how many items are to be discussed, and this helps me to set the pace for the meeting according to the agenda.

When a staff meeting is to be held here, someone should send the agenda to the manager one day in advance, so that the manager can be better prepared for it. The agenda can be on any topic which employees want to talk about. We always go through the agenda at the start of the meeting, and add the manager's points at the end. We always complete the agenda before we start the manager's points.

Now we take the staff meeting as our communication system. We want to work more to improve such a system, so as to make it more effective for our business.

Questions:

1. What do you think of the group meeting practice in the case above? Do you think such practice is workable in your company?

2. What is your opinion of an effective communication within a company?

2. Role Play

Frank Li, a market researcher with China National Everbright Import & Export Corporation, is telephoning Men's Fashion Magazine Office in New York for more specific information about men's shirts after having narrowed down the scope of market selection by "desk research".

Editor: Good morning. *Men's Fashion* Magazine. May I help you?

Li: Good morning. May I speak to the editor, please?

Editor: Yes, this is the managing director speaking. What can I do for you?

Li: I'm Frank Li, a market researcher with China National Everbright Import & Export Corporation. We know your magazine is very prestigious, and highly specialized. I'd like to ask you for a special favor.

Editor: Yes, go ahead.

Li: We'd like to know, according to your last survey, what kind of men's shirt will be fashionable this year.

Editor: Aha, you've found the right place and the right person for your market research. Our Statistics show the cotton print shirt is becoming popular here this year. So there's a potential market.

Li: You mean the cotton shirts with bright colors or light ones?

Editor: Probably, both. Our survey shows that most youngsters like bright colors while the older people like gray or slightly dark ones.

Li: I see. And what about the style?

Editor: I think the style is almost the same as usual, that is, the looser ones. You know, the temperature will be comparatively high this year.

Ll: Yes, I see your point. How about other kinds of shirts?

Editor: If you need any more specific information, you can refer to our current issue of *Men's Fashion*. It's probably available this week.

Li: Yes, that's a great idea. Thank you very much.

Editor: You're welcome. Good-bye!

Li: Good-bye!

3. Mini Negotiation

The fuzzy wording strategy has multi-faced functions, but the most striking is that it is persuasive and convincing without any force upon others. Discuss how the fuzzy wording strategy is used in the following negotiation.

A: Mr. Wang, I am anxious to know your offer.

B: Well, we've been holding it for you, Mr. Smith. Here it is. 80 dozens of woolen sweaters, at $160 per doz, CIF New York. Shipment will be in May.

A: That's too high! It will be difficult for us to make any sales.

B: I'm rather surprised to hear you say that, Mr. Smith. You know the price of woolen sweater has gone up since last year. Ours compares favorably with what you might get elsewhere.

A: I'm afraid I can't agree with you here. Japan has just come into the market with lower price.

B: Ah, but everybody in the woolen sweater trade knows that China's is of top quality. Considering the quality, I should say the price is reasonable.

A: No doubt, yours is of a high quality, but still there has been competition in the market. I know some countries are actually lowering their price.

B: So far our commodities have stood the competition well. The very fact that other clients keep on buying speaks for it. Few other woolen sweaters can compete with ours either for quality or price.

A: But I believe we'll have a hard time convincing our clients at your price.

B: To be frank with you, if it weren't for our good relation, we wouldn't consider making you a firm offer at this price.

A: All right. It seems that I have no other choice but accept it.

B: I'm glad that we've settled the price.

Negotiation Tips

● Enjoy the Negotiation Process 享受谈判过程

Negotiation is a process, not an event. There are predictable steps: preparation, creating the climate, identifying interests, and selecting outcomes that you will go through in any negotiation. With practice, you will gain skill at facilitating each step of the process. As your skill increases, you'll discover that negotiating can be fun.

● Find out the Interest of the Other Side 不失时机练谈判

Give the hardballer plenty of airtime to talk about what they value, what they are looking for, and any "hot" items the company has to have. To keep them talking about their interests, ask plenty of open-ended questions.

Extended Activities

Ⅰ. Situational Group Talks.

Search local newspapers or the Internet for some job vacancies，and then analyze the advertisements. List any possible questions will be asked in the interview and simulate it with your group member or by a panel of people in your group.

Ⅱ. Here are some problems which may arise during a presentation. Match the problems with the appropriate solution.

Problems	Solutions
1. Lack of focus	A. Explanatory title / prior discussion with key people
2. Lack of rehearsal	B. Learn and rehearse the use of equipment
3. Audience not prepared to enter open your discussion	C. Define the point your case illustrates and build presentation around this
4. Poor use of visual aids	D. Practice aloud and time your presentation
5. Inappropriate discussion	E. Plan the discussion properly；consider omitting discussion completely；always leave 8 – 10 minutes free for audience participation

Ⅲ. Complete the following telephone conversations according to the cues provided in the brackets.

1. A：This is Directory Assistance. ＿＿＿＿＿＿＿＿（您需要帮忙吗）?

   B：Hello. ＿＿＿＿＿＿＿＿（我想挂个电话给……）Italy-American Chamber of Commerce. But I don't know their phone number. Can you help me?

   A：＿＿＿＿＿＿＿＿（请稍候）. It's 310 – 826 – 9898.

   B：310 – 826 – 9898. Thank you.

   A：You're welcome. Good-bye!

2. A：Good morning. ＿＿＿＿＿＿＿＿（这是马丁律师事务所）. Can I help you?

   B：Good morning. This is Donald Hoover from Import and Export Office of Electrical Appliances. ＿＿＿＿＿＿＿＿＿＿＿＿（请接 Iris Hocking 小姐的办公室）?

   A：＿＿＿＿＿＿＿＿（对不起，占线）. Would you leave your phone number and she can call you back in a minute?

   B：OK. 2573846.

   A：2573846. Thank you. (After a while) Miss Hocking，＿＿＿＿＿＿＿＿＿＿＿＿＿＿ （有位 Donald Hoover 先生的电话。要不要接过来）?

   C：Yes，please.

   B：Hello. ＿＿＿＿＿＿＿＿＿＿＿＿（我想找 Hocking 小姐接电话）?

   C：Speaking. Oh，is that you，Donald? How are you?

   B：Fine，thank you. How about you?

C: Not bad.

B: Iris, _____ (我打电话想与你商讨一个法律文件). When are you free?

C: Let me see. _____ (明天上午十点钟行吗)?

B: All right. Thank you. See you then.

C: Bye-bye.

B: Bye.

Ⅳ. Fill the dialogue with the given words.

office	trip	bought	offer	handbag	style
maximum	fashionable	reference	shopping	acceptable	catching

1. A: A few more questions. What do you think of the _____?

   B: Mm. It's a bit out of date now. I personally prefer something more _____. That kind of stuff fits me quite well.

   A: By the way, what kind of price do you think is _____?

   B: For this kind of sunglasses, 200 *yuan* a pair is the _____ I will accept.

2. A: Morning.

   B: Good morning. I'm Jane, Jane Brown from Nanjing Haler Sales _____. I'm calling just to see how the refrigerator you _____ last month works these days.

   A: Oh, thank you very much. It works quite well and we all like it.

   B: Good. Our company has presented a series of new household electric appliances recently. I'd like to send a pamphlet for your _____.

   A: Thank you.

   B: And if there's anything we can further _____ our help, please let me know. Our office phone number is 4437268.

   A: 4437268. Thank you very much.

3. A: Excuse me. Your _____ looks very beautiful.

   B: Thanks.

   A: Where did you buy it?

   B: The Phoenix _____ Center.

   A: May I ask you a few questions about the handbag? I'm Jack Thomas, a marketer from Janna Co.

   B: Sorry. I'm afraid I can't. / I wish I could. You see I'm _____ an 8:30 train to Huangshan. It's 8:00 already.

   A: OK. Have a nice _____. Hope to see you again.

Ⅴ. Study the following telephoning conversation about complaints and fill in the blanks with the sentences given in the boxes.

1. it's my fault	2. I'm sorry to hear that
3. it will not happen again	4. She told me about this
5. I don't want this kind of thing to happen again	6. You seem unhappy
7. it would take me so much time	8. she should at least say something

A: This is Robert from ABC Company of China.

B: Oh, Robert, how's everything?

A: I'm glad you asked.

B: Oh? _____?

A: No, I'm not happy because I have a complaint to make.

B. Really? _____ Now please tell me about it.

A: I phoned you at 9:30 your time this morning and your operator said you were on the phone. She asked me to call you after ten minutes.

B: Ah! _____.

A: Did she? I called you after ten minutes but she could not find you. Then she put me on hold for almost two minutes. You know it is very expensive to make an international call.

B: Oh, _____. After I finished the first call by chance, my boss asked me to go to his office for a short talk. I didn't know _____.

A: _____. You should let her know _____.

B: I know. I promise _____.

A: OK, now let's come to . . .

Ⅵ. Translate the following passage into Chinese.

The "yes" / "no" questions should never be asked unless the questioner has prepared the ground in advance, and is satisfied that the answer he will obtain is the one he wants to hear. They are designed to set up a direct attack. The attacking questions are designed to force a concession based on the answers to the specific questions and other data, such as "How can that be valid?"

Chapter 6

Written Communication in Business(1)

Learning Goals

Upon completion of this chapter, you will be able to:
☞ identify the different styles and layout of business letters;
☞ master ways of writing common business paper;
☞ learn to write social correspondence in business.

Lead-in Words

the block style 段落齐头式   postscript notation 附言
the modified style 改良式   letterhead n. 信头
receipt n. 收条，收据   the indented style 段落首行缩进式
optional parts 选择项   complimentary close 信尾客套话
attention line 经办人   subject line 事由
enclosure notation 附件   copy notations 抄送

Section I   Business Letters

Business, as a kind of human communication, is often conducted in writing. Traditionally, the most common form of commercial correspondence is the business letter.

Every business letter is written for a specific purpose. Normally, business letters perform three functions. Some are designed to influence readers' attitudes and actions, including sales letters for promoting products or services. Some of them, such as those which give responses to request letters, place orders, or make complaints, are intended to inform the readers, and others are prepared to entertain them, that is, to establish good relationships with them and / or convey goodwill to them. Many business letters combine two or three functions. In short, business letters are used to keep business going smoothly, efficiently, and productively. This section will deal with the ways of business letters writing.

1. Styles of Business Letters

The layout of a formal letter can be in three styles: an indented style, a block style and a modified style. People tend to use the block style to save time. Here are examples of the three styles.

(1) The Indented style

In this style the first line of each paragraph is indented five spaces. The indention is necessary because there is not a blank line between paragraphs. and the indented letter-space should be the same in one letter. When either attention or subject lines are used, they are generally indented to comply with the paragraph indentation as shown herewith the following sample.

Figure 1

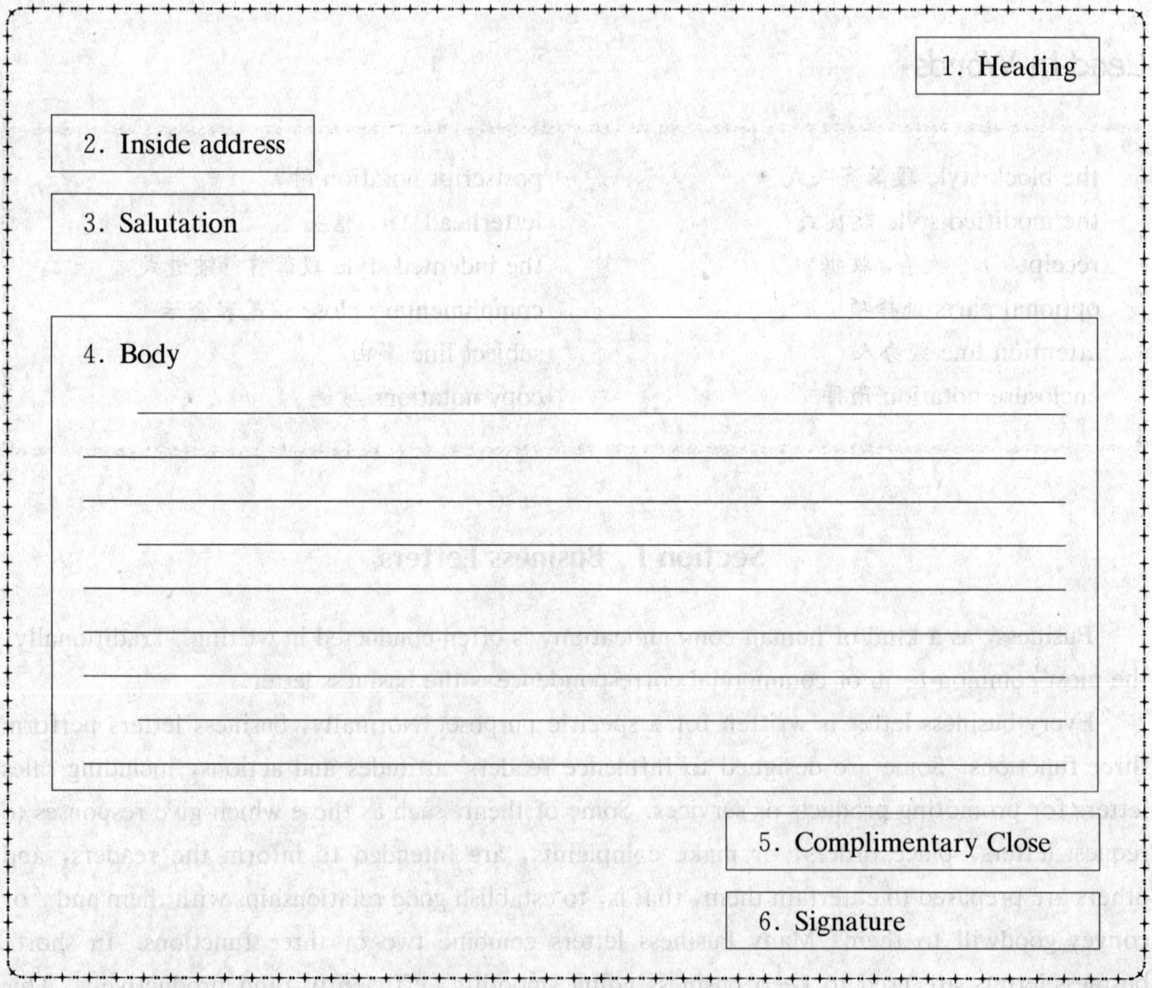

```
                                                              1. Heading

    2. Inside address

    3. Salutation


    4. Body
    _____
    _____
    _____
    _____
    _____
    _____
    _____

                                              5. Complimentary Close

                                              6. Signature
```

Sample 1

P. O. Box 121
Nanjing University, Jiangsu, China
May 31, 2007

Peace Hotel
Ling Gong Road 1818
Beijing, China

Dear Mr. Johnson Smith,

    I learned from your ad in *China Daily* that your hotel needs a typist. I am very interested in the position and would like to apply for it.

    I am a second-year student at the Financial Department in Nanjing University. I have passed the National College English Test (Band 4) with the score of 82. I have also received professional training in typing in a training school. My typing speed is 248 letters per minute. I worked as a typist at the Holiday Inn in Shanghai during the summer vacation. The duplication of my certificate of CET4 and a recommendation letter from Holiday Inn are attached to this letter.

    I am looking forward to an arrangement of interview from you. To contact me, please call me at 025 - 2233456.

    Hope to hear from you soon.

Yours sincerely,
Lin Hua

(2) The Block Style

    The block style is the most popular one for letters. It is now being increasingly adopted in Britain and is more popular in America. In this format, each line should be begin at the left margin — no colon after the salutation and no comma after the complimentary close. There are two line-spacing between paragraphs. When components of the letter begin at the left margin, it is quick and easy to control and practice. However, it looks very formal and the page looks off balance.

Figure 2

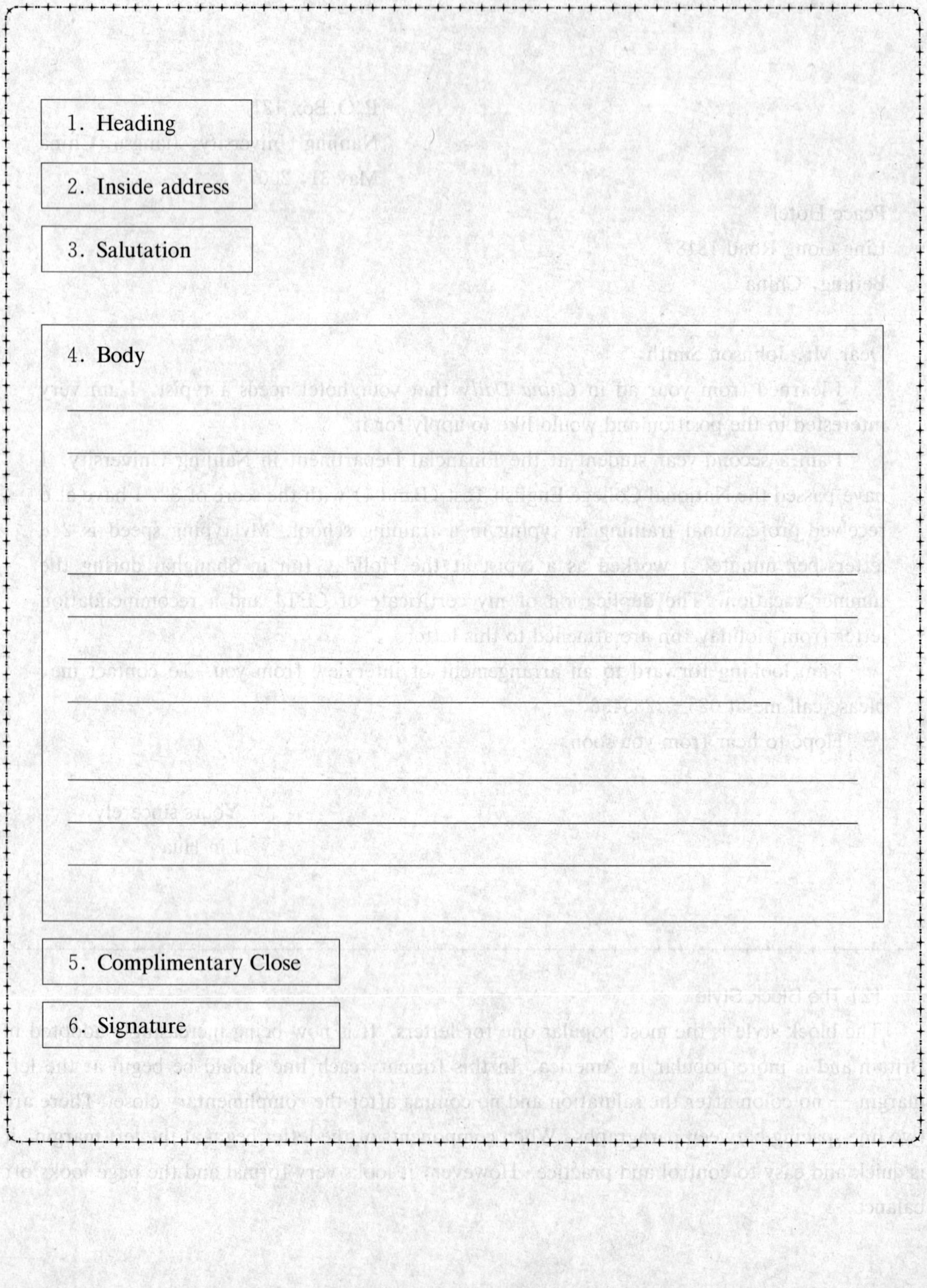

1. Heading

2. Inside address

3. Salutation

4. Body

5. Complimentary Close

6. Signature

Sample 2

Flat 6G, 6th Floor
28 Mount Davis Road
Hong Kong
15th July, 2000

The Personnel Manager
Hong Kong Traders Ltd.
39 Leighton Road
Causeway Bay
Hong Kong

Dear sir,
I have seen your advertisement for the post of executive secretary that appeared this morning in the *Morning Mail* and wish to apply for it.

I have pleasure in enclosing my personal resumé. As you will be able to see from this, I have been working on a full-time basis for seven years as a secretary and for the past three years I have been the private secretary to Mr. Charles Chen, Chief Accountant of Smith Brothers Ltd. Therefore feel that I have the experience to carry out the duties of an executive secretary satisfactorily, and undertake, if you decide to employ me, to give the company my complete loyalty.

I will be able to attend an interview any time at your convenience, but would be grateful if you could give me one or two days' notice so that I can apply for leave from my present employer. I also enclose a recent photograph of myself.

Yours faithfully,
Sophia Ma

Enclosure: Resumé

(3) The Modified Style

The Modified style has blocked-like and indented-like characteristics. All the paragraphs of the body begin at the left margin in block. Double-spaces are used between paragraphs. The inside address, the salutation and other extra parts use blocked style, while the heading, at the right-hand top，the complimentary close and signature in the right-hand corner at the bottom of the page.

Figure 3

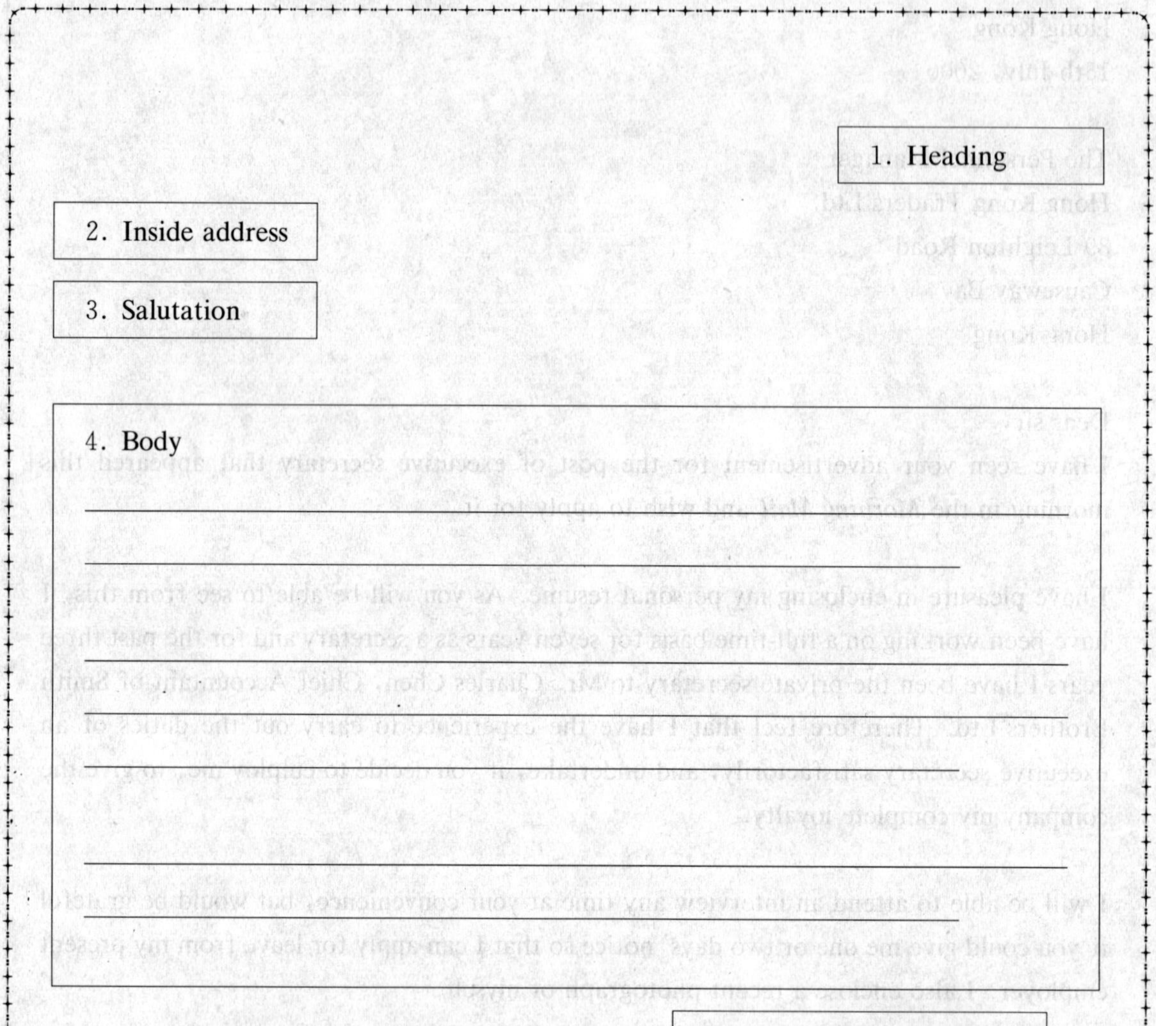

1. Heading

2. Inside address

3. Salutation

4. Body

5. Complimentary Close

6. Signature

7. Enclosure notation

8. Carbon Copy

Sample 3

HE Heibo Electrexpt co.
35 Sanlihe street, Beijing, China
Tel: 28154554   Fax: 28154555
May 21, 2007

Weston Co. Ltd.
88 Sutherland Street
Johannesburg
South Africa

Dear Sir or Madam,

Through the courtesy of Messrs Anderson & Co. , we are given to understand that you are handling the import of electric appliances in your country. As one of the largest manufacturers and exporters of the above products, we wish to take this opportunity to express our desire to enter into business relations with your firm.

We have been in this business line since 1985 and have vast and wide experience in the production and marketing of the commodities. We can assure you that our products are superior in quality and reasonable in price. They sell well in this country and we trust they wilt have a good sale in your country too.

Enclosed we are sending you a catalogue covering the items we are currently dealing in. Please advice us what articles you are interested in at present. Upon receipt of your specific enquiries, we shall send you sample books and quotations.

We are anticipating your early reply.

Yours faithfully,
Jiang Lin
Jiang Lin (Miss)
Sales Manager

Encl. As stated.

2. Essential Parts of Business Letters

A well-organized letter is made up of six or seven essential parts: letterhead (heading), date inside address (addressee), the salutation (greeting), main body, complimentary close (ending), and the signature.

(1) Letterhead

The letterhead tells the reader the name of the firm and often what it makes or sells, often omitted in personal letters.

The letterhead contains the following:

✦ the name of the sender;

✦ the address of the sender;

✦ the telephone, the fax number, e-mail address of the firm;

✦ the firm's number at the commercial register;

✦ the emblem or trade of the firm, the name of the directors;

✦ the name and address of the branches or offices of the firm;

✦ the date.

It can be written in two styles: (1) the indented style (each entry is indented by one to three letters); (2) the block style. In the indented style or modified block style, it is placed in the upper right-hand corner at the top of the first page, about one inch from the top edge, with each line either beginning with equal indention from the preceding line or aligned with it. In the block style, it is put in the upper left-hand corner at the top of the first page. It must be written in the following order: number of house, name of street, name of city or town, province (state), postcode, country (for letters abroad).

(1) Xinhua Bookstore   (2) Xinhua Bookstore
122 Zhongshan Road   122 Zhongshan Road
Chongqing, 400700   Chongqing, 400700
P. R. China   P. R. China
Nov. 9, 2006   Nov. 9, 2006

Be sure that when you are using stationery with a letterhead, that is, the name and the address of the company are already printed, the heading should be omitted. The printed heading is usually centered at the top of the sheet.

Never omit the date line because it plays a role of evidence of an arrangement or contract in case of dispute in courts of law. Usually type the date on the right hand side a double space below the last line of the letterhead.

✦ Difference between an American and British letter in heading:

US: gentleman: Br: dear sir,

US: block style   Br: indented style

US: Dear Jack (familiar)

In a formal letter, both will use surname or full-name.

(2) Inside name and address

The inside address is used, as a rule, in formal letter-writing, often omitted in personal letters. It always gives both the names of the person and the company to whom the letter is written properly. The layout of the inside address agrees exactly in style and form with the envelope address. It should be also governed by the style of the letterhead, indented or block.

The receiver's name and address in the inside address must be written with the proper title, correct personal titles put before the name such as:

Mr. James Allen	Miss Elizabeth Henry
Ms. Mary Smith	Mrs. John Blank

There are also professional and business titles. The professional title in the inside address is before the name:

Professor Richard Clanwell	Mr. Adam Clark Vice-President
Dr. Adam Clark	Mr. Adam Clark Export Manager

In formal letters the name and the address of the recipient are usually written at the left-hand top of the page and lower than the date, for example:

Mr. Philip Ashley	Mr. Jiang Shaocheng
Advertising Manager	Export Manager
Vermont Electronic Appliances Co. Ltd	New Asia Glass Manufacturing Corporation
23 Garden Street	88 Xin Hai Street
New York 10202, N. Y.	Dalian, China
USA	

Do not omit country when the letter is written to someone in another country. When you know the name of the person to whom you are writing, you should use it with his or her title instead of "the Manager".

(3) The Salutation

The salutation, also greeting, is placed two spaces below the inside address and should be in line with the inside address against the left margin. The British tend to use a comma after the salutation and Americans use a colon. The first name may be used in friendly personal letters, but surname or full name of the receiver is often used in business letters such as:

Dear Mr. Green,	Dear Mrs. Mary Smith:
Dear Prof. Black,	Dear Dr. Henry White:

When writing to individuals, always use their names if you know them. In business letters or letters to organizations, or to persons whose names you do not know, the most formal greetings are "Dear sirs" or "Gentlemen" or "Ladies and Gentlemen" when two or more persons and all personal companies are addressed. And use "Dear Madam" or "Dear Mesdames" to address a woman or a lady. But you can never use "Madam" with a woman's name. When "Mr.", "Ms.", "Mrs." or "Miss" are used, they must always be followed by a name. You should try to avoid using "Sirs" alone and "Gentlemen" in singular form. And never write "Dear Miss" or "Dear Mrs.". If the correspondent is a professor or a doctor, the proper terms of addressing are:

Dear Professor Black   Dear Doctor Manson

The usual forms of salutation in personal letters contain the word "Dear":

Dear (My dear) Henry

Dear (My dear) Elsie

Dear Mother (Father, Uncle)

In business letters the most formal greetings are: Sir, Sirs, Gentlemen, Madam. If the correspondent is a professor or a doctor, the proper terms of addressing are:

Dear Professor Campbell

Dear Doctor Manson

(4) The main body

The main body is the most important part of the letter, which carries the subject matter. It is two spaces below the salutation and there are two forms of the body: the block style and the indented style. As a rule, paragraphs in the block style are double-spaced between any two paragraphs, but single-spaced in the indented style. The body of the letter customarily consists of three paragraphs:

A. The first paragraph acts as an introduction or an acknowledgement of the previous correspondence if any;

B. The middle usually discusses matters or gives information;

C. The last paragraph expresses a hope or refers to the future action either by the writer or the reader.

(5) The Complimentary Close

The complimentary close is merely a polite way of ending a letter, a double space below the body of the letter. It is put on the right-hand side or even in the middle of the page in the indented style and put on the left-hand side in the block style. The first letter should be capitalized and the close is usually followed by a comma. But always be sure that the close and the salutation in one letter should agree with each other. Different complimentary closes used in different types of letters, such as

✦ Business letters: Yours (very) truly, / (Very) Truly yours, Yours sincerely, / Sincerely yours, Yours (very) faithfully, / (Very) Faithfully yours,

✦ Official letters: Yours respectfully, / Respectfully yours,

✦ Personal leffers: Sincerely yours, / Yours very sincerely, Yours affectionately, / Yours ever,

✦ Leffers to family members: Love, / All my love, / With love, / Lovingly yours, / Your (ever) loving son / daughter, / Your affectionate father / mother / sister,

Most English letters end the following ways:

Person Addressed	Salutation	Close
Mr. T. Smith	Dear Mr. Smith	Yours sincerely
Dr. A. Smith	Dear Dr. Smith	Yours sincerely
The Manager	Dear Sir	Yours faithfully
The Secretary	Dear Madam	Yours faithfully
Ms. Smith, Secretary	Dear Ms. Smith	Yours sincerely
Messrs Smith and Jones	Gentlemen	Yours faithfully
	Dear Sirs	Yours truly

(6) The Signature

The signature comes under the complimentary close. It should always be handwritten. In business letters, both typewritten and handwritten signatures are necessary. The handwritten signature should be between the closing and the typed name, below which the sender's title may appear. The typed name can prevent the possibility of mistake or confusion, for example:

(1) Yours sincerely,

Rene M. Hewitt

Rene M. Hewitt

(2) Sincerely yours,

Loraine Holloway

Loraine Holloway

Put the writer's job title, name of the writer's department or division in the company for which he works immediately following the type-written name. Put the company's name either immediately below the complimentary close or below the typed name and the titles of the writer in all capital letters. Don't put any courtesy title for a man before the man's name in the signature line but the abbreviations of his academic degrees.

Yours faithfully,	Yours very faithfully,
ASTON POTTERIES LTD	
G. Heathcliffe (hand written signature)	*Dr. Joseph Clernson* (hand written signature)
G. Heathcliffe	Dr. Joseph Clernson
Sales Manager	Managing Director
	HERCULES ENGUEERING CO. LTD.

Indicate whether you are married or single if you are a woman either by writing "Miss" or "Mrs." in parenthesis before your handwritten signature or by including either of them in your typewritten name.

Yours sincerely,	Sincerely yours,
(Mrs.) (handwritten signature)	(Miss) handwritten signature
Mrs. Robert Mack	Lois B. Kawecki

3. Optional Parts

Apart from the above essential parts, a business letter may also has some other parts, i. e. the reference line, the attention line, the subject heading, the enclosure notation, the carbon copy notation (C.C.) and the postscript (P. S.). Some of these special parts are rarely used and others are used often in the light of specific conditions.

(1) Reference number

The reference line is required for the purpose of convenient reply to the previous correspondence and easy filing and classification.

The reference line always appears in line with the date but against the left-hand margin. Sometimes the reference line does not only contain the numbers or the initials of the department's name but also gives the initials of the persons who dictate and type the letter.

— Your ref:

— Your ref: Dept B / 56

— Your ref: ALW / PS

— Our ref: SEL / CHEN / JVD / Z. 1119

Your ref: M. 306 / 0038

24th June, 2007

Our ref: LW / PB 534

Our ref: BL / RP

(2) Attention line

The attention line means "For the attention of" or simply "Attention" used to indicate that the letter is for a particular person or department within a firm so as to speed the delivery of the mail. It is typed two line-spacing above the salutation, underlined, and centered or on the left over the salutation.

① For the attention of Mr. Smith

　 Or Attention: Mr. Smith

　 The Secretary

　 Victory Toys, Inc.

　 892 Jones Road

　 Westwood, Ca 89232

② For the attention of Mr. T. Waterhouse

Dear Sir:

Plymouth Manufacturing Company

412 Atlantic Avenue

Boston, Massachusetts 02210

Attention: J. P. Scovill, Chief Engineer

The attention line is set between the inside address and the salutation with a single space above and below. There are several styles for typing the attention line.

Examples

— Attention Mr. ...

— Attention of the Sales Manager

— ATTENTION: Personnel Department

— ATTENTION — Ms. ...

— Attention of the Advertising Manager

(3) Subject Line

Functioning as a kind of title for the letter, the subject heading always tells the reader at a glance what the letter is about and saves the dispatcher's time to pass the letter quickly and directly to the person of a department in charge of the matter mentioned in the subject heading.

The subject heading may be centered on the page between the salutation and the body of the letter with a double space above and below.

— Dear Mrs. Merino,

Subject: Claim No. MA — 457972

— Dear Sirs,

Re: Order No. 010 — PR8 - 9907

78551 - 704 T

The subject heading may be preceded in the following ways:

— Subject: April Inventory Reports

— Re: Machine Tools

— Re: Catalogues for Simons Equipment

— Subject: Your Order No. 3045

— Lab Instruments

— DEFECTIVE WIDGET MODEL ♯ 123

(4) Enclosure Notation

When there is something enclosed with the letter, type the word "Enclosure" or the abbreviated form "Enc.", "Encls" or "Encs." (plural) in the bottom left-hand, two or three lines below the signature.

The use of the enclosure notation varies from company to company. Some companies indicate the number of the enclosures while the others only list the items being enclosed.

① Enc. Two letters of recommendation

One application form

One resume

② Encls: 2 Invoices

③ Enc. : 1. Invoice#98123

2. Check#13570(Photocopy)

④ Encl. : a / s(As stated)

⑤ Yours truly,

Lippert S. Young

Sales Manager

LSY: cg

Fncl. Two

(5) Copy Notations

When you want your correspondent to know that a copy of a letter is to be sent to a third party, it is usual to indicate this by typing CC, standing for "carbon copy" followed by the name of the receiver; the usual position is two lines below the signature or the enclosure.

① CC: Bob Owens, Linda Valencia, Tom Morgan

JB / ft

Encl. : One check

② CC: Mr. William Carter, Vice-President

③ CC Ms. Tracy Wadsworth, Personnel Director

(6) Postscript notation

The P. S. is used to emphasize the importance of a special point to which the writer of the letter wishes to call the reader's attention. If the writer wishes to say something more after finishing the letter, he may add a postscript (P. S. for short) — a few lines below the signature. For example,

① P. S. Please send all the material by air mail.

② P. S. — I'll be away from my office June 6 through June 18. My assistant, Bob Robbins, will be happy to assist you during this period.

4. Envelope Addressing

The layout of the envelope address agrees exactly in style and form with the inside address. Therefore it can be addressed in two styles: the indented style and the block style, and the latter is more popular in formal or business letters. The receiver's address is written in the center of the envelope following the order of the inside address in style. The title and full name come first, then the address follows, which is arranged in the following order: house number, name of the street or road, name of the town or city, name of the state or province, post code, and name of the the country. The sender's name and address are written at the left-handed top of the envelope (See Figure 1). If sender's name and address are not appeared on the cover, it can be written on the back of the envelope (See Figure 2).

The indented style

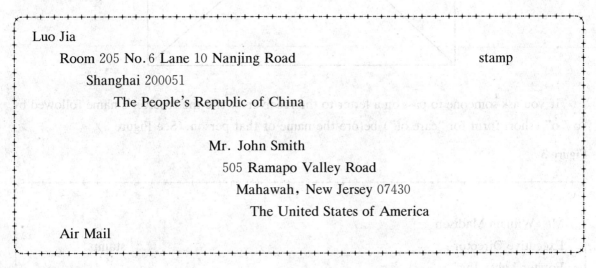

```
Luo Jia
        Room 205 No.6 Lane 10 Nanjing Road              stamp
              Shanghai 200051
                  The People's Republic of China


                  Mr. John Smith
                     505 Ramapo Valley Road
                        Mahawah, New Jersey 07430
                           The United States of America
        Air Mail
```

The block style

```
Harry Johnson
1568 G Orchard Place                                      stamp
Urbana IL61834
United States of America

                  Mr. Peter Stone
                  325 Green Street
                  Greenfield, London
                  U.K.
Air Mail
```

Figure 1

Figure 2

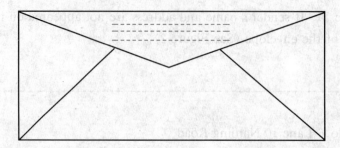

If you ask someone to pass on a letter to the receiver, write the receiver's name followed by "c / o" (short form for "care of") before the name of that person. (See Figure 3)

Figure 3

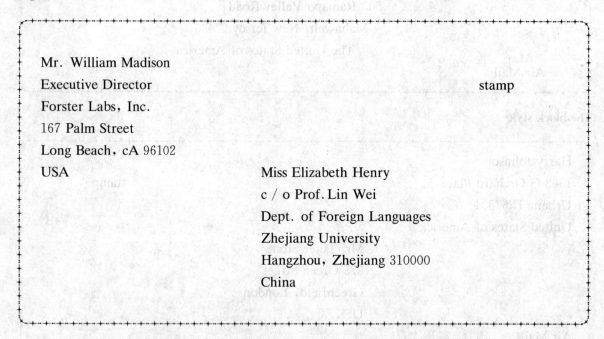

Section II   Social Correspondence in Business

Building up and maintaining business associates has been always an important routine and a main task for everyone in business. Social letter is just such a device widely used to fulfill that need.

1. Features of Social Letters

Social letters do not talk about business affairs directly. Instead, they are regarded as a kind of communication between firms or organizations. As most business people are very busy, and they may not have time to read carefully a letter which doesn't convey any important business information, one would better keep his / her social letter short and concise. Purpose of the letter should be stated clearly at the very beginning of the letter so that the recipient can be informed efficiently at first glance. Social letter should be sincere in tone. An improper tone may arouse suspicion on the motivation of the writer and even a feeling of antipathy. Social letters mostly follow the format and the style of a business letter. So the features of a well-written social letters are: briefness, clarity and sincerity.

2. Types of Social Letters

There are many kinds of social letters, coveting from invitations, thank-you letters, letters of congratulations to letters of apologies, and letters of condolences. Here we just focus several most commonly used social letters.

(1) Invitations Cards and Letters

An invitation letter is a kind of social letter, either used in the official commercial activity or unofficial social occasion to invite customers colleagues or friends to attend a ceremony or a party and so on. According to the occasion, it is divided into formal invitation and in formal invitation as follows.

① Formal invitations and replies

Formal invitation is usually applied to grand occasion such as opening ceremony or evening function. There are two types: invitation card and invitation letter, which include the following main points:

- ✦ purpose of invitation;
- ✦ necessary (headline, program, time and place);
- ✦ the hope that guests can be present;
- ✦ whether any suggested dress code.

The invitation card is a most formal invitation letter, though very short in length, usually less than 14 lines. It pays great emphasis on choice of words and the setup of letter paper. Due to its formality, the card would involve complete names instead of abbreviations, and salutation is very formal, for which Mr. and Mrs. are most preferred. In addition, the card is written in third person so that we do not use "I" or "we" in invitation cards.

A formal invitation letter or invitation card requires the guest's reply, so it usually adds "RSVP" or "r. s. v. p." (initials from French) at below on the right side or "Please reply", "Please send reply to (address)" above the address. The written form of an invitation card is fixed, without a letterhead, salutation or complimentary ending even without signature, which can be filled in or typed on well printed cards.

Sample 1

Mr. and Mrs. John Blank

request the pleasure of the company of

Mr. Paul Cotton

at dinner

on Monday，6 May 2007，at 7:00 p.m.

45 Park Avenue

New York，N.Y.

Please reply Tel. ××××××

Suggested dress code：formal

Sample 2

The Deputy Prime Minister of Australia

And Minister for Overseas Trade

Dr. J. F. Cairs

Requests the pleasure of your company

At a Banquet

On Friday，11 October，2006

From 12:30 to 1:30 p.m.

In Hall Three of the Beijing Exhibition Center

To mark the opening of the Australian Exhibition

Suggested dress code：formal

R. S. V. P.

The reply to a formal invitation is also in the third person and should follow as closely as possible the wording of the invitation.

Sample 3（Acceptance）

Mr. and Mrs. White Harrison Smith have the honor

to accept with pleasure Dr. and Mrs. Thomas White's

kind invitation for dinner，next Sunday，the eighth of April，

at 6:30 p.m. at the Bluesky Hotel

Sample 4（Regret）

> Miss Jane Cotton thanks Mr. and Mrs. John Blank
> for their kind invitation to a cocktail party on 6 May.
> but regrets that she is unable to accept owing to
> a prior engagement

② Informal Invitations

Informal invitations are simply handwritten brief notes in the first person to acquaintances or friends for simple, informal social affairs like small dinners and luncheons. (Of course, informal invitations may also be made in person or by telephone.) They are similar to ordinary personal letters but a bit shorter. Nowadays, it is far more popular than formal one, even for important occasions.

Sample 5

Bluestone Engineering Corp.
2 Aston Road
East Finchley
London
April 15, 2005

Mr. Green
Pacific Foreign Trade Company
12 Holly Road
North Walsham
Dear Mr. Green,

We greatly appreciate your cooperation and assistance in the business of recent weeks. We are cordially inviting you to an evening function on Saturday, April 23, 2005, at London Hotel at 7 o'clock sharp.

I do hope that you will be able to spare the time to share this occasion with us.

Yours faithfully,
Leo Burns
General Manager

Sample 6

Dear Sirs，

　　I take pleasure in telling you that we are going to hold a footwear and headgear fair in Jinan from May 1st to May 15th，2007. A great variety of samples，newly designed by our manufacturers，will be on exhibition. We take pleasure in inviting you to come to the fair. Please inform us about the date of your arrival，so that we can make necessary preparations.

Yours faithfully，
(Signature)

Sample 7（Acceptance）

Dear Mr. Suzuki，

I appreciate your thoughtfulness in extending all invitation to me for your 20th anniversary cocktail party. I am happy to be able to accept your invitation and would be an honor to celebrate this memorable occasion with you.

I am looking forward to seeing you there.

Sincerely，
(Signature)

Sample 8（Regret）

Dear Mr. Suzuki，

I very much appreciate the honor of being invited to your cocktail reception to celebrate your anniversary. Please accept my congratulations on this wonderful occasion.
Unfortunately，due to a previous commitment on that particular day，I am unable to attend the reception. I hope you understand.
I have long admired your achievements over the last twenty years and hope you will continue in your role as one of the leaders in your field.
Again，thank you very much for your kind invitation.

Yours sincerely，
(Signature)

(2) Congratulation Letters

Letters of congratulation are usually written to congratulate the receiver on something, and the writer and the receiver are usually business partners or friends.

This kind of letters should make clear what is being congratulated on, and usually put at the very beginning of the letters. So congratulation letters often start with sentences like this: "Please accept my congratulations on ..." or "Please allow me to congratulate you on ..." Besides the congratulating message, letters of congratulation usually also include wish for the future. For business partners, the writer may wish for better cooperation, for closer relation, everlasting friendship, and etc.

Letters of congratulation use the same layout as common letters, and are usually short. Generally, replies to letters of congratulation are also very short. The purpose of writing this reply is to thank the writer, so it usually starts with sentences like "Thank you for your letter of congratulation on my ..." In addition, the writer often expresses a sense of modesty by either claiming that the success is the result of mutual cooperation, or indicating that what he has achieved does not count much.

Sample 1

Dear Mr. Burundi,

　　Our heartiest congratulations on your promotion!

　　Your promotion to national marketing manager certainly came as no surprise to us in view of your brilliant record of achievements while you worked as the regional sales manager in the Central Region, and we always knew that you would become a great success someday.

　　You came to know us and our service well during the past five years, and you know that we stand ready to be of continued service to you in the days ahead.

　　We extend every good wish to you in this challenging task.

Sincerely yours,

Liu Dawei

Sample 2

Dear Mr. Thomas,

On reading through this morning's *Times*, I came across your name in the "New Year Honor List" and hasten to add my congratulations to the many you will be receiving.

The award will prove delightful to many people who know you and your work. I am happy that the many years service you have dedicated to global travel and marketing has been recognized and appreciated.

People working around me are deeply impressed by your work in our mutual business transactions over the past years. What you have done has been quite outstanding and it is very gratifying to know that these have now been so suitably rewarded.

We wish you ever success in the coming year and look forward to better cooperation with you in the future.

Warm regards and best wishes to you and your family!

Yours ever cordially,

Guy Grant

Sample 3

Dear Mr. York,

It was delightful news for me to learn of the establishment of your own advertising agency. Please accept our heartfelt congratulations.

With your brilliant background and long record of fine achievements, I'm sure the new agency will be a great success. I sincerely hope you will find in this new venture the happiness and satisfaction you so richly deserve.

Should there be any way in which we can be of assistance, please do not hesitate to contact me personally.

Yours sincerely,

Adam Adel

(3) Letter of Thanks

A thank-you letter is written to express the sender's gratitude and appreciation to the addressee for presents given, for services done and for kindness or bravery shown by the receivers. Compared with other kinds of letters, they are the easiest to write. A letter of thanks does not need to be very long but it must be enthusiastic and sincere, expressing your gratitude and appreciation to the addressee. You should explain why you write the thank-you letter, make suitable comments on what the addressee has done for you and express sincere thanks for his /

her hospitality, kindness and generosity.

Thank-you letters tend to be short and usually can be divided into the following four parts:

+ state clearly the purpose of writing the letter in the opening paragraph;
+ give positive comments on the services provided / action taken / performance made by the receiver;
+ restate the purpose of writing the letter and / or look forward to future co-operation;
+ thanks again / offer to reciprocate the help.

Sample 1

Dear Sirs,

We appreciate the promptness with which you settled. You're always with us during the past year, especially as a number of them have been for very large sums.

It has been of great help to us at a time when we faced heavy commitments from the expansion of our business into the overseas markets. We hope you will continue to give us the opportunity to serve you.

Yours sincerely,

Sample 2

Dear Ms. Greene,

Thank you for your purchase of our ink jet printer last January. Now you'll probably want to know something about our newest product, the electronic controller for household appliances.

We are pleased to send together with our latest catalogue and the price list. Our controller is suitable for the average household and optimal for families having five or more rooms.

When used together with your mobile computer, it will save 45 percent of energy compared with a home that does not use one. The quality of the controller is assured since there is a warranty for five years.

Yours sincerely,

Sample 3

Dear Prof. Kang Yulan,

Many thanks for the proofread copy of our yearbook. You are the first to return, with detailed correction and revisions.

My managers and colleagues are all very grateful for your time and hard work. And we expect you to continue to assist us in this matter next year.

I'll be issuing it later on to the net when other references have arrived.

Based on other proofread copies, we may do a little editing if you don't mind. I'll let you see any changes for approval before I send it out.

Yours respectfully,

(4) Letters of Apologies

Letters of apologies are necessary when one wants to express his regrets for having made a mistake, having done something wrong or having caused a damage, trouble or inconvenience or having broken a promise, missing an appointment, failing to reply to a letter, or having found himself unable to satisfy the needs of others. And etc.

Letters of apologies should be written as soon as possible to show respect toward the receiver. Such letters generally include apologetic expressions, explanations for the mistake or damage, and, if it is possible for the writer, offers to make up for the offence. Above all, they must be polite and sincere. The only aim is to make peace. Try not to let the feelings between you and your friend get hurt. A letter of apology may include the following parts:

+ express regret or apology;
+ explain what has happened — the reason for your apology;
+ express the wish to make up for the loss caused or to promise to remedy the faults;
+ express the wish for gaining the addressee's forgiveness.

Sample 1（Apology for a late Delivery）

Dear Mr. Smith,

We have received your letter of August 20, and ask you to accept our apologies for the delay in sending your order for the leather bags. The goods are in fact still with the forwarder. We assure you that your order has been attended to in strict rotation, but we should inform you that ordering has been particularly heavy over the past six months and it has been as much as we could do to meet the demand.

We have instructed our forwarders to treat your shipment with absolute priority, and we are given to understand that dispatch will be effected on the Evergreen, due to arrive at London on the 20th of September. Owing to the increase in business, we are making a number of modifications to our organization which will ensure that such a delay will never occur again.

Yours sincerely,

Zhang Yan

Sample 2（Apology for an Overdue Payment）

Dear Mr. Turner,

Your inquiry regarding a $6,200 outstanding balance for legal services rendered in June, was immediately checked against our records.

Our records indicated that the $6,200 had, in fact, not been paid due to an oversight on our part. The amount concerned was forwarded to your account in the Chase Manhattan Bank by telegraphic transfer today.

Please accept our apology for any inconvenience this matter has caused you.

We look forward to the pleasure of working with you again in the future.

Yours sincerely,

Robert Faulk

(5) Ceremonial Speech

Welcome and farewell letters can be used to establish positive associations and friendships with other businesses and consumers in the area. When welcoming a new business, you may wish to invite the reader to participate in your organization or association. It may also be appropriate to offer whatever specific assistance you are willing to give. Whether you are welcoming a company or potential client to a new area or are welcoming a new employee to your firm, use language that conveys your enthusiasm or appreciation, and help the reader feel that he or she belongs. Meanwhile, carefully write farewell letters to be an act of goodwill and diplomacy.

Tips for writing farewell letters:

+ Keep the tone of your farewell letter good-natured and positive;
+ Refer to personal, positive memories of the person or place you are leaving;
+ Express your appreciation for opportunities you enjoyed in the past;
+ Express your sense of loss to a friend or job associate who is leaving;
+ If you are leaving a bad situation, avoid making negative comments;
+ Offer the reader best wishes for success and happiness in the future.

Sample 1（Welcoming Speeches）

Ladies and Gentlemen,

I am very happy that you are here on your visit to my company. My staff and I are very proud and honored to have such distinguished guests as you with us today at our company.

We will do our best to make your visit comfortable and worthwhile. In a moment my colleagues will show you around of our new factory and the research center. Please do not hesitate to ask any questions you might have.

I want to extend my warmest welcome to all of you, and sincerely hope that your visit here will be worthwhile and meaningful.

Sample 2（Toast Speeches）

Distinguished guests,

Ladies and gentlemen,

First of all, on behalf of my colleagues and the company, I wish to warmly welcome.

Mr. Pierre Chardon,

Mr. Teilhard Ibrahim, and

Mr. and Mrs. Rajiv Patnaik on your tour of Shangdi and other high-tech parks in and around Beijing.

We, the New Century Electronics Co., and Bandwagon Engineered Testing Systems, have been close partners since the late of 1980s. We are confident that your visit will surely further the development of our cooperation.

Now please raise your glasses and drink a toast,

to the health of our distinguished guests,

to the further development of cooperation between us,

to the health of all friends here, and

to the success of your current visit.

Sample 3（A farewell speech）

Ladies and gentlemen,

We feel greatly honored to be here today to have the opportunity to say sincere thanks to and bid farewell to our friends of Chongqing Automobile Corporation.

During the last few days, we have concluded a journey of visiting some remarkable places in this city, a tour around your production area, a visit of some of the important production lines, and a visit of your R & D center. We are indeed deeply impressed by your achievements and by your hardworking spirit, and, of course, also by the natural beauties and cultural traditions of the city.

We are leaving for home very soon. You can be sure we shall always cherish happy memories of your delightful people, your kindly hospitality, your warm and sincere friendship, and your hardworking spirit and the strong desire for development. In the meantime, we look forward to the opportunity of receiving you at the other side of Pacific Ocean.

Thank you, our Chinese friends, and good-bye.

(6) Business Appointment

Business appointment is always relevant company activities, when you want to visit a company or meet another person, you have to make an appointment beforehand.

An appointment letter should be persuasive, sincere and courteous, should point out that if the appointment brings any inconveniences to the opposite party, it can be postponed or cancelled. Meanwhile the appointment letter should be brief, which should only simply explain the reason of the appointment and present an appropriate time and place for the opposite's approval.

After the appointment correspondence has been received, a prompt reply is supposed to be made. If you accept the appointment you may request to discuss the scheduled time or place. If you don't accept the appointment, you should explain the reason why you can't keep the appointment in a friendly way and not hurt the opposite party.

Such kind of appointment letter should:

✦ express your arrangement clearly, giving definite time, place and people involved;
✦ be personal and friendly in tone;
✦ encourage or wish the receiver to accept;
✦ state the reason for this arrangement;
✦ state the reason, if to decline;
✦ reply promptly, if you get a letter of this matter.

Sample 1

Dear Mr. Smith,

Subject: request for an appointment

　　I am scheduled to visit the U.S. on business at the end of this month, and wish to call on you at your office on that occasion.

　　I will be arriving in Washington on or around August 20 and staying there for about a week. It would be very much appreciated if you would kindly arrange to meet me either on August 22 or 23, whichever is convenient for you. If neither is convenient, could you please suggest an alternative date by returning me an e-mail?

　　Thank you in advance for your kind cooperation. I am looking forward to meeting you in Washington soon!

　　Sincerely yours,

　　James Ferguson

　　ABC Trading Company

Sample 2

Dear Mr. Zhang,

Subject: Urgent-Need to Change Appointment

　　With regard to our appointment to visit your China's factory on August 2, I regret that I must ask you to change the date to August 3 due to an unexpected matter that requires my personal attention.

　　I'm awfully sorry for this last-minute request, but I hope you will be able to meet with me on August 3 at around 10:00 a.m. If you are not available, will you please let me know by e-mail? Hope this will not cause you too much inconvenience. Thank you.

　　Best regards!

　　Sincerely yours,

　　James Black

　　Director, Overseas Operations

　　Washington Motors, Inc.

(7) Reservation

If you are to travel or visit on business, sometimes you have to write letters to order a hotel, a conference room or a plane ticket and so on beforehand. Such kind of reservation letter mainly includes:

✦ presenting your order and the reason;

✦ asking for a reply for confirmation.

Letters of reservations should be promptly answered explaining whether the request is satisfied.

Sample 1

Dear Sir / Madam,

Subject: Reservations for a Flight

    Mr. Lin Jie, our Marketing Manager, would like to fly from Guangzhou to London, on the earliest flight possible.

    We would be obliged if you would book one economy class seat for him on a flight leaving Guangzhou on or about June 28.

    Bank of China has been instructed to pay the fare and booking fee, and we would ask you to submit your account directly to them.

    We appreciate your early confirmation.

Sincerely yours,

Li Yang

Secretary to Mr. Lin

Guangzhou Trading Company

Sample 2

Dear Li,

Subject: Confirmation of Reservation

    We have acknowledged your e-mail dated June 15 requesting us to book one economy-class seat for Mr. Lin Jie on a flight from Guangzhou to London.

    One seat has been reserved on flight S. A. 917 departing Baiyun Airport, Guangzhou at 10:00 a. m. on the 28th, arriving London at 11:00 a. m. local time on the 30th.

    The account will be sent to Bank of China, as requested.

Yours faithfully,

Tang Xiaogang

Reservations Manager

Section III　Practical Activities

1. Case Study

● Case Study 1

Directions

You are given a negotiation talk, in which Mr. Zhao and Mr. Ma of the South Import & Export Corporation of China are having a talk about how to build up their competitive distribution channels. Read it and analyze with your classmate what measures they take to promote.

Zhao: In the world, the cases where exporters sell directly to end-users are rare. They must sell through marketing channels. But what channels, do you think, we should use?

Ma: That depends on what products you deal in. If you handle consumer products, longer channels should be used because such products need to be sold extensively, while industrial products usually have shorter channels.

Zhao: Could you give me an example?

Ma: Certainly. Suppose you export shirts, it's impossible for you to sell them directly to the users. Instead, you sell them first to an importer; the importer sells them to several wholesalers; the wholesalers sell them to quite a few retailers and retainers sell them to the end-users. But if you export certain equipments, you may sell them directly to a factory — the end-user. Even if not to the end-user directly, the channels can't be that long as above mentioned.

Zhao: But do you agree with me that marketing channels are very important?

Ma: Of course! An efficient marketing channel could enable you not only to increase sales and product competitiveness, but also to save time and money.

Zhao: Our enterprise has just been given the right of export. We have found it not easy so far to build up proper marketing channels.

Ma: No, it's not easy. I can imagine. But we may do some marketing research and try to find enough necessary information. Then, things will be better.

Zhao: I agree with you. We have set up an office in Hamburg. On one hand, it works as our agent, pushing the sale of our products in the European market. On the other hand, it takes field research, trying to build up our competitive distribution channels.

Ma：   I'm sure we will be successful!

Zhao： I hope so.

● Case Study 2

Directions

You are given a negotiation talk, in which the matter of goods delivery is negotiated about. Read it and analyze with your classmate the reasons why an agreement is reached without much difficulty.

A： Now, let's talk about the date of delivery. How long does it take you to make delivery?

B： As a rule, we deliver all our orders within three months after receipt of the covering L / C.

A： What about a special order?

B： It takes longer for a special order, but in no case would it take longer than six months.

A： I wonder whether you can make delivery in June.

B： I'm afraid it would be until the middle of July.

A： Is it possible for you to make delivery more promptly? Delivery by the middle of July will be too late. You know, Mr. Ma, July is the season for this commodity in our market. The time of delivery is a matter of great importance to us. If we place our goods on the market at a time when all other importers have already sold their goods at profitable prices, we shall lose out.

B： I see your point, but we've done more business this year than ever before. It's difficult for us to get the goods from our manufacturers in large quantity as well as to make prompt delivery.

A： But can't you find some way to get round your manufacturers for an earlier delivery? I hope you can give our request your special consideration. A timely delivery means a lot to us.

B： You may take it from me that the last thing we want to do is to disappoint a customer, especially an old customer like you. We'll get in touch with our manufacturers and try our best to advance delivery to June.

A： Good. We certainly appreciate your close cooperation.

B： We also hope that you can make a timely delivery.

A： We are very happy to be of help. I can assure you of our cooperation. When do we have to open the L / C?

B： Let's open the L / C one month before the time that the goods are delivery.

A： And I hope that the goods can be dispatched promptly after getting the L / C.

B： That's all right. I'm very glad we've come to an agreement on payment and the date of delivery.

2. Role Play

Mr. Zhang (Z) of China National Everbright Import and Export Corporation continues his talks with Mr. Wood (W) in the showroom of Sino-American Information and Trade Center, Inc.

<h3 style="text-align:center">An Inquiry</h3>

Z: Here you are.

W: Thank you.

Z: From what I understand, this kind of style of men's shirt will be very popular this year and also there is no one else producing this yet.

W: Oh, I see.

Z: All materials used are cotton print, and I highly recommend this kind of shirt for its high quality and the latest design.

W: It looks very good, however, we need to study it a bit further.

Z: OK. Keep in touch.

W: I'll let you know probably this afternoon.

Z: Fine.

W: It was nice meeting you.

Z: It was my pleasure. See you this afternoon.

W: See you then.

. . . .

Z: Good afternoon, Mr. Wood. Nice to see you.

W: Me, too.

Z: What do you think of our products?

W: Well, we're very much interested in your cotton print shirts and this is a good chance for us to cooperate in this line.

Z: Good! What particular patterns do you like?

W: I've read your brochure and catalogue.

Z: Yes?

W: Here is a list of patterns. I think these patterns are quite good, and we shall find a ready market here. I'd like to have your best quotations, C.I.F. New York.

Z: OK. No problem. Would you mind telling us the quantity you require so that we can work out an offer?

W: I will, but what about the commission? From our European suppliers, I usually get a 3 to 5 percent commission. It's the general practice, you know.

Z：Usually we don't take it into consideration unless your order is large enough.

W：Well, I do business on a commission basis. A reasonable commission on your prices would make it easier for me to promote sales. Even 3 or 5 percent would do.

Z：We'll talk about it when you place your order with us, OK?

W：OK. When can I have your firm C. I. F. prices?

Z：If you can confirm the quantity you will order, we'll have them worked out and let you know tomorrow morning. Would that be all right?

W：Good. Our first order will be one 40' container and I'll be here tomorrow morning at 9:30.

Z：Perfect. See you tomorrow then.

W：Bye!

3. Mini Negotiation

Directions

You are given a negotiation talk, in which two parties are negotiating over the price. Read it and analyze with your classmate the reasons why an agreement is not reached.

A：I should like to purchase printed pure silk fabrics. Have you got the catalogue for this line?

B：Yes, we have. Let's go to our showroom. (Coming to the showroom) It is the printed pure silk fabrics produced.

A：I think these patterns are quiet good. Will you please give me an indication of your price?

B：Here are our FOB price lists. All the prices on the lists are subject to our confirmation.

A：What about the commission? I usually get 3 to 5 percent commission for my imports from other countries.

B：As a rule, we do not allow any commission. But if the order is large enough, we'll consider it.

A：Why, your prices have soared! They're almost 25% higher than last year's. It would be impossible for us to make any sales at such prices.

B：I'm surprised to hear you say that, Mr. Smith. You know that the cost of production has risen a great deal in recent years.

A：We only ask that your prices to be comparable with others. That's reasonable, isn't it?

B：As you wish. Well, if your order is large enough. we are ready to reduce our price by 2%.

A: If that's the case, there is hardly any need for further discussion. We might as well call the whole deal off.

B: What I mean is that we'll never be able to come down to the price you name. The gap is too great. You know our products are of high quality. Taking the quality into consideration, I think the price is reasonable.

A: I think it unwise for either of us to insist on his own price. Each will make a further concession so that business can be concluded.

B: What is your proposal?

A: Your unit price is 80 dollars higher than we can accept. I suggest we meet each other half way.

B: Do you mean that we'll have to make a reduction of 40 dollars in our price?

A: What's your suggestion?

B: The best we can do will reduce 20 dollars. This is our rock-bottom price.

A: That still leaves a gap of 20 dollars. It's impossible for us to bear a considerable loss if it is accepted.

B: Now that our talk is at a stand, I suggest another talk be held next time.

Negotiation Tips

● Treat the Other Side as Your Ally 谈判对方是盟友

Your negotiating partner may have to persuade others in her organization to agree to your deal. As your friend, this person can sell your deal. As your enemy, she can sink it.

● Be patient 倾注耐心

Don't be angry or insulted if the first offer you receive is not what you hoped it would be. Treat this proposal as the first of several in the negotiating proposal. Slow but steady movement creates momentum, which can lead to an agreement.

Extended Activities

Ⅰ. Situational Group Talks.

Situation: You own a chain of stores in a big city. In order to increase your business, you want to sign to be the franchiser for some big manufacturers. You have invited them to your head office to discuss a possible contract. You need to clarify payment and delivery terms, and negotiate the maintenance contract to ensure the regular servicing as well as emergency repair work.

Task: Please make a plan for this negotiation, brainstorm for a list of possible topics. Then exchange yours with a group.

II. Make corrections in the format of the envelope.

Carbonite Corp.
Robert Kastens
Second Avenue 1333
Connecticut，Milford 06460

                          Ms．Yvette Carlson
                          Haley-Richardson Company
                          12345 Detroit，Ml
                          One Perry Park Plaza

III. Translate the following Chinese into English.

1. 可否告知你们主要想谈哪些方面的生意？
2. 我们对你们的小五金感兴趣。
3. 这些商品有现货供应吗？我们希望先看一看样品。
4. 如果需要的话，我们可以按照你们的要求，接受特殊订货。
5. 这是我们的询价单。请您看一下，好吗？
6. 如果你方报价具有竞争性，交货期可接受的话，我们非常乐意向你订货。
7. 一旦收到你方具体询价，我们将就将报价传真给你。
8. 这种商品型号很多。你们要哪一种（几种）？
9. 能否告诉我方你方所需数量，以便我们算出报价？
10. 这个问题可否等你们订货时再讨论？

IV. Translate the following letter into Chinese.

Dear Mr. Green，

    Please accept our apologies for this error. It occurred in our packing and dispatch department，and was due to our reorganization program. We are in the process of installing a computer in the forwarding department，which we expect will provide a more efficient service to our customers.

    Regarding the extra case of handles，to save freight charges，we would prefer you to try to fix them with other bicycles. We authorize you to reduce the part price by 20% to help clear them.

Yours faithfully，
Liu Dawei

V. Situational writing.

请根据以下提示写一封致歉函：

1. 由于公司记录了对方有 8 950 美元未支付，通过询问，对方迅速回复说已付此款；
2. 根据对方资料向银行查核后，确认已于 7 月 4 日收到了这笔款，是由于银行疏忽，公司未得到通知；
3. 向对方表达歉意并希望得到理解；
4. 为对方的积极合作表示感谢。

Chapter 7

Written Communication in Business(2)

Learning Goals

Upon completion of this chapter, you will be able to:
☞ learn about the functions and types of common business paperwork;
☞ understand the format of notices, memos and minutes;
☞ know about the general functions and types of business reports;
☞ familiarize the format of a business report.

Lead-in Words

notice n. 通知, 布告	defaulter n. 违约者
announcement n. 通告, 布告	recommendation n. 推荐
report n. 报告书	appendix n. 附录
note n. 通知	bibliography n. 参考文献
memo n. 备忘录	straightforward adj. 直接的
agenda n. 议事日程	conspicuous adj. 明显的
minute n. 会议记录	parliamentary adj. 议会的
notification n. 告示	

Section I   General Business Paperwork

This part focuses on the improvement of writing ability in general business paperwork, explaining in details the types and formats of general business paperwork, emphasizing the use and writing skills of notices, reports, notes, memos, agendas and minutes of a meeting. The learners are required to get familiar with and master the format and writing skills of the mentioned paperwork through the study of the real business activity materials and practices, and also required to do good general business paperwork independently.

1. Notices and Announcements

Notices and announcements are the good ways to carry out the informative functions. They can be directed to people outside companies or to employees inside, both serving an important pedagogic purpose. As for the forms, they may include notifications, warnings and posters to inform the public of some important events or activities. The information provided may be various, usually related to employment, rename, office removal, opening of a new supermarket, lost items or people, etc. Different from other forms of business writings, notices are aimed to reach a comparatively large number of audiences. Generally, they should be presented in a brief and straightforward way so as to be understood easily by the public. The language of the notice should be easy, clear and concise. A notice focuses on one thing at a time. In most cases, notices are often put up on bulletin boards or walls, or published in certain section of newspapers, conspicuous to their target readers.

(1) Main Parts of a Notice

Not all notices have a set format. Some notices are made up of four parts: the title, the body, the signature and the date. Some notices, especially notifications and warnings, may omit the last part. Sometimes, even the heading is omitted.

A. Title

The title, also called the heading, helps readers to focus on the purpose as quickly as possible. A good title directs readers' attention immediately to the information or instruction notices want to convey. The usual title is "Notice," but other titles can also be used. For example, you can induce the organization which issues the notice and the reason, writing the title as "Class Meeting," "Lecture", or the title of a lecture like "Women's Position in America", or "Football Match," "Found," or "Lost," etc.

B. Body

The body is mainly about the information that is being conveyed, including three parts: the purpose for issuing the notice, detailed information about the notice, and rounding off remarks.

C. Signature

The name of the person issuing the notice, comes at the end of the body, usually centered or in the bottom right-hand corner.

D. Date

The date of announcing the notice, appears below the signature, centered or in the bottom left-hand corner.

(2) Types of Notices

Notices fall into three types: brief notices about meetings or activities, including the time, place and contents of the meetings or activities; notifications and warnings about certain events in formal terms, with precise structure and concise words; and detailed notices on activities with background information about a certain person (such as the lecturers or speakers), organizations, and arrangements of activities.

① Brief notices about meetings or daily activities

This kind of notices are most frequently used and observed in our daily life. On the notices, the time (the specific day, month, date, and even hour, usually the day of the week put at the very beginning, followed by the month, date, and hour) and the place for the meetings or activities should be clearly and exactly stated so that there will be no misunderstanding of them. A few words about the meetings or activities themselves should also be included in order that the readers of the notices can decide whether participation is compulsory or selective, or whether it is worth the time or not.

Sample 1

Notice of Meeting

The Routine Meeting will be held at 2 o'clock on Friday, June 16th in the conference room in the office building to discuss the financial program of the company. All the department heads are required to attend it on time and every one must prepare a copy of suggestions for the program.

Administrative Office

June 10th, 2007

Sample 2

Change of Location

Owing to the speedy expansion of our business, we find it necessary to remove our department store to more spacious premises. We beg to inform our customers that on and after May Day, we shall be at 103 Shanghai Road.

You are warmly welcome to our new address.

Kaile Department Store

April 25, 2007

---

② Notifications and warnings

As for the notifications and warnings, the passive voice and big words are frequently found in such kind of notices to show the seriousness and formality of the requirements so as to arouse the attention of the public.

Sample 3

> **NOTICE**
>
> Passengers traveling on this ferry are cautioned against disernbarking before the ferry is properly moored and the gang-plank is in position. Passengers disregarding this caution are hereby informed that they do so at their own risk. Passengers are also requested to stand clear of the gangway while the ferry is moored.

Sample 4

> **NOTICE**
>
> Selection of the wrong registration card leads to incorrect payment. To ensure that you receive payment for your grain, please check your receipt before leaving the weight-bridge.

Sample 5

> **NOTICE**
>
> Office Hour: 8:00 a.m. — 6:00 p.m.
> Please Check and See if the Money is Right. We are Not Responsible after You Leave the Store.

③ Detailed notices on activities

This type of notices often includes some details about certain persons, like the speakers or lecturers, details about certain activities, or some background information about them. Special attention should be paid to the choice of words and the organization of ideas.

Sample 6

> **New Chain Store Opening**
>
> Friday, Jan. 5th, 2007
>
> Seawoods Book City is proud to announce the opening of a new chain store on Saturday, Jan. 12th at Huanghe Road 465, just opposite the MacDonald's. The new chain store will offer you various books, ranging from classic books to modern ones, from prose to novels, from comic books to scientific ones. It also provides medical books for elder people, cooking materials for housewives, fashion magazines for young ladies, and knowledge-based books for students.
>
> To mark this special occasion, customers will be offered a special opening discount. Just fill in the following coupon and bring it to us between Jan. 12th to Feb. 12th, you will enjoy a 20% discount on any book you purchase.
>
> The Seawoods Book City Office

Sample 7

Manhattan Leisure Centre

Opening Soon . . .

Facilities will include：

- a library with daily and weekly newspapers and magazines；
- a recreation room for table tennis, billiards, listening to music；
- beautification shops and fashion boutiques；
- a cafeteria selling tea, coffee and light snacks；
- a park for children to play in；
- a day nursery for mothers to leave their babies while they go to work.

Sample 8

Announcement

With the effective management and the efforts made by all staff, our company is ranked as one of the Top-5 in the same industry both in scope and profits. We are going to celebrate the 15th anniversary of our company. A number of activities will be held to celebrate our great achievements. Your proposals are welcome and those adopted will be rewarded.

Please turn in your proposal to our office as soon as possible.

Thank you for your attention.

Public Relations Section

June 8, 2007

2. Memo and Minutes

Memos and minutes are the two most common forms of business communication. They are both effective vehicles and almost always used within an organization.

(1) Memo

Memo is the short form of memorandum, which is a simple and efficient message used to remind of or draw someone's attention to certain matters. It usually omits the letterhead, salutation, complimentary close and signature block that are commonly used in business letters. It is efficient because its format conveys the writer's ideas quickly and directly to the readers.

A memo may communicate information, announce policies, instruct employees, make request or offer advice, usually more direct and concise and less formal than letters. Similar with letters, memorandums can have many different structures and purposes.

① Basic elements of a memo

Title: Memorandum(Memo) — written at the top center of the paper;

To: Receivers' names and job titles — stated at the left margin, followed by the name of the receiver;

From: Writer's name and job title — also stated at the left margin, followed by the name of the sender;

Date: Date of the memo is written — stated at the left margin, usually written Day-Month-Year, better to write the full name of the month;

Subject: The central topic of the memo — brief and clear;

Message: The main body of the memo — written in limited number of paragraphs;

Complimentary close and signature: Few people prefer this element and seldom used.

Generally speaking, a memo has two basic parts: a heading and a body. The heading is a compact block of information at the top of a memo, which is usually a preprinted form, consisting of four parts. Different offices may prefer different layouts, but in general you should use an arrangement like the following:

Memorandum

Date:
To:
From:
Subject:

_____

Body of the memo

The body of the memo carries a clearly structured message, which is often written in short numbered passages. The body of a memo contains the message which can be a suggestion, a recommendation, a statement of policy, or a report or summary of results. For each case, the structure of the memo is determined by the nature of the message and the writer's purpose.

Sample 1

MEMORANDUM

To：Personnel Manager，Northern Branch

From：K. L. J.

Date：6 December，2006

Subject：Installation of Coffee Machines

　　The board is thinking of installing automatic coffee machines in the offices of each division in Northern Branch. Before we do this we need to know：

　　1. how much use our staff will make of

　　2. how many we will need

　　3. how much time can be saved from making coffee individually.

　　Can you provide us with your view on：

　　1. how the staff will react to the idea.

　　2. how we can deal with the union on the matter.

　　If possible，I would like to receive your report before the next board meeting on June 1.

Sample 2

MEMORANDUM

To：Export Department

From：Technical Department

Date：8 June，2007

Subject：Jarritos

Re：Repair of capping machine at the above factory

Work will begin: next weekend

Work will take: 1 - 2 days

Deposit required: US $800

Our repair will be guaranteed for half a year.

② Types of memo

Even though no two memorandums are identical，four common broad categories exist：information，feedback，activity arrangement and suggestion.

✦ **Information**

Memorandum

To: All Employees

From: Rick Smith, Human Resources

Date: December 28th 2006

Subject: Time Cards

After reviewing our current method of keeping track of employee hours, we have concluded that time cards leave a lot to be desired, so starting Monday, we will have a new system: a time clock. You will then just have to punch in and punch out whenever you come and go from your work area.

The new system may take a little while to get used to, but it should be helpful to those of us who are making a New Year's resolution to be more punctual.

Happy New Year to all!

✦ **Feedback**

To: All members of staff, Northern Branch

From: K. L. J.

Date: 5 December 2006

Subject: PERSONAL COMPUTERS

The board urgently requires feedback on our experience with PCs in Northern Branch. I need to know, for my report:

1. What you personally use your PC for and your reasons for doing this. If you are doing the work that was formerly done by other staff, please justify this;

2. What software you use, please name the programs;

3. How many hours per day you spend actually using it;

4. How your PC has not come up to your expectations;

5. What unanticipated uses you have found for your PC, that others may want to share.

Please Fax this information directly to me by 5 p. m. on Wednesday 7 December. If you have any questions, please contact my assistant, Jane Simmonds, who will visit you on Tuesday, 6 December. Thank you for your help.

✦ **Activity arrangement**

> From: Office of the GM.
> Date: Feb. 1
> To: Heads of factories
> Subject: Trip by GM
> Below are details of the factories that the general Manager will visit. In each one, the GM would like to speak to all members of the Production Dept. Please inform each factory and ask them to cancel all other appointment.
> March 8 Kuala Lumpur
> March 9 Singapore
> March 10 Singapore
> March 11 Jakarta

✦ **Suggestion**

> To: Project Planning Dept.
> From: General Manager
> Date: Jan. 5
> Subject: Aqua Warm BV
> I have looked through our records of the work that we did at Perfecta Ltd. The heating system was checked three times before it was turned on. We are absolutely sure that explosion is not our responsibility.
> I suggest, therefore, that Perfecta write to Aqua Warm to claim compensation.
> Please write to Perfecta (address: 61 Bath Road, Worester, England WR 53AB) and explain our position.

③ Tips for memo writing

✦ The opening and closing phrases of a memo are omitted, regardless of the routine of etiquette;

✦ The style of memos may be brief or long handwritten notes or word-processed letters;

✦ A memo to a customer or client needs almost much care and courtesy as a letter;

✦ A memo used within a company must follow the usual practice in style;

✦ The 6 Cs writing principles are also fit for memo drafting.

(2) Minutes of a Meeting

Minute is a summarized record of all business matters that happens in a meeting. Much of business takes place in meetings which can be conducted very informally, or very formally. Whatever the size, a written record may need to be kept for future reference. Minutes are important in that they keep the original and historical records of a meeting in the file. Whatever discussed and reached in a meeting can easily be traced in the minutes.

① Structure of Minutes

The structure of minutes of a meeting is uncomplicated and usually includes four parts:

✦ The heading of the meeting: usually includes the name of the meeting; the time, the date; the place of the meeting and the presiding officer;

✦ The basic situation of the meeting includes: attendance, defaulter, agenda and recorder;

✦ The body of minutes is the main part of minutes, including reports by officers, old and new business, solutions, the date and agenda of next meeting, the names of those who make motions and those who make second motions, the results of all votes, adjournment time, etc.;

✦ The usual ending consists of the complimentary close respectfully submitted, the handwritten and typewritten signature of the recorder.

② Basic contents of a minute

✦ Chairperson — the name of the person or the group holding the meeting;

✦ Time — the beginning and ending time and date of the meeting;

✦ Participants — the people who attend the meeting;

✦ Content — problems for discussion, opinions of the speakers, decisions in the meeting, etc.;

✦ Minutes Keeper — the person who takes minutes.

Of course, some parts of them can be omitted according to the character of different meetings.

After the minutes have been transcribed in rough draft form, the presiding officer, who will make changes, as considered necessary before they are distributed to members, should review them.

Sample 1

Minutes of the Meeting of the Marketing Department

Date: June 10, 2007

Present: John Smith(Chair), Brian Li, Carl Read, Mark Brown, and Stella Woods

Apologies for absence: Sandy Leonard

The regular monthly meeting of Shenyang Trading Co., Ltd. was held at Room No. 4008, the Imperial Hotel, 9:00 a.m. June 10, 2007. The meeting was presided over by John Smith, President.

Minute

The minute of the last meeting was approved.

New proposals

Brian Li reported the availability of exploring overseas market and his proposal was unanimously accepted.

Resolution

A resolution was announced by President John Smith that Mr. Carl Read was retiring on August 1st after 20 years of service to Shenyang Trading Co., Ltd. The whole team expressed their deep appreciation to him and best wishes for his happy retirement. A copy of the resolution was included.

Adjournment

The meeting was adjourned at 11:00 a.m.

Marilyn Lucy

Secretary

③ Types of minutes

According to their degree of formality, minutes can usually be classified into two types: informal minutes and formal minutes.

✦ Informal minutes

When a meeting does not follow parliamentary procedure, its minutes can be quite informal. Informal minutes are to have a comprehensive summary, taking down, one after another, the important events such as motions, plans, resolutions.

Minutes of a Monthly Meeting of Board of Directors

Time: March 5, 2007, 2:30 p.m.
Place: Meeting Room, fifth floor, the Central Building of Sun Hotel
Participants: All the directors
Chairman: Chairman of the board, Mr. Liwens
Minutes keeper: Lily

The chief items at the meeting:
After the meeting was declared open, Mr. Liwens, chairman of the board, made a report on the work and total sales of the company at this season, which was followed by a heated discussion.
All the directors agreed to hold a press conference for the company next month.
The meeting suggested inviting experts from Canada to give a training course to all the employees of the company.
The meeting adjourned at 6:00 p.m.

✦ Formal minutes

Formal minutes are those that follow parliamentary procedure. They concentrate on the specific actions taken at the meeting, including committee reports heard and accepted, and motions made and passed.

Firewoods Exporting Co., Ltd

Date: March 26, 2007
Present: Amy Welsh(Chair), Keith Sherwin, Larry Johnson, Bill Trotter and Rich Smith
Apologies for absence: David Oliver

A meeting was held by the R&D Department at Hilton Hotel at 8:00 a.m. March 26, 2007. The meeting was presided over by Amy Welsh, President.
Minute
The minute of the meeting held on February 24, 2007 was read and approved.
Month's sales record
A copy of the past three months' record is enclosed.
New proposal
Two proposals were presented at the meeting. Keith Sherwin suggested a lucky draw program and Bill Trotter recommended free gifts. It was unanimously resolved that Bill Trotter's proposal was accepted.
Adjournment
The meeting was adjourned at 11:00 a.m.

John Byrne
Secretary

---

④ Tips for writing effective minutes

✦ Choose the proper type of minutes according to the needs;

✦ Start with the time, date and place of the meeting;

✦ Clearly state who attended the meeting and it may also include the apology from the person who was absent;

✦ Describe what has happened at the meeting in detail and avoid omitting any important contents of minutes;

✦ Write down the speech accurately to be faithful to the original meaning and avoid adding any personal view or opinion;

✦ Remain the same main points from the beginning to the end;

✦ Put the signature of the minutes keeper in the record.

Section II   Business Reports

Business reports are detailed account or statement that serve not only as a way of relaying information but also as a basis for executive to make decisions, to keep track of normal operations, to learn about unexpected developments, and to judge whether progress is satisfactory on new projects. In any large corporation or organization, they perform an indispensable service, being one of the most frequently used types in business communication.

1. Types of Business Report

From different aspects business reports can fall into different kinds. In terms of functions, there are informational report and analytical one; in terms of purpose, we have periodic report, progress report, incident report and trip report, etc. As far as forms are concerned, it can be formal or informal. According to the length of reports there are long report and short report. Generally speaking, a long report, meanwhile, is a formal one. Short business reports take the form of a letter or a memorandum.

2. Structure and Contents of Short Report

The short business reports are by far the most common in business. They typically concern day-to-day problems — those used for routine information reporting that is vital to an organization's communication, so only short forms will be discussed.

(1) Whatever forms the reports are, they are composed of some basic components:

① Title

② Introduction

③ Main body (discussion)

④ Conclusion (Terminal section)

⑤ Signature and date

⑥ Appendix

(2) When a short report takes the form of a letter, it is often sent outside the organization following a letter style which contains three parts: Headings, Body and Closing.

① The Heading's components: Writer's address, Reader's address, Date and Subject line;

② The Body's parts: Introduction, Illustration, Discussion and Conclusion or Suggestion;

③ Closing: Signature, Appendix.

(3) When a short report takes the form of a memorandum, it is used within the organization and contains the following elements:

① To — Reader's name

② From — Writer's name

③ Date

④ Subject line

⑤ Body

As the heading parts of a report are just like what are for a letter or a memo, our focus is only on the body components' writing.

✦ The introduction

The introduction aims at informing the receiver what information will be carried in the report, that is, introduces the background relative to the report, states the subjects, purpose and method of solving the problem, and summarizes the findings. It includes: a. why it is written; b. what it is about; c. who is intended for; d. who asked for it; e. what investigation or other methods were used. For example:

Following your memorandum of 27 April, we carried out a small study of staff views in 3 selected department.

In this report I present the data collected for improving our new series products.

In this report I present the information you wanted to have before deciding whether or not to invest in New Horizon, Inc.

This report summarizes the collection-series research you authorized on February 15. It confirms the findings reported in the preliminary report sent to you on April 1. The new collection series does lead to a significantly improved rate of collection.

The introduction should be brief and clear. In another word, the reader of the report would be expected to get some idea of the report after reading the introduction.

✦ Illustration

This is a presentation of how the information is based on, or to say, the way you collect or acquire information, the source of your information. For example:

My personnel officer informally asked a representative sample of office workers (in 3 departments) a number of questions.

I obtained most information from Mr. Ronald Braun, the financial analyst, and Ms. Margaret Persasky the investment advisor. I also spoke with some of the senior staff in the financial department. I also read some report on ABC Company in some leading newspapers and trade journals.

✦ Discussion

The discussion of the report is the analysis on the facts collected, which summarizes your activities and the problems you encountered. It works as a key part of the report in effecting the future strategy making, and it should describe the detailed information of the subject objectively. It should also, if necessary, reason the factors, result and possible measures, as without a rational analysis, a sound conclusion can not be expected. For example:

We attribute the decrease of the sales volume to the following three factors:

① Rivals, drastic price-cutting to gain more market shares.

② Our reduced commission rate to sales representatives.

③ Bonus programs promoted by Welfare, one of our major rivals.

✦ Conclusion

A conclusion is a very important section that summarizes the major findings of the report and tells what the findings mean, it is drawn based on the analysis of the facts or discussion for the readers of the report. For example:

In conclusion, my investigation indicates that investment in the high-interest-rate bonds is not as reliable or beneficial as investment in the low-dividend-rate stocks.

✦ Recommendation

The recommendation suggests the future action, if the report is expected to provide reference or suggestion for strategy making, the writer should put forward his own point of view. The recommendations need to be based clearly on the evidence presented in the body of the report. If your recommendations are practical and reasonable, they will be most helpful. For example:

Therefore, I'd like to make the following recommendations for your reference:

① The Company should enter into negotiations with Sunrise to purchase its equity in the Larson Lake Development.

② The Company should undertake a marketing survey to determine maximal sales levels for completed residences.

③ Once the purchase of the development is completed, the Company should retain a project management division to oversee the quality and progress of the construction.

The supplementary parts consist of Appendices and Bibliography or References.

✦ Appendix

The appendix includes charts, graphs and diagrams. The pages of the appendices are numbered consecutively following the body of the report.

✦ Bibliography or References

The bibliography or references must include the author, the title, the publication and the date of publication, and other important data for all ideas or quotations used in the report.

Sample 1   Memo Form

To: Robert Olson, Safety Director
From: Terry Miller, Safety Training Coordinator
Date: May 3, 2007
Subject: Safety Training Program for April 2006

Introduction
The training staff held one advanced training course for supervisory personnel and one basic training course for rank-and-file workers in April. In May, we have scheduled one advanced course and two basic courses. Until enrollment increases, we will consolidate scheduled classes. The final version of the "Safety Manual," which is under revision, will be ready by May 10.

Work Performed during This Period
Two training sessions are not being well attended because this training is on a voluntary basis. Unless this training is made compulsory, attendance will continue to be a problem.

Project Plans
The following classes are scheduled for May:
May 15 Advanced Course
(Shop Superintendents and General Foremen)
May 22 Basic Course
(Rank-and-File Workers)
May 29 Basic Course
(Rank-and-File Workers)

Final editorial changes are being made in the Safety Manual. The cover and final artwork for several drawings are nearing completion. The manual will be ready for distribution by May 10.

Sample 2　Letter Form

Our Ref.: Joan / S.202823
Your Ref.: Steven / W.20412
October 3rd, 2006
Dear Sir,

Sales Performance of the Manchester Branch Office

You expressed concern and dissatisfaction at the poor sales performance. The Manchester office, Chamberlain Street, Manchester NL2 5QR, instructed me to examine the causes of the decline in sales, and to recommend possible solutions.

I visited the branch office and most of their major customers in the area, the following are my findings:

(1) Some of our major customers in Manchester have closed down, and some have moved to other areas;

(2) Other customers are thinking of moving to new towns, such as Skelmersdale. There are quite generous government incentives for movement to these and other development areas;

(3) The Manchester Branch has not kept an up-to-date mailing list for sending circulars to existing customers who have moved, or to potential customers new to the area;

(4) The customers I visited were interested in more advanced mobile phones instead of the present old models we supply them with.

With the flow of our customers to other areas, the sales became poorer and poorer, and the sales in the following months will be even poorer.

I, therefore, recommend that the Manchester Branch Office should appoint a traveling salesman, whose job will be to cover the North West of England. He should contact our old customers at their new addresses, and should help in keeping the mailing list up-to-date. He should cooperate with the Sales Department in the Manchester Branch to find new customers in the Northwest Area.

Finally, I recommend that we begin to supply our customers with the latest models of our products, as demand for them is certainly growing fast.

Yours sincerely,

Joan Sung

Section III   Practical Activities

1. Case Study

● Case Study 1

Directions

You are given an unfinished negotiation talk. Study it and try to get it to end with a result beneficial to both sides of negotiation, and then role-play it with your partner.

Mexican Auto Workers Union

VS.

The American Auto Corp. of Mexico

A: First of all, at this time you are paying our employees $2.50 for one hour, and we would like to increase that by 20%. That would mean $3.00. And we already know that in America you are paying $12.50, so we think that $3.00 is not too much for our employees, because our productivity is higher than in America.

B: We believe that this discussion will be in good faith. This is how we determine the salary. If we compare the prices in America and the cost of living in Mexico, it's like 5 times higher. So that's how we decide that we are going to make American salary for $12.50 and Mexican salary for $2.50 an hour, because the purchasing power of the money is different. I mean, you might be able to get the same as America with $2.50. It's the same as in America you can get with $12.50. Then, 5% is the most we can offer.

A: 5% is too low. Our production right now is 100,000. I think we can meet 120,000 per year, but we need 20%.

B: That, for this moment, doesn't seem possible for our company to give 20% for another 20,000 per year. But I believe I will be able to give you 10 or 15% increase for 120,000. And I will give you 20% if you reach 130,000.

● Case Study 2

Directions

The following is an example negotiation situation. You are required to make with your partner a simulated negotiation talk according to the given situation.

Example Negotiating Situation

My wife and I were flying to Hawaii for a vacation. We arrived at the Eugene airport at

4:00 p. m. to check in for our flight to San Francisco, which would connect to the flight to Honolulu. When we arrived we learned that the airplane taking us to San Francisco had been delayed and was still on the ground in San Francisco. By the time it arrived in Eugene, refueled and returned to San Francisco, we would miss our flight to Hawaii.

I first asked the agent to rebook us on another flight leaving later that night. He checked and found that nothing else was available. He offered to let us fly to San Francisco that night, stay the night (at our expense) and leave on the first flight in the morning to Hawaii. Or we could go home and come back the next morning, catch the early flight to San Francisco, then on to Hawaii. Neither sounded very appealing, as we were packed and ready to go. I recalled from my studies of negotiation techniques that you can sometimes get more concessions out of another party by not responding to their proposal(s). This silence makes them nervous and they will concede something to you without you having to ask for it. So I merely kept silent, pretending to be deep in thought and a bit perturbed about the whole situation. After about 20 seconds. the agent said "How about if we do this? To compensate you for your inconvenience, we'll upgrade you to business class for the flight to Hawaii. " I accepted this proposal, we flew to San Francisco for the night, and the next day had a very nice flight to Honolulu.

I felt that the airline needed to provide some compensation; I was pleased that this little negotiation technique had extracted quite a nice concession from the agent.

This seemed to be an acceptable move by the agent. I am sure he is used to providing compensation in similar situations.

Really, I didn't prepare for this particular event. It just happened on the spur of the moment. The time spent studying negotiation techniques was really my preparation for this situation.

I was surprised at the size of the concession he offered. I expected maybe a free nights lodging in San Francisco, worth maybe $100. An upgrade for both of us was worth considerably more than that.

2. Role Play

A Chinese Textile Import & Company has carried business with an Indian company for several years. The Chinese company wants to import some fabrics from the Indian company, but they haven't reached agreement over price terms.

You and your partner are supposed to represent the two companies and negotiate over the price dispute.

A: Let's have your offer now.

B: Gladly. Here's our offer, 300 dollars per metric ton, FOB Bombay. You will notice the quotation is much lower than the current market price.

A: I'm afraid I disagree with you there. We have quotations from other sources too, and they are much lower than yours.

B: Well, then, what's your idea of a competitive price?

A: As we do business on the basis of mutual benefit, I suggest somewhere around 250 dollars per metric ton FOB Bombay.

B: I'm sorry, the difference between our price and your counter offer is too wide. It's impossible for us to entertain your counter offer, I'm afraid.

A: I have to stress that our price is well founded. It is in line with the international market.

B: I don't see how I can pull this business through at this price. Let's meet each other halfway. Mutual efforts would carry us a step forward.

A: What we have given is a fair price.

B: Well, how's this? We accept your price provided you take the quantity we offer.

A: I'm surprised. Wouldn't it be better to settle on the price first before going on to the quantity? If you accept our counter offer, we'll advise our end-users to buy from you.

B: Then perhaps you could give me a rough idea of the amount needed?

A: It'll be somewhere around 50,000 tons.

B: All right. As a token of friendship, we accept your counter offer for 50,000 tons, at 250 dollars per metric ton FOB Bombay.

A: I'm glad we have brought this transaction to a successful conclusion.

B: I appreciate your efforts and cooperation and hope that this will be the forerunner of other transactions in future.

A: Thank you. We'll be waiting for your confirmation.

3. Mini Negotiation

A: Advance Reservations. Can I help you?

B: Yes, I'd like to book a single room with a bath from the afternoon of October 4 to the morning of October 10.

A: Yes, we do have a single room available for those dates.

B: What is the rate, please?

A: The current rate is $50 per night.

B: What services come with that?

A: For $50 you'll have a radio, a color television, a telephone and a major international newspaper delivered to your room everyday.

B: That sounds not bad. I'll take it.

A: Very good. Could you tell me your name, sir, please?

B: Yes, it is Moore.

A: How do you spell it, please?

B: It's M-O-O-R-E.

A: M-O-O-R-E. And what is your address, please?

B: It is 3,600 Montague Boulevard, Hattiesburg, Mississippi 39401 USA.

A: Excuse me, sir, but could you speak a little more slowly, please?

B: Sure, no problem. It's 3,600 Montague Boulevard, Hattiesburg, Mississippi 39401 USA. Have you got it?

A: Yes, so it is 3,600 Montague Boulevard, Hattiesburg, Mississippi 39401 USA.

B: That's right.

A: What about your telephone number?

B: (601)264 - 9716. By the way, I'd like a quiet room away from the street if that is possible.

A: A quiet room away from the street is preferred. OK. We'll mail you a reservation card confirming your booking as soon as possible. We look forward to your visit.

B: Thank you and good-bye.

A: Good-bye.

Negotiation Tips

● Attack the Problem, Not the People 攻克难题不是攻克对手

Focus on finding solutions to your shared problem. Screaming at the other party may let off steam, but it isn't conducive to effective joint problem-solving. Be courteous and tactful.

● Consider the Consequences of No Agreement 对无法达成一致考虑在先

Think about what could happen — both good and bad — if you are unable to agree. Can you afford to "walk away" from the table, or are you desperate to make a deal now?

Extended Activities

I. Situational Group Talks.

Pair work. Read the given information and act out the following meetings. In each practice, one student takes the role of chairperson, and the other takes the role of a participant who keeps moving off the topic to talk about an item which is not on the agenda.

A meeting about preparation for a business exhibition

Items on the agenda:

① Decide the pace and time of the exhibition;

② Make site arrangements;

③ Organize a reception for visitors to the exhibition;

④ Items outside agenda: Approve the cooperation plan with Rotaplex Co., Ltd.

Ⅱ. The sentences of the following Memorandum got mixed. Number the correct order you think they should be.

Memorandum

TO: Students in my class

FROM: Roscoe Tanner, 7th grade student

SUBJECT: Results of Phone Inquiry to Craig Air

DATE: June 2, 2007

1. At $180.00 per 207, it will cost the class $720.00 to go to Bethel;

2. Please talk to me if you have any questions;

3. Yesterday (June 1) I called Craig Air and talked to Joe Smith about the class field trip to Bethel;

4. The two planes would be able to fly us to Bethel on November 10 at 10:00 a.m. and return to Napaskiak the same day at 5:00 p.m.;

5. Mr. Smith said that it would take two 207s to fly the class (10 students and 2 chaperones) to Bethel, and two 207s to fly the class back.

Roscoe Tanner

http://www.dmtcalaska.Org.

Ⅲ. Fill in the blanks of the following minute with the words given, changing the form where necessary.

| release | enclose | request | adjournment | approve |

Minutes of News Product Designing Committee

Date: May 5, 2007

Chairperson: Jack Stevenson, President

Present: Lucy Anderson, Mary Jane, Peter Black, Alice Brown

Apologies: Lily Wang

Old business

None

New business

Chief designer Lucy Anderson _____1._____ her new designing Model XP504-GP506 (pictures _____2._____). She explained the new functions of the new model.

The team offered their opinions on these models. All agreed that model XP504 is more acceptable to customers and _____3._____ its trial production.

President _____4._____ that all designers study on the similar product line from other companies and release their new designs quickly.

_____5._____

Date of Next Meeting

June 5, 2007

Ⅳ. Directions: You are a supervisor of a big company. The chief of operations wants to adopt the "punch-in" system to increase productivity. Write a memo about 100 words to talk about this:

1. Does the "punch-in" system benefit the company?

2. If the company doesn't adopt it, what else can we do to increase productivity?

Ⅴ. Translate the following note into Chinese.

Dear Lily,

I am sorry I missed seeing you yesterday. I know that you must have been disappointed. I also feel worried and anxious in my heart. The fact is that my manager at the last moment asked me to prepare an urgent report, so I could not call you, and yesterday I worked late until about 8:30 p.m. I am terribly sorry.

However, I would like to ask you out this weekend to make up for yesterday. Please give me a chance and I am waiting for your reply.

Peter

Ⅵ. Write an English memo according to the following requirements in Chinese.

至：各部门经理

自：ABC 谷物公司

日期：2007 年 1 月 10 日

主题：降低糖含量，降低价格

最近几年，由于管理上的问题，公司销售额有所下降，一是因为部分消费者认为我们的产品含糖量较高不利于健康；二是由于在最近 3 年价格上涨了 5%。为了增加利润，必须要降低糖含量，并且降低价格。

Chapter 8

Electronic Communication

Learning Goals

Upon completion of this chapter, you will be able to:
☞ know the different kinds of electronic communication;
☞ master the writing skills of fax and telex;
☞ write an e-mail and telephone message effectively.

Lead-in Words

telex *n*. 电报	commission *n*. 佣金
simplified words 简化字	draft *v*. 起草
facsimile machine *n*. 传真机	vegetarian *n*. 素食者
medium（pl. media） *n*. 媒介，工具	acknowledgement *n*. 承认，确认
client *n*. 客户	subscriber *n*. 用户
transmission *n*. 传递	encode *v*. 编码

With the popularization and development of information technology, electronic business has been spreading far and wide. The main methods of electronic business remain the Internet and World Wide Web, but the use of electronic transmission media engaged in buying and selling of products and services are also prevalent. Electronic communications including telex, fax and e-mail are becoming an integral part in international business. This chapter will introduce the three main forms.

Section I Telex

Telex has been extensively used in recent years as a means of communication in negotiating business with clients abroad. The word "telex" is the abbreviation of words "teletype exchange", so telex is a teletypewriter exchange service. It is conducted between two parties that have access to a teletypewriter. With the machine installed in office and connected by the telegraph office, the subscriber only needs to type his message on the machine without going to the telegraph office for transmission.

Telex takes only two or three minutes to have the calling and the called parties connected. They can practically talk on paper as if they were negotiating business face to face. Moreover, since the telex equipment works automatically, it is possible to receive messages even if the machine is left unattended.

The telex message is transmitted faster than a letter. The message can be transmitted so quickly that it is typed on the machine of both subscribers practically at the same time. And it is cheaper than an international telephone call and can provide a written record of the message and the reply. Thought it has been much replaced by fax and e-mail, telex service now is still in use as a means of communication in some businesses.

1. Form of Telex

Telex form is different from that of telegram and letter. It can usually be shown as the following:

Telex No. _____
Urgent or Top Urgent _____ _____
Date _____
(To) Receiver's Company and Country _____
(From) Sender's Company and Country _____
Our Ref. No. _____
Attention Line (ATTN) _____
Subject of the Telex (RE or SUB) _____
Body of the Telex _____
The Complimentary Clause _____
The Closing Clauses _____
Name, Title & Telex No. _____
Time _____

Sample

```
+-+-+-+-+-+-+-+-+-+-+-+-+-+-+-+-+-+-+-+-+-+-+-+-+-+-+-+-+-+-+-+-+-+-+-+-+

  44097 KCACB CN                                                      (1)
  15 / 10 / 19 _____ 1:30 P.M.                                     (2)

  ATTN: MANAGER                                                       (3)

  OUR COMPANY WILL BE PURCHASING IN NOV. FROM VARIOUS PROVINCES OF CHINA

  APPROX. 6,000 SILK PAINTINGS. WOULD YOUR CO. BE ABLE TO SUPPLY
  APPROX. 2,000 PAINTINGS.                                            (4)

  REGARDS

  65606 LEON HK                                                       (5)

+-+-+-+-+-+-+-+-+-+-+-+-+-+-+-+-+-+-+-+-+-+-+-+-+-+-+-+-+-+-+-+-+-+-+-+-+
```

Notes:

(1) 44097: receiver's number; KCACB: receiver's company; CN: China

(2) 15 / 10 / 19 _____ 1:30 P.M.: date and time of sending

(3) ATTN: Attention line

(4) Message (body) of telex

(5) 65606: sender's number; LEON: sender's company; HK: Hong Kong

2. Types of Telex

Telex can be classified into two types in terms of writing styles. One is written in plain language, and the other with some simplified words. The former is much more like a short letter with natural words, and the latter is rather brief somewhat like a telegram in simplified words.

The following is an example of telexes for comparing telex message with its letter and telegram message.

Telex (in plain language):

WE THANK YOU FOR YOUR SHIPPING ADVICE REGARDING THE SHIPMENT OF GOODS UNDER OUR ORDER NO. 1234. PLEASE SEND US A CHECK TO COVER OUR 5% COMMISSION JUST AS YOU DID IN THE PAST FOR OUR PREVIOUS ORDERS. BEST REGARDS.

Telex (in simplified words):

TKS FR SHPG ADV RE GOODS UNDER ORDER 1234. PLS SEND US A CHECK TO COVER OUR 5 PCT COMM JUST AS U DID FR PREVIOUS ONES. RGDS

3. Rules for Simplifying Words and Phrases in Telex Messages

As the charge for a telex is based on the distance that the telex has to travel and the time spent in transmission, using simplified words to save time is the main technique in drafting telex. However, the following symbols are generally expressed in plain words or commercial abbreviations instead of using signs.

(1) Abbreviation

① Use the capital letters of a phrase to form all abbreviation, for example:

European Economic Community — EEC

As soon as possible — ASAP

European main ports — EMP

China Council for the Promotion of International Trade — CCPIT

%→PCT	$→USD	£→GBP
C→DEGREE	@→AT	&→N

② Some universally accepted methods to simplify the telegraphic words are regarded as regulations, for example:

-ed(verbs)	... D	SHIPD (shipped)
-ing(verbs)	... G	OFFERG (offering)
-ment	... MT	PAYMT (payment)
-tion	... TN	INSTRUCTN (instruction)
-able	... BL	WORKBL (workable)
-ible	... BL	POSSBL (possible)

(2) Capitalized

① to leave out vowels;

e.g. ABT — about   BFR — before   PLS — please

YR — your   RPY — reply   TKS — thanks

② to retain the first syllable;

e.g. ART — article   CERT — certificate   IMP — import

③ to retain the first and the last letter of a word;

e.g. FM — from   BK — bank

④ to retain the important consonants and last letter of a word.

e.g. ARVD — arrived   QLY — quality   QTY — quantity

(3) Some are not only used in telexes but also used in business letters

ETA — estimated time of arrival   ETD — estimated time of departure

ETS — estimated time of sailing   EMP — European Main Ports

B / L—bill of landing   L / G — letter of credit

S / C — Sales Confirmation, Sales Contract   DEM — GERMAN Mark

D / P — documents against payment   COD — cash on delivery

CAD — cash against documents   D / A — documents against acceptance

M / T — metric ton   OZ — ounce   DZ — dozen   LB — pound

S / S — steamship   KG — kilogram   M / V — motor vessel

JPY — Japanese Yen   GBP — British Pound

Section II Fax

Fax, the shortened form of facsimile, is one of the most popular methods of communication for many businesses. A fax machine transmits and receives any kind of written message over telephone lines. It uses a digital process to scan and encode whatever feeds into the transceiver. A receiving fax machine decodes the information and prints out the document on fax paper. So the operation of a fax machine requires little training. All you need to do is to place your original paper into the transceiver and dial the number of the recipient, then the transmission will be done within seconds.

1. Structures of a Fax

Some businesses have their names, addresses and contact numbers printed in the form of a letterhead. Underneath follows the fax message, which comprises two parts: headings and body.

(1) The heading

Fax heading includes the details of the receiver, usually consisting of the five basic parts:

① To: receiver's name / title;

② From: sender's name / title;

③ Date: write out, no abbreviation;

④ Subject line;

⑤ Pages: total number of pages;

⑥ Fax No. and country code or the phone number.

(2) The body

Message of the fax, which ends with the signature of the sender. In constructing the body of a fax message, you may follow the layout of a formal business letter, but the salutation and complimentary close are normally omitted.

Sample

Fax for Reporting Damage of the Goods

F. Lynch & Co. Ltd.
(Head office) Nesson House, Newell Street, Birmingham B3 3EL
Telephone: 021 - 236657 01 Cables: MENFINCH Birmingham
Telex: 341641

Fax transmission
To: D. Causio
From: L. Crane
Date: September 19, 2001
Pages: 1
Fax number: (06)4815473

Dear Mr. Causio,

This is an urgent request for a consignment to replace the damaged delivery which we received, and about which you have already been informed.
Please airfreight the following items:

Cat. No.	Quantity
RN30	50
AG20	70
L26	100

The damaged consignment will be returned to you on receipt of the replacement.

L. Crane
Chief Buyer

---

2. Features of a Fax

　　Unlike telex, in which combinations and simplified words are used, fax is available for transmitting words, figures, pictures, diagrams and patterns. The layout of fax is simple and the message is just same as a letter. It has the following advantages:

　　① It can be communicated as fast as international phone call and telex;

　　② It does not need to use abbreviations;

　　③ It is cheaper than telex;

　　④ It is a 24 hour service and the message can be received unattended.

Section III　E-mail

　　With the development of Internet, electronic mail (e-mail) is widely used in modern business circles, refering to computer-based system whereby one computer sends a message to another. E-mails become more and more popular for its convenience, fastness and free delivery. With e-mails you can send a message to any person in the world who has an e-mail address within a short time.

1. Layout of the E-mail

　　Like a business letter, an e-mail has its own layout, which is quite different from the layout of a business letter. The layout of an e-mail is made up of two parts: the e-mail head and body.

Sample

Inbox

From: Sam Morton smorton@foresight.co.uk　　To: Fritz Knaup fknaup@durchsicht.de
Subject: Visit to Germany　　Date: Thu, 25Nov 2007, 00:13:22+0100

Dear Fritz,
My flight on Friday has been rescheduled. New arrival time is 8:45, not 10:30.
Please DON'T meet me at the airport — I'll get a taxi to your office, arriving by about 10:00.

We'll have time to talk about the project before we go to meet Mrs. Green at 11:30.

Can you book a table at te Golden Gate Restaurant for the three of us for 1 o'clock?
By the way, don't forget to tell them she's a vegetarian.

See you on Friday. If there are any delays, I'll call you at the office.

Any problems, call me on my cell phone: 0789 923 81945.
Best wishes,

Sam

The e-mail head as shown in the above box consists of four parts. In the column of "To", the name, title or the e-mail address of the receiver must be accurate and correct. If there is any subject you want to mention, place it in the column of "Subject". In the column of "From" and "Date", the writer's e-mail address and the time of sending will be shown automatically. And if writer sends an enclosure with the e-mail, a column of "Enclosure" will indicate it.

Usually the body of an e-mail excludes the salutation as a business letter does. If it is the first time for the writer to address the receiver, the salutation and complimentary close can be added for the sake of good order and formality.

2. Features of E-mail

E-mail message can be same as a letter or can include sound and pictures as well. It has more contents and carries more information than a letter does.

Everyone who enters the Web will have an e-mail address. The typical form of the address is: abc @ xyz. The letters before @ represent the user's codes and the letters after @ represent the name of the service device which provide the user with service, for instance: *wxh8989 @ yahoo . com . cn .*

(1) Advantages of e-mail

① It can be communicated as fast as telex and fax;

② It is cheaper than an international phone call, fax, and telex;

③ The message and pictures can be sent easily;

④ Some of e-mail addresses can be applied for free of charge;

⑤ It is a 24-hour service and the message can be received unattended.

(2) Tips for writing e-mail

Compared with the traditional way of communication, e-mail messages are usually more convenient and informal, therefore, before the writer sends out his e-mail, he must consider the reader's need, interests, feelings, etc. Whether it is formal or not depends on your relations with the reader and your writing goals.

① Like other business letters, e-mails should also follow the 6Cs;

② Audience-centered: keep your message short as people don't like long e-mails;

③ Get to the point quickly and make sure your main points are clear;

④ Help the reader to answer each point easily;

⑤ Don't use abbreviations unless you're quite sure your reader will understand them;

⑥ Only use capital letters for special emphasis;

⑦ Make sure you have attached any attachments you want to send.

3. Smiley in E-mail

While you are unable to accompany your words with hand or facial gestures in an e-mail, there are several ways to describe body language. These are called "smilies."

A facial expression or emotion can be represented with what is called a "smiley" or "emoticon": a textual drawing of a facial expression.

Smiley	Meanings	Smiley	Meanings
:-)	User is smiling.	:->	User is winking.
:-D	User is laughing.	:~)	User has a cold.
8-)	User is smiling and wearing glasses.	:'-~(	User has a cold and is crying.
:-(	User is sad.	=:-o	User is very surprised.
:-O	User made a mistake.	:-/	User does not believe you.

Section IV   Telephone Message

Telephone is the modernist communication service which message is no more than a memo intended to give messages. For conveniences, it can be preprinted for use like a company's writing pad. People from all walks can use telephone messages.

1. Elements of a Telephone Message

Any form of a telephone message must contain such necessary elements as:

"To" or "For": who is wanted on the telephone?

"From": who is the caller?

"Phone": telephone number of the caller;

"Message": brief record of the telephone message;

"Date" and "Time": date and time of the telephone call.

Sample 1

> To: *Mr. Suzuki*
>
> Date: *26 March*
>
> Time: *9:45*
>
> From: *Mr. Blondie*
>
> Of: *Viva Agency*
>
> Message: *Please call him back on 68794568 before 4 p.m.*
>
> Message taken by: Helen

Sample 2

```
+-+-+-+-+-+-+-+-+-+-+-+-+-+-+-+-+-+-+-+-+-+-+-+-+-+-+-+-+-+-+-+-+-+-+-+-+-+-+-+-+-+-+
  Message：*none*
  For：*Mr. Harding*        ☐ Will call again
  Date：*3 / 6*            ☐ Please call
  Time：*9：45*            ☐ Wants to see you
  From：*Ms. Bella*
  Of：*Pella Travel*
  Phone：*2568640*
+-+-+-+-+-+-+-+-+-+-+-+-+-+-+-+-+-+-+-+-+-+-+-+-+-+-+-+-+-+-+-+-+-+-+-+-+-+-+-+-+-+-+
```

2. Tips for Telephone Communications

General speaking, four steps should be followed when opening a call：greeting；asking for a connection；identifying yourself and stating your purpose.

(1) Tips for Telephoning

The following are some etiquette required of a receiver for a pleasant and business-like manner in the telephone communications.

① Greet warmly and speak clearly and in a courteous and friendly tone with a smile in your voice；

② Announce your phone number, or your name and / or position, the name of your firm so as to make sure that the caller is connected to the right person or organization he / she wants；

③ Ask "Who's calling, please?" if the caller has not identified himself / herself. If there is likely to be any delay, ask him / her to "hold the line, please"；

④ Offer to ring the caller back if the information he / she wants is not available. If the caller decides to wait, keep him / her aware of what is happening；

⑤ Explain to your boss or colleague the nature of the call if you can't deal with the caller and must transfer to him / her.

(2) Tips for Telephone Notes

Telephone notes are the written record of telephone, which record the contents. When taking a message, pay attention to the following：

① Keep the notes brief and to the point, while taking a message；

② Give complete information including name, date and time, telephone number, and matters in the message；

③ When answering a business phone, try to pick up the phone within two or three rings and be sure to identify yourself；

④ You should never delete a message until you have successfully called the person back.

Section V Practical Activities

1. Case Study

● Case Study 1

The 1990s have brought on a revolution in the electronic media. This revolution is the result of the computer, telephone, fax, and television. These technologies can be combined to bring many conveniences into the school, home, and office. The following questions and answers focus on the Internet, a new electronic tool for communication and research used by millions of people around the world.

A Dialogue about Internet

Q: What is the Internet?

A: When two or more computers are linked together to share files and electronic mail(e-mail), they form a network. Some individual networks consist of thousands of computers. The Internet is a network of thousands of networks, linking schools, universities, businesses, government agencies, libraries, nonprofit organizations and millions of individuals. The Internet is much smaller in size than the worldwide telephone network, but because the Internet links computers instead of telephones it has vastly more power.

Q: What can I find on the Internet?

A: If you can imagine it, you can probably find it. You can check the card catalogue of the Library of Congress, retrieve free software, get the latest news, send and receive electronic mails, complain about the Mets with fellow sufferers, view NASA satellite images, reach the world's leading authorities on pandas, and so on. There are literally thousands of "interest groups" on the net.

Q: What do I need to get onto the Internet?

A: For now, the requirements are a personal computer, a device called a modem, a communications program, access to a telephone line and an account with an Internet service provider. The computer does not have to be too fancy, although the ability to use Windows software or the Macintosh operating system is a definite plus. The modem should be as fast as possible. A speed of 14,400 bits is OK, but a faster one — 28.8 or 56 KBPS — is better.

Q: What is my first step in getting onto the Internet?

A: Go to the bookstore and get an Internet introductory guide. There are at least two dozens of them out there now. Or ask a computer-literate friend to show you how to use the "net".

Q: Who owns the Internet?

A: Nobody owns it. It is a cooperative but often chaotic federation of independent networks. Some regulatory groups set standards for the way. The information flows over the Internet, but they are not too effective at present.

● Case Study 2

A: Mr. Chen? This is Mr. Paul. Have you received my letter concerning the items we plan to purchase?

B: I'm sorry to say we have not received your letter yet.

A: I see. We are waiting for the specifications and quotations for these products.

B: I'm very sorry. I have the quotations for you right now.

A: Good. Will all the items be available?

B: I'm afraid not. Item No. 120 is no longer made by our company. We'll see if it's available in Japan, and if so, what the price is. We are optimistic about this.

A: OK. Now, as for the quotations ...

B: Items No. 1 through 119 will be priced at $23 a unit.

A: Are these quotations CIF or FOB?

B: They are FOB. Also there will be an extra charge of $0.2 per case.

A: Can you tell me the reason for the extra charges?

B: No. We are investigating it, though.

A: We are waiting for the results of your investigation. Thank you for your information. It has clarified the situation completely.

2. Role Play

A: Hello, Mr. Chine? This is Mr. Marsh.

B: Hello, Ms. Marsh. What can I do for you?

A: I'm concerned about the order we placed with your company in April. I have not received a reply to the letter I sent requesting a price list yet.

B: I see. I'm sorry to say that we have not received your letter yet.

A: Could you please send me a price list right away? I have many customers interested in placing an order.

B: I'm afraid there's no price list available, with all the recent changes in currency exchange rates.

A: I hope the prices that we agreed upon in April will still be based on the exchange rate at that time.

B: All prices are subject to our final confirmation.

A: I hope you will give me an answer by Friday.

B: I'm sorry, but I am not able to make this decision. I'll have to refer it to my manager. He's out of town right now.

A: I'll talk to you again about this next Monday.

3. Mini Negotiation

A: Mr. Hsieh, this is Mr. Clark.

B: Mr. Clark, I'm glad you called. I'm sorry for the delay in answering you. I'm afraid there are still some difficulties concerning your shipment.

A: This is very important. Have you taken any action?

B: We haven't taken any concrete steps yet. It depends on the situation in the future. We are studying the subject and we will let you know the conclusion later.

A: Do you think my shipment will come under the new laws?

B: It may. You should pay attention to this regulation. They are going to start enforcing it from June 1st.

A: If the regulation is applied to my shipment, could you give me an estimated price and quotation?

B: The price may go up as much as 30%. But you can be assured that the quality I'm offering you in these items is the best you'll find here.

A: I'm sure they will be of good quality. Well, if there are any further details, please tell us as soon as possible. We are waiting for the results of your investigation.

Negotiation Tips

● Educate, Don't Intimidate 多开导不威胁

Be prepared to explain and justify to your negotiating partner why they would be well-advised to accept your proposal. Help them understand your position.

● Set aside the Major Impasse 暂时撇开严重僵局

Put a contentious issue on hold, find agreement on other issues to create momentum and a positive negotiating climate, then return to any major impasse issues.

Extended Activities

Ⅰ. Translate the following letter into Chinese and then convert it into a telex message.

X X CO.

We have received your Ls / C No...., ... and ..., in payment Contract No. .... covering ... goods, and found that some stipulations in your Ls / C are not in conformity with that in the relative contract:

① The contract stipulated that the business is done on the basis of net price, with no commission and discount. But in your letter of credit No.... a commission of 5% is included.

② As for payment, the contract requires sight L / C, while your three letters of credit all call for times Ls / C. We have specially written you on(date), asking you to amend Ls / C, but haven't received any news from you up to now. We cannot effect the shipment due to your failure in following the contract and amending the L / C accordingly.

At present, fresh orders for … are rushing in and there is a shortage of stock on the other hand. Therefore, the present prices of all brands are much higher than the contract prices. You are expected to agree on the following purchase prices and immediately amend your Ls / C accordingly so as to make it in accordance with the present prices and the contracted terms of payment. Meanwhile, you should also extend the shipment date and validity to March 30 and April 15 respectively, otherwise, we would not effect shipment. You will be responsible for the consequence.

The prices of all the brands are as follows: (omitted)

Ⅱ. Fill in a fax of complaint according to the following information in Chinese.

ADCO INDONESIA LTD.
Jl Lombok 44
Jakarta
INDONESIA
Fax: (62)21 3533368 Tel: (62)21 353420
传真

致:

传真
电话

由 _____

日期: 2006 年 12 月 18 日   页码: 1
_____

Dear Mr. Lee

No. 12345 - 01 - 18 订货延误交货

You will remember that last month we ordered 30 Tanson 1GHz Pentium Ⅱ Computers.

我方应于 12 月 2 日收到上述订货。 _____

However, the products are now two weeks overdue. 请速告知详情。 _____

We urgently need these computers to upgrade the administrative functioning of our offices, and 因贵方延迟供货已给我方带来了巨大不便。 _____

谨希望阁下对此进行调查 _____ and arranging for delivery of these computers within the next three days.

I am afraid that if you are unable to deliver within this period, we shall be compelled to cancel our order and purchase from another supplier.

您若给予特别关注将不胜感激。 _____

Yours sincerely,

Mr. Kadir Aboe
Office Manager

Ⅲ. Translate the following English abbreviations into Chinese.

1. AFAIK
2. F2F
3. BTW
4. CUL
5. ASAP

6. HIH
7. IMO
8. LOW
9. PLS
10. TTYL

Ⅳ. Fill in the blanks with the words given below and change the form where necessary.

| @ | edu | Thank you and best regards | Subject |
| smith | hk | Fainthfully yours | gov |

1. sam. ko _____ intertech. com. hk.

2. infor@civil. accounts. _____

3. james. _____ @speedmail. com

4. Dear Karen

   ....

   _____

5. _____ : Return Merchandise Request

   Dear Mr. Smith，

   ....

Ⅴ. Translate the following into English in an e-mail form.

非常高兴收到贵方 9 月 19 日电邮。

对贵方打算与我方建立直接业务关系一事，我方很感兴趣。这恰好也是我方愿望。我方一贯坚持在平等互利的基础上与国外企业或公司共同合作，以促进我们的业务和关系共同发展。现附上我方经营的项目及产品目录供贵方参考。期盼早日回复。

Ⅵ. Read the passage about how to take a telephone message and fill in the blanks.

When a telephone is answered on behalf of another person，a clear and concise message should be written. Most organizations have _____ 1. _____ specifically designed for that purpose.

Often it is possible to simple write _____ 2. _____ ; _____ 3. _____ the message is intended； _____ 4. _____ which asks the to call the caller; and _____ 5. _____ . Sometimes it is important to write down a specific direction or message. This falls into the category of a short message and must _____ 6. _____ what the caller wishes to communicate. (You may not be there to translate your message.)

Chapter 9

Sales Negotiation

Learning Goals

Upon completion of this chapter, you will be able to:
☞ understand the importance of quality and quantity in negotiation;
☞ learn the knowledge about packing and marking;
☞ talk about transportation and insurance;
☞ make payment;
☞ make claiming and arbitration.

Lead-in Words

stipulated *adj.* 合同规定的	identical *adj.* 相同的
tally *v. n.* 合计，筹码	ultimate *adj.* 最终的
constitute *v.* 组成，构成	clause *n.* 条款
transit *n.* 运输	marine *adj.* 海的，海洋的
appropriate *adj.* 合适的	convertibility *n.* 可兑换性
claiming *n.* 索赔，声称	arbitration *n.* 仲裁
refund *n.* 退款	sarcasm *n.* 嘲讽
dispute *n.* 争议	compensation *n.* 补偿

The conduct of negotiation on sales is around the main clauses of the contract. According to the varieties of tactics adopted, the negotiator shall discuss with several foreign companies simultaneously or separately in import business. Due to the status differences of the two parties, generally the negotiator shall discuss the export business on the basis of analyzing the relation between supply and demand in international market, making proper strategic objective to achieve the desired results.

Section I   Quality and Quantity

To achieve satisfying results in a sales negotiation, one must consider a variety of factors:

quality, quantity, packing, shipment, quotation, offer and counter offer, etc. However, quality and quantity arc the most important factors to be taken into account.

1. Quality

The quality of the product is a combination of the product, referring to the inherent nature, the constructing elements, and the outside form. It determines the function and the usefulness of the product. In international trade, buyers and sellers usually live far from each other and this creates a problem. It is impossible for the buyers to examine the quality of the imported goods. Thus there needs to be some means for the sellers to inform the buyers of the quality.

In international trade, four means are generally used to express the quality of products. They are sales by sample, sales by specification, grade or standard, sales by trade mark or brand, and sales by description.

A sample is a small quantity of the product which represents the whole. It is a specimen in fact. Through the sample, buyers are able to know the quality of the products.

Sales by specification, grade or standard are another way to show the quality of the products, namely through certain recognized specifications, grades or standards.

Sales by trade mark or brand are useful to the products that have already gained export markets and whose brands or trade marks are already widely known.

Sales by description are usually applied to whole set of mechanical or electrical products such as instruments or equipment. For these products, there must be a detailed description provided for the buyers so that the buyers are able to know the structure, function, usage of the products, and so the products can be used accordingly.

2. Quantity

Quantity can be found more related to practical trade, especially in international trade. Quantity of the goods delivered forms one of the important terms of a sales contract. In many countries, it is stipulated in the national legislation that the quantity of the goods actually delivered should be identical to the amount called for in the contract. The buyer has the right to reject the whole lot if the amount is less than agreed upon. Likewise the buyer is entitled to reject the whole lot, or the excess portion of the goods, if more are delivered than are stipulated in the contract.

Some of the units of measurement commonly used in international trade are as follows:

(1) Weight: metric ton, long ton, short ton, kilogram, pound, ounce, gram, etc.;

(2) Number: piece, pair, set, dozen, gross, ream, etc.;

(3) Length: meter, foot, yard, mile, inch, etc.;

(4) Area: acre, square yard, square foot, square inch, etc.;

(5) Volume: cubic meter, cubic foot, cubic yard, etc.;

(6) Capacity: liter, gallon, bushel, quart, etc.

Section II　Packing and Marking

1. Packing

Packing is a critical element of your export business. If the product does not arrive at its destination in good condition, it is almost as if your product had not arrived at all. Both manufacturers and freight forwards can help with proper packing, since they have experience with shipping hazards and with the specific product, respectively.

When discussing packing, the seller should keep the following in mind:

(1) The buyer is under certain conditions entitled to reject the goods if they are not packed in accordance with his instruction or with the provisions agreed upon. So, it is essential for the seller to remember that the good to be shipped should be supplied in the stipulated packing;

(2) Packing should be designed to suit shipping requirements. In case of anomalies in packing, the master of the ship has the authority to refuse to sign a clean B / L. Likewise, the buyer is empowered to refuse the acceptance of a B / L which refers to goods marked and branded not in strict conformity with the contract;

(3) Packing should tally with the regulations in the country of destination, because some countries levy very heavy import duties on particular kinds of packing materials.

2. Marking

When packing is finished according to the packing instructions from the buyer, marking should be done on the export packages. The buyer should make demands for the marking definitely in order to identify the shipment, which enables the carrier to forward it to the ultimate consignee. Old marks, advertising, and other extraneous information only serve to confuse this primary function for freight handlers and carriers. In negotiating an import contract, the buyer should require the seller to follow the following fundamental rules:

(1) Unless local regulations prohibit them, use blind marks, particularly where goods are susceptible to pilferage. Change them periodically to avoid familiarity by handlers. Trade names and consignees or shipper's names should be avoided as they indicate the nature of the contents;

(2) Consignee marks and port marks showing destination and transfer points should be large, clear, and applied by stencil with waterproof ink. They should be applied on three faces of the container. Letters should be a minimum of two inches high;

(3) If commodities require special handling or stowage, the containers should be so marked, and the information should also appear on the bills of loading;

(4) Cautionary markings must be permanent and easy to read. The use of stencils is

recommended for legibility — do not use crayon, tags, or cards.

The making clauses usually adopted are as follows: The Sellers shall mark on each package with fadeless paint the package number, gross weight, net weight, measurement and the wordings: "KEEP AWAY FROM MOISTURE", "HANDLE WITH CARE", "THIS SIDE UP", the shipping mark and etc.

Section III　Transportation, Insurance and Payment

1. Transportation

The mode of transportation the importer and exporter take is decided by the following factors: the quantity, the cost, the size of each shipment, the distance of transportation and the nature of the cargo. Close attention must be paid to routing and scheduling dates. Importers of seasonal merchandise must make sure that schedules are met. Meanwhile, both exporter and importer should not neglect the location of the commodity during the negotiation because it has a direct relation with transportation. Small, inexpensive packages are best dispatched by parcel post. Air transportation is suitable for shipping fragile, expensive items, and its speed is preferable. The ocean freight is the most economical way to ship large quantities of goods. In international trade negotiations, exporter and importer should reach agreement on the date of shipment, places of shipping and destination, transshipment and partial shipments before they put their signature on a contract.

2. Insurance

In the course of transportation, loading, unloading and storage, the internationally traded goods may be subjected to various kinds of risks that may damage the goods. It is, therefore, necessary for either the seller or the buyer to buy transportation insurance in order that they can get compensation for any losses that might occur to the goods. They need to agree on who buys insurance, what kind of insurance to be bought, what amount to be insured, how long to be covered and how to make an insurance claim, and etc. All these constitute the insurance clause in a contract.

（1）As an exporter, it is important to know the following tips when negotiating the insurance clause of a contract.

Export shipments are usually insured against loss or damage in transit by ocean marine insurance. Inland marine policies cover shipment to the point of departure, whether seaport, airport, or rail terminal inside your country. Two types of policies are popular in international trade: special (one-time) cargo policy, which insures a single shipment and open and blanket cargo policies, which are in continuous effect and insure automatically all cargo moving at the seller's risk.

The one-time cargo policy is, of course, more expensive since the risk cannot be spread over a number of different shipments. However, if your export business is infrequent, it may be wise to obtain this type of coverage.

Open and blanket cargo policies are similar. The open policy remains in force until it is canceled, covering all shipments of the exporter in transit within specified geographical trade areas. Premiums are paid "as they go" because the amounts can be determined only when the goods are shipped.

Blanket policies are closed contracts. The insured exporter pays a lump sum premium that is fixed in advance. The premium is based on the estimated total amount of shipping expected. It can be adjusted depending on whether the coverage exceeded the originally insured amount or fell below it.

(2) With regard to the import insurance, the buyer should pay attention to the following:

All shipments should be insured either by your company or by the shipper. If you have obtained CIF pricing from your supplier, you will not have to worry about insurance, since it is included in the price you pay for the merchandise. However, be aware that there are some insurance coverage taken out by foreign sellers that our importers do not find satisfactory. Therefore, before you accept a deal with a CIF price, check to see that the coverage meets your needs.

If you make infrequent purchases from a particular source, the price you pay may not include insurance. In such cases, or if the offered coverage is unacceptable, you should obtain an open marine policy from a local company or through your customs broker.

Generally, it is easier to process a claim through a Chinese insurance company rather than a foreign company. Also, it is preferable to have one company underwrite all risks for collection purposes. Most marine insurance companies, however, will not grant an open policy until your volume and experience are established. Therefore, you will have to arrange coverage through your broker or rely on the foreign shipper.

Regardless of how you acquire marine insurance, you must have protection against "General Average Agreement", which, simply stated, means that if the ship on which your freight is being carried sustains damage, or if any other cargo is damaged due to collision, fire, and so on, the ship owner has the option of collecting a share of the damage from each firm that has cargo on board. This claim becomes a lien on your cargo, and any such lien must be satisfied before you can obtain your cargo.

Finally, you should also acquire an open inland marine policy, which covers shipments of goods after discharge at seaport, international airport, or rail terminal to their ultimate destination inside China.

(3) In negotiating the insurance clause, both the seller and the buyer should pay attention to

the following items:

① Who is responsible for buying insurance for the internationally traded goods is generally decided by the seller and the buyer through choosing a specific price term. For example, the buyer is to look after insurance in FOB and CFR contracts, and the seller has to buy insurance in CIF contract. Generally speaking, an importer should strive to sign a contract in FOB and CFR terms and an exporter should strive to sign a contract in CIF terms.

② The responsibility of an insurance company is defined by the kind of insurance bought by a seller or a buyer. When choosing the kind of insurance, the insured should take into account both the amount of insurance premium (cost) and the risks to be covered. For choosing the risks to be covered, such factors as nature of the goods, packing, transportation and season should be considered.

③ Determining the appropriate amount to be insured. As an insurance company charges premium according to the amount to be insured, and pay that amount if the goods covered incurs losses, the amount to be covered should be set as appropriate.

3. Payment

Payment in international sales and purchases is much more complicated than that in domestic trade. Terms of payment is one of the most important things in a contract and it usually takes more time, energy and care to negotiate and reach an agreement by both involved parties. The first item to talk about is payment instruments.

Payment in international trade is often beset with more difficulties owing to the fact that either party to a business transaction has relatively limited knowledge of the financial strength and commercial reputation of his counterpart. To guarantee the punctual delivery on the part of the seller and payment by the buyer, different modes of payments have been created.

(1) Currency

In international trade, the currencies to be used are generally the currency of the seller's country, the currency of the buyer's country and the currency of the third country. When selecting a currency for payment, its convertibility and stability should be well considered. The seller should choose the stable or appreciating currency, while the buyer should opt for a relatively weak or depreciating currency.

(2) Bill of Exchange or Draft

Drafts are a popular and common method of financing. A draft is a written instrument drawn by one party (exporter) on a buyer for certain sum of money at sight or at some definite future time.

(3) Remittance

The buyer remits the money to the seller through banks respectively located in the buyer's or the seller's offices. It consists mainly of mail transfer and telegraphic transfer.

(4) Letter of Credit

It goes without saying that you, the exporter, want to be paid as quickly as possible, whereas your overseas customer may well want to defer payment for as long as possible. The answer, of course, is credit.

In third world countries, letters of credit are the rule in conducting export sales. A letter of credit is a financing instrument opened by a foreign buyer with a bank in his or her locality. The letter of credit stipulates the purchase price agreed upon by the buyer and seller, the quantity of merchandise to be shipped, and the type of insurance coverage to protect the merchandise during shipment. The letter of credit names the seller as beneficiary and identifies the definite time period the terms remain in force. The letter of credit authorizes the buyers to pay when the stipulated conditions have been met. Most export letters of credit are made payable in China.

(5) Collection

It is a payment method by which the seller issues a draft on the buyer after the seller makes delivery, and then entrusts a bank to collect the payment on behalf of the seller.

When using collection as the payment method, the seller and the buyer usually agree beforehand that the transaction will be on a sight draft basis or perhaps on a 60-day or 90-day deferred payment basis (60 S / D, D / A). The overseas importer orders merchandise directly from seller and the seller arranges to ship the goods. The seller then takes out shipping documents and his own draft, drawn on the importer, to the seller's bank. The seller's bank forwards all documents to its correspondent bank overseas. This overseas bank notifies the importer when the documents arrive. If terms are payment at sight, this arrangement would be called a sight draft document against payment (S / D, D / P), and the importer would be required to pay immediately to obtain the shipping documents so he or she can pick up the goods.

However, if importer has agreed to "accept" (pay later) (D / A) the draft, he or she is permitted to obtain the documents by accepting the draft and the merchandise, but is not obliged to make payments until the draft matures (e.g. 60 days D / A). The exporter will, of course, have established credit locally and made arrangements with his or her bank prior to undertaking the shipment.

Section IV Claim and Arbitration

In international business activities, no matter how perfect an organization may be, complaints are certain to arise. If the importer does not receive goods of the kind, quality or quantity he expects, or the exporter does not receive the due payment, they will complain. They settle disputes through claiming and arbitration.

1. Claim

Claims offer the opportunity to discover and correct defects existing in the goods and service. In making a claim, one of the major jobs is to keep negatives from worsening the situation. When making a direct claim, we should make clear what the claim is. We won't let our anger show and at the same time we avoid sarcasm. We give the facts calmly, specifically, and thoroughly. We request the action: a replacement, repair, refund or compensation.

2. Arbitration

Arbitration is different from amicable consultation. Arbitration is a means of settling a dispute between two parties through the medium of a third party whose decision on the dispute is final and binding. As a rule, the negotiators should specify the place of arbitration. This is of primary importance and a matter of great concern to both parties. They should also specify the number of arbitrations and their selection, how the cost of the arbitration is to be divided and quite often, the scope of arbitration, in case the parties may wish to limit the scope to a specific aspect of a particular dispute.

Section V Practical Activities

1. Case Study

● Case study 1

Study the following case and be familiar with the procedure of sales negotiation:

A Successful Sales Negotiation

A: Miss Li, do you have offers for all the products listed here?

B: Yes, this is our latest price list, and it serves as a guideline only. Mr. Smith, I wonder if there is anything you are particularly interested in?

A: I'm very much interested in your Hebei peanuts, but I can't be sure of their quality. Have you got any samples here?

B: Yes, here you are.

A: Mmm ... the quality is not bad. I'd like to have your lowest price CIF London.

B: The unit price is $200 per metric ton CIF London. I'm sure you will find our price most competitive.

A: Is there any commission included?

B: No, we usually don't allow any commission, but, if the order is large enough, we will consider it.

A: I'm afraid we can't do much right now. Could we have 200 metric tons for a trial? If the sales go well, big business is sure to follow. I hope you'll give me special consideration.

B: Well, as an encouragement of business, we'll allow you 2% commission. That's the top rate.

A: Thank you. When do you expect to make shipment?

B: By this coming September. Do you have any special request for packing?

A: Packing in ordinary gunny sacks with a little bit of flower design is the best in our market. A nice packing helps find a market.

B: Here are the samples of packing available now. You may have a look.

A: Wonderful! This one is just right. What about the terms of payment?

B: Letter of credit available by draft at sight.

A: How long will your offer be open?

B: 24 hours.

A: Fine, thank you. It's very nice to see you.

● Case Study 2

Negotiating Discount

A: Mr. Li, I have considered the offer you made yesterday. I must point out that your price is much higher than other quotations we've received.

B: Well, it may appear a little higher but the quality of our products is much better than that of other suppliers'. You must take this into consideration.

A: I agree with you on this point. Otherwise, we would simply stop doing business with you. This time I intend to place a large order but business is almost impossible unless you give me a discount.

B: If so, we'll certainly give you a discount. But how large is the order you intend to place with us?

A: 90,000 sets with a discount rate of 20%.

B: I'm afraid I could not agree with you for such a big discount. In this way, it won't leave us anything. Our maximum is 10%.

A: Oh, Mr. Li, you see with such a large order on hand, you needn't worry anymore. You don't have to take in new orders. Think it over. We are old friends.

A: Considering the long-standing business relationship between us, we shall grant you a special discount of 10%. As you know, we do business on the basis of equality and mutual benefit.

B: Yes. I also hope we do business on the basis of mutual benefit. But 10% discount is not enough for such a big order.

A: Only for very special customers do we allow them a rate of 10% discount. Besides, the price of this product is tending to go up. There is a heavy demand for it.

B: Yes. I know the present tendency. Anyhow, let's meet each other half way, how about 15%?

A: You are a real businessman! All right, I agree to give you 15% discount provided you order 100,000 sets.

B: OK, I accept.

2. Role Play

Can We Meet Each Other Half Way?

A: It's really a pity that we don't come to any agreement on price at our last meeting.

B: We also consider it a great pity to talk for so long a time but to come to nothing.

A: Well, in view of concluding a transaction, I'm ready to make some concessions.

B: How much are you to step down?

A: I'm going to step down by ... er 2%.

B: Your price is really not encouraging. I was thinking of 20%.

A: Oh, I'm afraid that won't do. It's the quality that counts. Our curtains are by far the best in Europe and probably in the world. You should take into consideration our curtains' superior quality.

B: That's precisely why we prefer to order from your company. Well, how about ... er ... meeting each other half way? Let's each step a bit backward so that business can be done.

A: What do you mean?

B: That means there is a gap of 5 dollars left. Mr. Smith, shall we make a joint effort, the last effort to fill the gap? Let's close the deal at 10 dollars per yard, CIF London.

A: You drive a hard bargain.

B: I'll make out the contract for you to sign tomorrow.

3. Mini Negotiation

Negotiating Price

A: Even with volume sales, our costs for Sun Computer won't go down much.

B: What are you proposing?

A: We could take a cut on the price. But 20% would slash our profit margin. We suggest a compromise of 10%.

B: That's a big change from 25! 10 is beyond my negotiating limit. Any other ideas?

A: I don't think I can change it right now. Why don't we talk again tomorrow?

B: Sure. I must talk to my office anyway. I hope we can find some common ground on this.

(next day)

B: I've been instructed to reject the numbers you proposed; but we can try to come up with something else.

A： I hope so. My instructions are to negotiate hard on this deal，I'm trying very hard to reach some middle ground.

B： I understand. We propose a structured deal. For the first six months，we get a discount of 20%，and the next six months we get 15%.

A： I can't bring those numbers back to my office，they'll turn it down flat.

B： Then you'll have to think of something better.

Negotiation Tips

● Role Play Negotiation Beforehand 事先演练谈判

Role-play before every negotiation. Especially include reverse role-play，where you try to determine how the other side will approach the negotiation.

● Understand the Meaning of "Win-win" 理解双赢的意义

Understand the real meaning of "win-win". "Win-win" does not mean equal win. One party may gain more than the other，but as long as you both gain more by negotiating，you come away with a win-win deal.

● Recognize That People Often Ask for More than They Expect to Get 知道人的欲望常常高于期望

This means you need to resist the temptation to reduce your price or offer a discount automatically.

Extended Activities

Ⅰ. Situational Group Talks.

Make a phone call to check the cost of attending the commodities fair.

Ⅱ. Multiple Choice.

Directions：There are ten incomplete sentences in this part. For each sentence there are four choices marked A，B，C, and D. Choose the one that best completes the sentence.

1. We offer firm as follows _____ the terms and conditions as the previous contracts.

   A. of   B. by   C. on   D. at

2. _____ an order of over 500 prices we would grant you a special discount.

   A. In case   B. In case that   C. In the case   D. In case of

3. No discount will be granted _____ you place an order for more than 1,000 tons.

   A. so that   B. till   C. unless   D. nevertheless

4. We feel _____ that we must decline your counter offer.

   A. regretting   B. regretful   C. regrettable   D. regretted

5. If you can decrease your price by 3%，we shall be prepared to _____ for 5,000 pieces.

   A. book with you an order   B. decline your order

C. be in the market   D. make your order

6. In case you can make a reduction of 5% _____ your price, we may strike the deal with you.

    A. of   B. by   C. in   D. for

7. For the time being, we cannot commit _____ to any fresh orders.

    A. us   B. our   C. oneself   D. ourselves

8. Since our prices are closely calculated, we regret _____ to grant the discount you asked for.

    A. are unable   B. being unable   C. be unable   D. being able

9. We would suggest _____ your own interest that you fax us your acceptance as soon as possible.

    A. with   B. in   C. for   D. at

10. We are sorry we cannot _____ your counter offer, as your bid is too low.

    A. agree   B. agree with   C. entertain   D. decline

Ⅲ. Read the following statements and fill in the blanks.

1. A _____ is a small quantity of the product which represents the whole.

2. According to international practice, the shipping markings are designed and determined by the _____.

3. If commodities require special handling or stowage, the containers should be so marked, and the information should also appear on the _____ of loading.

4. The _____ freight is the most economical way to ship large quantities of goods.

5. Payment in international sales and purchases is much more _____ than that in domestic trade.

Ⅳ. Decide whether the following statements are true(T) or false(F).

1. It is impossible for the buyers to examine the quality of the imported goods. Thus, there needs to be some means for the sellers to inform the buyers of the quality.

2. Since quantity plays a very important part in foreign trade, it is not necessary to find out the units of measurement to be adopted in foreign trade.

3. It is essential for the seller to remember that the goods to be shipped should be supplied in the stipulated packing.

4. The letter of credit stipulates the purchase price agreed upon by the buyer and seller, the quantity of merchandise to be shipped.

5. In the course of transportation, loading and unloading and storage, the internationally traded goods may be subjected to various kinds of risks that may damage the goods.

Ⅴ. Translate the following sentences into Chinese.

1. We very much regret that your offer is 5% higher than those from the American suppliers.

2. As the market of wool is declining, there is no possibility of business unless you can reduce

your price by 5%.

3. We regret to inform you that our customers here find your price is too high.

4. As our price is quite reasonable, it has been accepted by other customers at your end.

5. As regards Men's Shirts, we look forward to doing business with you at a figure close to our quoted price.

Chapter 10

Investment Negotiation

Learning Goals

Upon completion of this chapter, you will be able to:
☞ grasp the features of different joint ventures;
☞ understand the management and operation of joint ventures;
☞ distinguish various parts of joint venture investment negotiation.

Lead-in Words

equity *n*. 公平	feasibility *n*. 可行性
respectively *adv*. 分别	expiry *n*. 到期
implementation *n*. 贯彻，执行	termination *n*. 终止
attain *v*. 达到	practice *n*. 惯例
breach *n*. *v*. 违约	dissolution *n*. 分解，瓦解
compensate *v*. 补偿	incur *v*. 引起，招致
hybrid-type *n*. 混杂型	provision *n*. 规定
stipulate *v*. 写入条款	distribution *n*. 分配
liability *n*. 责任，义务	station *v*. 驻扎，外派
manner *n*. 形式	nature *n*. 性质

Numerable foreign investment in China has taken the form of joint venture. In a joint venture agreement, your company is in a position to expand resources, export experience and market knowledge while spreading the risk and laying a distribution framework. There are also some forms of tax advantages or waivers offered by foreign countries for joint ventures. Compared to that of sales of goods or services, the negotiation of joint venture contract has more potential for difficulties and disputes. In this chapter the negotiation of joint venture is taken as an example to illustrate the essence of investment negotiation.

Section I   Types of Joint Ventures

1. Equity Joint Ventures

An equity joint venture is a liability-limited company formed by investors who make investments to the company respectively according to their share proportion as agreed in the agreement. The company is funded and operated jointly by investors who will assume responsibility for losses and profit according to the proportion of their shares in the venture.

A Sino-Foreign equity joint venture is a limited liability formed by foreign companies, enterprises, other economic organizations or individuals together with Chinese companies, enterprises or other economic organizations according to the Law of the People's Republic of China on Sino-Foreign Equity Joint Venture within the territory of the People's Republic of China, on the principle of equality and mutual benefit, and subject to approval by the Chinese Government. Within the equity joint venture, matters such as the conditions for cooperation, the distribution of earnings or products, the sharing of risks and losses, the manners of operation and management are decided according to the proportions of the shares of the investors.

2. Contractual Joint Ventures

A contractual joint venture is a joint venture formed by investors who make investment in accordance with the provisions of the contract signed by the investors. All matters concerning the contractual joint venture such as the investment, the conditions for cooperation, the distribution of earnings or products, the sharing of risks and losses, the manners of operation and management etc. are not decided according to the proportion of their investment, but rather prescribed by the contract.

A Sino-Foreign contractual joint venture is a joint venture formed by foreign companies, enterprises, other economic organizations or individuals together with Chinese companies, enterprises, other economic organizations according to the Law of the People's Republic of China on Sino-Foreign Equity Joint Venture within the territory of the People's Republic of China, on the principle of equality and mutual benefit, and subject to approval by the Chinese Government. Within the contractual joint venture, matters such as the investment or conditions for cooperation, the distribution of earnings or products, the sharing of risks and losses, the manners of operation and management and the ownership of the property at the time of the termination of the contractual joint venture are prescribed in the contractual joint venture contract.

Section II   Management and Operation of Joint Venture

1. Form of Organization

According to the Law of the People's Republic of China on Sino-Foreign Equity Joint Venture, the equity joint venture shall take the form of a limited liability company.

2. Registered Capital

According to the Implementation Rules of Law of the People's Republic of China on Sino-Foreign Equity Joint Venture, the registered capital of the equity joint venture is the total sum of capital registered at the registration management organization for the establishment of the equity joint venture. It should be total amount paid in by all the investors. The registered capital shall not be reduced during the term of the equity joint ventures.

3. Form of Investment and the Proportion of Investment

The parties to an equity joint venture may make their investment in cash, in kind or in industrial property rights. The proportion of investment of each party in an equity joint venture may vary in different cases, but the proportion of a foreign party shall be, in general, not less than 25 percent of its registered capital.

4. Board of the Directors and the Management Body

According to the Law of the People's Republic of China on Sino-Foreign Equity Joint Venture, the equity joint venture shall have a board of directors that is the highest decision-making body of the company. The number of the directors of equity directors may vary in different cases, but it shall not be less than three. The board of directors is responsible for the decision of great matters of the venture. The chairman and the vice-chairman (vice-chairmen) shall be determined through consultation by the parties to the venture or elected by the board of directors.

The general manager manages the daily business, the general manager and the deputy general manager(s) are appointed by the board of directors. The positions of the general manager and the deputy general manager(s) can be held by the Chinese party or foreign party (parties). In China, usually an experienced person from the foreign party with scientific management is appointed as the general manager at the beginning of an equity joint venture, and after some time of operation of the venture, the general manager will be transferred to the Chinese personnel.

5. Distribution of Profits

According to the Law of the People's Republic of China on Sino-Foreign Equity Joint Venture, the net profit of an equity joint venture shall be distributed among the parties to the venture in proportion to their respective contributions to the registered capital, after payment out of its gross profit of the equity joint venture income tax, pursuant to the provisions of the tax law of the People's Republic of China, and after deduction from the gross profit of a reserve fund, a bonus and welfare fund for workers and stuff members and a venture expansion fund, as stipulated in the venture's articles of association. The net profit within the territory of China may apply for partial refund of the income tax already paid.

6. Technology Introduction of Joint Venture

Equity joint venture is one of the best ways for the introduction of technology, through the establishment of an equity joint venture, not only advanced technologies are introduced, but also advanced production mechanics and scientific management.

7. Procurement of Materials and the Sales of Its Products

According to the provisions of Article 9 of the Law of the People's Republic of China on Sino-Foreign Equity Joint Venture, its purchase of required raw and semi-proceeded materials, fuels, auxiliary equipment, etc., the equity joint venture should give first priority for making purchases in China. It may also make such purchases directly on the world market with foreign exchange raised by it. An equity joint venture shall be encouraged to market its products outside China. It may sell its export products on foreign markets directly or through associated agencies or China's foreign trade agencies.

Section III   Other Issues of Investment Negotiation

1. Labor Management

The labor contract is required to contain provisions regarding employment terms, dismissal and resignation, wages, working hours, labor insurance, discipline and other matters.

2. Management of Land

The Chinese party to the joint venture may supply the land needed by a joint venture for its plant and office facilities as part to its capital contribution. Alternatively, the joint venture may lease the land from the local government a site in the place where the joint venture conducts its operation. In either case, the joint venture obtains only a leasehold interest the site and not ownership, and assignment of this interest to third parties is not permitted.

3. Foreign Exchange Controls

The foreign exchange balancing regulations introduced by the States Council formalize five mechanisms for foreign investors to resolve foreign exchange imbalance. They are: exports; domestic sales under certain conditions; exports of other products under certain conditions; the transfer of foreign exchange between joint ventures subject to approval by the state foreign exchange authorities and both parties to the joint venture; the reinvestment of earnings in local currency in other joint ventures that would generate foreign exchanges.

4. Taxation

Each party to the cooperative joint venture is required to pay its own taxes on profits earned from the distributions of the joint venture. For the foreign party, this means that net income is taxed under the Joint Venture Income Tax Law of the People's Republic of China at progressive rates, including a local surtax. As a matter of practice, however, some hybrid-type cooperative joint ventures have applied for and received tax treatment under the provisions of Joint Venture Income Tax Law and the Detailed Rules issued by the States Council.

In addition to the enterprise income tax, cooperative joint ventures are also subject to China's other tax laws. For example, individual income tax is imposed on the income of personnel stationed in China in connection with the joint venture.

5. Terms and Termination

The terms of the equity joint venture may vary according to different circumstances, but in principle, it is between 15 to 30 years. However, for projects with large investment, long construction period and low profit ratio, the term of the joint venture may exceed 30 years. If the parties of the joint venture agree, they may, before 6 months of the expiry of the term, apply to the administrative department for the extension of the term of the joint venture.

Chinese law does not specify any fixed term for joint ventures. The Implementing Act provides only that in principle the average term should be between ten and thirty years, although longer terms may be permitted. Under an amendment made to the Implementing Act, the maximum term may now be extended to fifty years or more in certain circumstances. Moreover, joint ventures are permitted to extend their life beyond the scheduled term, subject to the agreement of the parties and government approval. As a result, the duration of the venture is left to negotiation between the parties, taking into account the nature of the project, the wishes of the parties, and the attitude of the Chinese government.

The early dissolution of a joint venture is permitted in the event of a breach of contract by one of the parties, where the enterprise suffers heavy losses or is unable to attain its stated business goals, or upon the occurrence of other events stipulated in the joint venture contract. In the event that the reason for the termination is a breach of contract which makes the joint venture unable to continue its operations, the breaching party is liable to compensate the venture for the losses incurred thereby.

Section IV　Practical Activities

1. Case Study

● Case study 1

> *Zhang Ming(Z), director of a starch factory in China, is explaining China's laws and regulations governing foreign investment to Mr. Smith(S), manager of the marketing department of a German starch company that is thinking of setting up a joint venture in China.*

Setting up a Sino-Foreign Trade Company

S: We have a mind to establish a starch factory here with you as partner in a joint venture. Our market study shows that there is a great demand for starch in China. If you could improve the quality of your products, there would be a great possibility to enlarge sales.

Z: We're quite interested in your investment and cooperation.

S: But before we go into the details of the project, we would like to know the general practice of doing this kind of business in China.

Z: China is an ideal place for foreign investors. It not only provides an environment for overseas investors of low taxation, a comparatively low-wage work force and other preferential terms, but also an investment environment that's stable. What in particular would you like to know?

S: We would like to know what regulations the Chinese government has drawn up on the proportion of foreign money in the total investment?

Z: The proportion of foreign investment must not be lower than 25%.

S: Is there a ceiling?

Z: No. In fact, if you use advanced technology, you can even establish a wholly-owned foreign business.

S: Well, at this point we are interested in establishing a joint venture with a 50 / 50 split. We'll provide necessary exchange and production equipment and technology. What will the contribution from the Chinese side be?

Z: We'll provide factory buildings, premises, labor and funds in RMB. The right to use the site under a leasing arrangement is also part of our investment.

S: I see. How long will the duration of the joint venture be?

Z: It depends on the intention of both parties. To start with, the two parties can set the duration at 20 years. The contract can be extended if both parties agree.

S: What about the composition of the Board of Directors?

Z: Usually its composition will be decided by the proportion of the capital contributed.

S: Understood. Thank you for your explanation. I'll discuss the matter with the head office first and have a more detailed talk with you later.

Z: Good. We are looking forward to the next meeting.

● Case study 2

In the following case, a foreign company wants to set up a joint venture in China. Study the case and learn something about the process.

A: I think we could together set up a luggage and bag factory as a joint venture here in China.

B: Oh, your suggestion makes good business sense. For foreign investors, China is really an ideal place. It not only provides many preferential terms for them, but also a stable investment environment.

A: But this would be the first time we make investment in China, so we would like to know more about China's policies and practice regarding a joint venture.

B: We would be very happy to provide you with the necessary information.

A: Is there any regulation in your country regarding the proportion of the respective investment of the two parties?

B: Yes. According to the relevant laws and regulations of China, with regard to the registered capital of a joint venture, the proportion of the investment contributed by the foreign investor must in general be not less than 25%.

A: Is there an upper limit?

B: No. In fact, our government now encourages the establishment of wholly-owned foreign businesses.

A: How long is the term of a joint venture contract?

B: There is no fixed rule concerning the term of the contract. It will be determined by mutual agreement by the parties to the venture in the light of the venture's particular line of business and conditions. If the joint venture runs successfully, the term of the contract may be extended on expiration so long as both sides agree.

A: What about the division of labor in terms of the administrative responsibility of a joint venture?

B: A joint venture must have a board of directors. The size and composition of the board will be stipulated in the contract and articles of association after consultation between the parties to the venture. Generally speaking, the number of directors representing a party as well as their rights and responsibilities will be determined on the basis of the share of the investment made by it in the venture.

A: I see. Thank you very much for your explanation. I'll go back and have some further discussion with my company. I'm sure I'll come back again soon to discuss the matter with you in detail.

B: We hope we will have an opportunity to work together with you.

2. Role Play

The talk covers the total amount of investment, forms of investment and the administrative responsibility of the two parties.

S: Hello, Mr. Zhang, nice to see you again.

Z: Nice to see you again too so soon.

S: Do you mind my coming straight to the point?

Z: Certainly not. It's in fact welcome. That's the way business should be done.

S: Firstly we need to talk about how much each party should contribute to the project.

Z: What's your estimate of the total amount of the investment?

S: What do you say to U.S. $6 million?

Z: I'm afraid this figure is not large enough to cover the construction funds and circulating capital. For such a project as ours, we need at least a total of U.S. $8 million.

S: If so, how much should the registered capital be then?

Z: For a project with a total investment of from U.S. $3 million to U.S. $10 million, the registered capital should account for 50% of the total investment. So the registered capital for our project must be no less than U.S. $4 million.

S: I see. Then we agree to your proposal that the total investment should be U.S. $8 million.

Z: How much are you going to invest in the project?

S: Do you think a 60 / 40 split in your favor is OK with you?

Z: That'll do, I think. What are the primary markets for our products?

S: We think China should be our primary market because according to our market research there is a great demand for high-quality starch on the Chinese market.

Z: But in our opinion we should sell at least part of the products on the international market.

S: Shall we discuss this problem in detail at our next meeting?

Z: I don't think I have any reason to disagree to that.

3. Mini Negotiation

A: Our project proposal has been approved. Now we can discuss the details of the joint venture arrangement.

B: That's good news. We are going to contribute 40% of the investment. It includes equipment, patent rights and some funds.

A: Good. We will contribute 60%, in the form of land, buildings, equipment and machinery and some cash in RMB.

B: How should we decide the administrative responsibilities of the two parties to the joint venture?

A: The board of directors will decide all the important matters of the venture. The chairman will be appointed by the board. If the chairman is from the Chinese side, the vice chairman will be from your side and vice versa.

B: How many people will there be on the board?

A: Since we have the larger share, we'd like the board to have an odd number of directors, in our favor.

B: How about 7 directors then, four to be appointed by the Chinese side and three by our side?

A: We have no objection to that.

B: What's the duration of their term of office?

A: It should be a three-year term, in most cases. If any director should be disqualified, we should be able to dismiss and replace him at any time.

B: Good. That's settled then.

A: How long do you think the term of the joint venture will be?

B: We may temporarily fix the term at 15 years for the joint venture. If we run it well, we should extend the term at expiration.

A: That's sensible. We agree.

Negotiation Tips

● Balance Must Be Achieved 必须达到平衡

As we noted, every negotiation is a trade. You want to gain something; others want something from you. Concessions often become critical to closing a deal. But successful negotiators understand that a balance must be achieved. Every concession you make must be matched by a similar concession from the other side. Never make a concession without asking for one in return. If you give without getting anything back, you reinforce the behavior of asking for the concession.

- **Not Make Huge Concession 不能大幅度让步**

Don't make huge concessions, especially on the first go-around. Making a large initial concession undermines your credibility and sends the message that you still have plenty of room to come down.

- **Decrease the Amount of Concession Gradually 逐渐减少让步幅度**

Make concessions in decreasing increments. This establishes more credibility for your opening position and signals that you have little room left in which to move.

Extended Activities

Ⅰ. Situational Group Talks.

Mr. Smith comes to China for the first time with the intention of setting up a joint venture. Try to explain some policies to him.

Ⅱ. Multiple Choice.

Directions: There are ten incomplete sentences in this part. For each sentence there are four choices marked A, B, C, and D. Choose the one that best completes the sentence.

1. Please advise any change in the situation _____.

    A. at your end   B. in your end   C. on your end   D. by your end

2. We are glad to say that we can supply any quantity of dried seafood _____ stock to the exact specifications of your sample.

    A. at   B. for   C. from   D. in

3. The stocks are running _____.

    A. low   B. stop   C. little   D. limited

4. If we had been informed in time, we _____ them for you.

    A. would have reserved   B. would reserve

    C. will reserve   D. had reserved

5. We know nothing _____ the market condition there.

    A. regard   B. regards   C. regarding   D. as regard

6. We confirm _____ the following transactions with you.

    A. to conclude   B. concluding   C. concluded   D. having concluded

7. _____ at the beginning of March, we should be able to ship your order by S.S Peace.

    A. Your L / C shall reach us   B. Had your L / C reached us

    C. Should your L / C reach us   D. Your L / C reaching us

8. Much to our _____, we cannot accept any fresh orders at present.

    A. regret   B. regretful   C. regrettable   D. regrets

9. We thank you for your letter of Nov. 25 _____ your purchase from us of 100 tons.

    A. confirm   B. confirmed   C. to confirm   D. confirming

10. In most cases, goods are ordered on _____ order forms.

　　A. print　　　　　　B. printing　　　　　C. to print　　　　　D. printed

III. Read the following statements and fill in the blanks.

1. According to the Law of the People's Republic of China on Sino-Foreign Equity Joint Venture, the equity joint venture shall take the form of a limited _____ company.

2. An equity joint venture shall be encouraged to market its products _____ China.

3. The terms of the equity joint venture may _____ according to different circumstances.

4. If the parties of the joint venture agree, they may, before 6 months of the _____ of the term, apply to the administrative department for the extension of the term of the joint venture.

5. Each party to the cooperative joint venture is required to pay its own taxes on profits earned from the _____ of the joint venture.

IV. Decide whether the following statements are true(T) or false(F).

1. An equity joint venture is a liability-limited company formed by investors who make investments to the company respectively according to their share proportion as agreed in the agreement.

2. Before getting approval for the report of feasibility study, the parties of the joint venture should begin to negotiate for the contract and prepare the articles of association, and then submit them for approval.

3. The parties to an equity joint venture can only make their investment in cash.

4. The proportion of investment of each party in an equity joint venture may vary in different cases, but the proportion of a foreign party shall be, in general, not less than 25 percent of its registered capital.

5. The board of directors is the highest decision-making body of the joint venture.

V. Translate the following sentences into Chinese.

1. Enclosed please find our order No. 04 in duplicate, one of which please sign and return for our file.

2. As we are in urgent need of the goods, you are requested to effect shipment during May as promised in your offer.

3. Please note that the stipulations in the relative credit should fully conform to the terms in Our Sales Contract in order to avoid subsequent amendments.

4. Shipment should be made during August to October in three lots, with 100 tons each.

5. We can't accept any fresh orders because we are fully committed. But as soon as fresh supplies come in, we shall contact you without delay.

Chapter 11

Technology Trade Negotiation

Learning Goals

Upon completion of this chapter, you will be able to:

☞ grasp the features of technology trade negotiation;
☞ understand the content of technology trade negotiation;
☞ use terms of payment;
☞ make delivery of documentation;
☞ draw training program.

Lead-in Words

advisable *adj.* 合理的，适当的	annex *n.* 附件
obsolete *adj.* 过时的	acquisition *n.* 获得
specification *n.* 规格	emission *n.* 排放
installment *n.* 分期付款	lump-sum payment 一次性付款
royalty *n.* 专利使用费	interval *n.* 一段时间
sophisticated *adj.* 复杂的	evaluate *v.* 评估
potential *adj.* 潜在的	entail *v.* 蒙受
alternative *n.* 替换物，替换方式	invoice *n.* 发票
initial *adj.* 最初的	down payment 首付
remuneration *n.* 报酬，补偿	criterion *n. pl.* criteria 标准

Technological advances in different countries have always been unequal. It is this different nature of technological progress throughout the world that provides the very basis or technology transfer. In the past few decades, international technology transfer has multiplied in leaps and bounds. In technology trade negotiation, we need to understand its features, scope of technology, terms of payment, delivery of documentation and training program.

Section I Principal Legal Forms of Technology Trade

Generally, three principal legal methods can be used in technology trade: assignment, a license contract and a know-how contract.

1. Assignment

This method, i. e. through assignment, refers to the sale by the owner of all his or its exclusive rights to a patent, trademark or know-how and the purchase of these rights by another person or legal entity. The transferor — the owner of the patent, trademark or know-how, is called the "assignor" and the entity or the transferee who acquires all the exclusive rights, is called the "assignee". When an assignment takes place, the assignor no longer has any right in respect of the patent, trademark or know-how, while the assignee becomes the new owner and is entitled to exercise all the exclusive rights conferred by the grant of the patent, trademark or know-how.

2. A License Contract

When licensing takes place, the owner gives his a patent, trademark or know-how to the legal entity of the permission to perform, in the country and for a limited period of time. Once that permission is given, a "license" has been granted. Where a license is granted, the legal document evidencing the permission given one or more acts covered by the exclusive fights of the transferor to the transferee, is usually referred to as a "license contract" or more simply as a license. The owner of the patent, trademark or know-how who gives that permission is referred to as "the licensor". The receiver that permission is referred to as "the licensee". The licensee can only get the right to use the patent, trademark or know-how and the rights of manufacture and sale of the relative products in a limited territory over a limited period of time. The licensor remains the owner of the patent, trademark or know-how.

3. A Know-how Contract

Through a know-how contract, it is possible to include provisions concerning know-how in a license contract. It is also possible to include such provisions in a document that is separate from a license contract. In the case where the know-how relates to a patent or trademark, the provisions are usually found in the license contract which deals with that patent or trademark. This is particularly so when the owner of the patent or trademark is also the developer and holder of the know-how. However, for a variety of reasons, even in such a case, the provisions concerning the know-how might be placed in a separate or distinct writing or document. Whenever provisions concerning know-how appear in a separate or distinct writing or document, that writing or document is normally called a "know-how contract". Through such provisions, the supplier of the know-how promises to communicate the know-how to the recipient for the use by the latter.

In short, among the above three principal legal methods, the first one, i.e., through assignment, is the most expensive as it entails the purchase from the owner all his exclusive rights to a patented technology, trademark or know-how. When an assignment has taken place, the assignee becomes the owner of the patented technology, trademark or know-how. Nobody else, not even the former owner is allowed to use it without his permission. The second form, through licensing agreement or contract, is more flexible and less expensive. Hence more suitable to our national condition. By signing a license contract with a licensor, we can obtain permission to use his patented technology, trademark or know-how to manufacture a certain product or products needed in China. The third method is signing a know-how contract. But more often than not, the purchase of know-how alone is not enough. It takes place together with the purchase of equipment or technology and therefore can be included in the license contract.

Section II   Features of Technology Trade Negotiation

Technology transfer is a means of transferring research findings from within the institution to and for the benefit of the public. There are a number of unique features in technology transfer.

1. Monopolists

Commercial technology transfer is highly monopolistic. In order to maintain the advantage of its technology and products, the owner of a technology does not normally transfer the technology, except in some special situations, for example, when a transfer is necessary for penetrating the market, when the transfer can bring huge profits, or when the transfer does not threaten its monopoly.

2. Multiple Transactions

Usually, a single technology can be traded multiple times, as the transfer does not involve ownership but only the right to use. The number of transfers will have a direct impact on the value of the technology. When a technology is transferred to a variety of end users, the price the transferor charges will drop accordingly. Only in specific situations is ownership transferred, but the price is usually very high and conditions very rigid.

3. Profit-oriented

As technology transfer does not simply follow the basic market rule of exchange. The price of the transferred technology is not simply determined by its value, i. e., R & D costs plus margin, but heavily influenced by the profits it can bring to the transferee. The price of the technology transferred is the licensor's share of licensee's profits. When the transferor is in a monopolistic position, he will tend to charge higher prices. When the transferor is not in a monopolistic position, he will tend to settle on a price for the technology that is far lower than the price needed to recapture the full cost of the technological effort, simply because the marginal costs associated with an additional sale are usually very low and the costs of generating the technology itself are sunk costs.

Section III   Content of Technology Trade Negotiation

The principal legal methods that can be used for technology transfer include assignment, licensing, and a know-how contract. Signing licensing agreement is currently viewed as the most suitable method to import technology. The objects of license contracts can be patented technology, know-how and trademark and quite often a combination of patented technology and know-how. For this reason we will lay more emphasis on the study of China's import of technology through licensing negotiation and contract. The major provisions of license contracts that need to be negotiated includes:

1. Scope of Technology

To separate the technical part of the contract from the legal part, it is always advisable to put all the technical details in an annex, say, Annex A. Annex A can provide two kinds of specifications: product specifications and process specifications, to describe the product itself and all its properties and characteristics. In addition, the output, efficiency and emission of pollutants of the process, etc. may also be clearly specified therein. It may run something like this: The licensor agrees to transfer the know-how used by the licensor at the date the contract coming into force for the manufacture of the goods listed and specified in Annex A. The know-how is to confirm in all respects to the specifications of output, efficiency and emission of pollutants in Annex A.

The licensees are naturally afraid of purchasing out-dated or obsolete technologies. A provision about the know-how being used by the licensor at the date the contract coming into force provides some protection. If the licensor agrees to this, the licensee can be sure that the technology is current. But it does not guarantee that the technology is the most up-to-date or that the same technology is not available more cheaply elsewhere. Under such circumstances, a careful background research on the technology should be made either through government agencies or international agencies, which may be time-consuming and expensive but worthwhile.

2. Terms of Payment

Payment for the licensed technology can take different forms: lump-sum payment, royalties or a combination of both.

(1) Lump-sum Price

A lump-sum price is a pre-calculated amount to be paid once or in installments. The lump-sum amount may be paid, upon the conclusion of the license contract or shortly after it, either in a single payment staggered in relation to certain events such as the execution of the license or on the delivery of certain technical information.

Lump-sum payment is often made for the outright acquisition of license, where the technology can be transferred all at once and the licensee can readily and fully absorb it. Such payment is made for the transfer of rights and know-how concerning technology which is less sophisticated and quite adequate from the licensee's viewpoint, and a continuing supply of technical information concerning the technological advances or the marketing of the products or technical services or assistance in support of the licensee is no longer required of the licensor. For example, a lump-sum payment may be made to obtain the rights in a patented product, or to patented process or to sets of drawings that are sufficient in themselves to enable the licensee to manufacture and sell a certain product. This may, however, entail risks for the license if the production or the sale of the product falls short of expectations or if it is disproportional to the economic value of the performance of the licensee.

(2) Royalties

Royalties are post-calculated, recurring payments, the amount of which is determined as a function of economic use or result. In order to establish this functional relationship between the recurring amounts and the economic use or result, the provision may refer to the value of production, to the sales prices of the product that is manufactured incorporating the technology or to the profits of the license.

Royalties are paid at regular intervals, say every 3 months, 4 months or 6 months. When the licensee sends to the licensor a statement of royalty supported by the number and type of product sold, the gross invoice price and the net selling price and remits the royalty payment later on. An alternative is that the licensor, after he receives the statement, sends the licensee an invoice for the royalty due. Only after the licensee's receipt of the said invoice is the payment due. This follows the principle of commerce: payment against invoice only.

(3) Remuneration

In many cases, the remuneration for a license is a combination of a lump-sum payment and royalties. The lump-sum payment is often treated as an initial payment for disclosing information that enables the potential license to evaluate the technology. The licensor frequently views this payment as the initial remuneration for its basic research and development. The actual initial payment varies a great deal from transaction to transaction and may range from a small sum for the delivery of initial technical information to a very large amount for a sophisticated technology that has required much research and development. In some instances, the initial lump-sum payment may be viewed as a minimum payment or regarded as a down payment against royalties.

In negotiating remuneration in the form of a combined lump-sum payment and royalties, the licensee will need to evaluate carefully the total outflow and incidence of the payments that may be likely for various combinations. The burden of interest charges, for example, is important in determining the size of the lump-sum figure. In the meantime, projections of production estimates and cash flow from sales during the period of the license are essential in assessing the percentage rate of royalties.

3. Delivery of Documentation

Documentation, training and technical assistance are three separate yet related aspects in the process of transferring technology through licensing. Without them, the technology may not be transferred.

Documentation means the instructions, drawings, computer software, and so on, which are necessary for the transfer. In license contracts, the following provisions concerning the scope, form and other aspects of documentation are often found:

(1) Scope of Documentation

Documentation for the manufacture of the products includes but not limited to: drawings, blueprints and designs for manufacture and assembly; technical specifications; material list; general calculation sheet; procedures and data for inspections, trials and quality control procedures; manufacturing and assembly procedures; operating and maintenance manuals; flowcharts and formulae and other documentation as appropriate.

The list of documents given above is obviously not complete. Most license contracts add some other items. However, as the licensee, we should be cautious about removing any item or items from the list, for if litigation is raised about a certain missing item later on, we will be thrown into a very disadvantageous position.

(2) Requirements of Documents

It should be stated clearly that the documentation should be complete, correct and readable. It allows the licensor no excuses for missing pages, bad translation and so on. Documentation must be in a language that the licensee understands and English is often the chosen language. Not only the texts but also the drawings and blueprints should be standardized, preferably the metric system for Chinese businessmen. It is advisable not to convert measurements from one system to another: mistakes easily occur and figures become inexact. Such mistakes can be very costly. It is the licensor's duty to provide usable documentation.

Any defects in documentation are to be remedied without delay, by modification, amplification, completion or any other appropriate means. Computer software that fails for any reason during the lifetime of the contract is to be replaced immediately by the licensor at no cost to the licensee. For most licensees, technology is frozen as soon as they sign the contract. In order to stay up to date, they need a clause to guarantee that they can receive the newest information concerning the technology transferred from the licensor. Since the most basic principle of technology transfer is that the licensee acquires full manufacturing know-how, it is justifiable to include a clause in the contract which says: upon delivery, all documentation delivered to the licensee in connection with this contract becomes the property of the licensee.

4. Training Program

This simply means that the licensor agrees to train the licensee's personnel in all the techniques necessary to manufacture the products, that is, at the end of the training period, the licensee's people should be able to manufacture the products without further assistance from the licensor. Otherwise, the licensee has not acquired the technology.

With XXX days the coming into force of the contract, the parties shall agree on all elements for the training program such as the place and time, training curriculum, testing procedures, training language expenses, and etc.

It is usual for the parties to agree on a training program when they negotiate the contract. It is only a general outline. The details are to be clarified later, such as:

(1) Replacement of Trainers

No agreed trainer may be replaced by another trainer without the express written consent of the licensee. It protects the licensee against the danger of getting an unqualified trainer, not the one agreed upon between both sides.

(2) Language of Training

The language of training should be the language which the trainers and the trainees can understand. The trainers and the trainees should have a common language to work in. And all training manuals and other aids should be written in the agreed training language.

(3) Cost of Training

There should be a clause which suggests a specific hourly rate for training, which includes all the trainers' overheads: training material, preparation time, and etc. By paying for the training against invoice, the licensee has direct control over the cost; he can keep the cash in his pocket as long as possible; if the training is not successful, he still retains part of the bargaining power.

(4) Expenses for Trainees

Travel, living expenses and all other expenses for the trainees are to be borne by the licensee. If the licensor sends trainer outside licensor's country, travel and living expenses for such trainer are to be borne by the licensee.

(5) Completion of Training

At the end of the training period, the licensor and the licensee or their representatives are to administer the agreed tests. If the agreed percentage of the trainees meets the criteria, then the licensor and the licensee are jointly to issue a Certificate of the Completion of Training when the training is completed. The certificate ensures the licensee that training is successful and relieves the licensor of further responsibility of training.

(6) Failure to Complete Training

In case too many trainees fail the training, it is difficult to decide who is at fault, the teachers or the students. Since the objective for the licensee is to obtain the technology, it should have the right to ask for additional training for nothing. In case of additional training, the costs should be shared by both parties. Each party can bear its own cost or they can agree upon some other ways to split the costs.

5. Technical Assistance

Technical assistance is necessary to ensure the successful transfer of technology. Normally it takes place in three stages of a project:

(1) Before Start-up of Production

Project planning and design; project implementation; efficiency and environmental protection.

(2) During Start-up

The licensor makes qualified technicians available in the licensee's factory to advise, guide, help and assist the licensee to ensure the manufacture of the products.

(3) During Routine Production

At the request of the licensee, the licensor provides immediate technical assistance at any time during the life of the contract by telephone, by mail, by sending qualified technicians to the place of manufacture, and etc.

Section IV   Practical Activities

1. Case Study

● Case Study 1

Wendt(W) represents a French Textile company and Jiang(J) represents a Chinese Textile Import and Export company. Study their negotiation dialogue.

The Technology Would Soon Be out of Date

J: Yesterday we talked about the general idea of the documents of our joint venture. It is high time for us to discuss the details of technology transfer thoroughly.

W: Oh, yes, I'm just coming to that point. If you want to produce the competitive products which successfully meet the need of the international markets, you have to acquire advanced technology.

J: You are extremely right. The technology you are going to introduce to our new project should be advanced and appropriate to China's needs.

W: We promise that we transfer the advanced technology — what we are adopting in our production at the present. As a result, you'll pay for it in the form of royalties, except for a certain initial down payment. Am I right concerning that?

J: You are partly right and partly wrong.

W: Why?

J: Of course, we will pay for the imported technology. But you can't expect to labor for something that holds good for all time. If you transfer only the existing know-how, this company's technology would soon be out of date.

W: Then what kind of solution to this question can you think of?

J: My solution is simple. That is during the 20 years of our cooperation we hope you keep on renewing your know-how in other words, you continue offering us your improved technological expertise. I suppose we should not be requested to pay extra money for that.

W: Oh, no, that is too much. We can't promise that. You certainly understand that technology has a price tag. Your proposal is as different as chalk from cheese from ours. Such an unreasonable clause would drive our business to dead end.

J: Well, Mr. Wendt, we consider you as the partner of our company. Your share is 46% of the registered capital of the company, which means you will get almost half of the profit.

W: I should say what you've mentioned just now is correct, but I still want to make it clear that technology itself can produce new value. It makes sense that we ask for payment in some way for our technology.

J: No, no, Mr. Wendt, as you know, there is a famous saying "you can't eat your cake and have it too". If I were you, I would introduce the up-to-date technology to our project without considering to charge any extra dollars.

W: OK, let's hold back our discussion for the moment. We agree that we will share developments and costs fairly.

J: Super! Thank you so much.

● Case Study 2

An Australian business man Mr. Welch (W) talks with Ms. Lin (L), a Chinese manager, at transferring the skill of making jiao zi.

W: Well, Ms. Lin, your jiao zi is so good that it is one of my favorite food.

L: If you stayed here in China, you could have jiao zi everyday!

W: Well, that's fine. However, I wonder if it is possible for me to join your company. I mean you call have a branch in Australia. I want to introduce this food to people in Australia.

L: Are you serious?

W: Definitely.

L: You Australians have quite a high level of skills in food processing and cooking. If you get the skill you could make it yourself.

W: What do you mean? Are you suggesting you transfer the skill rather than let me join your company?

L: Exactly. It is easier and more convenient for us.

W: Then what kind of transfer would you suggest? What I say is that the right to manufacture does not include the skill required to produce it correctly. So could you make it specific?

L: Sure. How about my selling you the brand? I mean you name yours after mine, which is Lu Bian Jiao Zi.

W: Yes, and ...

L: And this means I'll provide you with the full information about the making of Lu Bian Jiao Zi.

W: It sounds good, but even so, we may still have difficulties in making Lu Bian Jiao Zi. Say, the taste may not be the same as that of yours, and it'll certainly spoil my fame and reduce the sale.

L: You are right. To solve it, we'll send some specialists to your country to train your cooks and managing personnel, or if you like, you send your people here to receive all these trainings. You could choose whichever way you like.

W: Thank you. So buying your brand and technique suits us better. I'll consider it.

L: Right, I'll draw a specimen of our agreement for today's discussion in detail.

W: Thank you. I'll study it. Shall we meet again sometime next week to discuss the details and other issues?

L: Yes. How about next Wednesday morning at 9:00?

W: Fine.

2. Role Play

In this dialogue，Mr. Smith（S）is explaining to Mr. Zhang（Z）the difference between the right to use the invention and the purchase of the relative know-how.

S： Mr. Zhang, we can get down to business now.

Z： Yes，certainly. We are interested in your offer to sell know-how of oven-manufacturing.

S： I'm glad to hear that. And what conclusion have you reached?

Z： This type of cooperation suits us perfectly. But before we give our final reply，I still have some questions.

S： I'm at your service，Mr. Zhang.

Z： Would you please distinguish the right to use the invention from the purchase of the relative know-how?

S： The difference is that at present time it's not enough to buy only the right to manufacture，when know-how licenses go to licenses completely with the so-called production secrets.

Z： I see. Thank you for the clarification.

3. Mini Negotiation

A： We'd like to buy your know-how.

B： What kind of know-how?

A： Software.

B： So you also know that buying know-how is better than buying the right to use the patent.

A： The know-how tells one all the details of how to manufacture and develop the software and technical level.

B： But it's far more expensive than the right to use the patent.

A： Then how much will you ask for?

B： Four times the price for the patent.

A： I'm afraid your price is much higher than I expected. I'll consult my home office and talk with you later.

Negotiation Tips

● Beware of Insignificant Concession　当心微小的让步

Great negotiators can take you to the cleaners by constantly asking for small concessions.

Always wait until you have the whole story before agreeing to a small concession.

- ● Be Good at Asking Questions 善于提问

Open ended "why" questions are best for obtaining information on interests. "Dumb" questions keep the other side off guard and usually lead the other side to help you rather than compete with you in the negotiation. Questions can also be used as a non-confrontational way of making a point. A question may even lead the other side to adopt your unexpressed point of view as their own.

- ● Don't Argue 不要争论

Arguing or expressing outright disagreement creates confrontational negotiation. Never say "I disagree with you" — it's often perceives as insulting to the other person. Look for an aspect of the other's statement that you do agree with, state that you agree on that aspect, and expand on that aspect with additional facts that support your interests.

Extended Activities

Ⅰ. Situational Group Talks.

Student A plays the role of a manage of a Chinese company who intends to buy some know-how from a British company. Student B plays the role of the British businessman.

Ⅱ. Multiple Choices.

Directions: There are ten incomplete sentences in this part. For each sentence there are four choices marked A, B, C, and D. Choose the one that best completes the sentence.

1. We find your terms _____ and now send you our order for 2 sets of generators.
   A. satisfied
   B. satisfaction
   C. satisfactory
   D. of satisfaction

2. We have _____ at 30 days' sight for the amount of the invoice.
   A. written to you
   B. called on you
   C. sent to you by air
   D. drawn on you

3. We regret _____ to accept your terms of payment and therefore have to return the order to you.
   A. cannot
   B. being unable
   C. us inability
   D. not able

4. We will consider _____ your D / P terms for this transaction.
   A. accepted
   B. be accept
   C. accepting
   D. accept

5. _____ an order for one hundred or more we allow a special discount of 3% for payment by L / C.
   A. At
   B. In

C. On　　　　　　　　　　　　　D. From

6. We would like to make _____ that we would accept 30 days D / P terms for your present order.

　　A. clear　　　　　　　　　　　B. it is clear

　　C. that clear　　　　　　　　　D. it clear

7. A 5% discount will be granted only _____ your order exceeds U.S. $15, 000.

　　A. depends on　　　　　　　　B. for condition that

　　C. on condition that　　　　　D. subject to

8. An exporter cannot receive payment until the goods on consignment _____ sometime in the future.

　　A. have offered for sale　　　B. are quoted

　　C. arrive at destination　　　D. have been sold

9. In view of the small amount of this transaction, we have decided _____ your D / P payment terms.

　　A. accept　　　　　　　　　　B. to accept

　　C. acceptable　　　　　　　　D. accepted

10. Your payment proposal for the order is quite _____ us.

　　A. satisfactory to　　　　　　B. satisfied with

　　C. satisfy　　　　　　　　　　D. of satisfaction

Ⅲ. Read the following statements and fill in the blanks.

1. To separate the technical part of the contract from the legal part, it is always advisable to put all the technical details in an _____.

2. The licensees are naturally afraid of purchasing out-dated or _____ technologies.

3. Royalties are paid at _____ intervals, say every 3 months, 4 months or 6 months.

4. The lump-sum payment is often treated as an initial payment for disclosing information that enables the potential license to _____ the technology.

5. Royalties are post-calculated, recurring payments, the amount of which is _____ as a function of economic use or result.

Ⅳ. Decide whether the following statements are true(T) or false(F).

1. The know-how is to confirm in all respects to the specifications of output, efficiency and emission of pollutants in Annex A.

2. Payment for the licensed technology can only take one form.

3. Lump-sum payment is often made for the outright acquisition of license, where the technology can not be transferred all at once and the licensee can readily and fully absorb it.

4. Only after the licensee's receipt of the said invoice is the payment due.

5. In many cases, the remuneration for a license is a combination of a lump-sum payment and royalties.

Ⅴ. Translate the following sentences into Chinese.

1. We'd like to transfer the right to use the patent in form of license.

2. I think you shall ensure that the technology provided is complete, correct and effective.

3. We hope you can explain know-how, its instructions and other technical data of the technology provided.

4. You shall undertake the obligation to keep the technical secrets confidential.

5. We expect that you may make some improvements and feed them back to us.

Chapter 12

International Business Contract Negotiation

Learning Goals

> Upon completion of this chapter, you will be able to:
> ☞ understand concepts of business contract;
> ☞ grasp types of business contract;
> ☞ master terms of business contract;
> ☞ draft and sign business contract;
> ☞ implement business contract;
> ☞ settle contract disputes.

Lead-in Words

define *v*. 明确	lease *n*. 契约
impose *v*. 强加	credit *n*. 信誉
arbitration *n*. 仲裁，调解	loom *v*. 悬，浮，游荡
peek *v*. 细看，窥视	consent *v*. 认同
horizon *n*. 地平线	binding *adj*. 有约束力的
rescind *v*. 废除，取消	remedial *adj*. 补救的
discord *n*. 混乱	inherent *adj*. 固有的
receipt *n*. 收据	

Section I An Introduction to International Business Contract

Before we go to the International Business Contract negotiation, we need to learn something about the factors involved: the required terms and structure, culture issues, matters affecting drafting, signing and enforcing a contract, how to make stipulations on transferring, altering, rescinding and terminating a contract and how to resolve disputes.

1. Concepts of Business Contract

A contract, in the broadest sense, is simply an agreement that defines a relationship between one or more parties. A business contract, in simplest terms, is just an agreement made by two or more parties for the purpose of transacting business. A contract may be oral or written, formal or informal. The contract which is generally adopted in import and export business is the formal written contract. Written terms may be recorded in a simple memorandum, certificate, or receipt. Because a contractual relationship is made between two or more parties who have potentially adverse interests, the contract terms are usually supplemented and restricted by laws that serve to protect the parties and to define specific relationships between them in the event that provisions are indefinite, ambiguous, or even missing.

When one party enters into a business contract with an unfamiliar and distant party across a country border, a contract takes on added significance. The creation of an international contract is a more complex process than the formation of a contract between parties from the same country and culture. In a cross-border transaction, the parties usually do not meet face-to-face, they have different social values and practices, and the laws to which they are subject are imposed by different governments with distinct legal systems. These factors can easily lead to misunderstanding, and therefore the contracting parties should define their mutual understanding in contractual and preferably written terms.

2. Types of Business Contract

As the international trade develops, more and more business contracts are involved in business negotiation. The most common ones are:

+ Sales Contract;
+ Purchase Contract;
+ Joint Venture Contract;
+ Contract for Cooperation;
+ Contract for Business of Processing (Party B's) Material into Finished Products;
+ Agreement on Compensation Trade;
+ Lease Contract (Agreement);
+ Service Contract (Contract for Foreign Labor Service; Contract for Employment);
+ Contract for Work;
+ Contract for Technology Transfer and Importation of Equipment and Materials;
+ International Loan Agreement;
+ International Tender and Bid;
+ License Contract;
+ Agency Contracts (General Agency Agreement; Agency Agreement; Sole Agency

Agreement).

3. Terms of Business Contract

If the contract does not provide the terms that are necessary to complete the transaction, in some jurisdictions the contract will not be enforceable. In others, the courts will imply terms into the contract, terms that may or may not have been intended. Therefore, always review the contract to see if it includes the required terms.

A business contract shall, in general, include the following terms:

- ✦ The corporate or personal names of the contracting parties and their nationalities and principal places of business or domicile;
- ✦ The date and place of the signing of the contract;
- ✦ The type of contract and the kind and scope of the object of the contract;
- ✦ The technical condition, quality, standard, specifications and quantity of the object of the contract;
- ✦ The time limit, place and method of performance;
- ✦ The price, amount and method of payment, and various incidental charges;
- ✦ Whether the contract is assignable and if it is, the condition for its assignment;
- ✦ Liabilities to pay compensation and other liabilities for breach of contract;
- ✦ The ways for settling contract dispute;
- ✦ The language(s) in which the contract is to be written and its validity.

Section II　Procedures of Business Contract Negotiation

1. Drafting and Signing of Business Contract

One may not be able to create the perfect contract, but nevertheless draft the contract provisions as clearly as possible. The more definitive the terms, the fewer the disputes. Use very precise language. Look for the weak links. Ask, "If something will go wrong, where will it go wrong?" And remember, when things do go wrong, correct the contract provisions to avoid the same mistake in the next transaction.

One should review one's contract from the point of view of the other party: What weakness in position might the other party find advantageous? And then, from one's own point of view: Are the contract requirements for performance and enforcement feasible, sufficient, and efficient?

In drafting international contracts, it is extremely wise to go through each contract provision with each party and expressly ask them to indicate their comprehension, such as: "Do you understand that you are assuming the responsibility for packing these goods according to our shipper's instructions?" If one is concerned that misunderstanding over performance is likely, one may want to have each party initial all or some paragraphs, and it is common practice to have each party initial every page. Some multinational contracts have every paragraph initialed after the parties have spent weeks negotiating the contract through interpreters.

Contracts that involve capital goods, high credit risks, or industrial or intellectual property rights will require special protective clauses. In preparing such contracts, it is essential to obtain legal advice from a professional who is familiar with the laws and practices of both countries.

Before signing a contract, one may have not even read it all the way through from beginning to end. Maybe one has just peeked inside at a few provisions, in particular the payment clauses. Does it state the intentions? Does it cover all of the basics? Does it cover all of the extras? And the most important question looms on the horizon: should one sign the contract?

It is best to review and understand every term before signing. It is wise to read the contract several times, keeping in mind different concerns each time to be certain that the contract states the entire agreement. First read it to become familiar with organization of the provisions. The next review should include a comparison with the terms that have already been negotiated and with which there is an oral agreement. On the third review, consider whether the contract defines every aspect of the relationship that is intended in terms of the practices in the industry and in one's own particular business. Finally, always be certain that the legal and business issues common to all international contracts have been covered.

2. Implementation of Business Contract

A contract becomes legally binding when both parties have put their signatures to it. The parties must perform the agreed obligations of the contract, and neither party may alter or rescind the contract without the other party's consent.

When one party has actual evidence that the other party cannot perform the contract, it may temporarily suspend performance of the contract, but must immediately inform the other party. When the other party provides a full guarantee of performance of the contract, the first party must perform the contract. When one party, without having actual evidence that the other party cannot perform the contract, suspends performance of the contract, it must bear liability for breach of contract.

When one party does not perform the contract or its performance of the contractual obligations doe not comply with the agreed conditions, it is in breach of contract, and the other party has the right to demand compensation for losses or adoption of other reasonable remedial measures.

In the context of enforcement, the balance of power can work against the stronger party in a contract negotiation. Courts and arbitrators often refuse to enforce terms that unreasonably burden one party or that are otherwise unconscionable.

Because of the problem with enforcement, parties to cross-border transactions should avoid taking unfair advantage. A contract that is in accord with fair business practices will encourage both parties to perform their obligations, and therefore the need for enforcement — and the need to outlay the costs attendant to enforcement — may be avoided.

3. Contract Dispute Settlement

Parties who enter into a contract are in effect putting aside their adverse interests and joining in a transaction for their mutual benefit. If that benefit is reduced or eliminated for either or both parties, dispute is inevitable. Although the majority of contracts are completed without any, or at most minor, disagreements, advance planning for dispute resolution is essential because the parties are most unlikely to come to an agreement on this issue after they have fallen into discord.

In an international contract, the methods of dispute resolution selected will depend on what is most familiar to and preferred by the nationals of the country where the transaction takes place. In addition, parties must consider the costs involved in cross-border contract enforcement, the delay inherent in obtaining certain types of relief, and the extent to which available mechanisms have developed into efficient means of dispute resolution. Americans are quick to resort to court actions, while Chinese and Japanese nationals are loath to do so. Binding arbitration is favored in some countries, while others prefer informal negotiation and conciliation. One must know the options and their usefulness in the country where business is done.

Communication between one and the foreign business partner is essential to keeping the relationship smooth. For minor discrepancies, or even major calamities, the business relationships and reputation will benefit if one approaches the problem with understanding and a view toward resolving it such that everyone will be satisfied. A good rule to remember: create a working relationship with the foreign business parties, not an adversarial one.

Negotiation, followed by written confirmation of any waiver or modified contract team, is the most effective means of resolution in terms of cost and time. It is generally an informal, unstructured process, subject only to the limitations imposed by parties themselves. Its success depends on the desire of both parties to participate and settle their differences.

The very characteristics that make negotiation advantageous — lack of structure, formality, and neutral assistance — can also contribute to its failure if parties are unable to communicate without formal procedures. If a dispute continues despite informal attempts to resolve it, one should take steps to protect one's rights. The most imminent concern will probably be to recover one's own property quickly or to find an immediate replacement supplier so that one can honor commitments to third parties.

Section III　Practical Activities

1. Case Study

● Case Study 1

> *Mr. Liu(L) represents a Chinese fruit import and export company while Mr. Allen (A) represents American fruit export company. They are talking about signing a contract.*

Signing a Contract

A: Good morning, Mr. Liu. Here is our contract. Please go through it and see if everything is in order.

L: Let me read it over and consider it. Don't you think we should insert this sentence here? That is, if one side fails to observe the contract, the other side is entitled to cancel it, and the loss for this reason should be charged by the side breaking the contract.

A: That's good. I think all the terms should meet with unanimous agreement. Do you have any comment to make on this clause?

L: I think this clause suits us well, but the time of payment should be prolonged, to say, two or three months.

A: We are accustomed to payment within one month, but for the sake of friendship, let's fix it at two months.

L: No wonder everyone speaks highly of your commercial integrity.

A: One of our principles is that contracts are honored and commercial integrity is maintained. Anything else you want to bring up for discussion?

L: There's still a minor point to be cleared up. Whom will this commodity inspection be conducted by?

A: The first inspection should be carried out by New York Administration for Quality Supervision and Inspection and Quarantine, whose decision is the final basis and binding on both sides. The reinspection should be carried out by Changsha Administration for Quality Supervision and Inspection and Quarantine, whose decision is the basis for the buyers to a lodge claim.

L: It contains basically all we have agreed upon during our negotiations. I have no questions about the terms.

A: Other terms and conditions shall be subject to those specified in the formal S / C signed by both parties.

L： Mr. Allen, your terms and conditions can be accepted. Then, when shall we sign the contract?

A： Would 9:00 tomorrow morning be all right for you?

L： That's OK. See you tomorrow.

A： See you tomorrow morning.

● Case Study 2

Mr. Smith (S) is discussing with Mr. Liu (L) the problems of materials to be purchased, marketing of the products and the balance of foreign exchange.

Negotiating a Purchase Deal

S： Mr. Liu, we need to discuss the problem of marketing with you today.

L： Oh, this is really an important issue.

S： What do you think are the specific kinds of shoes to be produced?

L： Mainly ladies' leatherwear of the latest designs of great popularity.

S： What do you estimate will be the annual volume of production after the venture gets into operation?

L： It will be somewhere around 5 million pairs.

S： In your opinion, what would be our primary markets?

L： The products should be mainly for export. Our government encourages joint ventures to sell their products outside China. That's because a joint venture is expected to balance its own foreign exchange receipts and payments.

S： But according to our market research, China is a huge potential market. Because of their superior quality and fashionable design, we're sure our leather shoes will enjoy great popularity in China.

L： There's something in what you said. But the balance of foreign exchange will be a great headache for us. You know, some of the raw materials will have to be imported. Moreover, you need to remit your legitimate profits abroad in U. S. dollars or pound sterling. You certainly don't want to remit your profits back in RMB, do you?

S： Of course not. Perhaps through our sales agents we could sell 30% of our products in North America and Europe.

L： I'm afraid 30% is not enough. Although we can find some substitute things in China for imported raw materials, I don't think that would be enough to ensure a favorable foreign exchange balance, not to say your profits.

S： What do you have in mind then?

L： We suggest that 50% be sold internationally. When we can balance our foreign exchange revenues with expenses, we can then consider enlarging the sale on the

Chinese market.

S: Well, as the situation stands now, we can promise 40% at most at the moment. Perhaps in the future we can agree to more.

L: OK, we'll consider this settled.

S: How will the price be fixed?

L: We suggest that for products sold in China, the price will be set by us. As for what's sold on the international market, the price will be set according to the international market price.

S: But we propose that the price should be fixed by mutual agreement no matter whether the products are sold in China or on the international market because we are co-producers and should make decisions together.

L: All right. We agree the price will be fixed through negotiation.

S: It seems that we have covered almost all the major points. Is there anything else that needs to be discussed?

L: Yes, one more thing. What about the trade marks and the packing of the products?

S: As we have mentioned, our investment will be, partly, in the form of equipment and the use of our patent rights. So the products will use our trade marks. As for packing, those sold in North America and Europe can use our packing while those sold in China can either use our packing or have a new packing designed for the Chinese market.

L: Good. We shall first put this to the test of the market before making any final decision.

S: I'm very pleased that we have reached an agreement on all the major points. If everything goes as planned, I've no doubt our cooperation will be very fruitful.

L: Yes. We firmly believe that our cooperation on this project will be good for both of us.

2. Role Play

A: We need to discuss three issues today, that is, the sale of our products, the purchase of the needed materials and the balance of the foreign exchange. Let's begin with the sale of the products. In your opinion, what are our primary markets?

B: We believe China is a large potential market. With our advanced technology, we are sure that our products will be very competitive on the Chinese market.

A: Your remarks make good sense. But the problem is that we have to import part of our raw materials and pay foreign employees in foreign currencies. Besides, you also need to remit your legitimate profits back home in foreign exchange. We think the only way to balance the receipts and payments in foreign exchange of the joint venture is to sell our products on the international market.

B: Balance of foreign exchange is indeed a problem. May I suggest 60% of the products of the joint venture be sold on the Chinese market and the remaining 40% be sold on oversees markets?

A: To ensure the balance of foreign exchange and your share of the profits, we think at least 50% should be sold on the international market, and you should be responsible for the sale of the products abroad.

B: Well, it seems that to ensure the foreign exchange balance, we have to accept this. What about the purchase of needed materials?

A: In purchasing required raw materials, parts, means of transportation and articles for office use, the joint venture should give priority to local supply in China if conditions are the same.

B: That's reasonable we agree.

A: In case the joint venture is unable to find substitutes in China and must make purchase in overseas markets, we think a representative appointed by us should be invited to take part in purchasing what's needed.

B: We have no objection to that.

A: I'm very glad that we've reached agreement on all the major points. We'll draft the contract according to the results of our talks and we'll have a copy sent to you for you to go through after we have done it.

B: That's great! Thank you very much.

3. Mini Negotiation

A: This is the first time we have met and I feel very pleased, Mr. Zhu.

B: The same with me, Mr. Black.

A: I'm sure your visit will contribute a lot to the setting of the payment problem that concerns both of us.

B: Yes. I'm willing to cooperate with you to the maximum.

A: Then, have you got any specific proposal?

B: I wonder if we can make payment for this order by documentary collection.

A: I'm sorry to say the only term of payment we can accept is 100% irrevocable letter of credit payable against shipping documents.

B: But our order this time is very large. To open an L / C for such a large amount at a bank is costly. Can you be a bit more flexible and bend the rule a little?

A: I'm afraid not. We insist on a letter of credit, because as seller, we also have the problem of funds being tied up.

B: To be frank, a letter of credit would increase the cost of my import. When I open a letter of credit with a bank, I have to pay a deposit. That'll tie up my money and add to my cost.

A: My suggestion is to consult your bank and see if they will reduce the required deposit to a minimum.

Negotiation Tips

● Negotiation Involves Bargaining 谈判需要讨价还价

Bargaining is competitive; negotiating is co-operative. Bargaining focuses on whom is right; negotiating focuses on what is right. Negotiating creates long-term deals and relationships. Bargaining agreements never last because the losing party always insists on the chance to come back and get even.

● Negotiation Always Involves Compromise 谈判总是需要妥协

Nobody wins in compromise because both sides end up getting less than they want or need.

● Establishing Good Relationship 建立融洽的关系

Most CEOs focus on price, terms and conditions because that's what they know best. Plus, those areas are easy to quantify. But the key to most negotiations is building communication, relationship and trust because those elements most often determine the outcome. People have a pressure and a need to tell you what they want. If you don't hear them out, you won't understand their point that your company can't meet their needs. If they don't feel that your company can meet their needs, they will give the business to someone who will.

Extended Activities

Ⅰ. Situational Group Talks.

Student A plays the role of Mr. Zhu while Student B plays the role of Mr. Black. Continue the talk on payments.

Ⅱ. Multiple Choices.

Directions: There are ten incomplete sentences in this part. For each sentence there are four choices marked A, B, C, and D. Choose the one that best completes the sentence.

1. Everyone in this trade knows that China's bristles are superior _____ quality _____ those from other countries.

   A. in, with   B. in, to   C. on, for   D. of, than

2. We specialize _____ all kinds of metals and are always ready to buy in large quantities.

   A. at   B. from   C. on   D. in

3. We will see to it that the L / C _____ within the stipulated time.

   A. should be opened   B. must be opened

   C. is opened   D. will be opened

4. Your claim for shortage of weight _____ U.S. $1,000 in all.

   A. accounts to   B. amounts to   C. is accounted to   D. is amounted to

5. The two sides failed to _____ an agreement owing to their big difference in the price of the deal.

A. include   B. have   C. result   D. reach

6. We ask you to compare our prices with _____ of other houses; we are confident that you will appreciate the exceptional values we offer.

 A. that   B. this   C. these   D. those

7. For the time being, we cannot commit _____ any fresh orders.

 A. ourselves to B. us to   C. ourselves with D. us with

8. You don't have to worry about the time of delivery because we can supply this item _____ .

 A. with stock B. in stock   C. from stock   D. in stock

9. All orders by post will receive our best attention and, whenever possible, will be _____ on the day of receipt.

 A. booked   B. placed   C. expedited   D. given

10. It _____ if you _____ the L / C fro another 15 days.

 A. is appreciated, extended   B. will be appreciated, could extend

 C. shall be appreciated, could extend D. should be appreciated, can extend

Ⅲ. Read the following statements and fill in the blanks.

1. The contract which is generally _____ in import and export business is the formal written contract.

2. A contract, in the broadest sense, is simply an agreement that _____ a relationship between one or more parties.

3. When one party enters into a business contract with an unfamiliar and distant party across a country border, a contract _____ on added significance.

4. Binding _____ is favored in some countries, while others prefer informal negotiation and conciliation.

Ⅳ. Decide whether the following statements are true(T) or false(F).

1. These factors can easily lead to misunderstanding, and therefore the contracting parties should define their mutual understanding in contractual, and preferably written terms.

2. If the contract does not provide the terms that are necessary to complete the transaction, in some jurisdictions the contract will not be enforceable.

3. The more definitive the terms, the more the disputes.

4. A contract becomes legally binding when both parties have put their signatures to it.

Ⅴ. Translate the following sentences into Chinese.

1. We promise to give more commission if you order bigger quantity.

2. It doesn't conform to international trade practice not to allow a commission.

3. To compete with business from these firmly established competitors, a strong sales drive and various advertising should be stepped up.

4. Could we have some subsidy for sales promotion?

5. To help your products enter into a new market, I think the best way of doing it is to find a sales agent in this district.

Intercultural Awareness in
Business Activities

Part

4

Intercultural Business Negotiation & Communication

Chapter 13

Intercultural Awareness in Business Activities

Learning Goals

Upon completion of this chapter, you will be able to:
- ☞ learn about the culture influence;
- ☞ recognize relevant cultural factors;
- ☞ identify different business culture types;
- ☞ understand the culture and business etiquette.

Lead-in Words

compliment *n.* 赞扬	taboo *n.* 禁忌
etiquette *n.* 礼仪	intercultural *adj.* 跨文化的
diversified *adj.* 多样化的	tactically *adv.* 策略地
concrete *adj.* 具体的	implement *v.* 履行,实施
oriental *adj.* 东方的	occidental *adj.* 西方的
masculinity *n.* 男性化	manifest *v. adj.* 显然,展示;显而易见的
protocol *n.* 草案,协议	femininity *n.* 女性化

Section I   Impact of Culture Differences

Nowadays, the world economy tends to be more and more global. Organizations, especially those multinational corporations, are culturally diversified in the formation of their staff members and in handling all kinds of business activities. This culturally diversified workforce has brought greater vitality to the business, but at the same time, business people are facing many problems in their cross-cultural business communication. International business negotiations take place across national boundaries, which means understanding the different cultural environments among nations and considering cultural differences in all respects of business are very important to the operation of international business negotiations. Now more and more business people have become aware of the strong impact from culture and come to realize the significance of cross-cultural business communication.

1. Cultural Influences

An ancient Chinese philosopher points out that human being is identical in nature but different in customs and habits. Because of interconnection of human nature, it is less difficult to comprehend human being as a whole, however it is truly a great challenge to understand people better from every culture. Every person is a product of a particular culture, learning the "right way" of doing things, as a result, everyone bears strong identification and marks of his own culture. This inherently limits one's understanding of foreign cultures. When two people from the same country are negotiating, it is possible to expedite communications by making cultural assumptions. The situation is reversed when two different cultures are involved. Most people, unconsciously, use their own habitual cultural lenses as a guide for judging the actions, views, customs, or manners of others. We may often condemn someone because his or her views do not coincide with ours and fail to see the fact that our words and actions may also be misunderstood in the same way.

Some cultural influences are difficult to predict. For example, an American businessman once presented a clock to the daughter of his Chinese counterpart on the occasion of her marriage, not knowing that clocks are inappropriate gifts in China, which are associated with death in Chinese culture. This led to the termination of the business relationship.

Culture not only affects the range of strategies that negotiators develop but also the many ways they are tactically implemented. For example, the difference between the Israeli preference for direct forms of communication and the Egyptian preference for indirect forms exacerbate relations between the two countries. The Egyptians interpret Israeli directness as aggression and insulting; the Israelis view Egyptian indirectness with impatience and consider it insincere.

Therefore, cultural difference should be regarded as a challenge rather than a problem, which may mean a little more investment of time and funds, but it is more likely to produce international workable teams, systems and products. It can also help cultivate the deep awareness of international markets.

2. Relevant Cultural Factors

As whatever the technology and whatever the benefits of a particular product, all business deals are made by people, and understanding cultural differences affects almost every part of the negotiating process, in terms of international business negotiations, what are the concrete cultural factors in play?

The issues to be taken into consideration about cultural differences when entering into international business activities are social values, attitudes towards roles and status, ways for making decisions, cultural context, manners and customs, and etc.

(1) Social Values

Different nations have different views about social values. Social values are the standards by which a culture evaluates actions and consequences. They affect perceptions and can have a strong emotional impact upon people. In different cultures, social values may vary significantly. One's proper actions in one culture can be seen as wrong in a moral sense in another culture. For example, the Americans are goal-driven, i. e. they want to finish their work nice and quick. People who can do it this way are regarded as capable persons, otherwise, they will be considered as incapable or being low-efficient. But things are different in countries like Pakistan and India, where the rate of unemployment is rather high. Therefore, management there will think more about employment creation than about efficiency.

Thus, it is important to understand the prevailing values in a particular society and the extent to which they are respected in the everyday behavior of individuals. Values affect the willingness to take risks, the leadership style, the superior-subordinate relationships, and etc. This is true for the relationships between negotiators. Our discussion here will focus on values critical for understanding the economic performance of a society, more specifically, the values that deserve attention in order to develop intercultural communication skills.

(2) Attitudes towards Status

People's attitudes to status differ from culture to culture. The Occidental culture, generally speaking, ignores status, which is manifested by their way of addressing each other. Mr., Mrs., and Miss are applicable to people of all social status and levels, whereas in the Oriental culture, like China and Japan, people ale inclined to address each other according to their official titles, like "General Manager" or "Director". People appear to be quite formal and polite in negotiations while Westerners behave in a casual and informal way. They value easy-going, friendly, relaxed relationship. They dislike ceremony, tradition, or formal social gestures. They greet people with a firm handshake and look directly at them. They like to get on a first name basis as soon as possible. They consider formality and protocol to be pretentious obstacles to negotiations.

In the Oriental culture countries, due to high respect to status, business is half done if you may find someone working in the government section related directly with the project or the transaction. If there is no such relation, it is still worthwhile finding someone having indirect connection with government officials. In the Oriental cultures, relationship also consists of complicated social connections and interrelations like relatives, fellow countrymen, town men, schoolmates, comrade-in-arms and friends, a huge net of relations functioning in business world. Ignorance or neglect of the net will sometimes bring trouble, while accepting and making usc of the net will facilitate transactions — a fact that makes some, especially western, business people uneasy. In the western countries relationship seems to be secondary, which does not mean establishing a good relation is unnecessary, but rather it carries different connotation. A British manager once explained that a good relation requires correct attitude, respecting distance and being reasonable. In some Pacific-rim countries, extended social acquaintance and the establishment of appropriate personal relationship are essential to conducting business. It is necessary that one should know one's business partner on a personal base before transactions can occur. Therefore, rushing straight to business will not be rewarded, because deals are made on the basis of not only the best products or price but also the personal relationship or person deemed most trustworthy. Contracts may be bound on handshakes, or dinner tables.

(3) Ways of Making Decisions

Decision-making procedures differ from culture to culture. When faced with a complex negotiating task, people in different countries may use different approaches to make a decision. For example, business people from Latin America prefer to have more discussions before reach any agreement, while the Americans and Canadians like to make decision as quickly as possible, as they give great priority to the efficiency business. Besides, decision-makers in the United States and Canada are interested in reaching general agreements, with details left behind to be discussed by their subordinates. But countries like Greece are just the opposite — insist that details should be discussed before reaching any agreement.

As far as the decision-maker is concerned, countries like China and Japan prefer collective agreement, with a little difference between them — China practices the majority rule, while Japan asks for a complete agreement. But things are different in Western countries where the decision is often made by top person.

(4) Manners and Customs

Understanding manners and customs is especially important in negotiation. To negotiate effectively abroad, all types of communication should be read correctly. Americans often interpret inaction and silence as negative signs. As a result, Japanese executives tend to expect that their silence can get Americans to lower prices or accelerate a deal. In the Middle East even a simple agreement may take days to negotiate because the Arab party may want to talk about unrelated issues or do something else for a while. It is nothing surprising in Finland if a Finnish businessman proposed to continuing negotiations in the sauna or if a Japanese counterpart proposed a karaoke performance be in order.

Section II   Features and Context Orientation of
Main Streams of Cultures

Due to the difficulties to look into every culture and its impact on individual's behavior, the discussion will concentrate on the typical features of two main streams of cultures: the Oriental culture and the Occidental culture starting from two types of cultures connected with negotiation pattern.

1. Oriental Culture and Occidental Culture

The Oriental culture and the Occidental culture are the typical features of two main streams of cultures. In the Occidental culture, oneself consciousness is emphasized whereas in the Oriental culture where group consciousness is stressed. Loyalty to central authority and placing the good of a group before that of the individual is held valuable. The different focuses in the two types of cultures have even led to misunderstandings. In Western societies there has been a perception that the subordination of the individual to the common good has resulted in the sacrifice of human rights, however on the other hand it may explain the economic success of Japan and "the Four Tigers" of Singapore, South Korea, Hong Kong (China) and Taiwan (China).

A Dutch expert Gilt once conducted a research on self-consciousness of managers in selected countries from the major parts of the world and the result drawn indicates American values individualism most, which is manifested in their daily life and social activities, taking the example of the rewarding system in sport competition. If the price for the champion is $150, 000, then the person in the second place will get only half of the price the champion is rewarded. In contrast, in countries of strong collectivism, say in China, athletes winning the first place habitually announce that they owe their success to the country, the leader, the coach, their coworkers, their family and finally their own efforts. Different focuses on oneself or group bring about an impact on outcome of negotiations. When talking to people from Japan or Mexico, it is important to stress the benefit, the deal may bring to his company or his community or country, but the emphases will not work so well with a Canadian or an American.

2. Context Orientation in Major Cultures

There is a paired concept according to Anthropologist Edward T. Hall's theory, i.e. high-context and low-context culture which helps us better understand the powerful effect that culture has on negotiation. A key point in his theory is context relating to the framework, background, and surrounding circumstances in which communication or an event takes place.

High-context cultures are relational, collectivist, intuitive, and contemplative. People in these cultures lay emphasis on interpersonal relationships. Developing trust is the first and for most step to any business transaction. These cultures are characterized by collectivist, preferring group harmony and consensus to individual achievement. That means people in these cultures are less governed by reason than by intuition or feelings. High-context communication tends to be more indirect and more formal. Flowery languages, humility, and elaborate apologies are typical. People are more dependent on the non-verbal cues than on the verbal ones. Much of the Middle East, Asia, Africa, and South America belong to the high-context culture.

Low-context cultures, are logical, linear, individualistic, and action-oriented. People from low-context cultures value logic, facts, and directness. They pay more attention to what you say and prefer the verbal context to the circumstances of communication. They solve a problem lining up the facts and evaluating one after another. Decisions are on fact rather than intuition. Discussions lead to actions. Communicators are expected to be straightforward, concise, and efficient in telling what action is expected. These cultures are individualistic cultures, which are very different from communicators in high-context cultures who rely less on language precision or legal documents. High-context business people may even distrust contracts and be offended by the lack of trust they suggest. Canada, the United states, other countries of North America and much of Western belong to the low-context cultures.

3. Communication Style

Human beings are by nature people of society. They communicate with other people around by different means, basically languages. People longing for communication need access to conveying their ideas. The way through which people communicate, including verbal and non-verbal, directly affects international business negotiation. As partners may have different native languages, they need to use interpreters in negotiations. To guess the meaning of the other side's non-verbal behaviors, and to write contracts in a foreign language(at least foreign to one side). All these require smooth communications.

(1) Verbal Communication

Verbal communication, in accordance with cultural patterns, consists of two models: high-context model and low-context model.

In high-context model, such as China, Japan and Saudi Arabia, context is at least as important as what is actually said. The speaker and the listener rely on a common understanding of the context. Often what is not being said can carry more meaning than what is said. The speaker composes his messages in a way similar with telling a riddle, providing most of clues of a riddle, or leaving a gap between what is said and what is hidden and let the listener to make up the missing part.

In the low-context model, however, most of the information is contained explicitly in the words. Countries like U.S., Canada and UK engage in low-context communication. Unless one is aware of this basic difference, messages and intention can easily be misunderstood. For example, criticism is more direct and recorded formally in the United States, whereas in Japan it is more subtle and verbal. American prefers asking, "Frankly speaking, what is the bottom line?"

People from high context cultures would consider this way of speaking "arrogant", "superior" and "pressing". On the contrary, people from low context cultures regard "riddle-guessing" way of speaking is not reliable, cunning and insincere. They may say "The guy is slippery." He doesn't want to say "Yes" or "No". They expect people to "stop beating about the bush" and "get to the point".

(2) Non-verbal Communication

Language goes beyond the spoken word, encompassing non-verbal actions and behaviors that reveal hidden clues to culture. Non-verbal behavior may be defined as any behavior, intentional or unintentional, beyond the words themselves, which can be interpreted by a receiver as having meaning. Non-verbal communication is important in two aspects: ① helpful to decide the counterpart's intention, and ② helpful to convey one's own message. Non-verbal language practices differ greatly from country to country, and carry totally different messages. Three key topics — time, space, body language are dealt with.

✦ Time

Different cultures have different understanding of value of time. In some countries, such as Japan, the United States and Germany, people are so particular about time that even one minute is valuable. In "time is money" culture, idleness is wasteful and inefficient. Delay and avoidance are particularly irritating. However in many other parts of the world, time is flexible and not seen as a limited commodity; people come late to the appointment or may not come at all. In India, for example, a driver was asked to arrive at 2 o'clock to send a World Bank project mission to visit a water plant, the driver failed to make the appearance until 3:30. When asked to explain the reason for the delay, the driver declared that India was a democratic country and everyone was entitled to a good rest after meals. Values towards time and how they shape the way people structure their actions have a pervasive yet invisible influence on negotiations. Differences in punctuality, reflected in everyday business negotiation behavior, may probably appear as the most visible consequence. But differences in time orientations, especially toward the future, are more important as they affect long-range issues such as the strategic framework of decisions made when negotiating.

✦ Space

Space orientations differ across cultures. Space relates to comfort with personal distance. There are large differences in spatial preferences according to gender, age, generation, socioeconomic class, and context. These differences vary by group, but should be considered in any exploration of space as a variable in negotiations. A survey shows that Northern Europeans are quite reserved in using their hands and maintain a good amount of personal space, whereas southern Europeans involve their bodies to a far greater degree in making a point. The amount of space separating some people from others is one key element in non-verbal expression. Arabs and Latin Americans like to stand close to people when they talk. The space between them is about 1 foot, whereas the comfortable space between Americans is much larger, about 3 feet, and for Chinese 2 feet is the usual choice. If an American, who may not be comfortable at close space, backs away from an Arab, this might incorrectly be taken as a negative reaction.

For example, an American etiquette manual advises this about personal space: "When you meet someone, don't stand too close. An uncomfortable closeness is very annoying to the other person, so keep your physical distance, or he'll have to keep backing off from you. A minimum of two feet away from the other person will do it."

✦ Body Language

Every culture has a set of body language. Insights into non-verbal behavior will add to your negotiating strength. You learn to interpret what the other side is saying in addition to their words. At the same time you can become more aware of what your body language is saying to your opponent. Body language has a vocabulary and grammar of all its own. Likes and dislikes, tensions, and assessing an argument are shown by numerous signs such as blushing, contraction of facial muscles, giggling, strained laughter or simply silence.

Whenever a party negotiates, the negotiator must watch and observe the other party. People, when seated, lean forward if they like what you are saying or are interested in listening. Whenever a party negotiates, the negotiator must watch and observe the other party. People, when seated, lean forward if they like what you are saying or are interested in listening. They sit back with crossed arms if they do not like the message. Nervousness can manifest itself through non-verbal behavior, and blinking can be related to feelings of guilt or fear. For example, an American manager may, after successful completion of negotiations, impulsively give a finger-and-thumb OK sign. In southern France, the manager would have indicated that the sale was worthless and in Japan, that a little bribe had been requested, the gesture would be grossly insulting to Brazilians.

In negotiation, information is what you are pursuing. The best way to gain information is through communication. Clear communication using common-sense questioning and listening skills is your best way for eliciting information. However, you should learn more with your mouth closed and your ears open. Being a good listener is a better way to learn than being a good presenter. If there is effective communication, both parties' perceptions will likely be clearer. The clearer and more comprehensive your perception of what's at issue and what's going on, the more likely you will reach a wise agreement.

Section III   Cultural Pattern

Beliefs and behaviors differ between cultures because each develops its own means for explaining and coping with life. Due to the varieties and multifaceses of cultures, it is very conducive to study each individual cultural features and cultural patterns to better understand people's behavior in negotiations. The discussion focuses on the cultural patterns connected with negotiation patterns.

1. Individualism vs. Collectivism

In individualistic cultures, people tend to put tasks before relationship, see negotiations as a competition with a win / lose outcome, so it is important to be a winner. People in these cultures are expected to take care of themselves and to value the needs of the individual over those of the group, community, or society. People of strong individualism or self-centered people expect that one should pursue his interests in the first place. They assert their differences with others and take action when they feel others are unreasonably blocking him from reaching his goals.

Individualistic cultures prefer linear logic and tend to value open conflict. Members from individualistic societies expect the other side's negotiators to have the ability to make decisions unilaterally.

By contrast, cultures that value collectivism emphasize solidarity, loyalty, and strong interdependence among individuals. Relationships are based on mutual self-interest and are dependent on the success of the group. Collectivist cultures define themselves in terms of their membership within groups. Maintaining the integrity of groups is stressed so that cooperation, conflict avoidance, and conformity dominate the culture. Collectivist societies tend to stress abstract, general agreements over concrete, specific issues.

Collectivist negotiators tend to assume that details can be worked out if the negotiators can agree on generalities. Collectivist societies show more on group goals than do individualistic societies. Members of collectivist societies chafe when members from individualist societies promote their own positions and ideas during negotiations.

Negotiation decisions are usually made by the highest ranking executives. Because of this reason, American negotiators prefer talking with someone who has enough authority and can make decisions, an expectation often frustrated in face of negotiators from countries of strong group consciousness, because Americans find they have to persuade the whole group instead of just one or two adversaries.

Negotiators from countries of strong collectivism take a long time to arrive at a decision because they have to ask everyone's opinion in order to achieve group consensus, which also explains why there are often more than a dozen of Japanese or Chinese participants around the table while on the U.S. side there are only three.

2. Uncertainty of Avoidance of Cultures

The idea of uncertainty avoidance has to do with the way cultures relate to uncertainty and ambiguity, and, how well they may adapt to changes. People with high uncertainty avoidance of cultures always take security into consideration and tend to avoid conflict. They have a need for consensus. In general, countries that show the most discomfort with ambiguity and uncertainty include Muslim countries and traditional African countries, where high value is placed on conformity and safety, risk avoidance, and reliance on formal rules and rituals. Trust tends to be vested only in family and close friends. It may be difficult for outside negotiators to establish relationships of confidence and trust with members of these cultures.

People with low uncertainty avoidance are quite comfortable with ambiguity and they are ready to take risks and more tolerant of individual differences. They see conflicts as constructive, and accept dissenting opinions. Some countries in the world such as United States, Scandinavia, Singapore, Australia and Norway, are characterized by low uncertainty avoidance. This can be seen in their value placed on job mobility. Members of these cultures tend to value risk-taking, problem-solving, flat organizational structures, and tolerance for ambiguity. It may be easier for outsiders to establish trusting relationships with negotiating partners in these cultural contexts.

3. Power Differential

The idea of power distance describes the degree of deference and acceptance of unequal power between people. Cultures where there is a comfort with high power differential are those where some people are considered superior to others because of their social status, gender, race, age, education, birthright, personal achievements, family background or other factors. Cultures with low power differential tend to assume equality among people, and focus more on earned status than ascribed status. Generally speaking, the more unequally wealth is distributed, the bigger will be the power differential in any national setting. High power-distance cultures are status conscious and respectful of age and seniority. In high power-distance cultures, outward forms of status such as protocol, formality, and hierarchy are considered important. National cultures with a high power differential include Arabian countries, Malaysia, the Philippines, Mexico, Indonesia, and India. Negotiators from these countries tend to be comfortable with.

In low power-distance cultures, people strive for power equalization and justice. A low power-distance culture values competence over seniority with a resulting consultative management style. Low power distance may be related to the sharing of information and the offering of multiple proposals as well as more cooperative and creative behavior.

4. Masculinity and Femininity

Cultures can be classified into masculinity and femininity types referring to the degree to which a culture values assertiveness or nurturing and social support. The terms also refer to the degree to which socially prescribed roles operate for men and women. Masculinity culture typically values assertiveness, independence, task-orientation, self-achievement. Masculinity societies tend to have a rigid division of sex roles. The competitiveness and assertiveness embedded in masculinity societies may result in individuals perceiving the negotiations situation in win-or-lose terms. In masculinity cultures, the party with the most competitive behavior is likely to gain more. Countries and regions such as Japan and Latin America are rigid rated as preferring values of assertiveness, task-orientation, and achievement. In these cultures, there tend to be more rigid gender roles and "live to work" orientations. In countries and regions rated feminine, such as Scandinavia, Thailand, and Portugal, values of modesty, cooperation, nurturing, relationship and solidarity with the less fortunate prevail. Femininity is related to sympathy and social relation.

Section IV　Business Protocol and Etiquette

Nowadays, the world economy tends to be more and more globalized. Organizations, especially those multinational corporations, are culturally diversified in the formation of their staff members and in handling all kinds of business activities. The culturally diversified workforce has brought greater vitality to the business, but at the same time, business people are facing many problems in their cross-cultural business communication, one of which is to know a good deal about international business protocol and etiquette.

Etiquette refers to manners and behavior considered acceptable in social and business situations. Exchanging business cards, dining practices, tipping and giving gifts all belong to etiquette.

1. Exchanging Business Cards

A business card always gives the information like your company name, your name, your position or title, your company address, telephone, fax number, e-mail address or Web site. The recognized etiquette is to present and receive cards with both hands to show respect to others. Glance at the business card and promptly put it in the pocket.

More formal cultures tend to treat the name card with more respect. For instance, in Japan the "meishi" or business card is exchanged with great ceremony. It is always presented and received with both hands, scanned carefully for four or five seconds, placed respectfully on the conference and then put reverently into a leather card wallet.

Business visitors to the Pacific Rim will note that the ceremony of the meishi has spread to most parts of East and Southeast Asia. There, one is expected to treat the name card with the same respect as they treat the person who gave the card.

Many visitors to the United States are struck by how casually Americans treat that little piece of card. The East Asian who politely offers his business card with both hands should not be offended if his U. S. counterpart stuffs the card in his back pocket, tosses it onto the desk, scribbles on it or even picks his teeth with it at the lunch table.

2. Dress Code

Proper attire at business meeting is essential for it is a sign of respect for the person with whom you meet. The following are the etiquette guidelines for attire at business meetings, presentations, receptions and information sessions:

(1) Formal Business Dress

Both men and women should always wear a suit. Consider dark navy and gray. Men should wear shirts that are nicely starched and not taken right out of the dryer. White shirts should be white, not yellowish. Men's ties should be seen and not heard. Women should avoid wearing several pieces of jewelry, especially dangling, chunky sorts. Wear accessories and jewelry that make you look polished and professional. Make sure skirts are at least knee length. Women should always wear hosiery, and shoes with heels. You should try to be on the conservative side rather than trying to look glamorous.

(2) Business Casual

In most parts of the world, business women can choose between a good dress, suit or blazer and skirt. For men, a dark suit, conservative tie and dark socks will cover most meetings with high-status individuals. Men should avoid Khaki pants and "loud print" shirts. Consider dark-colored slacks with a nice Oxford shirt with muted colors and a conservative matching tie. If the weather is cold, put on a nice solid color sweater. Another option is to wear dark slacks, solid or bold striped shirt, and a nice dark colored sports coat or blazer. Belt and shoes should match.

Women should consider wearing business skirts with appropriate blouses, such as silk, polyester, or rayon with attractive prints. Nice slacks with a blazer or pants suits are also acceptable. Larger pieces of jewelry are acceptable for business casual. Shoes with flat heels or small heels are appropriate, and of course, always wear hosiery.

(3) Casual

It is acceptable for men to wear nice khaki, navy or some other basic color slacks. Polo type shirts, "Camp" shirts or collared shirts, long or short, sleeved, would be appropriate. Stay away from blue jeans, denim, and Sweat suit material. Shirts should be crisp and colorful but not flashy. No cut-off jeans or shorts.

Appropriate attire for women might be a skirt and a blouse, or tailored slacks, a blouse, and a nice belt. Wear attractive coordinated accessories flats, and always hosiery. No cut-off jeans or shorts.

(4) Culture-specific Hints

+ Visits to Latin Europe and Latin America require special attention to the style and quality of both men's and women's apparel and accessories.
+ In the Middle East, the business contacts often judge one partly on the quality and price of one's briefcase, watch, pen and jewelry. One should wear and carry the best one has.

- Germans feel more comfortable doing business with men whose shoes are brightly polished.
- Throughout Asia, it is a good idea to wear slip-on shoes such as high quality loafers because custom requires removing footwear when entering temples, peoples' homes and some offices as well.
- Americans pay special attention to the condition of one's teeth, so some Europeans include a visit to their dentist for a cleaning as part of their preparation.
- In Muslim countries, female visitors should dress so as to show as little bare skin as possible.
- Americans vary somewhat according to location and type of business; visitors are well advised to wear a suit and tie to the first meeting with a new contact.
- In China, suit, white shirt, conservative tie for men and a conservative suit or dress for women.
- In India, men wear a dark suit when meeting government officials. For most private sector meetings, they wear a suit in the cooler months, shirt and tie or bush shirt without a tie in summer. Women wear a conservative dress or blouse and skirt (below-the-knee length) and avoid revealing garb such as thin T-shirts, sleeveless blouses and tank tops.

3. Forms of Address

The more formal the culture, the more likely you will use the person's family name plus any applicable title or honorific.

Visitors to Japan who interact with women should remember that the polite prefix "san" can mean "Miss", "Ms." or "Mrs.", as well as "Mister".

Many cultures employ standard expressions as verbal greetings. For instance, Americans often say, "Hi, how are you?" and some Asians and Europeans seem to be confused by this rhetorical question, thinking the Yank is actually asking after their health. In fact it's a meaningless expression calling for the automatic response "Fine! How are you?" Whereupon everyone gets right down to business.

In the USA the saying goes, "I don't care what you call me just as long as you call me for dinner."

In fact, Europeans also employ various meaningless syllables when being introduced to someone for the first time. Germans will say something meaning "it is a great pleasure to meet you". How do they know whether it is going to be such a great pleasure when they don't even know the person yet?

4. Dinner Party Etiquette

Dinner party is an important social activity in business negotiation. Dinner party etiquette is about how to behave in a proper and gracious way when attending a dinner party. Many American negotiators prefer to maintain a separation between their professional and private lives as well as between business and pleasure. If invited to the cocktail party, expect to mix informally with a large number of complete strangers.

✦ Etiquette guidelines for attending a dinner party

Knowing the fundamental element of business protocol shows your counterpart that you are serious and committed potential supplier or partner. And making fewer blunders gives you an edge over your less conscientious competitor. Here are some etiquette guidelines that are applicable to attending a dinner party:

(1) Upon Invitation

Upon receiving an invitation to a dinner party, you should inform the host of your decision by telephone or mail at your earliest convenience. Once accepted, you should keep your word. If for some special reason you cannot make it, you owe the host an immediate explanation and an apology. Call the host at his house if necessary (may not be appropriate in North America).

(2) Being Time Conscious

Arrive on time or early. Being late, leaving early or staying for a very short period of time are examples of poor etiquette. If you must leave early, unless you have notified him in advance, you should offer the host an explanation and leave quietly.

(3) On Arrival

Go to the cloakroom first to take off your hat and overcoat. Then go to the reception room to exchange greetings with the host.

(4) Seating

Take the seat assigned by the host. Assist senior and female guests beside you to their seats first.

(5) Getting Ready to Eat

The host will announce that the dinner starts when everyone is seated. Do not begin to eat or drink before the host does.

(6) Communication

Communicate with people at the same table, especially with those sitting next to you. Introduce yourself if they do not know you.

(7) Toasting

Raise your glass when the host and the guest of honor clink their glasses. When the host proposes a toast and the guest of honor responds to a toast, you should stop eating, drinking or talking and listen to them. If the host and the guest of honor come to your table, be sure to stand up and raise your glass. Keep good eye contact to show your respect when clinking glasses with them. Avoid excessive drinking.

(8) Taking off Your Coat

No matter how hot it is, it would not be appropriate to take off your coat in public. At a small-sized informal dinner, with the permission of the host, you may take off your coat and put it on the back of your chair.

(9) At Table

Maintain a natural sitting posture and keep proper distance between your body and the table. Try to keep the table clean while eating. Place your napkin on your lap; do not use napkin to clean your face or take food from your mouth. When cutting meat, hold the knife in your right hand and the fork in your left hand and avoid making noises. Cut the meat one piece at a time and eat it with the fork. Put the knife and fork in the plate when you finish a course.

+ Do not use a spoon to eat; it is for soup only.
+ Be sure to sample all the food served to you and finish the food in your plate.
+ Do not talk when you have food in your mouth.
+ Avoid talking to your neighbor when he has food in his mouth.

+ Food and drink taboos

Some food and drink taboos are really serious, such as offering the Muslim guest a pork chop or the Hindu friend a T-bone steak. Other taboos are simply amusing. Italians, for example, only drink cappuccino in the morning, before about 10 a. m.

Smart visitors rely on local advisers or culture-specific guides about food and drink taboos.

+ Observant Muslims do not drink alcohol or eat any pork product. Many avoid shellfish as well. Jews share some of these food taboos.
+ Hindus avoid both beef and pork; most are strict vegetarians.
+ Buddhists are often strict vegetarians, but many Thai Buddhists enjoy beef as long as someone else has done the slaughtering for them.

5. Business Gifts

Business gifts in negotiation are an important part of etiquette in business negotiation which create an opportunity to build a relationship between negotiating parties and help a negotiator to achieve his goal. However, the nuances of gift-giving among different cultures are important.

(1) What to Give

Watch out for culture-specific taboos. Avoid sharp objects such as knives; in some cultures they symbolize the ending of a relationship. In China, avoid clocks and watches, which bring bad luck because the word for clock sounds like another Chinese word which refers to death. Good choices are quality writing instruments, branded whisky, picture books about one's city, region or country and products one's home country is famous for.

(2) When to Give

In Europe, after the agreement is signed. In Japan and most other Asian countries, gifts are given at the end of the meeting. Note that North America is not a gift-giving culture. Many companies have strict policies concerning gifts, especially for people with purchasing responsibilities. Many American negotiators feel uncomfortable if presented with an expensive gift.

(3) How to Give

In Japan the wrapping of the gift is at least as important as the gift itself. In Japan and the rest of Asia, present and receive any gift with both hands, except in Thailand where the present is landed over with one right hand supported by the left. In Asia and North & South America, the gift will more likely be opened immediately.

The nuances of gift-giving are important; however, not every blunder is fatal.

Section V　Practical Activities

1. Case Study

● **Case Study 1**

Li Hong-zhang's Embarrassment

Li Hong-zhang, one of the top officials in Qing Dynasty, was invited to visit the United States. He was warmly welcomed. One day, Li was hosting a banquet for the American officials in a popular restaurant. As the banquet started, according to the Chinese custom, Li stood up and said, "I am very happy to have all of you here today. Though these dishes are coarse and not delicious and good enough to show my respect for you, I hope you will enjoy them ..."（今天承蒙各位光临，不胜荣幸。我们略备粗馔，聊表寸心，没有什么可口的东西，不成敬意，请大家多多包涵……）

The next day, the English version of his words was shown in the local newspaper. To his shock, the restaurant owner flew into a rage. He thought it was an insult to his restaurant and insisted that Li should show him the evidence of which dish was not well-made and which dish was not delicious. Otherwise, Li intentionally damaged the reputation of the restaurant, and he should apologize. All the fuss made Li rather embarrassed.

Comment: What Li said is just some formulaic polite expression common in type; almost all Chinese people know this and could hear that nearly everywhere. As far as the literary meaning is concerned. Li's words are inappropriate, but they do convey the meaning of respect. Here, the language form is different from its content, a phenomenon only found in the Eastern culture. However, this case happened in America, and the audience was Americans. America is a country with highly valued individualism and they express themselves rather directly. They could not understand the Easterners' over-modesty, for they tend to comprehend what they hear literally, and a clash was inevitable. If one day, you entered an American company, and said "My ability is limited（我的能力有限）". Then, most likely you would be refused. A common response may be, "If you have limited ability, why should I hire you?" On the contrary, if you said how capable you were, he may hire you. So the reaction of the restaurant boss was nothing unusual. If Li Hong-zhang's words were changed into "The cuisine of your country is really great. It is my great honor to have a chance to entertain you with them … （贵国的菜看真是好极了。今天能有机会借花献佛，不胜荣幸之至……）", then everyone would have been happy.

Question：

Could the Westerners understand Chinese modesty?

● Case Study 2

Cross-cultural Differences — Different Styles

A commonly held belief is that men and women are fundamentally different in negotiations. Some studies have shown that men more commonly enjoy the "competitive" aspect of negotiation and will continue to bargain even after their objectives have been met. These studies portray women as being on the other end generally more in tune with the interpersonal aspects of negotiation, striving to build a cooperative relationship, and sometimes settling earlier than necessary, forgoing additional gains for the sake of harmony.

In the same way, slight differences exist in negotiation styles among various cultures and ethnic groups. Ardent, a German businesswoman, and Diana, a British businesswoman, are doing a business negotiation. The German is a buyer for a large chain of department stores and is interested in purchasing clothes manufactured by the British company. The following is a part of the negotiation. Read it and answer the questions.

Ardent：　… good, I'll take your advice and try that restaurant this evening. On my last few visits to England I've been very impressed by the general standard of restaurants, not at all like the bad image many people in Germany have of English cooking.

Diana：　I'm very pleased to hear that. There has been, I think, big improvement in recent years. Anyway, shall we get down to business?

Ardent：　Yes, good. My position is that I'm prepared to offer you an item price of 285 for your spring range dresses — up to orders of 2,000 we would expect a discount of at least 5 percent.

Diana：　I wonder if we could go back a couple of steps and talk about what we hope to achieve in this session.

Ardent：　I'm afraid I don't quite follow you …

Questions：

① What goes wrong?

② Why does it go wrong?

2. Role Play

For Your Information

How to discuss time of delivery in a negotiation?

A: Now that we've settled the payment terms, shall we decide the time of delivery?

B: Certainly.

A: Is it possible to deliver the goods in October?

B: In October? I am sorry to say that's impossible because we are fully scheduled in that month.

A: Mr. Roberson, you must realize that the prompt delivery is of great importance to us.

B: I see your point. Well, maybe we can deliver the goods in two parts. That is, in October we deliver 50% and the balance will be shipped in the following month.

A: Thank you for your kindness. But I still hope you can ship the whole in October.

B: Mr. Smith, please trust me that we don't want to disappoint our customers. Anyway, we really are fully committed and your goods are not very seasonal ones.

A: But, could you make it better? Say, 80% to be delivered in October?

B: Well, I'm afraid we can't agree to that right now. May I suggest I contact our producers to see if they could manage it?

A: I will accept your suggestion. When can you give me your decision?

B: May I phone you tomorrow morning about 8:00?

A: Great. Thanks for your help.

B: Now it looks fine to me. All we have to do is sign the contract.

3. Mini Negotiation

Mr. Wilson(W) is negotiating with Mr. Hu(H) on the loss due to untimely delivery.

W: Mr. Hu, we'll have to lodge a claim for all the losses incurred as a consequence of your failure to ship our order in time.

H: I'm very sorry for all the losses you suffered, but we should not be held responsible for any delay due to force majeure. It is definitely stipulated in the contract, Mr. Wilson.

W: What evidence do you have to support that the delay was caused by force majeure? I'm told that the delay was caused by your carelessness.

H: That's not true. We can show you the weather reports of the last month. They are respectively issued by China's central and local meteorological stations.

W：Well，I'll take them back and I suggest we meet again sometime tomorrow.

H：How about 10 o'clock tomorrow morning?

W：I suppose it'll be OK.

Negotiation Tips

- **Separate People from Problems 分别对待人和事**

Put yourself in your opponent's shoes and don't take disagreements personally.

- **Focus on Interests, Not Position 着眼利益而不是立场**

When discussing each other's interests, bargainers can maintain flexibility and allow for compromise. As soon as anyone locks into a firm "position", the other side must take it or leave it.

- **Never Make the First Offer 不要首先报盘**

Let's say that after all of your analysis you conclude the company you are looking to buy is worth $500,000. You decide to break this rule and make the first offer：$400,000. Sounds reasonable, right? Well, yes, unless the owner of that company would be happy to get $400,000 for this business. All of a sudden, once he hears your initial $400,000 offer, he knows he will get even more than that. By making the first offer, you will likely be paying at least $50,000 more for that business than you had to if you had kept your mouth shut.

Extended Activities

Ⅰ. Situational Group Talks.

Study the following examples of business etiquette. Discuss with your partner other examples appropriate to dealing with visitors.

> Etiquette in Business
> - Learn how to say, "Please", "Thank you" and "Goodbye" in every foreign language you will use.
> - Show appropriate for the culture, music, and art of the country you are visiting or the country your guests are from.
> - Don't make comparisons of dietary customs, holidays, religion, and forms of government.
> - Keep in mind that business is more formal in all countries other than the USA Conduct yourself accordingly.
> - Be punctual.
> - Be well groomed.
> - Hand-shaking is very important in Europe. Wait for ladies to extend their hands first.
> - Be courteous and respectful and do nothing that would offend your guests' pride.

Ⅱ. Multiple Choice.

Directions: There are ten incomplete sentences in this part. For each sentence there are four choices marked A, B, C, and D. Choose the one that best completes the sentence.

1. That is a(n) _____ topic. We needn't spend so much time on it.

    A. old   B. habitual   C. habitable   D. habitant

2. Lightning is a sign of thunder and enables us to _____ thunder.

    A. precede   B. predict   C. prepare   D. prescribe

3. Two executives were sent to _____ the policy set by the government.

    A. complement   B. supplement   C. implement   D. compliment

4. His refusal to attend the ceremony is an _____ to the host.

    A. insult   B. insulting   C. instruct   D. insure

5. My opinions _____ with this.

    A. cash   B. cry   C. clash   D. shout

6. The ambassador personally _____ the president's message to the premier.

    A. exchanged   B. delayed   C. carried   D. conveyed

7. The landlady asked her lodgers to be _____ in the payment of their rent.

    A. punctual   B. permanent   C. protective   D. preferable

8. I think we can _____ Mr. White to support us.

    A. count up   B. count out   C. count off   D. count on

9. None of the other planets in our solar system are capable of _____ life at present.

    A. remaining   B. maintaining   C. sustaining   D. retaining

10. She is only a(n) _____, not a friend of mine.

    A. acquaintance   B. familiarity   C. announcement   D. family.

Ⅲ. Imagine you are going to prepare a dinner for six people. Study the following principles of seat arrangement for a western dinner. Then discuss with your partner and propose seat arrangements for the two different tables below.

Principles for Seat Arrangement

- Host and hostess should be seated separately at each side of the table to take care of the table.
- Male and female should be seated separately around the table.
- The right hand seat is more important than the left hand seat.
- The people near the host and the hostess are more important.
- The most important person should be seated at the right hand of the host.

---

1. host

2. hostess

3. VIP

4. VIPs' wife

5. guest(female)

6. guest(male)

Ⅳ. Decide whether the following statements are true(T) or false(F).

1. Every culture has a set of body language which has a vocabulary and grammar of all its own.

2. Both Americans and Chinese accept apologies with a smile.

3. In Western countries, women and men are not supposed to have eye contact.

4. In many cultures, people who are of the same age and sex take less personal space than do mixed-age or mixed-sex groups.

5. Every human being is surrounded by an invisible envelop of air called a "space bubble" which varies in size according to where in the world they grew up and the particular situation.

Ⅴ. Translate the following sentences into English.

1. 文化冲突会导致交流失败。

2. 时间作为一种文化价值，我们只有处于该文化中，才会理解它的不同含义。

3. 在外国经营业务，宗教是另一个需要考虑的重要问题。

4. 从某种程度上讲，谈判者的成功取决于他对不同文化的敏感性。

5. 对文化差异的熟悉与敏感对国际谈判至关重要。

Ⅵ. Translate the following sentences into Chinese.

1. A close culture-strategy match is crucial to managing a company's people resources with maximum effectiveness.

2. The value and attitude of the people in a foreign culture are important considerations for the multinational corporation.

3. Cultural clash refers to uncertainty, anxiety, fear, and tension which accompany the forced union of two dissimilar cultures.

4. People in different society organize their social relationships and activities in a manner that is consistent with their society's value, religions and economies.

5. Individuals should also do all that they can to learn how cultural and business practices differ in the countries where they want to do business.

Chapter 14

Different Culture and Business Negotiation

Learning Goals

Upon completion of this chapter, you will be able to:
☞ learn about negotiating style of different cultures;
☞ deal with cultural conflicts management in business negotiations;
☞ master two approaches to conflicts;
☞ organize effective conflict management.

Lead-in Words

straightforward *adj.* 不兜圈子	rigid-time 时间观念严紧
subsume *v.* 包含	indigenous *adj.* 本地的
sanction *n. v.* 制裁	task-centered 成就型
people-oriented 人本型	intermediate *adj.* 居中的，中间的
attune *v.* 和谐，协调	polychromic *adj.* 多向的
bureaucratic *adj.* 官僚的	collaboration *n.* 合作、协作
entrepot *n.* 贸易中心	monochromic *adj.* 单向的
rupture *n.* 破裂，断绝	fluid-time 时间观念松散

Section I   Different Business Culture Types

International business negotiations cover various levels of negotiators from multi-nations and multi-nationalities. Due to different cultural background and customs there exist evident differences of values and negotiating styles among people all over the world. Therefore a business negotiator should have some business conventions of different countries.

The skilled negotiator, usually meeting many other parties, recognizes that each has its own distinct way of negotiation. He attunes to the differences and adjusts his preparation and his conduct. Here we shall examine differences of style which reflect the ways in which different organizations work.

1. Task-oriented vs. People-oriented Cultures

People who are purely task-centered are concerned entirely with achieving a business goal. They are not at all concerned about the effect which their determination will have on the people with whom they come into contact. They will pursue their business objectives relentlessly; they will go to the limits of morality; as negotiators, they will be very tough, very fighting, very aware of tactical ploys and anxious to make maximum use of them. The outcome for them is more important than process.

It is known to all that task or achievement-oriented culture is quite characteristic of Americans, no matter what they do or where they go; so is the case with American business people. To understand this helps to explain many behaviors on the side of the American business people. They don't want to waste time with the social niceties; they want to get down to business. Another point is to say that it is very specific. People who adopt this approach tend to focus hard on specific issues — this should mean that time is saved and objectives reached most effectively. Very often the emphasis on self-interest and freedom of the individual can run counter to cooperation. The business firm values the person who is mobile, energetic, creative, and ambitious. However, there is always a danger that the larger picture may be missed and that personal issues can be ignored. These personal issues may be the ones which make or break the deal.

People-oriented managers, on the other hand, are highly concerned about the well-being of those who work for them, or alongside them or above them. This concern about people dominates their activity, says the theory, and it can lead to an almost total neglect of the business goals.

In this case, they give time to some small talk before the meeting starts because they believes this will improve communication and lay the basis for possible future relationships. Another way of looking at this is to call it diffuse. A diffuse approach to business will place great importance on all the events which surround the actual discussion of the deal, for example, lunch together, social conversation on the way to the airport, or a chance to meet your partner's family.

There are intermediate points between total task-orientation and total people-orientation. It splits this central area into three parts:

① low-orientation both to task and to people;

② medium-orientation both to task and to people;

③ high-orientation both to task and to people.

From the above three parts, we recognize also three styles of negotiators we are likely to meet in practice:

　　① the fighter (highly task-oriented);

　　② the collaborator (aiming to get everything into the open, confront issues and make a creative deal);

　　③ the compromiser (looking always to compromise to settle deals).

These three distinctive styles of negotiation will influence the way we conduct our negotiation.

2. Pioneer vs. Bureaucrat

As for pioneer, it means the strong individual. This kind of negotiator is characterized by prominent in his own organization, good at seizing an opportunity, spotting a market, making a profit. He tends to be very dominating, good at improvising, intuitive in his thinking, charismatic in his personality.

A negotiator of this type will be aggressive, forceful, and ready to take decisions and to come to agreements. He will be distinguishable particularly in the way he acts as a team leader; the focal point of the team, the one who speaks for the team on all issues, the one who use his team members to obtain information for himself which he then transmits to other party.

Negotiating with a "pioneer" can be exciting, enjoyable and highly productive. It demands that we should recognize his highly intuitive and instinctive nature. We should ourselves retain a consciousness of the negotiating processes through which we are going, trying to sustain our normal degrees of control.

Bureaucracy is the pattern most found in large organizations. The style of working is systematized. There are books of rules, standardizations, planning, numerous committees, lots of checking, double-checking and cross-checking. The organization is governed with a clear hierarchy. It is classified and co-coordinated by the system, the rules, the procedures and the objectives.

Advantage within a bureaucratic organization comes to the people who are most good at playing the game according to the rules. This means that their negotiators may be expected to have both objectives and styles of working which are bureaucratic. In setting up a deal, it is more important for the bureaucratic negotiator to fit into the budgetary provisions than the total sum of money involved. For stylized bureaucrats, precise statements are to be agreed at each step. Elegance and conformity are maintained as they go along the negotiating process.

To better deal with bureaucratic negotiators, the other party should do well to select a team which has both the personality and experience to handle this manner of operating. The team will readily accept the system of approach we have advocated to negotiations. Bureaucratic organizations thus tend to have distinctive objective and to negotiate in the pattern "to our advantage".

3. Relationship-focused vs. Deal-focused Cultures

Deal-focused people are fundamentally task-oriented while relationship-focused folks are more people-oriented. Conflicts arise when deal-focused export marketers try to do business with prospects from relationship-focused markets. Many relationship-focused people find deal-focused types pushy, aggressive and offensively blunt. In return, deal-focused types often consider their relationship-focused counterparts dilatory, vague and inscrutable.

The major differences between relationship-focused and deal-focused markets impact business success throughout the global marketplace. The vast majority of the world's markets are relationship-oriented: the Arab world and most of Africa, Latin America and the Asia / Pacific region, where business people get things done through intricate networks of personal contacts. They prefer to deal with friends and persons or groups who are well known to them and can be trusted. They are uncomfortable doing business with strangers, especially strangers who also happen to be foreigners. Likewise, relationship-oriented firms typically want to know their prospective business partners very well before talking business with them.

In contracts, the deal-focused approach is common in only a small part of the world. Strongly deal-focused cultures are found in northern Europe, North America, Australia and New Zealand, where people are relatively open to doing business with strangers.

Moderately deal-focused cultures could be found in Great Britain, South Africa, Latin America, Central and Eastern Europe, Chile, Southern Brazil, Northern Mexico, and Singapore.

In deal-focused cultures, people are relatively open to dealing with strangers. The marketer can make initial contact with prospective buyer without any previous relationship or connection. Having an introduction or referral is helpful but not essential. Let's take the United States as an example. Perhaps because they are raised in a highly mobile immigrant society, most Americans are open to discussing business possibilities with people they don't know. Each year Americans buy over $300 billion dollars worth of goods and services from total strangers, and half of it is business-to-business selling.

In relationship-focused cultures, firms do not do business with strangers. The proper way to approach someone who isn't yet known is to arrange for the right person or organization to make an introduction. A third party introduction bridges the relationship gap between one and the person or company one wants to talk to. The ideal introducer is a high-status person or organization known to both parties. A good second best might be the commercial section of one's country's embassy in the target market. Embassy officials tend to be accorded high status in relationship-oriented cultures, and of course it is part of their job to promote export. Chambers of commerce and trade associations are other potential introducers.

4. Formal vs. Informal Business Cultures

Formal cultures tend to be organized in steep hierarchies which reflect major difference in status and power. Formal cultures are practiced in most of Europe and Asia, the Mediterranean Region and the Arab World, Latin America. In contrast, informal cultures value more egalitarian organizations with smaller difference in status and power. Countries like Australia, USA, Canada, New Zealand, Denmark, Norway, and Iceland belong to informal business cultures.

Many promising international deals have fallen through when a negotiator from an informal culture confronts counterparts from more formal cultures because these contrasting values cause conflict at the conference table. Business people from formal, hierarchical cultures may be offended by the breezy familiarity of counterparts from informal, relatively egalitarian societies. On the other hand, those from informal cultures may see their formal counterparts as stuffy, distant, pompous or arrogant.

Formality actually is about status, hierarchies, power and respect. Whereas informal cultures are supposed to value status equality, formal cultures value hierarchies and status differences. Ignorance of this distinction can cause serious problems across the bargaining table.

Such misunderstandings can be avoided if both sides are aware that differing business behaviors are the result of differing cultural values rather than individual idiosyncrasies.

5. Expressive vs. Reserved Cultures

Expressive people communicate in radically different ways from their more reserved counterparts; they tend to be uncomfortable with more than a second or two of silence during a conversation. In contrast, people from reserved cultures feel at ease with much longer silences. Japanese negotiators, for example, often sit without speaking for what seems like an eternity to voluble Mexicans, Greeks or Americans. After three or four seconds the latter feel compelled to say something, anything to fill the awful silence. For another example, Americans are known for being fond of talking. They have, therefore, the title "talkative Americans". However, those expressive Americans feel puzzled and frustrated when they talk to the Japanese — sometimes they get a "hai" in return, sometimes a nod, still sometimes they simply get no other response but silence. For that reason, many Americans feel frustrated when they meet situations mentioned above. Actually, the reason leading to their frustration is their lack of understanding about the Japanese culture.

As far as the American culture is concerned, an eloquent speaker is regarded as a good communicator. For that reason, many Americans assume that one should be eloquent, and this should be the standard applicable everywhere in the world. However, what they do not know is that such a standard does not fit into the Japanese context. The Japanese culture, on the contrary, silence as an earnest way to think about what others have said (or are saying).

Unfortunately the loquacity of expressive people tends to irritate the reticent Japanese, who seem to value the space between the spoken words just as much as the words themselves. Negotiators from reserved cultures do not feel the need to engage in constant blabbing the way many of their expressive counterparts do.

6. Rigid-time vs. Fluid-time Cultures

People look at time and schedule differently in different parts of the world. In rigid-time societies, punctuality is critical, schedules are set in stone, agendas are fixed and business meetings are rarely interrupted. Edward T. Hall invented the term "monochromic" for these clock-obsessed, schedule-worshipping cultures.

In direct contrast are "polychromic" cultures, where people place less emphasis on strict punctuality and are not obsessed with deadlines. Polychromic cultures value loose scheduling as well as business meetings where meetings-within-meetings may be taking place simultaneously.

However, culture does change, for example, Japan was classified as polychromic by Edward T. Hall in the 1960's, but today the Japanese are as schedule-obsessed and clock-conscious as the Swiss. Another example, Singapore, a polychromic Southeast Asian entrepot just 30 years ago is now a moderately monochromic business culture. Both countries are proof that culture does change, though, slowly. Some typical business cultures are as following:

(1) Monochromic business cultures: Nordic and Germanic Europe, North America, Japan;

(2) Moderately monochromic: Australia / New Zealand, Russia and most of East-Central Europe, Southern Europe, Singapore, China, Korea, South Africa;

(3) Polychromic business cultures: The Arab World, most of Africa, Latin America, South and Southeast Asia.

Orientation to time varies not only among different countries but often within a given country as well. In Brazil, São Paulo is relatively monochromic whereas Rio is strongly polychromic. Similarly, people in the more industrialized southern coastal provinces of China are more clock-conscious than those in the less-developed interior. And a Korean meeting is more likely to start on time if it takes place in Seoul rather than in a small town in the countryside.

Section II Business Negotiating Style of Different Culture

People from different countries have different values, different attitudes and different experience. These different notions of culture yield different understandings of the culture-negotiation link. Researches and observations by most scholars indicate fairly clearly that negotiation practices differ from culture to culture and that culture can influence "negotiating style" — the way persons from different cultures conduct themselves in negotiating sessions. A competent negotiator should develop a style appropriate for his own strengths of his particular culture. The following will provide some typical negotiating styles of different countries.

1. American Style

The American style of negotiating is possibly the most influential in the world. It is characterized first by personalities which are usually outgoing, and quickly convey sincerity. Personalities are confident and positive and talkative. Generally, Americans are very direct, openly disagree and try to demand the same from counterparts. They tend to make concessions throughout the negotiations, settling one issue, then proceeding to the next. They are particularly high in the bargaining phases of negotiation, make decisions based upon the bottom line and on cold, hard facts. Thus the final agreement is a sequence of several smaller concessions. They usually ignore establishing personal relation prior negotiation. In their minds, good business relation brings about good personal relation, not vice versa. American's high individualism is manifested through their decision making process — individual has the right to make the decision. Personal responsibility is stressed.

2. Australia Style

The Australians are tough breed and they enjoy competition. They encourage long-term relationships and prefer to work with people they count as friends. Being direct while negotiating, the Australian are keen to spot deception and they feel no hesitation to walk away from the table if they feel one is holding back information.

Australian will bargain, but only to a small degree. Waiting for the price to drop is an Australian pastime. Since Australian tend to dislike bazaar haggling, visiting negotiators will get better results by opening discussions with a realistic bed. The negotiating process may take more time than it would in some other deal-focused business cultures, though less than in strongly relationship-focused markets such as Japan.

Australians have well developed commercial law. Handshakes are an amenity. Signatures mean business. Because of their relatively small population and remote location, the Australians have become experienced travelers and negotiators. They research the target economies and companies in great detail, with an eye toward reducing surprises at the table. Be assured that they will know all about the prospective company and culture before the first meeting.

3. German Style

German negotiators are highly prepared, low in flexibility and compromise. In other words, in particular the German preparation for negotiations is superb. They are also well known for sticking steadfastly to their negotiating positions in the face of pressure tactics. They tend toward a factual approach when conducting business. Instructions and preliminaries are brief, so be prepared to get right to the point. They always identify the deal he hopes to make, and then prepare a reasonable bid, carefully coverting each issue in the deal. When selling, make straightforward presentations. They will be interested in the reasons for purchasing goods or services, rather than the image that surrounds the purchase. They observe strictly schedule, punctuality go for meetings, payments and social gatherings as well, and therefore, will not trust those who fail to keep good time. As to the time of negotiation, they take more time than Americans but perhaps less than the Japanese and most other Asians. Decisions are made after careful, thorough and precise analysis, thus risks are minimized.

Therefore, German negotiators are characterized by the following generalizations:

(1) Do their homework very well before negotiations;

(2) Make poor conversation partners as they see no points in small talk;

(3) Frankness is honesty and "diplomacy" can often mean deviousness;

(4) Consider formality and use of surname as signs of respect;

(5) Stick to the facts and expect organization and order in all things;

(6) Be slow at making decisions for taking time to have a consensus decision-making process.

4. Japanese Styles

Japanese belonging to high context culture communicate with others in implied and roundabout way. The most effective way to achieve the purpose is to find an "insider" who can introduce or establish a tie between you and your Japanese partner. If there is lack of such a go-between, special business agency or government and other organizations can serve the purpose.

Japanese negotiators are famous for their ambiguous responses to proposals. They view vagueness as a form of protection from loss of face in case things go sour. They are also known for their politeness, their emphasis on establishing relationships, and their indirect use of power. To maintain surface harmony and prevent loss of face, Japanese rely on codes of behavior such as the ritual of the business cards. Japanese negotiators rarely come to the table in groups smaller than three. The negotiating communication focuses on group goals, interdependence, and many Japanese companies still make decisions by consensus. This is a time-consuming process, one reason to bring patience to the negotiating table. So quick answers to any question or problem are almost impossible. Japanese negotiators are also known for their politeness, their emphasis on establishing relationships, and their indirect ways consistent with their preference for harmony and calmness. In comparative studies, Japanese negotiators were found to disclose considerably less about themselves and their goals than French or American counterparts.

5. Russian Style

Russians may be new to international commercial negotiations but they're old hands at negotiation with foreign powers. They have clear agenda and no strategy or tactics is off-limits. Russia is no place for negotiation amateurs. Generally, Russians view compromise as a sign of weakness. Often, they will refuse to back down until the other side agrees to make sufficient concessions or shows exceptional firmness. Russians decision-making is rather bureaucratic. Even the simplest deals will take a great deal of time to analyze and decide. Numerous trips will be required for medium to large ventures. Just as the geography lies between Europe and Asia, so does Russia's attitude toward contracts. It's best to get as many details written into the document as possible. Important points must be stressed continually as the Russians tend to look at the totality rather than the details of a contract.

6. French Style

French negotiators are reputed to have three main characteristics in international dealings: a great deal of firmness, an insistence on using French as the language for negotiation, and a decidedly lateral style in negotiating. That is, in contrast to the American piece-by-piece approach, they prefer to make an outline agreement, then an agreement in principle, and then headings of agreement repeatedly coverting the whole breadth of a deal.

The French are verbally and non-verbally expressive. They love debate, often engaging in spirited debate during business meetings, but not intense criticism to avoid direct confrontation. The French will discuss every point at length and will have a position on every topic. They think proper use of the language is a sensitive cultural issue. All contracts must be completely in French, and commonly used foreign words cannot be substituted. They consider friendship as important in doing business, so they will not place large order before trustful and friendly relation is established. French decision-making takes longer time than German and have a well-known weak point: often late or changing schedule unilaterally, but they will not forgive their partner's delay.

7. British Style

The British are old hands at international business. Their history of negotiation in international business goes back centuries. The depth of their knowledge is without comparison. They may put a wide safety margin in their opening position so as to leave room for substantial concessions during the bargaining process.

Britain is an orderly society, punctuality is mandatory and presentations should be detailed. Englishmen always arrange appointments in advance and present an agenda as early in the process as possible. British business moves at a more deliberate pace than American business.

British negotiators' style is calm, balanced, confident, cautious and not flexible. They tend to keep silent in the beginning in business talks, they are reserved rather than expressive or demonstrative in the way they communicate and start the bargaining at a point only slightly distant from the projected goal. They are not used to showing off in public and keep a distance with others. They will not confuse personal relation with business relation, so business affairs go first. They also attach great importance to protocol and ceremony, before negotiation exchange of greetings and courtesy may sometimes last for a couple of hours. This is evident in their use of understatement, low-contact body language and restrained gestures.

8. Latin American Style

In Latin American contexts responsibility to others is generally considered more important than schedules and task accomplishment. People in Latin America consider relationship a very important element in doing business. If a good relationship is established between the two sides, they will not hesitate to help their counterparts. It is conceived that business people there have a poor record of credibility and commitment, because it is not unusual that they postpone payment without any reason or make use of the delaying to cut prices. Their negotiation approach relates to the patterns of high-context communication. A common term for conflict in Central America is *enredo*, meaning "entangled" or "caught in a net". When Latin Americans need help with negotiations, they tend to look to partial insiders rather than neutral outsiders, preferring the trust and confidence of established relationships. Thus, negotiation is done within networks, relationships are emphasized, and open ruptures are avoided.

9. African Styles

Many African nations have indigenous systems of conflict resolution that have endured to the present. Some of these systems are quite intact and some are fragmented by rapid social change. These systems rely on particular approaches to negotiation that respect kinship ties and elder roles, and the structures of local society in general. In Nigeria, for example, people are organized in extended families, villages, lineages, and lineage groups. A belief in the continuing ability of ancestors to affect people's lives maintains social control, and makes the need to have formal laws or regulations minimal. Negotiation happens within social networks, following prescribed roles.

In the Nigerian Ibibio context, the goal of restoring social networks is paramount, and individual differences are expected to be subsumed in the interest of the group. To ensure that progress or an agreement in a negotiation is preserved, parties must promise not to invoke the power of ancestors to bewitch or curse the other in the future. The aim of any process, formal or informal, is to affect a positive outcome without a "residue of bitterness or resentment". Elders have substantial power, and when they intervene in a conflict or a negotiation, their words are respected. This is partly because certain elders are believed to have access to supernatural powers that can remove protective shields at best and cause personal disaster at worst.

In other African contexts, arrange of indigenous processes exists in which relationships and hierarchies tend to be emphasized.

Section III   Cultural Conflicts Management in Business Negotiation

Negotiation is a conflict-solving process. Different cultures solve problems in different ways. You must ask yourself what your expectations are when you enter a negotiation setting. The expectation of different cultures, even within an organization, can be very different. Those expectations relate directly to their view of what the problem is and what the values are surrounding the problem and the options for solving it.

1. Approaches to Conflicts

Different approaches to conflict reflect different underlying cultural values. According the Stella Ting-Toomey, there are two approaches to conflict resolution. In western cultures conflict is viewed as fundamentally a good thing. Working through conflicts constructively results in stronger, healthier, and more satisfying relationships. Similarly, groups that work through conflict can gain new information about members or about other groups, defuse more serious conflict, and increase group cohesiveness.

However, many culture groups, especially many Asian cultures, regard conflict as ultimately destructive for relationships and see conflict as disturbing the peace. These groups also think that when members disagree they should adhere to the consensus of the group rather than engage in conflict. In fact, members who threaten group harmony may be sanctioned.

These two approaches to conflict resolution reflect different cultural values involving identity and face-saving.

2. Effective Conflict Management

Each nation has its own culture. It is not difficult for us to find that wherever they go, people bring along with them their culture and stick to their cultural norms. In many cases, business people find that it is not easy at all to communicate with people from different cultural backgrounds. Sometimes, people may mistake someone as a culturally identical person, which often ends in troubles. In order to communicate effectively negotiators should:

(1) learn to respect each other's culture;

(2) be objective about the culture differences;

（3）pay attention to the language barriers;

（4）use skills when communicating cross-culturally.

3. Rules of Conflict Management

The key to effective conflict management is to take positive rules to prepare for the decision-making process, to monitor our own behavior as the process goes forward. By following a few common-sense rules, conflicts can reduce and turn it into cooperation and reach solutions that really work for all the participants.

(1) Separate the People From the Problem

When viewing the problem as something that needs to be resolved rather than someone, holding a contrary viewpoint, to be defeated, the odds of a successful collaboration increase.

(2) Distinguish between Interests and Position

When preparing for a negotiation, or after it has begun, don't just ask, "What do they want?" or "Why do they want it?" Many successful negotiators find they will be more successful if focusing on understanding their interests as they enter discussions. If they haven't started out with a perfect package, the ideas of others may actually improve their final result.

(3) Consider Your Best Alternative to a Negotiated Agreement

If you do not reach an agreement with the other side, does that really make things worse for you? In determining your best option, a straightforward review of your interest will give you the clearest picture.

(4) Silence Is Golden

This is true that most people are troubled by silence in the midst of a heated discussion. Sometimes silence is viewed as disapproval — but since no specific disapproval has been voiced, it cannot be treated as an attack. It has happened on many occasions that, when met with silence, people have modified their previous statements to make them more palatable.

(5) Pursue Fairness

If all the participants view the process as fair, they are more likely to take it seriously and "buy into" the result. Moreover, the focus on fairness can have an important impact on the substantive result. If the parties to a negotiation can agree on standards against which elements of the agreement can be measured, it can give each a face-saving reason for agreeing.

(6) Only One Person Can Get Angry at a Time

This is yet another means to help individuals keep a cool head and pay attention to the process and the strategy, as well as the substance of the negotiation. If it's not your "turn" to be angry, the exercise of restraint can be turned into a positive opportunity to observe what is going on with a clear view. No less important, yelling at each other is not negotiation; it is confrontation. In those situations there may possibly be a "winner"; but it is even more likely there will be a "loser".

Section IV Practical Activities

1. Case Study

● Case study 1

> *For the sake of business, I was sent to study in Canada for two years. During my stay there, I encountered all sorts of inconveniences, especially the "no etiquette" custom which almost drove me crazy.*

The Embarrassment Caused by "No Etiquette"
No Seeing out When Guest Leaves

Having just recently arrived in Canada, I paid a visit to my boss. When I was leaving, to my bewilderment, the door was shut with a click the moment I stepped out of his house. I was upset about this for several days. Gradually, I came to know it was not only me who received such "treatment". When their boss or parents are leaving, the Canadians will not see them out of the door as well.

No Stand-up When Your Leader Comes in

When my boss came into my office for me first time, I stood up immediately to show my respect. The boss misunderstood my behavior, thought I was going out, and said he would talk with me in a while. I was accustomed to respecting all those in authority. For instance, at an academic conference, if some academic experts came in late, and unfortunately had to stand behind me. I would feel uncomfortable and offer my seat to him. On one occasion, I offered my seat to the Head of the Department of Internal Medicine. He said "Thanks" and sat down. During the conference, he kept turning around and looking at me, which made me feel ill at ease. When the conference was over, he came over and apologized to me, "I thought you were leaving the conference. You don't have to offer me the seat."

Questions:

If you were the counselor of "I" in the case above, how would you help him?

● Case study 2

How to Start Your Work

A U. S. production manager, Joe Sorrels, is sent to manage a manufacturing facility in Mexico. Upon arrival, his assistant production manager, Juan Lopez, suggests they go to the factory to meet the workers who have been awaiting his arrival. Joe declines Juan's offer and chooses instead to get fight to work on determining why the quality and production rate of the Mexican plant are not equal to the U.S. plant's. Juan stresses the importance of getting to know the workers first, but Joe lets Juan know he was sent to Mexico to straighten things out, not to form friendships with the local workers. Without further comment, Juan gets Joe the figures and records he requests. Joe made a number of changes and felt sure the plan he had prepared would improve quality and increase production. After a couple of months, no improvement has been made; Joe cannot understand why the workers seem to resist his plans.

　　Questions:

　　1) What went wrong with Joe's working style?

　　2) If you were Joe, how would you start your work?

2. Role Play

　　Mr. Brown(B) got a fax before he was leaving for his headquarters, which required him to modify the shipment terms a bit. Now he is talking to Yang(Y) about it.

B: Mr. Yang, before my leaving, I've got something urgent to discuss with you.

Y: Go ahead, please, Mr. Brown.

B: Yesterday evening I received a fax from my headquarters. Here's the fax. You may read it now.

Y: OK. you'd like to modify the shipment terms, Yap? Instead of two equal partial shipments, you want to have 80% of the goods delivered for the first shipment and the balance for the second.

B: Can that be arranged?

Y: Well, I'm not sure whether our factory can rearrange its production schedule.

B: It's really troublesome. I know, especially when everything has been according to the contract.

Y: I'll try my best. As soon as I get a reply from the factory, I'll send you a fax.

B: Thank you so much, Mr. Yang. By the way, is it possible to avoid transshipment for further deliveries?

Y: That much depends on the shipping available. Anything else, Mr. Brown?

B: Nothing more. Again, I'd say "thank you very much".

3. Mini Negotiation

　　The following is a part of mini negotiation. On one side there are two representatives of Setel, a U.S. company producing software systems for use in production process in the optical fibre industry. On the other side are two representatives of Nippon Glass, a Japanese electric manufacturer.

A: As Mr. B was remarking, our latest software control systems are proving very popular with both medium and large-sized manufacturers.

B: That's right — our customers are particularly pleased with the flexibility they offer. And, as I understand one of the main purposes of your visit is to look at how our range of software would suit your developing needs in the optical fibre area.

(Silence)

Mr. A, would you like to run through the day's programs at this stage?

A: Sure. But first, have you guys got any questions? Yeah, Mr. C?

(Silence)

C: No, everything is clear.

A: Oh, OK. Mr. B.

B: Thanks, Mr. A. As you can see on the programs in front of you, I will first be making a short presentation of our product range, concentrating on the new control systems. Then there is a space for you to present to us your future needs and how we may be able to help you. We will then be breaking for lunch. After lunch we plan to go to our facility in which you will see the new system, as well as some of our other products, in operation. How does that program sound to you?

(Silence)

D: It's fine. We are here because we are interested in your software system.

(Silence)

B: Well, Mr. D, we think you will be even more interested by the end of the day . . . Well, you can see our programs are really powerful and convenient. Would you please tell us your decision?

(Silence)

D: Fine, fine. I'm afraid we have to have an internal discussion, so we will inform you tomorrow.

The comments below were made after the meeting by members of the negotiation teams. If you think a comment was made by an American, circle A; if you think it was made by one of the Japanese, circle J. And then explain why.

(1) Get the impression they don't like U.S. A / J Reason: _____

(2) Why are they telling U.S. obvious things? A / J Reason: _____

(3) They're very sales-oriented. A / J Reason: _____

(4) I've no idea what they're really thinking. A / J Reason: _____

Negotiation Tips

● **Never Narrow Negotiation Down to One Issue** 别把谈判局限在一个问题上

Doing so leaves the participants in the position of having a winner or a loser. When single-issue negotiations become a factor, broaden the scope of the negotiations. If immediate delivery is important to a customer and you can't meet the schedule, maybe a partial shipment will resolve their problem while you produce the rest.

● Use Different Gambits 使用不同的谈判策略

Knowing one gambit and using it always is not enough. It may not work on some people. These people may have an affective counter to the gambit. Then you are lost or may not recognize tactics being used on you.

● To Negotiate with Someone Who Has the Authority 只和权威人士谈判

Sometimes, the person you are negotiating with does not have the authority to close the deal. He or she will say, "I have to talk to my manager." In fact, the so-called manager might not even exist! The best way to deal with this tactic is to insist on negotiating only with someone who does have the authority to close the deal, and walk away if this condition is not met.

Extended Activities

Ⅰ. Situational Group Talks.

Student A is from Britain and Student B is from France. Try to settle the dispute on the punctuality for the negotiation.

Ⅱ. Multiple Choices.

Directions: There are ten incomplete sentences in this part. For each sentence there are four choices marked A, B, C, and D. Choose the one that best completes the sentence.

1. We suggest that you file a claim _____ the shipping company for all the losses incurred as a consequence of the failure to ship the goods _____ Order TC21 in time.

  A. against, unless　　B. for, under　　　　C. to, in　　　　　　D. against, under

2. We are offering firm _____ on the same terms and conditions as the previous contract.

  A. as following　　　B. as follow　　　　 C. as follows　　　　D. as is followed

3. Please note Items Nos. 1 – 10 can be certainly promised for immediate shipment _____ receipt of your order.

  A. if　　　　　　　　B. whether　　　　　C. at　　　　　　　 D. upon

4. There is a steady demand in Europe _____ leather gloves _____ high quality.

  A. for, of　　　　　　B. at, with　　　　　C. for, with　　　　 D. in, of

5. We regret our inability to agree _____ your proposal to pack the goods _____ cartons, because transshipment has to be made at Hamburg for the goods to be shipped to our port.

  A. to, by　　　　　　B. with, in　　　　　C. to, in　　　　　　D. on, in

6. Every week hundreds of companies and entrepreneurs are setting up sites or "homepages" _____ the World Wide Web, a popular part of the Net with user-friendly graphics.

  A. in　　　　　　　　B. on　　　　　　　　C. at　　　　　　　 D. of

7. We refer you _____ our bankers, the Bank of China, Beijing Branch to inquire about our

financial standing.

   A. to go to   B. to contact   C. to consult   D. to

8. The sugar was dispatched by rail two weeks ago from Ningbo and _____ you by now.

   A. should have reached   B. should reach

   C. have reached   D. shall reach

9. We hope that you will see your way to grant us your order, and assure you _____ advance _____ its most careful execution.

   A. in, of   B. by, for   C. in, for   D. in, at

10. _____ pessimistic, it may be several months before we see a strong upturn.

   A. Be   B. Being   C. Very   D. To be

Ⅲ. Read the following statements and fill in the blanks.

1. High-context business people may even distrust contracts and be _____ by the lack of trust they suggest.

2. Japanese people tend to use power in muted, indirect ways consistent with their preference for _____ and calmness.

3. The German business culture takes the rule of law _____.

4. Americans prefer a storied, holistic approach to conflict and negotiation, rather than a linear, _____ one.

5. In other African contexts, arrange of indigenous processes exists in which relationships and hierarchies tend to be _____.

Ⅳ. Decide whether the following statements are true(T) or false(F).

1. U.S. negotiators tend to rely on individualist values, imagining self and other as autonomous, independent, and self-reliant.

2. Japanese negotiators are known for their politeness, their emphasis on establishing relationships, and their indirect use of power.

3. German approaches to negotiations are surprisingly akin to some interpretations of the German character: thorough, systematic, highly prepared, and low in flexibility and compromise.

4. Not many African nations have indigenous systems of conflict resolution that have endured to the present.

5. Few culture groups view conflict as ultimately destructive for relationships.

Ⅴ. Translate the following sentences into Chinese.

1. The American style is very direct and they try to demand the same from counterparts.

2. German negotiators are known for their thorough preparation for negotiations.

3. Britain is an orderly society and punctuality is mandatory.

4. The French love debate but not intense criticism. It will be taken as a personal attack.

5. The Australians are tough breed and they enjoy competition.

Key to the Exercises

Chapter 1

Ⅰ. (open)

Ⅱ. 1. T 2. T 3. F 4. T 5. T 6. T 7. F 8. T 9. F 10. T

Ⅲ. 1. 永远记住，每个人都为了一个简单的原因坐在谈判桌前：他们想从另一方得到某种东西。

2. 如果你用知识武装自己，你就可以充满自信地面对你的对手。

3. 谈判的成功与否并不以击败对手来衡量，而是以促进整个交易活动的成功为标准，这一点贯穿于谈判的整个过程之中。

4. 谈判的整个过程的前提是建立在双方相互依靠的基础上的，也就是说，任何一方在获取自己所需的同时，必须将对方纳入考虑之列。

5. 谈判不过是为交易双方的商业利益而服务的工具，是为了帮助交易各方实现各自的目的而服务的。

Ⅳ. 1. Negotiation is not treated as an isolated event but as an integral part of the total business activity.

2. Negotiators need to adjust themselves by exchanging their ideas on the common interest.

3. Common and complementary objectives leave direct and positive effects while conflicting objectives have negative ones on the negotiation process.

4. Good negotiators consider it very important to promote a constructive climate and respectful personal relationships.

5. What matters in negotiation are results. Everything else is decoration.

Ⅴ. 1. agreement 2. objective 3. lower 4. cooperation 5. lost 6. mutual 7. interests 8. negotiator 9. risk 10. bargain

Chapter 2

Ⅰ. (open)

Ⅱ. 1. B 2. C 3. B 4. B 5. A 6. B 7. A 8. C 9. B 10. A

Ⅲ. 1. helping 2. Equality 3. destroy 4. agreements 5. collaboration

Ⅳ. 1. T 2. F 3. T 4. F 5. T

Ⅴ. 1. 谈判不过是为交易双方的商业利益服务的工具。

2. 我建议我们大家折中一下，这样就能做成生意了。

3. 我很高兴这笔交易圆满成功了，希望以后能达成更多的交易。

4. 谈判并非独立于整个交易之外，而是整个交易活动的一部分。

5. 谈判高手认为创造一个建设性的氛围和建立彼此尊重的人际关系是至关重要的。

Chapter 3

Ⅰ. (略)

Ⅱ. 1. B 2. A 3. B 4. D 5. B 6. B 7. C 8. A 9. B 10. A

Ⅲ. 1. trunk code 2. subscriber's number 3. directory 4. **Yellow Pages** 5. receiver 6. dial 7. dialing tone 8. engaged 9. operator 10. exchange 11. automatic

Ⅳ. 1. T 2. T 3. T 4. F 5. F

Ⅴ. 1. 请报我方 100 公吨大米的最低价 CIF 广州，并表明最早交货期。

2. 为了便于你方了解我方的产品，我们立即航寄目录本厂份，样品书两份。

3. 按惯例，我们通常从欧洲供应商处得到 5%的佣金。

4. 如果你方价格有竞争力的话，我们打算订购 30 万码棉布。

5. 若产品质量好，价格与我方市场相符，我们愿意向你方订一大笔货。

Chapter 4

Ⅰ. （略）

Ⅱ. 1. D 2. D 3. A 4. C 5. D 6. B 7. A 8. A 9. B 10. B

Ⅲ. 1. e 2. a 3. h 4. d 5. f 6. g 7. c 8. b

Ⅳ. 1. T 2. T 3. T 4. T 5. F

Ⅴ. 1. 我们正在仔细研究你方报盘，希望将此盘保留到月底有效。

2. 由于此盘需求量甚大，所以该盘有效期不能超过 5 天。

3. 请接受此难得再有的报盘，最近可望有大笔订单自美国方面来，届时将导致价格猛涨。

4. 所有报价须经我方最后确认，除非另有规定或达成一致意见，所有价格都不含佣金。

5. 为复你方 7 月 21 日询价，现报儿童自行车盘如下。

Chapter 5

Ⅰ. （略）

Ⅱ. 1. C 2. D 3. A 4. B 5. E

Ⅲ. 1. May I help you; I'd like to make a call to; A moment, please

2. Martin's Law Office; Could you put me through to Miss Iris Hocking's Office, please; Sorry, the line is busy / engaged; I have a Mr. Donald Hoover on the line. Shall I put him through; May I speak to Miss Hocking; I'm calling to discuss a legal document with you; How about 10 o'clock tomorrow morning.

Ⅳ. 1. style, fashionable, acceptable, maximum

2. office, bought, reference, offer

3. handbag, Shopping, catching, trip

Ⅴ. 6 2 4 1 7 5 8 3

Ⅵ. 不要轻易提出只能回答"是"或"不是"的问题，除非提问者已事先做好准备，并很有把握答案就是他想要的。此类问题意在发起直接进攻。进攻性的问题是在对具体问题的回答以及对其他情况的了解的基础上提出的，旨在迫使对方让步，如："这有什么根据吗?"

Chapter 6

Ⅰ. （open）

Ⅱ.

```
Robert Kastens
Carbonite Corp.
1333 Second Avenue
Milford, Connecticut 06460

                                        Ms. Yvette Carlson
                                        Haley-Richardson Company
                                        One Perry Park Plaza
                                        Detroit, MI 12345
```

Ⅲ.　1. May I know what particular line you are interested in?

2. We are interested in your hardware.

3. Are these commodities available right now? We would like to see the samples first.

4. If necessary, we take special orders according to your requirement.

5. Here is our inquiry. Would you like lo have a look?

6. We shall be very glad to place our order with you if your quotation is competitive and delivery date acceptable.

7. As soon as we receive your specific inquiry, we will fax our quotation.

8. There are different models for this particular product. Which model(s) do you want?

9. Would you tell us the quantity you require so as to enable us to work out the offers?

10. Can we discuss this problem later when you place the order?

Ⅳ.　亲爱的格林先生：

关于此次错误,请接受我们的歉意。差错发生于本公司的包装及发货部门,是因重组计划之故。我们正在承运部门安装电脑,希望能对本公司顾客做更有效率的服务。

关于多出一箱手把之事,为了节省运费,希望您能将之试装于其他脚踏车上。本公司授权您减价百分之二十,以便清理余货。

刘大维敬上

Ⅴ.　Dear . . . ,

Thank you for your prompt action on our inquiry regarding an $8,950 outstanding balance on our records.

Subsequent checks with the Bank in line with you information have confirmed that the amount was duly received on July 4. This had not been reported to us due to an oversight on the part of the Bank.

We know this matter has caused you some inconvenience but hope you will understand the circumstances. Thank you again for your positive cooperation.

Yours sincerely,

Chapter 7

Ⅰ.　（open）

Ⅱ.　3.　5.　1.　4.　2.

Ⅲ.　1. released　2. enclosed　3. approved　4. requested　5. Adjournment

Ⅳ.　To: David Green, Chief of Operations

From：Tony Party，Supervisor

Subject：Comments on the "Punch-in" System

Date：March 22，2007

This is further to your memo dated March 20，2004，in which you proposed that employees adopt the "punch-in" system.

I fully agree with you that we must increase productivity. As far as your proposal that if the "punch-in" system is adopted，we would have a tighter control over the employees is concerned. However，I don't think so. I personally think that，to accomplish this，we should give the employees more incentives to work faster，I feel that if we（the supervisors）could meet with you，we could discuss different possibilities to create such incentive.

Your consideration of this suggestion would be appreciated.

Tony Party

Secretary

Ⅴ. Translate the following note into Chinese.

亲爱的 Lily：

很抱歉我昨天没能跟你见面，我知道你当时一定觉得很失望，我心里也一样感到不安。我的经理突然让我准备一份紧急的文件，我甚至连打电话给你的时间都没有，而且我昨天也一直工作到晚上八点半。我真的觉得很抱歉。

不过我想这个周末请你出来作为补偿，希望你能给我一个机会。期待你的回复。

彼得

Ⅵ. To：Department managers

From：President of ABC Cereal Company

Date：January 10，2007

Subject：Reduce sugar amount and price

Sales of Better Bran have declined in recent years，for reasons that management has now identified. First，Better Bran is a cereal with high sugar content，and recent research studies have found that most consumers say they are concerned about the amount of sugar added to their breakfast cereal. Second，the price of Better Bran has increased by 5 percent in each of the last three years. Therefore，to increase our company's profits we need to reduce the amount of sugar in Better Bran and lower Better Bran's price.

Chapter 8

Ⅰ. ××公司：

第×号合同项下有关×货的第×、×、×号三份信用证已收到，来证中一些内容与合同有关规定不符：① 合同规定按净价成交，并无佣金及折扣，而第×号信用证内却列有佣金5%；② 合同规定以即期信用证付款，而上述三份来证全为远期。我公司于×月×日特函通知改正，而你公司迄今未予办理。由于你公司不遵守合同规定又不按照我公司要求修改信用证，致使我公司无法履行装运。

目前×货订单踊跃，供应十分紧张，且各品种现行价格已超过原合同价格很多，除非你公司同意按下列现行价格订购，并立即按下列现行价格及合同规定之价格条件及付款条件修改上述信用证，同时将各证最迟装运期及有效期分别延展至3月30日和4月15日，否则我公司不能装运。后果由你公司负责。

各品种现行价格如下：（略）

（Telex）：

RCVD YLC ···, ···, ···,FR CONTRACT NO ···. N FOUND FLWG DISCREPANCIES

（1）ACDG TO CONTRACT，BIZ ON BASIS OF NET PRC，NO COMM N DISCNT. BUT 5 PCT COMM LISTD IN YLC NO ····.

（2）SIGHT LC NEEDED ACDG TO CONTRACT BUT ALL YLC DEMAND FORWARD. V HV NOTIFIED U OF AMDG LC.

HWEVER U HV NOT DONE. V CANT SHP DUE TO YR FAILUR IN FLWG CONTRACT N AMDG LC. MANY ORDRS NOW. STOCK LIMITED. PRESNT PRC MUCH HIGHER. U SHUD ORDER ON FLWG PRC N AMD YLC. EXTND SHPMNT TO MAR 30，VALIDITY TO APR 15. OZWS, U SHUD B RESPONSBL FR CONSEQUENCE. PRESNT PRCS AS FLWS：

Ⅱ.

ADCO INDONESIA LTD.

Jl Lombok 44

Jakarta

INDONESIA

Fax：(62)21 3533368   Tel：(62)21 353420

FAX

To：Mr. Lee Jung Hyun   Fax：(82)2431 6678

    Sales Manager，Interface Computers   Tel：(82)2431 6688

From：Mr. Kadir Aboe, Office Manager

      ADCO Indonesia Ltd.

Date：18 December 2006   Pages：1

Dear Mr. Lee

Delayed Delivery of Order No. 12345 - 01 - 18

You will remember that last month we ordered 30 Tanson 1 GHz Pentium II Computers.

We should have received the above order by 2 December. However，the products are now two weeks overdue. Would you please let me know what the status is right away?

We urgently need these computers to upgrade the administrative functioning of our offices，and your delayed delivery has caused a great deal of inconvenience to us.

I should appreciate your looking into this matter and arranging for delivery of these computers within the next three days.

I am afraid that if you are unable to deliver within this period，we shall be compelled to cancel our order and purchase from another supplier.

Thank you for giving this order your special attention.

Yours sincerely,

Mr. Kadir Aboe

Office Manager

Ⅲ. 1. 据我所知　2. 面对面　3. 顺便说一下　4. 再联系　5. 尽快　6. 希望这能帮上忙　7. 依我之见　8. 换句话说　9. 请　10. 稍后再联系

Ⅳ. 1. @　2. gov　3. smith　4. Thank you and best regards　5. Subject

Ⅴ. From：

To：

Date：

Dear Sirs,

　　We are very pleased to have received your e-mail message dated September 19.

　　We are very interested in your suggestion of establishing business relations with us, for this just coincides with our desire. We always adhere to cooperate with foreign enterprises or companies on the basis of equality and mutual benefits, in order to promote the development of our businesses and relationship.

　　For your reference, we are enclosing with our catalogues covering the items we deal with at present. Hoping to receive your early reply.

Yours faithfully,

Ⅵ. 1. a message pad　2. the caller's name　3. the person to whom　4. tick the box　5. fill in the caller's telephone number　6. communicate clearly and briefly

Chapter 9

Ⅰ. (open)

Ⅱ. 1. C　2. D　3. C　4. B　5. A　6. C　7. D　8. B　9. B　10. C

Ⅲ. 1. sample　2. seller　3. bills　4. ocean　5. complicated

Ⅳ. 1. T　2. F　3. T　4. F　5. T

Ⅴ. 1. 我们很遗憾你们的发盘比美国供应商的价格高出5%。

　　2. 羊毛行市目前疲软，除非你方能降价5%，否则无法成交。

　　3. 兹遗憾通知你方，本地买主认为你方报价太高。

　　4. 我们的报价相当合理，且已为你的其他客户所接受。

　　5. 至于男式衬衫，我们盼望能够按接近我们的价格达成交易。

Chapter 10

Ⅰ. (open)

Ⅱ. 1. A　2. C　3. A　4. A　5. C　6. D　7. C　8. A　9. D　10. D

Ⅲ. 1. liability　2. outside　3. vary　4. expiry　5. distributions

Ⅳ. 1. T　2. F　3. F　4. T　5. T

Ⅴ. 1. 随函附上我们第四号订单一式两份，请签退一份供我方存档。

　　2. 由于我们急需该货，请在你方报盘所承诺的5月份装船。

　　3. 请注意有关信用证的条款必须与合同条款完全一致，以避免日后修改。

　　4. 该货分三批提出，每月100吨，从8月份开始。

　　5. 由于订单太多，我们不能接受新订单。但一旦有新货，我们将立即与你方联系。

Chapter 11

Ⅰ.（open）

Ⅱ. 1. C　2. D　3. B　4. C　5. C　6. D　7. C　8. D　9. B　10. A

Ⅲ. 1. annex　2. obsolete　3. regular　4. evaluate　5. determined

Ⅳ. 1. T　2. F　3. F　4. T　5. T

Ⅴ. 1. 我们想以许可证的形式转让专利使用权。

2. 我想，你们应保证所提供的技术完整无缺，正确有效。

3. 我方希望你方能讲解所提供的技术、有关说明和其他技术数据。

4. 你方应承担保守我们提供的技术秘密的义务。

5. 我们希望你们可以进行一些改进，然后反馈给我们。

Chapter 12

Ⅰ.（open）

Ⅱ. 1. B　2. D　3. C　4. B　5. D　6. D　7. A　8. C　9. A　10. C

Ⅲ. 1. adopted　2. defines　3. takes　4. arbitration

Ⅳ. 1. T　2. T　3. F　4. T

Ⅴ. 1. 如果你们订货量加大的话，我们肯定会提高佣金。

2. 不给佣金与国际贸易惯例不符。

3. 与这些已站稳脚跟的对手竞争，必须推出强大的促销行动和各种广告。

4. 可以给我们一些津贴做促销费吗？

5. 为了帮助你方产品打入新市场，我认为最好的办法就是找一个这个地区的代理商。

Chapter 13

Ⅰ.（open）

Ⅱ. 1. B　2. A　3. C　4. A　5. C　6. D　7. A　8. D　9. C　10. A

Ⅲ.（open）

Ⅳ. 1. T　2. F　3. F　4. T　5. T

Ⅴ. 1. Culture clash can lead to breakdown in a communication.

2. Time as a culture value is something we don't understand until we are in another culture.

3. Religion is another important consideration in conducting business in foreign countries.

4. To some extent, a negotiator's success depends on his sensitivity to different cultures.

5. Awareness and sensitivity to cultural differences is vital in international negotiation.

Ⅵ. 1. 文化与策略的紧密结合对最有效管理公司人力资源是至关重要的。

2. 外国文化中人们的价值及态度对跨国公司来说是重点需要考虑的。

3. 文化冲突指两种不同文化结合的同时所带来的不确定性、焦虑、恐惧及紧张的状态。

4. 不同社会组织的人们的社会关系及活动的方式与社会价值、宗教和经济一致。

5. 商务人员要尽可能了解所做交易国的文化及商务惯例与本国有何不同。

Chapter 14

Ⅰ.（open）

II. 1. D　2. C　3. D　4. A　5. C　6. B　7. D　8. A　9. A　10. D

III. 1. offended　2. harmony　3. seriously　4. analytical　5. emphasized

IV. 1. T　2. T　3. T　4. F　5. F

V. 1. 美国人的风格是办事直率,并希望对方也能做事爽快。

2. 德国人谈判前的准备非常周密。

3. 英国人做事井井有条,守时观念非常严格。

4. 法国人喜欢争论,但不喜欢严厉批评,因为严厉批评会被认为是人身攻击。

5. 澳大利亚人性格倔强,喜欢竞争。

主要参考文献

1. 余慕鸿，章汝雯 《商务英语谈判》 外语教学与研究出版社 2005
2. 徐宪光 《商务沟通》 外语教学与研究出版社 2001
3. 曹 菱《商务英语谈判》 外语教学与研究出版社 2001
4. 韩江红，钟乐平 《敢说商务谈判英语》 机械工业出版社 2006
5. 丁衡祁，张 静 《商务谈判英语》 新时代出版社 2003
6. 丁文京，刘明宇 《当代国际商务英语教程》 北京大学出版社 2001
7. 白 远 《国际商务谈判》 中国人民大学出版社 2003
8. 何 英，郑 敏 《商务英语谈判》 清华大学出版社，北京交通大学出版社 2006
9. 金 英，肖云南 《国际商务谈判》 清华大学出版社 2003
10. 张立玉，王卫红 《实用商务英语谈判》 北京理工大学出版社 2004
11. 秦 川 《商务谈判：轻松与外商洽谈》 中国对外经济贸易出版社 2003
12. 柯 霖，邹晓东 《贸易英语》 机械工业出版社 2005
13. 盛 之，李白清 《实用英语谈判与辩论口语》 中南大学出版社 2003
14. 吴云娣 《国际商务谈判英语》 上海交通大学出版社 2002
15. 杨静宽 《商务谈判英语高级》 上海外语教育出版社 2002
16. 秦 川 《商务英语谈判》 中国对外经济贸易出版社 2004
17. 郑 欢 《谈判技巧与句型》 西南交通大学出版社 2000
18. 仲谷荣一郎，洪沁玫(译) 《谈判英语》 中华工商联合出版社 2001
19. 邱革加，杨国俊 《双赢现代商务英语谈判》 中国国际广播出版社 2006
20. 翁风翔 《商务谈判》 浙江大学出版社 2002
21. 陈 倩 《商贸英语对话》 对外经济贸易大学出版社 2005
22. 王正元 《商务谈判英语口语》 大连理工大学出版社 2005
23. 刘法公 《国际贸易实务英语》 浙江大学出版社 2002
24. 邹 莉 《专业商务谈判英语》 远方出版社 2000
25. 江 春 《商务谈判英语》 首都经济贸易大学出版社 2000
26. 张中倩 《谈判英语一日通》 科学出版社 2005
27. 吴云娣 《国际商务谈判英语》 上海交通大学出版社 2002
28. 戚云芳 《新编外贸英语函电与谈判》 浙江大学出版社 2002
29. 高瑞伶 《商贸英语脱口说》 中国宇航出版社 2006
30. 诸葛霖 《外贸英语对话》 对外经济贸易大学出版社 1998
31. Jeremy Comfort,王关富,宿玉荣改编 《成功谈判》 牛津大学出版社,复旦大学出版社 2001

32. Coulson,J. 等 《牛津当代百科大辞典》 北京：中国人民大学出版社　2004

33. Pearsall,Judy，The New Oxford Dictionary of English，上海：上海外语教育出版社 2001

34. Raiffa，Howard. et al. Negotiation Analysis：The Science and Art of Collaborative Decision Making，Cambridge，Mass.：Belknap Press，January 1，2003

35. Camp，Jim，The Negotiating Tools that the Pros Don't Want You to Know，New York：Crown Business，1st edition，July 15，2002

36. Goodman，Peter J.，Win-Win Career Negotiations：Proven Strategies for Getting What You Want from Your Employer，Harmondsworth：Penguin Books，September 1，2002

37. Jeffery Curry，2000，A Short Course in International Negotiating，Shanghai Foreign Language Education Press，Shanghai

38. Lewcki，Roy J. et al.，Essentials of Negotiation，Boston：McGraw-Hill / Irwin，3 edition，June 13，2003

39. Lewicki，Roy J. et al. Negotiation：Readings，Exercises，and Cases，Boston：McGraw-Hill Irwin，4th edition，June 4，2002

40. 网站：
http://www. Negotiation.com
http://www. Negotiations.org
http://www. Business balls. com
http://www. Professionalpractice. asme. org / communications / negotiation
http://www. moftec. gov. cn
http://www. cietac. org. cn
http://www. iccwbo. org
http:// www. unctad. org
http://www. wto. org